THE
UNGRATEFUL
BASTARDS

T. STYLES

NATIONAL BESTSELLING AUTHOR OF *RAUNCHY*

ARE **Y**OU **O**N **O**UR **E**MAIL **L**IST?
SIGN UP ON OUR WEBSITE
www.thecartelpublications.com
OR TEXT THE WORD: CARTELBOOKS
TO **22828**
FOR PRIZES, CONTESTS, ETC.

By T. Styles

The Ungrateful Bastards
By T. Styles

Library of Congress Control Number: 2015941060

ISBN 10: 0989084531

ISBN 13: 978-0989084536

Cover Design: Davida Baldwin www.oddballdsgn.com
www.thecartelpublications.com
First Edition
Printed in the United States of America

What's Up Fam,

The talented T. Styles has brought another exciting tale to your fingertips!
'The Ungrateful Bastards' is classic T. Styles with the benefit of her experience and expertise. You will laugh and love this one, I promise!

I know we have had some tough times over these past couple of years with our black boys/men being killed, but I have faith that a change will come. We have made our voice clear and will no longer stand by and let them assassinate us. Hold on family, stay strong and stand up to save our boys/men.

Baltimore and Ferguson we stand with you!

With that being said, keeping in line with tradition, we want to give respect to a vet or trailblazer paving the way. In this novel, we would like to recognize:

MARILYN MOSBY

Marilyn Mosby is an African-American lawyer and on January 8, 2015 she became the newest and youngest States Attorney for Baltimore Maryland. She comes from a long line of law enforcement, over five generations lead by her grandfather who was one of the first black police officers in Massachusetts. She won all of our hearts and respect when she filed charges against six Baltimore police officers in the death of Freddie Gray on May 1, 2015. Marilyn Mosby is a mother and a brave soul. We salute you Mrs. Mosby, thank you for taking a stand and we will be praying for you.

Aight, Get to it. I'll catch you in the next novel.

Be Easy!

Charisse "C. Wash" Washington
Vice President
The Cartel Publications
www.thecartelpublications.com
www.facebook.com/publishercwash

Instagram: publishercwash
www.twitter.com/cartelbooks
www.facebook.com/cartelpublications
Follow us on Instagram: Cartelpublications
#PrayForCeCe
#PrayForSeven

ATTENTION: TWISTED BABIES

Where you at?

Let me see you! Let me hear from you!

Join your Twisted Siblings home via Facebook at: TWISTED BABIES' READERS GROUP.

Get to know your family and shout me out by using the name, Twisted Baby!

I want to meet you!

Love,
T. STYLES aka THE TWISTED MOTHER

#TheUngratefulBastards

The Ungrateful Bastards   10

PROLOGUE

M o murda, mo murda, mo murda...," Martha Gregory sang as she marched down the street on a mission.

A gang of wilted yellow dandelions hung out her brown church hat as she stomped. The service she attended earlier was a blessing and she left feeling inspired.

The edges of her worn imposter leather purse were busted open, revealing a grayish-white cotton fabric beneath. But she clutched it tightly against her, for fear that the many thugs who dressed the street curb of the Washington DC block would relieve her of her possessions, including the twenty-two dollars and sixteen cent she had to her name.

When she made it to a gathering of young men they parted like the Red Sea, unveiling Pierce Guns— a 22-year old hooligan with nothing to lose and limited respect for those he didn't know.

"You Guns," she asked with authority, clutching her purse closer when a vandal passed the blunt to his comrade that at first she thought was a gun.

"If he is, what you want with him?" Five-feet five Jordan Marx asked, blocking her path.

The moment he stepped her way, Martha raised her tattered purse and knocked him in the head repeatedly until he was as flat as a stick of gum. Although any of the men could've pulled her off they were all too intrigued to stop her.

When she was done, with most of her flowers now pressed against the grungy concrete, she stood up, wiped the sweat off her brow and took a few deep breaths.

By T. Styles   11

vas about to repay her with a blow
a few of the men on the sidelines
t. He would be forced to be the
f the neighborhood on this one
Jdy was willing to see him hit an old
t, not under their watch.

"Are you Guns?" she repeated.

Guns removed a chewed toothpick from his mouth and threw it on the ground. Grimacing he said, "You doing a whole lot aren't you?" he asked.

"I come in peace."

He laughed. "You call that peace?" he looked at Jordan and shook his head. "Yeah...I'm Guns."

She nodded satisfactorily. "Then you just the man I'm looking for."

He ran his hand over his lips before dropping it at his side. "How so?"

"Because you're going to do a job for me." She cleared her throat. "A job I can't do myself, otherwise I wouldn't be here." She readjusted her church crown.

"And what's that?"

"You're gonna kill for me."

He laughed and looked at his homies. "And exactly who do you want dead?"

"My kids...and you have my sincere blessings."

CHAPTER ONE
TROUBLE COMES TO THOSE WHO CALL

The moonlight filtered through Shane Projects in Washington, DC., shining it's light on two pre-teens who were in search for trouble. The summer heat was horrendous but a non-factor to fourteen-year-old Dodson Gregory and his cohort Bear as they played behind their apartment building.

Dodson's cinnamon colored skin seemed to sparkle as sweat drifted through the two stylish shaved lines on the side of his head. His thick eyebrows, sat over a set of wide brown eyes and his nostrils spread with each heavy breath. Although he was fourteen, he acted younger than his age, having developed a slight mental disability earlier in life.

Enveloped in clandestine he was beyond excited about the mischief he was about to dive into. "Look at this shit, slim," Dodson said opening the large red firework box before him. He ripped at the sides until it busted open— the sulfur smell suddenly filling the air. "It got everything in it!"

Bear, who was perched on a yellow milk crate, with a lidded brown box next to him, waddled toward Dodson. Bear earned his signature limp a year ago after he and Dodson decided to ride their bikes down the steps behind the high school.

Bear lowered his body and picked up a large red and silver firework. Wide eyes gleaming with malice he said, "Please say you got fire."

Dodson reached into his back blue jeans pocket and removed a book of matches. "Don't leave nowhere without 'em!"

The boys spent the next few minutes going over everything inside. There were bottle rockets, skyrockets, roman candles, sparklers, and shells. But what was also present, and the most dangerous of them all, was six M80's.

"Can't believe your moms bought you all this stuff," Bear said excitedly.

"I keep telling you she do anything I want," he bragged as he focused back on his act.

When the smell of fireworks took over the air Dodson was ready for the next level— extreme violence. "Grab the cats," Dodson said pointing to the brown paper box to his left.

Bear slid the box over and removed the lid, revealing five yellow kittens inside. Looking down at them he said, "Now what?"

"Take them over there," Dodson frowned. "I don't want them too close to me."

Bear, who hated to move more than two steps in an hour breathed heavily as he rearranged the box. "Hurry up and do it! You acting scared." He placed his hands on his hips.

"Suck my dick!" Dodson yelled. Grabbing an M80 he rushed toward the cat box. "Betta back up!"

Bear ran some feet away, just as Dodson lit the M80 and dropped it inside the box. Not even a second later it exploded and small kitten fragments splattered everywhere.

"That shit was like that!" Dodson cheered, clapping his hands and jumping around, courtesy of no home training. With wide eyes he asked, "Did you see it?" he looked at the bloody cat and box fragments. "I wish we had more cats! I'd do it again."

Bear wasn't as excited about the gore as Dodson, as a matter of fact he hated it. Whenever they did anything violent it was Dodson's idea and most times he went along for the ride.

"I want to light one," Bear said as he rifled through the box until he located another M80. He picked it up and examined it, understanding full well the danger it held.

"Let me do one more first," Dodson said as he rifled through the box.

"Aight, but after that I'm next!" Bear responded as if he put in on the explosives.

Dodson clutched the M80 in his palm, struck a match and focused on the fiery tip. He was mesmerized by its glow and strong rotten egg odor. How could such a small thing be so powerful?

He was still in a trance when Bear yelled, "You better throw it before it—"

His words were halted.

Unfortunately Dodson wasn't fast enough to hurl it and it detonated before his eyes.

****

The music boomed out of the car stereo speakers with Nicki Minaj's latest song...

Fifteen-year-old Berry Gregory danced in place inside of her mother's red Honda Civic, within a crowded mall parking lot. Bags from Macys and Nordstrom, loaded to the rim with clothing, were thrown in the backseat.

Her best friend Liberty was her passenger and a thick blunt was pressed against her lips, while her other hand squeezed her nipple, something she did to gain the ultimate high.

"Bitch, we loaded up," Berry said as she pulled out of the parking lot and onto the street. "That receipt scam shit worked!" She turned the music up so loudly she could barely hear Liberty's response. "Wait 'til school tomorrow! We gonna outshine bitches!"

Berry whipped her long five hundred dollar black weave over her right shoulder as the streetlight bounced against the huge fake diamond earrings weighing down her lobes. When Liberty handed her the blunt, she accepted with her free hand while maneuvering the car with the other. Her light brown skin reddened as she inhaled, sending powdery smoke clouds into the car. The appropriate high in place, she handed it back and grimaced when Liberty pinched her nipple again while inhaling.

"Why you always do that gross shit?" Berry asked.

With flaming red eyes and a dopey smile she said, "Ain't nothing like your heart pumping and your pussy tingling at the same time." She winked. "Try it, you'll love it!"

They danced so hard the car rocked down the street. Arms flailing, hips gyrating and mouths contorted - they looked more like they were fighting than dancing.

"So what we gonna do tonight?" Liberty asked, lowering the music. "I'm not ready to go home." she pulled the visor down and gazed at her light skin in the reflection of the mirror. "Let's ride around a little longer. Maybe we can book some niggas."

The Ungrateful Bastards   16

"Let's play it by ear," Berry said as she teased her hair.

When she pulled up at a light a black Honda eased up next to them and stopped. Feeling high and devious Liberty said, "Watch this shit."

With the announcement made she lifted her waist and pushed her jeans down to her ankles. Her red lace panties were revealed as she buried her knees in the passenger seat— pressing her butt cheeks against the cool window on her side of the car.

"Bitch, you so crazy," Berry laughed having been with Liberty when she'd pulled the stunt in the past. "I can't believe you doing that dumb shit!"

"But you love it though," Liberty laughed as she moved back and forth. And when she was sure the female driver in the next car was watching, she flapped her ass cheeks back and forth like an American flag.

Unbeknownst to them, the joke was over.

Suddenly an angry woman with stones for fists pushed open her car door and made a beeline for their vehicle. Realizing the joke had gone too far, Liberty quickly stuffed her ass cheeks into her jeans. When she glanced ahead the light was still red but how she wished it wasn't. "Oh shit, we got problems."

Berry looked across Liberty and outside the window. Eyes glued on the angry woman who was holding a yellow iron steering wheel lock club in her hand and stomping in their direction, she knew things were about to escalate. When she noticed her angry male passenger still in the car, she pleaded with him with her eyes to stop the woman but there was no haps. He welcomed whatever was about to happen.

Faking tough Berry said, "I know that bitch not about to hit my mother's car!"

"I wish she would touch this car," Liberty added, equally frightened despite the light barking. "I'ma stomp the fuck outta—"

Before she could respond the woman brought down the club on the top of the car...multiple times. Although the light was green, and had been for a few seconds, Berry was too stunned to drive. And if the Angry Woman hadn't done enough, she reached into her pocket and pulled out a switchblade.

Berry turned fifty shades of pink wondering if the woman would take their lives like she had the integrity of her mother's car. Instead the Angry Woman pressed the tip of the blade two inches from the gas tank and rolled it all the way to the bumper, leaving a deep white scratch in the paint job.

Since the car was only two months old Berry knew her mother would never allow her to use it again, and as far as she was concerned without wheels her young life was over. To make matters worse Berry had to pick her up from work in a few hours.

Outraged, Berry pushed her door open and stomped toward the woman harshly. "What the fuck is wrong with you?" She yelled, spit bubbles flying from her lips and onto the woman's nose. "You a crazy black—"

Suddenly Berry was thirsty...

Her momentary delirium was due to the Angry Woman slapping her so hard in the mouth that her lips flattened under the blow. When

The Ungrateful Bastards   18

Berry got her wits about herself and attempted to hit the woman back the Angry Woman raised the knife and pressed it against the vein of her throat.

"Do it, young bitch," she threatened. She swallowed as if she was a rabid dog salivating. "Put your hands on me so I can have a reason to go back to prison. I got ten more years in me easy."

Berry was as still as stone.

When the Angry Woman saw that Berry was afraid she lowered the weapon. "Word of advice. The next time you and your friend want to tease a bitch's husband, please be sure she didn't just get out of jail for attempted murder." She gazed at Liberty whose forehead was squished against the window in anticipation, before focusing back on Berry.

Having said her piece, the Angry Woman sauntered back to her car and pulled off, leaving Berry stuck and stupid in the middle of the street.

Cars whizzed by as she turned around to observe the damage made to her mother's car and her jaw dropped after realizing how bad things really were. "Oh my, God," Berry said covering her mouth. "Mama's gonna kill me."

Real danger out of the way, Liberty slowly stepped her punk ass out and stood next to her friend. Together they discerned the obvious, that the car was ruined.

"Move ya'll's funky asses out the middle of the street, young bitches!" a woman yelled, having to drive around them.

Berry and Liberty rushed back into the car and pulled to the side of the road. Distraught about her circumstances she parked and leaned her head against the steering wheel. "I can't deal with this shit right now!" She farted due to her stomach twerking causing Liberty to frown.

"You gonna be alright," Liberty said, feeling slightly guilty at her part in the problem. Although not guilty enough to apologize. Had she not pressed her naked ass against the window none of this would've happened.

Berry raised her head and looked outward. "She told me the last time I crashed her car that if something happened I would be cut off. It took her three months to let me drive this one."

"Girl, Ms. Martha loves you. She can't stay mad at you like other people's mothers'." She dug into her purse, grabbed a rolled blunt and lit it. "If I would've crashed my mother's car like you did hers she would never let me drive." She paused pulling on the weed. "Trust me...even if she punishes you, you'll be fine."

"The party is in two weeks. How we gonna get there?"

"Who gonna stop you if you sneak out? Your mother can't be in the house for five minutes without falling to sleep. Zoom always in the shower and Dodson too busy with his gay best friend to check for you. All you gotta do is take the keys."

"Naw, this time gotta be different." She paused gazing at the man walking two German Shepherds in front of the car.

Frustrated Liberty sat back into her seat and folded her hands. "Then what's your plan?"

Berry's eyebrows rose. "If she think I got hurt then she won't ground me." She swallowed and blinked a few times— her plan coming to life in her mind.

"Okay, so what you want me to do? Slap the shit out you or something?" Liberty asked, a little too excited about the prospect.

Berry stared out into the street. "No, it gotta be worse..."

"What's worse than me beating your ass?"

Slowly Berry's head rolled toward her. "I don't have all the details yet...but I'ma tell her I got raped."

****

Huddled in the corner of a DC Project, a game amongst thugs was in session...

The white dice felt cool in eighteen-year-old Zoom's hand as he shook them several times. His long black cornrows hung down his back and were dressed with one black crystal bead apiece. Since it was rare to find him wearing anything other than long jean shorts, a pair of new Nike Foamposites and no shirt during the summer, today was no exception.

Zoom was definitely easy on the eyes but it was his brave heart and gangster mentality that made him so appealable.

With the dice still in hand Zoom gazed at his brown Gucci watch. In fifteen minutes he would have to ride with his sister to pick Martha up from work, which he hated. Unlike some he despised his mother and wanted nothing to do with her but he promised Berry.

When he studied his competitors, Perch, the biggest drug dealer in the city and Barney, he was sure he could beat them. After all he'd done it before and nobody knew how to stop him.

"Will you hurry the fuck up?" Perch yelled. "You holding onto the dice like they titties. Roll them mothafuckas!" Perch plucked his bushy mane with the Afro fist pick that stayed in his hair.

"I got you, baby boy," Zoom winked. "Ain't no need in rushing to get all your money taken."

"Nigga please," Perch chuckled. "It'll take the rest of your life to take my money." He pressed a stiff finger in Zoom's chest. "Don't forget, I pay your salary."

Zoom was just about to roll when Shakes, a local dope head from up the block yelled, "Zoom, you holding?" His steps were hurried and rushed as if someone were after him, causing all around to go into distress mode.

So uncomfortable, five of Perch's soldiers reached for their weapons preparing to cut him down until Perch raised his hand and told them to lower them. Perch knew Shakes and knew he meant no harm...at least he hoped.

"I'm busy right now," Zoom said. "Hit up Money Mooch down the block." He turned his back preparing to play the game.

"He ain't out there," Shakes said trembling. When his foot moved again his big toe shot through the hole in his grungy Nike and everybody was disgusted. "Come on, man. Tonight ain't for me. I need to get right in the next few minutes. Help me out. I'm dying!"

While Shakes waited on Zoom's response Nay came strutting up the block and Zoom could care less about his sickness. The black tank top she wore was oversized but failed to hide the phat ass in her jean shorts. Her sandy brown hair was pulled back into a tight ponytail and the only thing she wore on her face was a smile.

"Aye, Nay, when you gonna let me get in them jeans?" Zoom said, fully aware that he sounded corny. He gripped his dick and waited for an answer.

She stopped, put her hands on her hips and shook her head as if she was not amused. "You always faking, everybody know where your heart at."

Perch and the others laughed, having bared full witness to the broken heart he held two years earlier, courtesy of his first love, Dookie. It was because of her that although he may have fucked a female or two, relationship status was no longer in the cards. Zoom admired his freedom, money and unlimited pussy. Anything that compromised those medium goals was detonated.

"All I'm trying to do is make you feel good," he paused. "When you gonna let me do that?"

"When you kill yourself and meet me in the next life."

Everyone laughed. Even Zoom.

"Damn, all that for the pussy?"

"I've seen the bitches you fuck with. Trust me it's worth the wait."

Nay continued her walk and Zoom turned around to face Perch who was looking at him disapprovingly. "Nigga, throw the dice! I don't know why you busying yourself with that whore anyway." He paused. "She fuck anything moving."

"And all I want is my turn," Zoom winked.

"What about me?" Shakes interrupted.

Zoom blew air into his hand, rolled the dice and went over to serve Shakes. He didn't need to look at how the dice fell to know he won the pot. Luck was always on his side and he didn't expect that moment to be any different.

Besides, the sound of Perch's long sigh told him everything he needed to know.

He won again.

"The money?" Zoom said to Shakes.

Shakes pushed the cash into the center of his hand. Zoom counted it and moved to his stash, a Pepsi soda can with the bottom cut out, which was positioned a few feet over from the crap game.

The moment he grabbed a small bag of heroin and handed it to Shakes three police cars pulled up on the block and jumped out on Zoom.

Perch and the others peeped the move seconds earlier and already caught wheels...fleeing the scene.

Caught slipping, Zoom was thrown to the ground, arms yanked behind his back and cool cuffs slapped against his wrists.

"Fuck!" he yelled. His luck must have blinked.

CHAPTER TWO
ROTTEN

Martha Gregory stood in the middle of the kitchen of *Heart & Bowl* and diced onions quicker than a machine. Sweat poured down her underarms and alongside of her body and she hoped no one caught a whiff of the sour smell of her vagina, due to working almost thirty hours straight without bathing.

As head chef, people came from miles around to enjoy Martha's meals and she earned a good salary and would've had the money to open up her business long ago if it wasn't for her greedy children. Martha did everything they asked but it wasn't good enough.

Years ago Martha was married to Steven Gregory.

The marriage didn't start as a fairytale and she wasn't use to real love considering her upbringing. She came from a single parent home in which her mother used crack on an hourly basis. Martha an impressionable teenager, at the time, followed her mother's lead.

Before Martha knew it she was abusing crack cocaine and selling her body and mouth no less than six times a day to support her habit. After awhile her life went spiraling out of control until the night she tried to steal pieces of scrap metal from Riley Construction Company.

Since the business appeared to be closed that night, she popped open a flimsy back door, eased into the dark garage and pilfered through a pile of metal pieces that sat in the corner.

"What are you doing here?" Steven Gregory asked stepping out of the darkness. He flipped on a light and continued to wipe his hands using a soiled white cloth.

Martha turned around, hand still gripping a long scrap metal piece. A tall handsome man, with skin the color of cherry wood made her instantly attracted to him. The thought was fleeting, besides who would be attracted to a crack head?

"I'm...I was...looking for someone."

"Is that so?" he asked through squinted eyes.

"Yes..." she paused. Realizing she was caught her shoulders collapsed forward. "Please don't call the cops." She scratched her wooly wild hair. "I'll go away and never come back."

Instead of turning her in, he took one look at her beautiful but grotty face and said, "I can't let you take that." He stuffed the cloth into his back pocket. "It's not that I don't want you to have it but if you take it I'll lose my job."

"Okay," she said although she didn't drop the metal.

Martha was about to run until he said, "If I hadn't caught you, and you made it out of here, how much would you have earned for it?"

She looked down at it and then back at him. "About seventy bucks," she lied, eager to leave. Although the nosey man was attractive he was also creepy.

"Alright then," he said reaching into his pocket and removing seventy bucks. "Take it."

She released the metal and quickly snatched the money. Suddenly she knew what he wanted and it was time to get down to business. She walked toward him, dropped to her knees and made a move for his belt buckle. "What you want...a dick suck? An ass lick?" she paused. "Whatever it is lets hurry up because I don't have all day."

He gripped her hand and helped her to her feet. "No, nothing like that." She snatched away. If he didn't want sex what did he want?

"I don't get it." She frowned.

"Just come here every Friday and I'll give you a little something."

"Something *like money?*"

He nodded yes.

With raised brows she asked, "And the reason you would do all of that?"

"Because I can."

"What are you a fag?"

Steven smiled and walked away, leaving her alone with her unhealthy thoughts.

She may have behaved crassly but he maintained a cool demeanor. Intrigued, she played along and every Friday Martha returned to his job to receive cash. Although she thought he was queer at first before long she preferred to think of him as gullible.

Until the sixth month.

She came into the building during the same time and instead of a payday she was met with something else. "Sorry, Martha. Today I'm not giving you any money."

Since she was physically sicker than she had been in the past he was better off giving her a death wish. "What do you mean?" she frowned, eyebrows pulling tightly together. "You told me to come here every Friday and I did!" she carried on as if she earned the money and wanted her paycheck. "Why you holding out on it now?"

"You have to get clean, and I have already chosen a place." He said looking into her eyes. "If you're serious about getting your life together all you have to do is climb in the passenger seat and I'll take you myself. I'll even stop to get you a rock. But you have to get clean or I'm cutting you off."

"I don't understand!" she screamed, spit flying from her mouth like a wild animal. "What does my lifestyle have to do with you? Huh?"

"Everything...I care about you," he said plainly. "And I want to see you better."

Not recognizing the gift, Martha picked up a piece of scrap metal and tossed it toward him. When he tried to defend his face the shred cut one of his fingers badly.

"Oh my, god," she screamed upon seeing the gushing blood. Her eyes widened as she saw firsthand how much of her life the drugs claimed. He could've been killed. "I'm so sorry, Steven. Please forgive me!"

Steven tore off his shirt, covered his injured finger and looked down at her face, which was plagued with guilt. "I'm okay, Martha." He grabbed the back of her hair with his other hand and looked into her eyes. "If you get yourself together and stay in the program I will provide a home for you." He paused. "You're not alone anymore."

At first Martha was frightened. But his support got her through one of the most difficult periods in her life.

Four months later Martha got out of bed in the rehab center. As she was getting dressed she realized she didn't have a desire for the drugs anymore. She was officially rehabilitated.

On the last day a heavy cloud of worry hovered over her. Would Steven continue to be the crutch she had come to depend on? She hadn't spoken to him since she enrolled in the program because it was against the rules. So her concern was warranted. But the moment she opened the door to leave the facility there he was, standing in front of his white pick up truck with a bushel of red roses in hand.

"You waited," she said looking at the all black suit he wore before staring into his eyes.

"I told you that you're not in this alone," he walked up to her and they embraced, although it was friendlier more than romantic. He proved his trueheartedness by moving her into his home.

Three months later life got even better. He asked if she had any dreams and she told him of her desire to be a chef. Quickly he enrolled her into a culinary program and she graduated with flying stars. It didn't take long for him to see she didn't have minor skills but that she was the best. With her passion in place they immediately went into plans to open a restaurant and Steven asked her to marry him.

Although excited by the proposal, Martha was quite all right with the arrangement because she adored him and didn't see a need to press marriage. As a matter of fact she was afraid she would jinx their bond and their relationship wouldn't last. But Steven knew what he wanted...a wife.

"Yes, Steven," she said as they sat next to each other on the sofa. "Of course I will marry you."

"Before you agree I have something to tell you," he replied.

"Please don't tell me you're married," Martha said as she looked into his eyes.

"No," he chuckled. "It's nothing like that." He cleared his throat. "Before I met you, years earlier, I was a catholic priest. I devoted everything to my religion but I left the church for personal reasons and I've always felt guilty. I begged God for forgiveness and promised to do one more favor for Him when the time was right. I prayed for a sign and then you walked into the construction company."

Her eyes widened. "So I was some charity case?" she asked with trembling lips. "Something for you to do to make yourself feel better about turning your back on your faith?"

"Yes. At first it was a way for me to get right with God," he admitted. "But after awhile I fell in love. I'm still in love."

Martha couldn't lie, she felt slight disappointment but what was his crime? Being an ex-priest who cared and helped her when no one else did? She realized it was better to forgive than to miss out on the best thing that ever happened to her.

Before long they were married in a small ceremony and then came Zoom, Berry and Dodson. Suddenly her family was complete.

The first thing Steven did was bought them a beautiful home in suburbia Maryland. Each of their children had their own room and they were the envy at school. Both of their parents were in their lives and they had every toy, fashionable clothing and all the money they could spend.

But soon, on June 14th, tragedy struck.

A crane holding a piece of iron weighing over a ton crashed into Steven's car and his body was crushed instantly...the damage so severe there was a closed casket funeral.

The Ungrateful Bastards 30

After his death Martha did all she could to keep the children happy. She bought them anything they wanted even at the expense of paying the house bills. Before long even though she had a high paying job at the restaurant she couldn't afford rent. So she moved into the projects so that she could continue to spoil them and provide them with a semblance of the lifestyle they were accustomed.

Martha accepted the responsibility for their father's death and after a while, they took full advantage. She was at the mercy of her children and as a result grew weaker everyday.

No longer a mother or wife, she moved into her new position as slave.

When Martha finished dicing onions she prepared the other meals at the restaurant. She was about to start on her signature chili when her boss walked into the kitchen with a crinkled expression. "Martha," he said with an evil eye. "It's the phone...again!"

Martha wiped her hands on her apron and walked slowly into his office. With the scent of onions heavy on her fingertips, she picked up the handset and said, "Yes..."

"Hello, is this Mrs. Gregory?" a white man asked on the other end.

She swallowed and could feel her heart rate increasing. "I am."

"This is Dr. Corey from Children's Hospital. I'm calling to tell you that your son Dodson is here. We need you to come right away. He's been injured."

Martha placed her hand over her heart and sat on the edge of her boss's desk. "Is he alive?"

"Yes, but he...well...I really prefer if you come in so we can talk face to face."

By T. Styles 31

"Just tell me what the fuck has happened!" she yelled.

Martha's Boss walked into the office and sat in his seat behind his desk and she had his undivided attention.

"Well he blew off one of his testicles in an accident," the doctor said. "And we need you down here right away before we can continue with surgery."

A tear rolled down Martha's face. When would it all stop?

She stood up, wiped her eyes, which immediately stung from the onions she chopped and turned around to face her boss. "Okay, I'll be there right away." When she hung up her gaze fell down on the phone. "I have to leave. I'm so—"

"Do you want his job?" he asked with an attitude, interrupting her. "I have to know right here and right now...what the fuck do you want to do?" he slammed his fist into his palm.

"Of course I want my job," she said passionately. "I love it here!"

"Well if you leave out of that door you won't have it, Martha. Do you hear what I'm saying? I will not sit by here and allow you to take this restaurant down any longer."

Martha lowered her head and quickly removed her apron. She threw it in his face and pointed a long finger at him. "There are two things you don't fuck with when it comes to me. My children and my God." She stood up straight and raised her head in the air. "If you want to fire me then so be it but I'm leaving to see my child."

Martha turned to walk away. "It should be three things," Taylor said before she left.

The Ungrateful Bastards 32

She spun around to face him. "What you talking about?"

"You said there were two things and I'm saying it should be three. Your children, your God and *your life*. Because I don't know what's going on in your world but I do know this...if you don't get a reign on those children they are going to be the death of you. That much I can promise!"

CHAPTER THREE
THE LYING PRINCESS

Martha sat on the edge of the bed placing Neosporin where Dodson's left ball use to rest. Thanks to the exploding M80, he lost one of his testicles and was in excruciating pain. Had he not moved his penis to the left after pissing moments before the accident, he would've lost all of his reproductive organs, never being able to experience sex or have children.

After Martha was done caring for him she re-bandaged the wound and pulled the covers over his body. Although disappointed, she didn't want him to see her frustration. Sitting down on the edge of the bed, it rocked a little under her weight. "What happened, Dodson? I don't understand how you could've gotten so injured." She was careful of his feelings but still felt the strong need to know.

In search of a lie, Dodson looked away and focused on the Kanye West poster on his wall. Martha's constant desire to find out why her children were disobedient was annoying. At the end of the day he did things because he could...because she allowed them so much leeway they felt grown and that wouldn't be changing any time soon.

"I don't know, ma," he shrugged dismissively. "We were playing and it dropped in my lap. You heard what the doctor said!"

She placed a tuft of hair behind her ear. "But, son, you could've been killed. When I bought you the fireworks I thought you would be responsible and not use them without me or Zoom. You promised."

Often Dodson found it hard to deal with his mother's emotions. With lowered brows he said, "It wouldn'tve happened if you got the right ones! I almost died because of you!"

She looked down at him. "What do you mean the right ones? You were with me when we bought them."

He readjusted in the bed and pulled the sheets up as if they were more important than speaking to her. "Well they were still wrong," he yelled louder. "Now get out of my face! I don't feel good!"

A tear rolled down her cheek as she stood up slowly, her back aching from all of the hours she put in at the kitchen. "Okay, son." Martha rubbed his head. "Try to get some rest."

"I can if you leave me alone! You just doing this nice stuff because..."

"Because what?"

He looked at her as if she knew the answer.

"Call me if you need anything," she continued.

Dodson rolled his eyes as she trudged out of his room, closing the door behind herself. Emotionally beaten she trudged into the living room and sat between Berry and Liberty who were sitting on the sofa. They were waiting for a detective who was coming to collect information on the rape case.

Frustrated, Martha leaned back and glanced at Berry who was filing her nails. She lovingly touched her daughter's leg. "How you doing, baby? I can't imagine what you going through right now."

"Ain't nothing wrong with me, ma," Berry frowned rolling her eyes. "What you talking about?"

Her eyebrows rose in confusion. "I'm talking about what happened to you yesterday, sweetheart," Martha said softly. "The rape."

Berry, finally remembering her lie dropped the nail file in her purse on the floor and tried to appear sad. "I'm fine I guess." She paused "My coody cat was hurting earlier but I put a cool rag on it and now I'm good."

Liberty did all she could to suppress her laughter. When she saw Martha watching her she cleared her throat and asked, "And how are you, Ms. Martha?"

"I'm fine. Just worried about Berry that's all. It was by the grace of God that you two are still alive."

Liberty looked at her lying friend then at the floor. "Won't He do it?"

Martha smiled, stood up and walked toward the window. "I just wish I knew where Michael is at this hour." She looked at the white clock on the wall in the kitchen as she thought more about Zoom. "Did he come home last night?"

"Yes, ma," Berry sighed.

"Then where is he now? He's never been out this late without at least checking in the house."

"Zoom, gonna be alright," Berry blurted out. "Just chill and stop asking a million questions."

"I hope you're right."

A few seconds later there was a knock at the door and Martha folded her arms over her chest, walked toward it and looked out of the peephole. She turned around and gazed at Berry. "He's here." She opened the door and realized it wasn't locked. Frowning she said, "Berry, you all have to remember to lock the door."

"Sorry, ma," she frowned.

Millin Scott, the investigating officer on Berry's rape case, walked inside. Martha locked the door, grabbed a chair from the kitchen table and placed it in front of the couch. "Please have a seat."

"Thank you for seeing me again," Millin said to Martha before sitting. He was a stocky white man with broad shoulders and serious aqua green eyes. "Before coming I heard about what happened to your son at the precinct...my apologies."

Martha smiled lightly. "Thank you. There has been a lot going on. If only we could find the man who raped my daughter I would rest a little easier." She sat between Berry and Liberty, while bringing him to the point of the meeting.

"Yes," Millin said as he gazed at Berry suspiciously. "We are definitely going to get down to the bottom of it." He'd been doing detective work for over twenty years and something felt extremely off about the case. He grabbed a blue pen and small pad from his shirt pocket. "Berry, I know this may be hard so I'll try to take it easy. I understand you were in the hospital all last night and I realize the testing they did on you was very invasive. It's just that we must be thorough with investigations such as this. Now I have a few questions."

"Go 'head," Berry responded trying to appear despondent.

The officer flipped a few sheets of paper on the pad before stopping at a blank one. "You said you were with your friend." He looked at Liberty. "But where were you coming from?"

"The mall," she said flatly.

He made notes and his gaze remained on the pad. "And what happened when you were there?"

"Nothing. We just went shopping and stuff."

"I think the officer wants a little more information, honey," Martha said in a loving tone.

"I know, ma, dang," Berry snapped. "Let him fucking talk! Shit!" she rolled her eyes and focused back on him. "Anyway, officer, what were you saying?"

Millin found the girl's attitude to be rude at best but he kept his comments to himself. Besides, if the woman couldn't handle her own child far be it from him to get involved. "Tell me what happened minutes before the rape."

"I told you already," she said with an attitude, smacking her lips. "We were driving down the street after going to the mall. I got a phone call so I pulled over." Berry looked at her mother. "I'm not allowed to talk on the phone and drive because mama says so." She focused back on the officer. "Anyway, while we were parking this man got into the car and raped me."

He stopped writing and squinted. If he thought something was off he was certain there was fraud now. "When you say he got in the car and raped you where did it happen?"

She shrugged. "In the front seat."

"But how?"

He pulled me out and took it from the back."

"*Took it from the back*?" he repeated.

"He did it doggie style! Stuck his dick in my ass! Dang! Why I got to tell you how somebody fuck?"

He was flabbergasted and took more notes despite being certain she was lying. "Okay, where were you, Liberty? During the rape?"

"In the car," she said under her breath.

"In the car doing what?"

"Watching I guess."

Great. So they're both liars. He thought. "Can either of you identify this man? If you saw him again?"

"Yeah," Berry responded. "I can remember his face and he was in a blue car. He was real ugly too. After he raped me he scratched the car just to be mean. He also banged it with his shoe boot...and that's why it's messed up, mama."

Martha touched her leg softly.

Millin despised the young lady because her story made zero sense. "Okay..."

"And Liberty got his license plate number," Berry blurted out.

First he thought she was a liar but now he believed he was wrong. If there was a license plate maybe he judged too quickly. It wasn't his nature but quite honestly, he wasn't a fan.

Although Berry was proud to have additional information to support her lie, Liberty was angry because she didn't warn her that she was throwing the man under the bus. She felt if Millin received the address he would surely find out they were *both* lying. Still, she gave him the information that she retained from memory of the Angry Woman's car.

"Now that I have the details we will try to locate him for questioning." He sighed. "Before I leave can you think of any reason he would target you? And your friend?"

"Target?" Martha responded. "Since when does a rapist need to target anyone?"

He exhaled deeply. "Generally I can see how this would be a bad question. But this event seems so random. It's one thing to rape one person but to have a witness in the same car, who isn't bound and could've run at anytime, is unheard of. All I want to do is make sense of it all." He stood up and placed the pen and pad back into his pocket. "Well I'm not going to waste any more of your time. I'll be in contact."

When the detective left Martha locked the door and looked down at Berry. "I'm so sorry, sweetheart. That you had to go through all of that." She rushed to her room, slammed the door and cried.

"She's so fucking weird," Berry said grabbing the fingernail file from her purse.

"No...you're mean," Liberty corrected. "And we not gonna get away with this. This shit gone too far."

"Trust me," Berry winked. "She gonna believe me and he will too."

A few seconds later after being in jail for one night Zoom came into the door, naked chest, white shirt over his shoulder. "Where's ma?" he whispered looking toward the back of the apartment.

"In her room crying again," Berry said.

If the Gregory children knew one thing it was that Martha was a crying woman. She cried for their souls. She cried for her job. She cried if her wig wouldn't sit right. She cried in prayer so that her husband could rest in peace. But she did most of her crying at Memory Baptist Church.

Although all of them had been given invitations to visit the small church, none accepted. It was whispered that the church was more of a cult than a place of worship and they wanted no parts of it.

Zoom placed his keys on the living room table. "Why she crying now?"

Berry shrugged. "Probably because Dodson blew one of his balls off in a freak fireworks accident."

"And because you got raped too," Liberty said dry snitching. "Remember?"

"Raped?" Zoom said in a condescending tone. "Who the fuck raped your pissy smelling ass?" He wiped his face with his shirt and tossed it on the couch.

"Some nigga at the mall," Berry said nonchalantly, the fingernail file gliding back and forth over her nails.

"You lying like shit," he laughed. "Ain't nobody raped your motherfukin' ass."

Berry's jaw dropped. "How you figure?"

"For starters you filing your nails like you waiting in a doctor's office. I don't know what kind of trouble you got into but you taking it too far now." He pointed at her forehead.

Berry threw the file down and jumped up in his face. "Oh yeah, what about you? Everybody knows you got arrested on a set up from Shakes. You the laughing stock of the neighborhood! You better hope Perch don't bust that back out with a few slugs since you fucking up his money."

Zoom was surprised at how much his sister knew in such a short period of time. Then again the hood talked consistently, often recycling information until everyone with a doorknob heard the latest gossip. "Mama know I got locked up?" he asked.

"No, unless you give me a reason to tell her."

Zoom waved her off, never bending to blackmail. "Sit your young ass down before I smack the shit out you." At first Berry remained standing until he squared up like he was about to drop her on the floor.

When she was seated he said, "I don't know what possessed you to lie to ma about being raped but you better make it go away. I don't feel like that bitch fucking with me cause you starting shit." He walked into the kitchen and pulled on the refrigerator door. "Hold up, you didn't pinpoint no nigga did you?"

"Pinpoint no nigga?" Berry repeated. "What you mean?"

"Did you say a particular dude raped you?" he said louder. "Did you give a name?"

"She said the dude who girlfriend slapped her in the middle of the street raped her," Liberty interrupted. The detective didn't even get that information but if she loved anything it was Zoom.

Berry looked over at her and frowned. "Fuck is wrong with you? Why would you tell him that?"

Liberty's eyes rolled over Zoom's body and chiseled chest. "Because he cool." She bit her bottom lip seductively and eyed him.

"You mean because you want to fuck," Berry corrected her. "If you think you gonna meet my brother's dick anytime soon forget about it," she continued as if she owned it.

Liberty smiled at Zoom who looked away in embarrassment. He cleared his throat and said, "The worst thing you can do is put a rape on a nigga who ain't do it. If you lying I suggest you correct that shit before you be in a casket." He drank his beer and bopped off.

CHAPTER FOUR
MOTHER SLAVE

Martha was sitting at her kitchen table holding an Ace Of Spades, and a three of Spades card in her hand. Contemplating her next move, she looked across the table at Dora, her long time spades partner, and then Vicky and her husband George. When Martha took her partner's book by throwing out a larger card, forcing them to bump, Dora went through the roof.

"Martha, what the fuck is wrong with you?" Dora screamed as she stuffed her fist into her beefy waist. "You could've thrown out the three and we would've won the fucking game!" She was so angry she was sweating. "Now we lost!" She slammed a fist into the table, shaking everything on top.

"I'm sorry," Martha said under her breath, tossing the cards down. "My mind been all over the place."'

"Leave that girl alone," Vicky said grabbing her share of the money while giving her husband George the other half. "You know she had a hard week."

"That ain't stop you from taking advantage either," Dora responded, legs crossed, foot wiggling.

"All's fair in a game of money." Vicky stood up and walked over to her husband. "Let's go, baby. We've done enough damage here."

They walked to the door and although she was halfway down the steps George looked back at Martha. "On another note...how you holding up, Martha?" he paused. "I mean really?"

Martha looked at Dora and then back at George as if he lost his mind. "I'm fine...go on out of here and see about your wife. I ain't your problem no more."

George nodded once and left.

"That man always worrying about me...he needs to tend to his wife," she said firmly."

Dora wasn't hearing shit she was saying. She didn't know whether to blacken her eye or murder her on account of the money she lost. Dora's light skin reddened the more she considered losing. Besides, they usually cleaned Vicky and George out. Since they played every week for the same amount she counted that money toward her light bill and now she was short. "Can you tell me what is on your mind?"

Martha stood up and walked to the refrigerator to grab two beers. When she realized Zoom drank them all she grabbed two cokes instead. Flopping back down she slid one to Dora and kept the other.

"It's my kids. They out of control and I don't know what to do about 'em no more. Dodson blowing himself up, Berry getting raped and now I'm finding out from a neighbor that Zoom got arrested on a drug charge."

"What you talking about? I saw Zoom outside earlier," Dora said.

"He's out on bail. I think Perch posted it for him." she sighed. "Since Steven's been dead life has been a living hell." She paused. "He ruled with an iron fist and we need some more of that around here."

Dora rolled her eyes, never liking her ex-husband or what he represented. "Martha, why you letting them kids run all over you?" she asked throwing her hands up before letting them flop by her sides. "I don't understand."

"Understand what?"

"That you are the mother but they in charge?" Dora opened her Coke and gulped a large amount. She wiped her mouth with the back of her hand. "If you don't get a hold of them they gonna drive you to the crazy house, Martha. Is that what you want?" she paused. "You know the saddest part...them kids fight each other up and down this apartment. But when it comes to outsiders, even their mother, they stick together. Who sticking up for you?"

"It's easy for you to say. You don't have children."

"I raised three... remember?"

"Dora, please!" she said waving her off.

"Please nothing! And it ain't about having kids. It's about demanding that the ones you slid out of your pussy show you a little respect. You run around here like you're their maid."

"I don't know what to do...I really think they need a man around here again."

"What you need is control!" she paused. "The only thing them kids fear is the police and snitching. Where is the discipline?"

"I got control, Dora," she exhaled.

"Hey, ma!" Dodson called out from the bedroom, interrupting the conversation. "I'm thirsty!"

Martha jumped up from the kitchen table like it was on fire, rushed to the counter and grabbed a large yellow cup. In automatic mode she filled it with ice and then Coca-Cola, adding a little milk like he preferred...since he couldn't get out of bed with his ball deficiency of course.

The Ungrateful Bastards   46

When Martha sat back down she was out of breath and Dora was disgusted. "Did you see that shit?"

"What shit?" Martha responded trying to catch her breath.

"You almost killed yourself for a cup of soda."

Martha held her head down, got up from the table and walked toward the stove. "I don't want to talk about this no more...I gotta cook dinner."

She loved Martha dearly.

Not only because she was her dearest friend but also because they did crack together. History went deep between those two.

Dora walked into the kitchen to accompany her while cooking. "I hope you not giving them kids the world on account of a mistake." She exhaled deeply reminding her of deep family secrets. "Martha, I'm begging you, please regain control of your family."

"It's not as easy as it seems," she cried softly. "Things have gone on too long and I'm afraid if I come down on them too hard...that they...that they ..."

"Won't love you?"

She shrugged. "Yes. That too."

"They will be brats but they will always love you. Now it's time for tough love on your part."

Martha placed the chicken on the plate and seasoned it. "I'm all they got left you know?"

"God did not mean for them children to carry on as such. If our church home saw how they treated you they wouldn't believe it. Colossians 3:20 says 'Children obey your parents *in everything, for this is well pleasing unto the Lord'*."

Upon hearing the Word Martha turned on the eye on the stove and said, "I know what the bible says. I'm just gonna have to pray a little harder for an answer that's all."

"Chile, praying to God alone not going to get you out of this mess. You gotta help yourself too."

"I'm not giving up on my kids, Dora," she turned around to the stove and grabbed the cooking oil. "Just let me handle things. An answer will come soon."

Mind in the wrong place, Martha poured the grease directly onto the fire without the pan and it exploded before her eyes.

CHAPTER FIVE
THE CRUCIAL

The sun seemed to fry the lotion on Zoom's skin as he sat on the steps of his apartment building and thought about his life. Would he beat the upcoming drug charge?

Things had been weird over the past few days. Ever since Martha burned the side of her face and Dora's arm in a grease fire there was something strange about his mother that he couldn't put his hand on.

Scalp throbbing, Zoom scratched between the rows of his newly braided hair, now dressed with a red crystal bead each.

When Zoom saw a customer, he jogged down the steps and served him before walking back. When the door to his apartment building opened, he saw Dodson wobbling outside. Since his injury he was still in a little pain and found it difficult to walk.

He stuffed the money he just made in his pocket and Dodson sat next to him. "Somebody broke into an apartment on the first floor again," Dodson said.

Zoom shrugged. "So...we don't live there."

"You got any more work on you?" Dodson asked.

Caught off guard, Zoom gripped him by his collar and pulled him toward his face. "Fuck you talking about, lil nigga? Huh? You must be crazy to be talking to me like that."

Dodson was taken aback by his brother's reaction and more than anything afraid. "I was just...I..."

"Just like I thought...you don't know shit 'bout what I do so don't speak on it," he said pointing in his face before releasing.

Embarrassed, Dodson looked around the neighborhood to see who was staring in his direction. Luckily for him no one was. "Dang, you didn't have to do all that." He rubbed the wrinkles out of his shirt.

"Don't tell me what I didn't have to do." Zoom turned around and focused ahead. "Lil niggas with one ball shouldn't comment on shit anyway."

He looked out ahead of him but the weight of his comment had him feeling guilty. Hurting his brother's feelings was the last thing on his mind so he gazed back at him, remembering that Dodson was someone touched. "You want something from the ice cream truck? I think it should be coming in a little while." That was Zoom's way of apologizing.

"Naw, I'm good." Dodson said trying not to cry. He spent half of his life attempting to impress his brother so rejection was hard.

When their neighbor known as The Creeper walked toward the steps, Zoom's expression immediately changed for the violent. He lived in the building on the first floor and everyone felt uncomfortable whenever he was around.

The Creeper, a Hispanic man who looked at little boys way too long, was to be avoided not respected. Zoom caught him rubbing his dick once when he was playing basketball and he beat him so badly he was in the hospital for three days, suffering a broken jaw and concussion. The

Creeper's guilt was evident by refusing to press charges.

When The Creeper saw Zoom he tried to rush into the building without confrontation. Of course Zoom allowed him while keeping his eyes on him the entire time.

When the door closed Zoom leaned over to Dodson and said, "You stay away from that nigga you hear me? And let me know if he stalking because he does that sometimes."

"Okay," Dodson said not knowing why everyone avoided him. He looked ahead and asked, "Zoom, is ma acting different to you?"

"I don't know. I ain't notice," Zoom lied.

"She seems like she kinda crazy or something."

"It's probably that church she be fucking with. They say they worship God but they act like the devil." He paused. "Long as the bitch stays away from me I'm good."

"Maybe you right," Dodson shrugged.

When Nay walked down the street wearing a tight red summer dress Zoom hopped down the steps and blocked her path. "So when you gonna stop playing games and get with a nigga?"

Nay's pretty brown eyes peered up at him. Pressing her hand against her forehead to see him despite the bright sun overhead she asked, "You got money?" The strap to the black leather purse she was wearing crossed between her breasts and hung at her side.

Upon hearing the question Zoom frowned and said, "Whoa, ma. You coming at me hard ain't you?" he tossed his white t-shirt on the other shoulder, rubbing his bare chest before dropping his hand. "I was hoping we could make each other feel good."

By T. Styles   51

"It's a beautiful day and I'm good regardless." She said. "I'm coming at you on the real. You got money or not?"

"What you trying to sell?"

She rolled her eyes and walked around him. "Just like I thought. You just like the rest of these stingy ass niggas around here."

Zoom rushed in front of her and blocked her path again. "What you gonna give me for my money?"

"What you want?"

He gripped at his pants. "My dick sucked."

Since he was finally talking her language she snatched him by the hand. "Follow me."

Zoom looked at his brother who was still sitting in front of the building. "I'm gonna take you to get your hair cut and get some sneaks later. But don't move off them steps! If you do I'ma crack your facial plates!"

Dodson rolled his eyes but he was certainly afraid of his big brother's harsh words. He wasn't even supposed to be outside because he wasn't healed but boredom was the devil's workshop.

On a mission, Nay continued the trek to her building before entering her apartment. Although she didn't say another word he allowed her to take him to the bathroom. When Zoom was there he looked around at the Dora The Explorer shower curtain and matching bath rug. "You got a kid?"

"No," she said leaning on the doorframe.

Since she didn't volunteer any other information he asked, "What am I doing in here?"

"You gotta wash your dick before I suck it."

"Are you serious?" he paused, thinking she was joking. "I been out the shower no more than two hours. Pissed one time today tops."

She crossed her arms over her chest. Let me be clear...no washed dick, no suck. And trust me, I can smell soap." She closed the door and he stared at it for a moment.

Although he was disappointed that she was actually a whore, he had to admit that he liked the fact that she had boundaries. When he was done he pulled his clothes up and opened the door only to see Nay standing there. "You done?"

"Yeah." He laughed. "Wow...you dead serious."

She grabbed his hand again and pulled him toward a bedroom in the back of the apartment. It was a large room with pink curtains, a pink comforter and a fluffy pink rug. Since it was the master bedroom he drew his own conclusion. "So you live alone?"

"Why?" she said pushing him down onto the edge of the bed.

"Because I ain't trying to be in your crib if your folks coming home," he said looking down at her.

She sighed. "I live by myself Monday through Friday. On the weekends I have to find some place else to live." She got on her knees and pulled down his zipper to get at his damp dick.

"How does that work?" he asked looking down at her. "The Monday through Friday thing?" Zoom had to admit; she was getting more interesting by the minute.

"All you need to know is this. It's Sunday and I have one hour to put you on cloud nine." She held her hand out. "Before we begin...money please..."

By T. Styles 53

He dug into his pocket and handed her fifteen bucks. He didn't expect her to accept it but she stuffed it in the purse on her hip and lowered her head to get down to work. The moment her warm mouth covered his dick he shivered in ecstasy. Her slick pink tongue ran up and down the shaft before it circled the tip multiple times.

As if he was a full time job and she was a star employee, she softly cuffed his balls while sucking on his stick. To make shit sexier she moaned loudly. Because she was on her knees her waist lowered and her ass rose into the air like the moon. Although she wore a dress he could still see the curves of her meaty ass cheeks.

When his dick was extra wet, she raised her head, spit on it three times and allowed thick globs of white saliva to run down the sides. She continued to lower her head and suck him until his cream exploded into her mouth.

Zoom did everything in his power to prevent from crying out like a bitch but it didn't stop his entire body from trembling. When she was done she stood up, wiped her mouth with the back of her hand and said, "Next time you gotta pay more."

"I figured the cash wasn't enough anyway so why you do it?"

She shrugged. "Because I like you I guess. Now get the fuck out of my house before my Sponsor comes back and kills you."

****

Zoom left the building feeling like he was floating on the Anacostia River. Although he knew he had no business dealing with Nay, he wanted to know more about her. Like what made her a whore? Why did she have to find some place else to stay on the weekends? And who was her sponsor?

He was bopping up the street to check on his brother and to sling some more dope when he realized Dodson was not there. "If your little ass ain't in the house I'ma crack your chest plate," he said to himself.

Zoom was walking up the steps when Perch pulled up in front of the house in a white Benz. He beeped a few times and when Zoom saw him he dipped back down the steps and approached the vehicle. Reaching into the passenger window he gave Perch dap.

"How's it looking out here?" Perch asked, observing the city for himself.

Zoom leaned into the open window. "It's kind of dry," he looked up and down the street. "But I'm on grind mode all night so we gonna be good. What's up?"

"You know you owe me right? For the bail?"

"Yeah, I got it," Zoom responded wondering how he was going to get Perch the paper.

He quickly received his answer.

"The next few packs belong to me. That means you work for free."

"I know, man," Zoom continued, tossing his shirt on the other shoulder. He may have said he knew but it was news to him that he would be working for free. "And I think I'm gonna get off too. My lawyer said they didn't read me my rights and the can coulda been anybody's."

"Whether you get off or not is your problem," Perch continued. "Just make sure I get paid." He paused. "But look, some strange shit been going around and I wanted you to hear it from me first."

"What's up?"

"Your mother just tried to cop some dope from Springman a few blocks from that church she go to. I ain't know she was on the rock again."

Zoom backed up from the car...his jaw dropped. "Damn...me either..."

CHAPTER SIX
THE GAMES BOYS PLAY

Dodson was inside of a large half empty dumpster in the back of FloorMart Superstore along with Bear. Although the smell of the wet garbage would've sickened the average person the two teenagers could care less. The small cracks in the dumpster's frame provided just enough light for them to see from the inside of the darkness to the outside world.

Dodson wasn't supposed to be off the steps and he knew he would have to catch one to the chest from Zoom for not listening. And yet in his mind for what he and his friend were about to get into it was worth it.

"Watch my work," Dodson bragged. "You can't shoot as good as me."

"Bet I do when I'm next," Bear whispered inside of the large can.

Although Dodson was in a little pain from his missing ball stitches, he raised the lid slightly to peer outside. When he saw a male FloorMart employee exiting the back door he aimed his BB Gun through the slot, tugged the trigger and fired into the flesh of the employee's arm.

"Ouch," the struck employee yelled, before looking around to see what happened. "What the fuck was that?"

Having met his mark Dodson quickly ducked into the dumpster and covered his mouth. He and Bear did all they could to prevent from laughing loudly but it was always difficult. To be sure they weren't seen they nestled their bodies deeper into the putrid garbage, with only their heads sticking out.

After a few seconds, Dodson peeked through the lid again and saw the employee rubbing his arm...nursing the wound Since they played this game before at the same store many times, he knew that the victim would assume that something bit him before going back inside.

When the employee went back into the store Dodson stooped back down. "I got him," he whispered to Bear. "You owe me five bucks."

Bear dug into his pocket and gave him the money.

"Maybe next time we can use real guns," Dodson said in a conniving manner.

"Real guns?" He paused. "I don't know about all of that but it's my turn," Bear whispered.

"It don't matter," Dodson said with an attitude. "You not a better shot than me. Not with them fat ass fingers anyway."

"That's cause it's your gun and you play with it more," Bear continued.

"Shut up, fatty. You just mad."

"At least I'm smart enough not to get my ball blown off."

Bear having stated facts caused Dodson embarrassment. "I ain't get my ball blown off," he lied. "Now shut up and shoot", Dodson said raising his voice, but not loud enough to be heard outside. "I dare you."

The boys waited fifteen minutes for the next employee, neither saying a word to the other due to being mad. A dare had been issued and it was time to follow through. Impatient, Dodson looked through the lid and saw a pretty white girl with hair the color of blood exit the back door.

The Ungrateful Bastards   58

The moment she turned around he aimed at her and pulled the trigger. The BB struck her in the side of her neck and she screamed out in pain.

Immediately she ran into the building and they laughed at how hilarious her cries sounded. "Told you," Bear bragged, tossing the gun into the garbage. "I got that bitch!"

"That's one shot to my fifteen," Dodson said hating a little. "Let's see if you can get another one."

"I can," he said confidently. "It's easy as—"

Bear's statement was cut when the lid flew open and the dude Dodson shot earlier snatched Bear out like he was in the matrix. Seeing his friend had been caught Dodson ducked deeper under the trash as the lid came slamming back down, hiding his body.

He was safe.

But what would happen to Bear?

"What the fuck is wrong with you?" The employee scolded. "You think it's funny that you shooting people and shit? Huh? You think it's cool?"

"No, sir," Bear said, scared for his life. He was trying to be polite hoping the dude wouldn't go off like his temper suggested. "I'm sorry. I was just playing."

"Sorry not good enough. You been doing this shit for a long time and now you caught! Don't be a punk! Man up!"

There was brief silence and Dodson wondered from the confines of the trashcan what was happening.

"Go inside, Amanda," the employee instructed.

"What are you about to do?" she asked worriedly.

"Just go!"

When Dodson heard the door close he also heard a thump and his friend exhale quickly. What he didn't see was that with a closed fist the employee slammed Bear in the stomach repeatedly as Bear tried desperately to pull for air. At first Bear was begging the man to stop but after awhile he wasn't saying a word even though the thumps continued.

Dodson stayed in the trashcan for one hour and when he didn't hear anything he finally crawled out. His air felt sucked from his lungs when he saw that his boy was in a motionless pile. Carefully he walked toward his friend who was bloodied and silent. "Bear, come on," he said shaking his arm. "We gotta go before he come back."

Bear didn't move.

"Come on, man," Dodson said pushing harder.

When he heard a noise from the side of the building he took off running, leaving him alone.

CHAPTER SEVEN
THE TRUTH ABOUT LIES

Millin Scott sat at his desk in the precinct and looked evilly at Berry and Liberty.

Martha sat next to the girls and she could tell whatever he was about to say wouldn't be nice. A bandage covered the side of her face where the grease fire smacked her and it was starting to itch terribly.

His tough facial expression, void of pleasantries made it evident how he felt. "Mrs. Gregory, I asked you hear because we have a serious situation that requires your attention."

Martha crossed her legs at the ankle, pulled her brown leather purse closer to her protruding belly and said, "Go on." She nodded. "I'm listening."

Detective Millin flipped a few sheets of paper that were pinned to a clipboard in front of him. "There's no easy way to say this so I'm going to just come out with it. Your daughter and her friend are liars." He stopped searching through the documents and looked directly into Martha's eyes. "A lot of work goes into investigating cases and there are many victimized people who need my help. Your daughter isn't one of them."

Berry pouted upon hearing his words and Liberty's jaw hung.

Martha wasn't so much shocked as she was angry. She leaned in with the disposition of a mother whose child had been insulted. "With all due respect, if you want to retain each one of your teeth, I suggest you explain yourself in a way I can forgive."

"I don't mean to be blunt but it's true. We were able to run the plates that were given to us by your daughter's friend." He gave Liberty the stank eye and focused back on Martha. "With the information we obtained we were able to apprehend the suspect. But when we brought him into custody he had an entirely different story."

"As well he would," Martha spat back. "He's a rapist."

"Not so fast, Mrs. Gregory. Before you go too far it's important for me to say that he's an innocent man!" He looked over at Berry. "Go ahead, young lady. Tell your mother what actually happened that day."

Berry looked over at her mother who was staring at her intently. The strap from Berry's yellow sundress kept falling down her shoulder and Martha pulled it up in a supportive manner. "Talk to me, Berry. Tell this man he wrong about you."

Berry considered telling the truth but she believed in seeing things through to the end. "I don't know what you talking about, officer. I was raped. Honest to God...on Jesus Christ and Mary Magdalene...I told the truth."

Without responding Detective Millin started punching at his keyboard diligently. When he located the website he wanted, he turned the screen so that Martha, Berry and Liberty could see it clearly. On a mission to catch a liar, he moved the mouse over the play button and clicked it. The video played smoothly and he sat back in his chair and waited for their response.

The video was taken the night of the alleged rape. At first Berry didn't know what she was seeing because the camera shot was taken from inside the car the Angry Woman was driving. But after awhile she knew exactly what she was witnessing. Someone from inside the accused rapist's car, a person she hadn't known was present, taped the entire incident.

The video was precise.

It clearly showed Berry being slapped by the Angry Woman and the Angry woman scratching her car. But afterwards it showed the Angry Woman getting back inside her vehicle and pulling off with her husband, the alleged rapist. The entire footage was done from an iPhone.

Having gotten caught Berry held her head down in shame and Martha clutched the top of her own shirt.

"Berry," Martha yelled as she continued to eye the video. "Why would you do something like this? I'm confused…" Nowhere in the picture did it showcase a rape.

When the video finished Detective Millin looked over at them. "The person you accused of raping you had his daughter in the car that night, Berry. And because you put your butt out of the window"— he paused and gaped at Liberty— "she felt offended and slapped Berry before scratching the car. She may have committed assault but she isn't a man and she didn't rape you. Neither did her husband who you described."

Martha was stunned silent.

"But that don't give her the right to hit me," Berry reminded him. Apologizing was not in her vocabulary. She'd rather bullshit her way out of a situation than admit any wrongdoing.

"It also doesn't give you the right to lie on her husband. So this is what we're going to do." He leaned back in his chair and it squeaked. "I'm going to give you her number Mrs. Gregory and she has assured me that she will pay to get your car repaired"— he wrote the information on a piece of paper— "and your daughter will be assigned community service for lying to police." He handed the sheet to Martha who took it slowly. "You too, Liberty."

She sighed.

"Community service?" Berry yelled with her bottom lip hanging. "Doing what? Cause I ain't cleaning no streets."

"You will clean the sidewalks, streets, highways and anything else you're assigned," he grinned slyly. "And if you don't you will be locked up, young lady! Be glad that's all I'm doing. This type of offense carries major time. The man you accused was a convicted felon who turned his life around and now is a service to his community. And had his daughter not taped the entire incident he would've been locked up for a crime he didn't commit. You should consider yourself lucky."

"Man, I hate people," Berry pouted. "Ya'll police always trying to put a young black—"

"Save the race card," he yelled raising his hand. "You haven't earned it." Detective Millin rolled his eyes. He was through with her. "Mrs. Gregory, do you have any questions?"

Even if she did she couldn't speak...instead she sat in her seat and stared out into space. Her life was quickly rolling out of control. It was as if some strange...evil...power was taking over her spirit and changing her for the worse.

In zombie mode, Martha gripped her purse and stood up.

The Ungrateful Bastards   64

"Mrs. Gregory, are you okay?" the detective asked.

When she didn't respond Berry said, "Mama, stop acting strange and shit! That white man talking to you."

Silence.

Martha continued to slog toward the exit of his office without a word. Berry and Liberty, afraid they would get left, followed behind.

"If you need anything let me know," the detective yelled. "Someone will be getting in contact with you soon with Berry's community service schedule." He paused. "Liberty, your mother will receive yours as well."

Although Martha was conscious she was tapping out of reality by the second. As she passed the other officers in the facility, her stone expression gave them the impression that something was off or about to blow. She was so unfocused that she didn't even blink.

When she made it to the car, her world spiraled further out of control as she noticed that her back tire was flattened. What she didn't know was that it was the work of the Angry Woman who was there earlier and recognized the car.

Instead of fussing Martha popped the trunk and removed the tire iron. It was time to fix the flat, get back to her apartment and cry her eyes out.

"Mama," Berry said softly. "What's going on? Why you not talking?"

"Just leave her alone, Berry," Liberty said not wanting Martha to snap, which in her opinion was a moment from occurring.

"Bitch, shut up! That's my mama." Berry focused back on Martha. "Mama, what's—"

When Berry parted her lips and revealed her teeth to speak, Martha came down on her with the tire iron causing her severe pain.

CHAPTER EIGHT
THE DIRTY ONES

Zoom walked into the apartment exhausted after slinging dope all night. And since his mother hadn't been home after learning about his sister's fake rape charge, he feared the household bills would soon be his responsibility.

"Dodson!" he yelled throwing the keys down on the table by the door before locking it.

He scratched his bare chest, tossed his shirt to the couch and bopped toward the refrigerator to grab a cold beer.

He flopped in the chair and yelled, "Dodson, where you at? You better be in his fucking house!" He popped the tab on the beer and downed half of it before sitting it on the table. Since he was seated he went through the mail and was angered when he saw the court date for his drug case.

"Fuck!" he yelled out of frustration. "They always trying to trap a nigga on some bullshit ass charge."

His car was broke. He didn't have any money because he owed Perch and now he needed a lawyer. Would his woes ever end?

More frustrated than ever, he slammed the letter down when he noticed his brother still hadn't answered. Not realizing he was about to take his anger out on him he went on the hunt.

"Dodson, where the fuck you at?" He stood up and bopped toward his bedroom. "I know you hear me calling you. I'm gonna fuck your young ass up."

Zoom walked to his bedroom and threw the door open but he wasn't in the bed. Afraid he wasn't in the house and he would have to hit the streets looking for him he moved toward the bathroom. Knocking hard, he pushed the door open without an invitation.

There Dodson was, in the tub holding his knees against his chest crying.

It wasn't his solemn mood that first caught Zoom but the putrid smell steaming from his body. The entire bathroom stank of garbage and feces and Dodson's gold Nike Foamposites were soiled. When he stepped further inside and gazed at the water he noticed it was completely brown.

Zoom pushed further inside and said, "What happened man? You shit on yourself?"

Dodson shook his head no and wiped his tears roughly away.

"Then what the fuck is up?" Zoom said sternly.

"Nothing," he responded trying to act tough and doing a poor job.

"Did you and Bear go at it again? Ma gonna stop letting you hang with him if ya'll keep fighting and shit."

Instead of answering Dodson burst out in tears with cries so deep they appeared to pull from his gut. He was devastated and although Zoom had known his brother all of his life he'd never seen him in such disarray.

Uncomfortable with how Dodson was acting, he rushed out of the bathroom and toward the kitchen. He grabbed the red phone on the wall and dialed a number that rang two times before someone answered. "Hey, Mrs. Charles." He clutched the phone tighter. "Is Bear in the house?"

"No!" she yelled as if she'd had enough of her son's shit. "I'm looking for his ass right now. Why you asking'? The boys got into another fight?"

"I think so," Zoom said as he could still hear his brother crying in the bathroom. "I was hoping to get some more info from you since he act like he can't talk."

"I swear they have the weirdest relationship." She giggled. "One minute they the best of friends and the next they can't stand each other. What are we going to do with them?"

"I can't call it. But I'll hit you later. Let me know if you find out what happened before I do."

"Okay, son."

Zoom hung up and placed both hands on the counter for support. He had zero time for this type of shit. It was his mother's job to get the family together but what could he do? She took leave with no day of return in sight.

Taking two deep breaths, he scratched his chest and tried to think about how best to deal with the matter.

Standing up straight, he tapped the counter and walked back to the bathroom. Dodson was still the way he left him... an emotional pile of mess. Zoom sat on the toilet and looked ahead of him because he couldn't face his kid brother yet. When he was ready he asked, "What happen, man?"

"Nothing."

"Well if nothing happened why you sitting in here crying like a bitch?" he looked over at him. "Huh? Real niggas don't cry...didn't I tell you that before? Don't you know that shit by now? Real niggas do what they gotta no matter what.

We make the big decisions!" he paused. "Now tell me what happened."

Dodson's glassy eyes looked up into his big brother's. "It's Bear," he whispered.

"What about the fat ass youngin?" Zoom yelled.

"He killed him. He killed him and I saw the whole thing."

Zoom's heart rocked within the walls of his chest. When it felt like the room was spinning and he leaned against the sink for support. "Who killed who?"

"They killed Bear...behind the store."

Dodson spent the next five minutes telling him how they shot BB guns out the inside of a dumpster for fun. When Dodson was finished Zoom felt as if the breath had been sucked from his body. He didn't fuck with her but this type of shit would kill his mother. She already had problems because of his fast ass sister crying rape and if she were home she would be forced to deal with a child who witnessed a murder.

In clean up mode he asked, "Do ma know you involved?"

He shook his head no. "I haven't seen her."

"Good...where's the BB gun?"

"In my room. Under the bed."

Zoom exhaled. "Good." He nodded. "Did the police find Bear's body yet? That you know of?"

Dodson shook his head no.

"Then here's how it's gonna go down," he sat on the toilet and turned toward him. "You not gonna say nothing about this to nobody. If a nigga ask where Bear is you don't know shit."

"But Mrs. Charles gonna ask again. We left the house together."

"I don't give a fuck what Mrs. Charles gonna say! You don't know where this little nigga went do you hear me?" he roared. "Unless you want to get pulled up for questioning by the police and labeled a snitch. Is that what you want? Because you keep running your mouth the way you do and that's exactly what's gonna happen."

"I don't want that," he said shaking his head.

"Then hear me good. I better never hear you talking about that little nigga again. EVER! As far as I'm concerned you never knew him. When the cops call and ask...and they will...the last time you saw him ya'll were playing out front the house. Am I clear?"

Dodson wiped tears from his face again.

"Good," Zoom responded feeling one percent better that at least a plan, although weak, was put into action.

When there was a firm knock at the front door Zoom's eyes widened fearing it was the police. He lowered his body and pointed a stiff finger into the center of Dodson's nose. "Don't come out of this bedroom until I call your name," he whispered. "Understood?"

Dodson nodded.

With his kid brother properly threatened, Zoom exited the bathroom and closed the door behind him. Slowly he walked toward the door, hair beads clicking against one another. He was hoping that the knocks would stop and whoever was there would go away.

They didn't.

When he finally made it to the door he looked out of the peephole and exhaled in slight relief when he saw who it was. He stepped back, looked down at his jeans and opened the door. He was staring into Nay's eyes.

"Hey, you," she smiled, way more cheerful than he felt.

Although he was going through the motions with the kid murder beef in the air he couldn't get over how cute she looked. Wearing a pair of tight blue jeans, a pink halter-top and open toe sandals he wanted to fuck.

But as if he could care less he said, "I didn't know you knew where I lived." He walked deeper into the apartment and she followed, closing the door behind herself.

"I asked a neighbor."

Before sitting on the sofa Zoom turned around and looked at the open bathroom door...Dodson was standing in the doorway. Even though he told him to remain inside, he disobeyed and Zoom contemplated flattening his face with his fists. "Dodson, go to your room!"

Walking out with a towel wrapped around his lower body, he obeyed.

"Your brother okay?" She asked compassionately.

"He'll be aight." He flopped on the couch and she sat next to him. "So what you want, Nay? I'm not up for company right now as you can see."

She frowned. "Wow, I was hoping you would be happy to hear from me."

"Shawty, any other time I would but tonight ain't it." He paused. "Now what's up?"

The Ungrateful Bastards   72

Nay looked down at her hands. "Never mind... guess I'll leave then."

Zoom watched her move slowly to the door realizing once she was gone he would be free to handle other matters. But if he let that chick go he would be fucked up all day. "Don't leave. Chill with me for a—"

"Zoom, my stitches bleeding," Dodson said sticking his head out of the door.

"Well bandage it up," he told him. "I ain't no fucking nurse and I don't feel like looking at your dick!"

"But I can't see it by myself."

The last thing Zoom felt like doing was looking at his little brother's missing ball. "Well wait 'til ma come home."

"But it's bleeding bad."

"Let me do it," Nay said softly.

Zoom looked at her as if she were playing. Was she a pervert or helpful? If she was one or the other at this point he didn't care. "Are you sure? From what I heard it's bad."

"I ain't doing nothing else right now." She shrugged.

His silence was the answer and the first thing she did was wash her hands. As she walked into Dodson's room and cleaned and bandaged his wound, Zoom just stood back in the corner and watched her do her thing.

When she was done they walked into the living room. "As you can clearly see I like you," she said out of nowhere.

He laughed. "That was the grossest shit I've seen all night." He laughed. "Well tell me something about yourself. You make me suspicious so I need to know something personal."

"What you want to know?"

He folded his arms over his chest. "Anything."

"Okay," she swallowed. "Although I like you...if I were you I would stay away from me. Even talking to me can get you killed."

"I'm a Gregory, baby." He winked. "That's code word for danger."

CHAPTER NINE
OF THE WORST KIND

Only a core of herself, Martha wandered down the street, a few blocks from her house. Wearing the same clothes she had on the day she ambled away from the police station in a daze. It appeared that something clicked in her brain where she kept her common sense and it didn't look like she would return to her normal ways anytime soon.

When she first learned that her daughter was allegedly raped she did everything she could to make her feel better. Martha was willing and able to be the rock Berry needed but where was her support?

After learning that the rape was all a lie she felt betrayal of the worst kind.

How awful!

How mean!

For the life of her she couldn't understand how she could have bred such selfish children. She began to question everything she thought was safe and started to feel hate deeply in the center of her stomach where she kept her love.

Martha walked up and down the road never stopping not even to release her bladder. Instead she urinated in her dress and continued as if nothing was wrong.

Her trek continued down the streets of Washington DC until a white Subaru Outback pulled alongside her. The truck drove slowly careful not to hurt her but equally careful not to lose her either.

It was Dora, her best friend.

Dora rolled the passenger window down and yelled, "Martha, oh my God, where have you been? Your family has been worried sick. What's going on, suga?" Unconsciously she rubbed the small rippled patch on her arm where the grease fire had burned her skin.

Martha continued her zombie walk without an answer. Besides Dora had yet to say the words to get her to connect with reality. But she was a good friend...the best that a lifetime could buy...and she would not let go no matter what. "Martha, please talk to me. Whatever it is it can't be this bad!"

Silence.

Frustrated, Dora pulled her car in front of Martha, blocked her path and hopped out. Walking up to her friend, the first thing she smelled was the odor of dried urine so strong she started to say fuck it, get back in her car and be home in time to watch her soap operas.

Instead she stayed.

Gazing at Martha's state Dora was so beside herself that her body trembled and she felt she was about to have a seizure like she use to years ago.

There was history between them.

When they use to do drugs together it was Martha who got clean first when she met her husband Steven. Prior to that they were both out on the streets and lived in crack houses, selling stank pussy to buy their next hit.

When Martha got herself together she shared her life and home with Dora. The plan was to see her through her rehabilitation. Martha and Steven helped her into a facility and they both were there when she got clean. It was at that time that Martha introduced her to the congregation at Memory Baptist church and her life changed for the better.

They were more than friends. They were sisters and Dora could see herself killing somebody for her.

Martha was looking at the ground until Dora placed her hands on Martha's shoulders. When Martha's eyes finally met Dora's, and she recognized her friend, she burst into tears.

Dora pulled Martha into her body and held her tightly. At this point she could care less about the odor steaming off of her flesh. Considering all of the things they'd been through in the past she smelled worse. All she wanted was to support her friend and try to help her through whatever darkness was attempting to steal her soul.

"Come with me, Martha," Dora said holding her gritty, dirty hand. "Get in my truck and talk to me."

"But I'm wet." By knowing that she was too soiled to enter a car, Dora hoped she was finally touching a version of reality.

"I don't care," Dora said seriously. "Now come on."

Dora walked Martha to the passenger side and when she was tucked in she closed the door. She took a few more seconds to look at her through the window to be sure she wouldn't get out. When she was hopeful that Martha wouldn't leave, she carefully walked to the driver's side keeping her eyes on her friend the whole time.

Easing into the truck she looked over at her. "Tell me what's going on, Martha. Please. Because I'm having trouble understanding how a woman as strong as you could fall so hard."

Martha looked down at her sooty hands. "It's my kids." She shook her head and sighed. "I don't know what's going on with my kids."

Dora exhaled. Finally she was speaking a language she understood. But before going any further she had to know one question. "There is talk on the streets, Martha." Her tone was deep and serious. "Talk I don't like so instead of speculating I'ma just ask. Are you using again?"

Immense guilt consumed Martha. She looked out the passenger window and sighed. "I did a few times. A little rock here and there...nothing to go to rehab about if that's your question." She looked at Dora. "I think it got out of my system though. It just didn't seem to get me high enough to make my troubles go away."

Dora looked ahead, hoping she was speaking the truth. "Thank, God." She placed her hand on her friend's thigh. "You going to have to let your kids do them while you do you for a little while. Now I know you don't want to hear this but it's the only way. Zoom old enough to look after things anyhow. The boy over eighteen."

"It' so hard," she sobbed.

Martha proceeded to tell Dora how Berry lied about being raped. "There's nothing worse than wanting to help your child through something so horrible only to find out it was a lie."

Dora shook her head. "Martha, I'm gonna be honest with you and I don't want you to be angry. Your kids are holding the past against you. Now I know things happened to make you feel guilty, but you have spoiled them kids rotten and look at how you're repaid. Anybody with two eyes, two ears and a heart could tell that you have

The Ungrateful Bastards   78

some devil spawns for children. Don't trade your soul for them."

"Dora, please..."

"I'm serious. Now I know you wanted to raise some good God-fearing children but things took a turn for the evil. Maybe you should leave for a few days. You got to let them make mistakes so that they can see what happens when you not there to pick up their load. You understand?"

Martha looked out ahead of her. She filled her lungs with as much air as they could hold and released. Could she walk out of her children's lives if only for a little while? Was she that type of mother?

She turned toward her friend. "So you really think my kids are evil?"

Dora said with all certainty, "Yes, honey...of the worst kind."

CHAPTER TEN
THE UNFORGOTTEN

Zoom paced the living room as Dodson sat on the sofa crying.

He was getting on his nerves!

Earlier in the day he got him a haircut and bought him some silver Nike Foamposites since he fucked the other ones up in the garbage. He figured by then his mother would be home and he would be calm but she hadn't returned.

Zoom tried to fake hard and in most aspects he was, but it would be inauthentic to say that he wasn't worried about Martha, mainly for Dodson. Even though he talked shit to her, Dodson wasn't the kind of kid who could go without his mother for too long and it was evident by his erratic behavior.

The last few days had been pure madness and Nay stood by his side for every minute of it. But he wouldn't allow himself to get but so comfortable because he couldn't trust her. Add to his woes Berry was ripping and running the streets like she found out the second use for her pussy.

"She dead!" Dodson yelled. "She on the streets dead."

"Don't say that," Nay said softly, sitting beside him. "She's fine."

"She dead...dead...dead....dead!" Dodson chanted louder slapping the sides of his face with his hands.

It was final.

Zoom grabbed his mother's car keys off the counter. "I'm going to look for her."

"I'm coming with you," Nay said standing up.

Before leaving Zoom walked to his sister's room and knocked on the door. When she didn't answer he opened it without permission. As usual she was wearing a pair of shorts that hiked up between the lips of her coochie along with a white tank top that revealed the brown circles of her areoles. Her arm was wrapped in a sling because Martha's strike with the tire iron caused her a sprain.

He was disgusted at how she was posted up.

Although she saw him, instead of closing her legs she maintained the conversation on the phone she was having with Liberty.

Zoom stepped in and frowned. "I wish for once you would wear some clothes around here."

"Says the nigga without a shirt...*ever*." She rolled her eyes and removed the phone from her ear. "Sides...if you wouldn't come in my room unwantedly you wouldn't have to see it." She opened her legs wider and Zoom could see the pinkness surrounding the opening of her vagina.

Quickly he turned his head. "I should fuck you up for that nasty shit you just did!" he yelled. "Close your fucking legs before I break them!"

She giggled and obeyed. "What do you want, Zoom?"

"I'm going looking for ma and I got her car. Don't leave the house. I want you to keep your eyes on Dodson. He in his room tripping over ma."

Nay popped up and stood in front of him. "But I was gonna take the car. Me and Liberty going to the movies and stuff later."

"Ain't you listening? You not going nowhere. You gonna stay your fast ass here and watch Dodson."

She stomped and her foot smacked against the hardwood floor. "But you gotta a car! How come you can't use your own?"

"Do you hear yourself? I just told you that I'm gonna look for ma and you don't even care. Instead you in here talking to that ditsy ass bitch on the phone and flashing your pissy pussy 'round the house." His face reddened.

"Why should I care about that bitch. Look at what she did to my arm!" she raised the sling and dropped it, only wearing it for attention.

"You heard what I said, Berry." He said breathing heavily. "I'm taking the car and you better be here when I get back."

She placed her hands on her hips and leaned toward him. "And if I don't. What you gonna do?"

Zoom raised his hand and smacked her so hard her ass slapped against the floor and her arm popped out of the sling. "Then I'm gonna fuck you up." He pointed down at her. "You don't know me as much as you think you do, Berry. But you'll learn if you're not in this house when I get back!" He stormed out and slammed the door.

Before going back into the living room he leaned against the wall in the hallway next to her room. Frustrated with it all he looked up at the ceiling and sighed. He didn't want to hit her but she was being reckless and he was afraid she would continue if he didn't control her before their mother returned.

When ready he pushed off the wall, stood up straight and bopped down the hallway toward the living room as if nothing was wrong. He started to stop by Dodson's room but he didn't have enough energy to deal with him again.

Besides, Bear's mother had been by earlier that day asking about her son's whereabouts and she was hysterical. Since Dodson was the last one with him she had a few questions. With his body being dumped in a ditch a mile away from Floormart, it was difficult finding out how he was killed. But when Zoom told her Dodson hadn't seen or heard from Bear she requested to speak to him directly.

Zoom was smart. He knew his brother was too weak to be exposed to her line of questioning so he refused by telling her that he was sick.

Blair, Bear's mother, had skin the color of vanilla ice cream, but after witnessing Zoom's callous attitude she turned a shade of strawberry. "If you don't let me talk to that boy I'm gonna get the cops!" She yelled, her body trembling.

"He already talked to them...but you do what you gotta."

When he made it to the living room Nay was standing in the middle of the floor waiting on him with a smile on her face. There was a firm knock at the door that caused Zoom's blood to rumble. He crept to it, looked out the peephole and saw it was George, his father's old co-worker and Martha's spades friend.

Zoom opened the door slowly, not allowing him inside. "What you want?"

"Your mother here?"

Zoom frowned and pushed out into the hallway, with Nay following. She was confused. What caused him to be so angry with the stranger?

Knocking him up against the wall Zoom asked, "Why the fuck you keep coming around here askin' about my mother?"

He looked dead into his eyes. "You know why, young man..."

Zoom, not liking his response pulled his weapon and anchored it against his nose. "Give me everything you got."

George's eyebrows rose and Nay thought she would piss her pants. "So you gonna rob me?" He couldn't believe it was happening.

"Something is wrong with you, young man."

Zoom cocked the weapon as his answer.

Not wanting to die, George dug inside his pockets. "Give it to her," Zoom said referring to Nay. George complied and Zoom lowered his gun. "Don't come back here again. You hear me? Not even for cards."

George ran down the steps and bolted out the building's door.

"What was all that about?" she asked, trembling, before handing him the money.

"The less you know the better." They walked out the building.

****

Hours passed and Zoom had been everywhere looking for his mother. His mind was all over the place and he needed a release. What better way than to find out more information about his sidekick. "What's your thing?" he asked Nay as he steered down the road. "I mean really."

She ran her hands through her hair. "What you mean?"

"You been over my house for the past few nights. Haven't left my side except the couple hours you leave in the afternoon. What you into?"

She sighed and rubbed her own thighs briskly. "My situation is unique, Zoom. Even if I told you...you would never understand. And since we trying to look for your mother I would love if we kept our minds on that."

"Let me worry about my mother...I got a few seconds for a history lesson. So talk to me."

She looked at him and smiled. "You're real persistent."

He shrugged. "If that's what you want to call it."

"Well, I got myself into some trouble when I was twelve years old."

"Twelve. What kind of trouble can a kid get in that ain't an adult's fault at that age?"

"The kind I'm into. I keep telling you my situation is unique." She sighed. "Anyway when I was younger my mother—"

Her story was interrupted by the ring of Zoom's cell phone. His eyes widened when he realized it was Dora's number so he quickly answered. "Please tell me you found my mother," he said in lieu of hello.

"I got her."

Zoom slapped the steering wheel five times in relief. "I don't know why I didn't stop by your crib earlier. I'm on my way."

"We'll be waiting," she said, voice heavy with attitude.

****

Zoom made it to Dora's house in five minutes and when the door open he saw Martha sitting

By T. Styles   85

innocently on the sofa wearing a pink robe with yellow flowers. As if she hadn't pissed herself some days earlier. The burn mark on her face was uncovered and looked a little healed.

He looked up at Dora whose arms were crossed over her chest like a bodyguard. She looked as if she wanted to smack the shit out of him.

"Where did you find her?" he asked.

"Does it matter?" She said in a gruffly tone. "You and your siblings done did everything you could to make her life miserable. Including break her heart. Why should I tell you shit?"

His brows lowered as he reconciled whose side she was on. "Can I spend a few moments with my moms?"

"Nigga, if you think I'm leaving you alone with your mother you got another thing coming."

He frowned. "How you sound? This is my moms! What you think I'm gonna do...fuck her?"

"Zoom," Martha yelled. "It's been a long time since I heard foul language from one of my kids and I'm not trying to hear it now."

Zoom stepped back, lowered his head and sighed. "All I want to do is find out what's going on. Can you give me a few seconds?"

Martha turned toward Dora. "It's okay. I'll talk to him."

Dora gave one more menacing look to Zoom and then focused her attention on Nay. "You like wine?"

"If you gotta glass I'll drink anything."

"My kind of girl," she said. "Join me in the kitchen."

As they walked away Zoom sat next to his mother. He could sense that he needed to be careful and choose his words wisely, or risk pushing her away even more. "Ma, what's up? Where you been? Dodson running around here tripping and you act like you don't care."

She crossed her arms over her belly. "I've been around." She avoided eye contact and kept her focus on the picture of black Jesus on the wall.

"Why haven't you been home to see about your kids?"

Martha was silent for a moment. When she was prepared to talk she turned her body toward him and exhaled. "Son, your soul is compromised and the Lord is going to take you from this place if you don't get it together."

Zoom hated when his mother went on a religious rant and he would rather drink piss out of a urinal than talk about God. Truthfully he had a love hate relationship with the Man upstairs.

"If anything you need to check yourself. Family secrets don't remain secrets if the family is divided."

"You threatening me again, boy?

"Stating truth," he said firmly. "Now get up. It's time to go home and see about Dodson."

"Son, I'm serious. The devil is real and he wants you and your sister and brother. The way you acting it looks like you've chosen him already."

"Do you hear yourself? You haven't been home in days and you want me to respect a God that would condone that? Where was your God when I was up at night with Dodson because he thought you were dead on the side of the road. And don't think I don't know you've been doing rocks again."

Martha was embarrassed and she gripped at the collar of her robe. "I did backslide once but I'm fine now. I'm a firm example of what He can do and I want you to come with me and walk in the Lord's way. Please."

Zoom wanted his mother home but he wasn't sure if he could sit through a minute more of her testimony. "What *exactly* you want me to do, ma?"

"Go to church with me and I promise not to bother you again about it."

This wasn't what he wanted but he had to meet her half way. "Just one time?"

"All I'm asking is for one day, Michael."

"If I do will you come home?"

"Son, if the Lord sees fit I will return that day."

****

After getting almost nowhere with his mother he went home, only to see a candy apple red Porsche sitting out in front of his building. "What the fuck?" he said to himself, having been familiar with the car.

Parking sideways, he jumped out and made a beeline for his apartment. All while Nay followed, too afraid to ask what was going on.

Removing the keys from his pocket, he could hear heavy laughter and loud music playing inside as he unlocked the door. His blood felt like it was boiling as he entered. His eyes widened with disgust at the department store shopping bags on the couch and grocery bags on the kitchen counter.

The Ungrateful Bastards

When he gazed to the left he saw Dodson and Berry sitting next to Marine "Dookie" Patterson on the sofa. When they saw Zoom's angry face, Berry stood up and turned the music down as they waited for his wrath.

Stomping up to Dookie Zoom yelled, "What the fuck you doing in my crib?"

Nay, not knowing what was happening hung by the door.

"She bought us some clothes and stocked the fridge," Berry said excitedly, hoping Zoom wouldn't fuck things up. "Cause ma not here and stuff."

"I told you to stay away from my family," he yelled, ignoring Berry. His nose flared, as he looked dead into Dookie's eyes. "Didn't I?"

Dookie slowly rose, as if trying to determine if she should smack the shit out of him or not. He could tell she was angry because her light skin was reddening.

She whipped her long hair over her shoulder, crossed her arms over her chest and leaned back on one foot. "Nigga, you heard your sister. I'm here because I heard what was happening to your family. Instead of coming at me like you wanna box you should be on your knees thanking me. It ain't like you haven't done it before."

He blew out a noisy breath. "No!" he pointed in her face. "You here because you don't get the picture that it's over between us."

"Is that what you think?" she asked sarcastically. "It ain't never over between us, Zoom. I'm the one who gave you your nickname because when I called you always came in a hurry," she laughed.

"Get the fuck out my face," he said.

By T. Styles

89

"You love me in your face," she continued. "Can't nobody fuck you like I do and we both know it." She looked at Nay. "And I do mean nobody." She paused. "Now I'm here to talk to you about something in private. You coming with me or not?"

"We have no words for each other," he said firmly. "Now get the fuck out my spot." He pointed at the door.

When Nay opened it Dookie walked up to her, looked at her clothing and laughed. "Damn, Zoom." She gazed at him and back at Nay. "I guess the rumors are true. You have fallen on hard times." She walked past him to pick up her Celine purse and hit it for the door. Before walking out she stopped. "I'm leaving...but not without a warning. Be careful how you talk to me, Zoom. You and I both know who runs DC...and it damn sure ain't Perch." She hugged Berry and Dodson and bounced.

When she left Berry looked at her older brother. "I know this the wrong time and stuff, but can I borrow the car tonight?" she played with the strap on her sling.

Zoom shook his head and stomped toward his room, slamming the door behind himself.

CHAPTER ELEVEN
MOMMY WEIRDEST

Zoom trudged behind his mother along with Berry and Dodson as they made their way into the church.

Visiting the steeple was nothing like they expected.

It was worse.

As Martha crossed the threshold, a woman holding a fistful of coconut scented lit incense spread the smoke over her head. The odor was so thick that it caused Zoom to cough and gasp as if he just hit the best weed money could buy.

Before the family could make it to their seats, five women approached and dropped to their knees in front of Martha. One woman removed her shoes while the other four wiped her legs with a wet lavender scented cloth. They didn't clean down Zoom and the others because they weren't members, but they were handed a plastic white bag for their shoes.

Berry and Dodson quickly removed theirs but Zoom had already contemplated leaving the church if he was forced to part with his sneaks. Bad enough she made him wear a blue plaid button down shirt.

"I'm good," Zoom told them with a half a smile. "Thanks anyway."

Martha looked back at him. "Son, please. It's disrespectful to come into the house of the lord with unclean shoes. Remove them now! You're embarrassing me."

To keep the peace he did what she wanted but the woman still wouldn't move. "You're filled with animosity," she told him. "I have to clean your feet too. I'm afraid the demons that keep you company will spread over the others."

Having heard her explanation he certainly had enough. "But I washed already," he shot back.

"Boy, just do it," Berry said rolling her eyes. "I want to get this over with!"

Although Berry hadn't inspired him to move forward Martha had. "Son, do it for me," she said. "This is what I want and you promised you would at least try."

Zoom looked into Dodson's eyes and his heart softened. If he refused he was afraid he would find Martha roaming around the city back on drugs. He was already hearing different versions of what happened to Martha during her recent stint on the streets.

Some people said she was selling pussy. Some said her children were beating her and she was running for cover. He even had a nigga tell him that his mother was selling dope. Whatever the story told they were on to one truth. And that was that his mother was definitely different.

"Aight, ma." He paused. "Whatever you want."

The women walked over to him and cleaned his legs and feet. Afterwards they were escorted to the front of the church where a warm red velvet blanket was placed over their legs. Having gone through the process, Dora was already sitting up front waiting for them.

Once seated, when Zoom looked at his sister she was on her phone texting, and Dodson who was looking around in a confused fashion, he wondered if he wasn't making things worse by trying to bring his mother back home.

The Ungrateful Bastards   92

Was it too late? Besides, too much had happened and her weird behavior made him want to stay away from her.

As he sat next to her, the look on his mother's face as she waited on the preacher was priceless. She smiled in a way that Zoom hadn't seen since their father was alive.

Before long a very tall and lanky preacher stepped up to the podium. He was also barefoot and dressed in a gold pants suit. He waved his hand to all of the followers and they cheered as if he were a rock star. "God bless"— a head nod – "God bless" – two head nods. "God bless you all."

Martha clasped her hands over her heart and grinned widely.

"As you all know today is not just another day," the preacher continued. "Today is a blessed day because we are together. We are here to fellowship with one another. And we are here to *enjoy* one another."

He smiled even wider and Zoom was certain the edges of his mouth would crack and bleed.

"Before I begin are there any visitors here?" the preacher questioned.

Martha threw her head to the left to look at her children who were also looking toward their left and away from her. Surely she didn't expect them to say anything.

But she did.

"Stand up," she said happily. "Let the preacher take a look at you."

Berry propped her head up with a fist. "I don't want to, ma. This your thang not ours." She played with the sling on her arm.

She rolled up the sleeves of her church dress. "I don't care what you want to do," she said through clenched teeth. "Now stand up so the Preacher could lay eyes on you!"

Slowly her three children rose and the preacher looked down at them with much gratitude. "Welcome, children! Are you in for a treat this Sunday morning." He motioned his hands for them to sit down and they did so gladly. "I'm certain something I say will bring you closer to Jesus."

"The pastor ain't lying," Dora added. "If this man knows one thing it's God."

Zoom, along with his sister and brother sat through what could be arguably the worst day of their existence. The first hour was long and drawn out and Zoom was shocked at how quickly folks caught The Holy Ghost...even if it meant putting the eye out of their closest neighbor. But when one woman took off her skirt and a few other people followed suit, Zoom knew he'd seen it all. And if it was all the same to God, he hoped never to see it again.

He was just trying to stomach it all when Martha reached to remove her shirt due to catching the spirit too. Zoom rushed in just before the first button popped and showcased all his mother's secrets. "What you doing, ma?" He asked as he gripped at her hands.

"The spirit is moving me son," she said excitedly. "And when that happens can't nothing stand in my way." She slapped at his hand and continued to remove her blue blouse, revealing her tan bra underneath.

Dodson covered his mouth while Berry's jaw hung. They couldn't believe the levels their mother reached.

Zoom couldn't take it anymore. "Let's get the fuck out of here. We'll get up with ma when it's over." He expeditiously escorted his siblings out of the church before they saw anymore. And since Martha had the keys to the car in her church purse, they sat on the steps and waited for the shenanigans to be over.

Needing some air, Zoom removed his shirt and tossed it over his shoulder.

When service was over, the church door's opened and the congregation spilled out. Martha walked up to her children and she spoke, as she hadn't just removed her skirt and bra.

"Are you kids ready?" she said with a smile. "It's time to grab something to eat." She turned around to walk away.

****

Zoom, Berry, Dodson and Nay stared at Martha who was in the kitchen slamming pots and pans on the stove. She claimed she was cooking macaroni and cheese, meatloaf and spinach, but her erratic behavior suggested she didn't feel like doing shit.

An hour later, when the meal was burnt, something Martha never did, they sat at the table and tried to eat as a family. Although no one was hungry except Martha, who was on her third piece of meat, the rest were too shocked to move as they observed the woman who use to be so kind and meek move with rage.

"Ma," Dodson said softly. He swallowed the lump in his throat before saying another word. "You okay?"

She placed her fork down, looked at him and rolled her eyes. "Even if I wasn't it wouldn't make a difference to none of you bastards." She gazed at all of them, eyes black with disdain. "Would it?" she grabbed her plate, walked to her room and slammed the door.

Nay, who remained quiet the whole time, was starting to realize the dynamics of this family ran deeper than she thought.

CHAPTER TWELVE
UNANSWERED KNOCKS

The house seemed eerie with everyone gone...

Dodson sat on the living room sofa wearing a white t-shirt and his underwear, while eating a mammoth sized bowl of Captain Crunch cereal...his favorite.

Earlier in the day Zoom bought him new clothes and got him another haircut with the hard lines on the side the way he liked, anything to appease him and make him feel better about their mother acting weirdly.

But nothing worked...Dodson wanted his mother.

Stuffed beyond the limits, he placed the half eaten meal on the floor, grabbed the remote and turned on the television. Boredom had him looking for something to pass the time and normally it would be the company of his best friend...but he was dead.

After being unable to find a channel to his liking, he stopped on the news, picked up his bowl and started eating again.

Until he saw *his* face.

With eyes glued on the newscaster's lips and ears on his words, he was in a trance.

"This case is getting sadder by the day. As we reported first, the suspect who murdered Vance Taylor, known as Bear to his family and friends, has yet to be found.

Vance was last seen in front of his mother's house playing ball with friends and as expected the family is devastated. When a child is murdered it's never easy but not having the killer in custody makes things more difficult.

If you have any information about what happened to young Vance Taylor please contact the number below. Let's bring this murderer to justice."

Tears streamed down Dodson's face and the spoon fell out of his palm. Although he realized he was dead, having seen the murder with his own eyes, it was easier to deal with when it was out of sight.

To make matters worse he didn't have support because he had to keep secret what he knew. And when the cops came to the house to question Dodson, Zoom was right there leading his testimony and giving him the evil eye as a reminder of what they talked about.

To say nothing to no one about what he actually saw.

Dodson hoped the command meant outsiders only but that was not the case. Whenever he tried to talk to Zoom when they were alone he was not receptive, threatening to knock out his teeth. So he was left to cry into his pillow while his family carried on with life.

He was just about to go into his room when someone knocked at the door. At first he attempted to ignore it but the knocking was so persistent it rattled his nerves.

Slowly he crept towards the sound.

Standing in front of the door, he was about to say hello until he heard Blair, Bear's mother's soft but desperate voice outside. "Dodson, I know you're in there," she cried softly, her voice quivering with every word. "You can't keep hiding in this apartment. You can't keep lying and saying you don't know what happened to my boy. Now I like you son...always have. But you have to tell the police the truth."

The Ungrateful Bastards   98

Silence.

"Dodson," she continued. "Please talk to me...I'm dying out here."

He stared at the door as if he could see her face. Suddenly his body collapsed Indian style on the floor and his young heart ruptured again with pain.

"Son, I know you're in there. I...I saw your brother and your sister leave earlier. Its twelve o-clock in the afternoon and usually by this time you are out here playing...with...with Vance." She choked up and pulled herself together. "I'm not mad at you, son. If you are in there listening, I know that things happen. And all I want to know is what went down that day. Tell me and I won't bother you again."

Dodson wiped the tears away, wanting so badly to stop the nightmares that took hold of him. Just last night he woke up in a cold sweat replaying everything that happened the day Bear lost his life. Deep down he felt if he told her everything he'd be honoring his friend...looking out for him as he often did in life.

It was time to be brave.

Dodson stood up and touched the doorknob, preparing not only to disobey Zoom but also possibly get himself in trouble for lying to police. But the moment he was about to unlock the door Blaire snapped. "I never liked you, you stupid ass nigga! I told my boy you were a snake...and not to trust you but he never listened. When I finally get my hands on you my boy is going to have you as a playmate again in death! "

Upon hearing her threat Dodson pissed on himself— his boy briefs soaked as he trembled in fear for his life.

When he heard the woman walk down the stairway only then did he breathe. His relief was short lived when there was another knock.

"Dodson," Dookie said softly. "It's me. Open the door." He didn't budge. "I know you in there. I heard that chick talking to you."

Although he hadn't said a word to Blair, he was slightly relieved he wasn't by himself. "Wait a minute." He ran to the kitchen, grabbed some napkins and wiped up his urine. When he was done he changed into some dry jeans, took a look down at himself and opened the door.

Dookie walked inside, wide smiled and possessing her usual strong but sexy demeanor. "Zoom here?"

He shook his head no.

She exhaled. "I was hoping I could talk to him alone. Away from his girlfriend."

Dodson sat on the sofa. "He doesn't want you here. I'm talking about Zoom."

She cocked her head to the side and shook it lightly. "He treats me like I'm an enemy when I'm anything but." She exhaled. "Look...I know what Zoom wants...but what about you? Do you mind that I'm here?"

He shrugged. "No...I mean...I don't know."

She walked in, switching her hips before flopping next to him. "I need your help, Dodson."

He looked at her. "With what?"

"Tell me about Zoom's new bitch."

"I don't know nothing about her." He scratched his head. "I don't even know if he's feeling her. Why?"

"Listen, I want you to keep an eye on her. Tell me whatever you find out and I'll give you a few bucks for the information."

The Ungrateful Bastards   100

"I guess," he said softly, Bear still on his mind.

Having heard what she wanted, she witnessed something else in his eyes that made her uncomfortable. Something was wrong. "Are you okay?" she remembered the woman. "And what did that chick want at the door? She looked serious on her way down the steps."

Dodson tried to pull himself together but it was difficult. Carrying what he knew around in his heart was too much weight. "Bear...I saw him get killed."

Dookie sat back and smiled thinking he was kidding. But when she realized he wasn't she exhaled deeply. "Tell me everything. Leave nothing out."

And he did. Delivering detail after detail until Dookie knew more than Zoom. In the end she was exhausted but confident she could help via the unlikeliest sources. "You should tell Zoom she came by."

He shook his head no.

"Your brother knows what to do, Dodson."

"He's going to be mad."

She laughed. "You don't know him like I do." She giggled. "Let me handle things...but trust me this will be taken care of." she said touching his leg. "I just need you to keep your end of the bargain." She stood up and moved toward the door. "I'll be in contact, Dodson. And Zoom was right...you shouldn't tell anybody else."

After she left, Dodson felt slightly relieved and decided to go to his mother's room. He wanted to be in her bed, next to her clothes in the hopes of getting one ounce of her love.

But when he opened the bedroom door and walked further inside, something felt different. Something he couldn't explain.

Moving toward her closet door, which hung open he glanced inside. He collapsed forward when he observed every stitch of clothing his mother owned was gone.

It appeared that Martha Gregory had left her children...forever.

CHAPTER THIRTEEN
LINES DRAWN

"Why your pussy so wet...huh?" Zoom asked as he stuffed his finger into Nay's box as she sat on his lap. They were at an empty park with the blanket they used earlier to lay on the cool grass draped over her legs to hide their indiscretions.

Looking down at him seductively she said, "It's juicy because you keep playing in it, nigga." She giggled.

"And you like this shit too don't you?" he asked flicking her clit again so that she received vibrations down deep. "Your body responding."

Nay laughed a little louder. "I can't lie it does feel good...but I'm tired of the finger fuck thing. How come you won't give me no dick?"

Zoom seemed uncomfortable. "Because..."

She frowned. "Because what?"

"Because you haven't told me what you're *really* about." He took his finger out of her wet vagina and rubbed it on the blanket. The mood ruined, she rose and sat next to him.

Sighing deeply she said, "Okay I'm ready to be one hundred."

"Should've did that before but I'm listening."

"I was sold to a man by my parents."

Zoom leaned closer, unsure he heard her correctly. "What you mean you were sold?"

"I know it's sounds weird but it's not what you thinking. It's like this...Dr. Cuba is a family practitioner in DC. He gets a lot of grants and things due to being a physician. His specialty is health care within the projects and he receives

By T. Styles   103

big money for his services. I'm talking hundreds of thousands. But to qualify he has to live in the projects. So he found this family who he paid to apply for a unit and during the week he pretends he lives there with a teenage daughter to get even more money for having a child. That daughter was me."

He was confused. "What type shit is that? He's a doctor? " He laughed. "You made it sound like dude was a gangster."

Nay didn't think shit was funny. "Zoom, he's use to receiving thousands of dollars a month in addition to what he gets from his regular job...just to fake like he lives in the projects instead of the suburbs of Maryland. If he thought his money would be compromised because I was spending too much time with you he would have you killed. Just because he's a white collar crook doesn't mean he's not a gangster."

Zoom was somewhat relieved although he was still confused. "I thought he was tricking on you. Making you sell your body and shit."

"Well you were wrong." She stood up and exhaled. "Anyway my duty to him is over next week and I'm gone. I'll be eighteen. After all these years I'll have to move on with my life and find another way to get paid. Besides he only pays me a little bit. He stingy as shit."

"Is that why you be tricking?"

Her head lowered and she kicked a big branch, which rested at her foot. "I gotta eat some how." She looked over at him. "You know?"

"I can dig it." He paused. "So where is home?"

"In Atlanta."

His brows rose. "So you going back after you done with dude?"

Her shoulders collapsed forward. "Yeah. Ain't nothing else here for me."

"It is if you want it to be."

She smiled. "You talking real fly but everybody in DC know you don't want no bitch."

"I want a friend," he paused. "I'm serious, Nay."

She removed the grin. "Well if you want me here then I have my reason. I guess we'll talk about that later." She looked into his eyes. "When are you going to tell me about her?"

"Who?"

"Dookie."

"What do you want to know?"

"Everything...starting with why her nickname is Dookie." She laughed.

He ran his hand down his braids, held and then released. "I met Dookie in high school...she was the first girl I ever fucked. We were in the 9th grade and everybody who met us separately said we had the same personality. After awhile I decided to see if the rumors were true and I met her through my best friend Ericko. They were. We were too much alike and she had a body that wouldn't quit...you know, fat ass, little waist and cute face."

"Unfortunately I'm not familiar," Nay said with an attitude.

He smiled a little, thinking her jealousy was a bit attractive. "Anyway from that point on although Ericko was my friend, and she was my girl we all grew close. Where you saw Dookie you saw me and the same with Ericko." He crossed his arms over his chest and looked out into the park. "Around the 11th grade her father got arrested for moving heroin and was shanked to death. Dookie was devastated and during the funeral was approached by his drug boss."

"Why? She use to sell drugs too?"

"Fuck no! Dookie ain't know nothing about moving no weight but she didn't have a choice when Felipe Ortega expected her to do it anyway."

"But she was a kid."

"She was also a goldmine. Nobody in DC outside of her pops knew more people and Felipe had an eye for new talent. Dookie pumped work up and down Southeast and was so good they nicknamed her Dookie...for moving the best brown heroin fiends had ever known. Her main place of business was a run down project in DC called Wonderland. It was a thirteen floor building that nobody was supposed to be living in but they were...and half of the tenants was her customers."

"Wow..."

Zoom shook his head and grew angry as if remembering more of the story. "I didn't want her moving the shit but I can't lie, we were kids. With the money Dookie made and the work Ericko and me put in, we didn't want for anything. I even got a little apartment that we spent most nights in."

"What happened to it?"

"My mother made me give it up." He smiled. "A little after that she moved us to the projects thinking she could buy me things if rent wasn't so high. She also thought I'd stop moving dope but I had gotten too good at it. Plus I was too invested in Dookie and Ericko. Until..."

"Ericko and her had an affair?"

He threw his head in her direction. "Don't ever disrespect like that!" he yelled. "Ericko loved me too much and he loved her too. We were kids but we knew the meaning of loyalty...at least I thought so."

"So what *did* happen?"

"The rule was to never have big work on us when we traveled. It wasn't like Dookie didn't have flunkies for shit like that. Anyway, Dookie and Ericko were buying me some new clothes for an upcoming birthday one night. The cops pulled them over for a broken tailpipe and found out that Dookie had over one hundred thousand dollars worth of work in one of the boxes she claimed was shoes."

Nay felt like there was more to the story for some reason but didn't understand why. "I don't get it."

"During one of them excursions to the mall, Dookie picked up work from one of Ortega's men but she didn't let Ericko know. She probably thought they would get away with it because there were so many shoe boxes in the car...except for the one he was holding in his lap." His neck bent forward. "She let him take the rap and they threw my man under the prison...won't be out until he's forty."

"That's fucked up!"

"I dumped her after that and she tried hard to get back right. Spoiling my sister and brother and shit. She's one of the reasons why Berry feels entitled. Dookie did all she could but when I'm done...I'm done. So that was it."

"Do you love her still?" Nay asked.

When Zoom's phone rang he saw it was the home number. Without responding to her question he answered the call. "I'm busy right now."

"You gotta come home," Dodson said. "It's an emergency."

****

With his jaw hung, Zoom sat on the edge of his mother's bed and looked into her empty closet. He was trying to understand what was happening which was hard considering Berry was crying hysterically behind him while Dodson sat in the closet with a look of confusion on his face.

"Where is ma, Zoom?" Berry asked with snot strings hanging out of her nose. "Where'd she go this time?"

"I don't know," he answered truthfully, wiping his hand down his face. "But don't act like you don't know how this bitch is." He exhaled. "Ya'll keep expecting her to be everything she ain't. We need to stick together like always! Ain't nothing changed."

"But is she coming back?" Dodson asked from the closet's floor.

Zoom was becoming annoyed with all the questions and he started to scream on them. Besides, who the fuck did they think he was? "I don't know! I just don't—"

Nay placed a soft hand on Zoom's shoulder, which interrupted his thoughts. She saw him unraveling and she wanted to do all she could to reel him back in. "I'm going to make dinner." She looked at Berry and Dodson. "Why don't you guys get cleaned up?"

The moment she gave the order Zoom was certain that Berry would snap on her because she was not her mother. Instead she stood up and

The Ungrateful Bastards 108

moved toward the door as if the weight of the world was on her lying ass shoulders.

Dodson followed closely behind.

When they were gone Zoom looked up at her and said, "Thank you. Because I don't know what to say to them right now."

"I don't mind helping," she paused. "You not fucking me around here. What else I'm gonna do but help?" she laughed.

He smiled but it disappeared when he thought about the seriousness of his life.

"What happened when you called Dora? Has she seen your mother?"

Zoom swallowed. "Yeah...but I couldn't tell them that."

Nay sat next to him on the bed. "What Martha say?"

"That she never wants to see us again and that as far as she was concerned we're on our own."

When Zoom's cell phone rang he answered although not recognizing the number. "Who this?"

"It's Dookie... I have to tell you something...it's important. Please don't hang up."

****

Although her son had only been dead for less than two weeks, Blair Charles looked a mess.

An extra slender face, splotched with red circles showcased sunken her eyes. She looked as unhealthy as her broken heart. Then again after losing a child no one expected her to be much more.

Angry at not being able to get through to Dodson, Blair walked up to her house, barely able to stand up straight. Days of not being able to eat full meals had worn on her body, causing her strength to diminish by the hour. No matter how decrepit, she was determined to pull more information out of Dodson, even if it meant through violence.

For now she had to get inside, take out the beef to thaw for tonight's dinner, since meatloaf was on the menu. Her youngest son Quincy was returning after staying with his father for a week and she wanted things in order. Besides, she hadn't been the nicest to him after Bear's murder and it was time for all of that to change.

Digging inside the blue purse hanging on her arm she removed her keys and entered her tiny apartment. At first she didn't notice the condition of her home. But when she did she stumbled backwards when she noticed that her house was a wreck.

The living room table was broken in the middle, forcing two parts in separate directions. The flat screen TV had the remote control hanging out of it and the shelf holding her DVD's was face first on the floor.

"Oh my..." her voice wafted softly in the air. She looked around where she stood, stunned and horrified.

Thinking she'd been robbed she stopped by the kitchen to grab a knife. And with it firmly in her palm she crept down the hallway toward her bedroom. Opening the door she realized her most private space was met with the same fate, disaster.

Her mirrors broken, necklaces popped and lipstick smeared upon the wall. It started to feel more personal than financial. Moving further, to her youngest son's room, she was heartbroken when she saw it was also vandalized.

Finally she approached Bear's room, her body convulsing once upon the door. After losing her son to murder she wasn't prepared to have his things disrespected. It would be as if she were going through his death all over again.

Slowly she opened the door and exhaled deeply. His things were as neat as the day he left them but her worries were far from over. Because there inside the room was Zoom, Berry and Dodson, staring in her direction.

Berry was sitting on Bear's bed, with her back against the headboard smiling wildly. Dodson was sitting on the floor, next to Zoom who was perched on the edge of the dresser.

Zoom was confident and in control.

She raised the knife but lowered it quickly when Zoom aimed his gun. "So the rumors are true about you three," she said softly.

"I don't know...what do they say?" Zoom asked as if no cares in the world.

Silence.

"This is how it's going to be," Zoom said plainly, "You're going to leave my family alone. Dodson don't know anything about what happened to Bear and you know he wouldn't hurt him."

"So why won't he talk to the police?" she said softly.

"He told them everything he knows." He corrected her. "And I just heard on the way over here that they found the person who killed Bear. He worked at Floormart."

"But I want to know what happened every second before he died! And Dodson knows more," she responded looking down at Dodson.

By T. Styles 111

Zoom stood up and walked closer to her. Looking down, his warm breath beaming on her forehead he said, "Stay away from us, Blair. You heard the rumors, don't experience the reality." He walked out with Dodson and Berry following.

CHAPTER FOURTEEN
WHEN A MOTHER'S FED UP

The air conditioner was off and the heat caused everyone inside to sweat, sending a beefy odor throughout the small chapel...

Martha sat in the front pew barefoot with her arms high in the air while she praised God and hung onto the pastor's every word. Her children were an emotional wreck but she didn't share their feelings. She felt as free as a man out of prison off a twenty-year sentence.

Life had gotten better ever since she made the decision to shake her responsibilities, and she was too mentally detached to realize the lasting damage she would do to them. In her mind it was just a matter of time before they burned in hell and she didn't want to be anywhere near them when it happened.

"We are one," yelled the preacher from the podium. His sparkling emerald green pants suit combined with his alluring smile had the women thinking unnatural thoughts. "We are united in faith and in God. Let no man tear apart the foundation that you have build with the Father, the Son and the Holy Ghost!"

"Praise be to God," Martha yelled louder all while wiggling her fingers in the hopes that he would look at her personally. "Glory be to his name!"

"He's on fire this morning ain't he?" Dora whispered leaning toward her friend. She looked at him again and smiled wider, "I swear I can't get enough of him."

Martha twisted her head so rapidly toward Dora that her neck almost snapped. "Well you should really try." Her brows lowered.

"What got you so frisky this Sunday morning?" Dora's hands dropped by her sides after the preacher finished his sermon. "And why you giving me the impression I said something wrong? You talk about the pastor all the time...why can't I?"

Martha took her seat when she noticed in her peripheral vision that the congregation sat down. "Just so you know, he don't want no woman like you. A man of God can't be with someone unclean. I know...I had me a man of the cloth once. And God may see fit to give me one again." She looked at the preacher once more.

Dora gave her the stank face. "And just what is that supposed to mean?" she whispered. "Far as I know we both led similar lives...outside of getting yourself a husband, who we both know wasn't shit, you were sucking the glass dick just like me." She focused on the choir who was now singing and then back at Martha.

"You don't know what you talkin' 'bout. My sins were forgiven when I married a man of God. You on the other hand ain't never been right. Only thing you do is whatever you see me doing." She leaned in and looked dead into her eyes. "Besides, I know you got Herpes. What you trying to do? Infect Pastor with that flapping pussy?"

Dora crossed her arms over her chest and leaned back in the pew. She could feel a ball of spit twirling at the base of her tongue but she thought better of shooting it in her face. "First off I wasn't even looking at Pastor like that. Second of all the fact that I got them things is a secret I

The Ungrateful Bastards   114

shared with you in a moment of low. Is you saying you gonna use it against me?"

Martha gave her a sly smile and then fixed her eyes back on the object of her obsessions. The pastor. She didn't know she was falling for him until that very minute. One moment she was coming to church and the next she was head over heals. She had to admit, the way she'd been feeling lately it felt good to desire another.

When her husband died she reconciled with being lonely for the rest of her life, with nothing but her mean children to keep her company. But if one man of God made her his wife, what was to stop her from getting another?

"I know what kind of man Pastor needs," Martha said eyes twinkling. "And I'm gonna make sure that he gets it too."

"You know what, something is *really* different about you," Dora said softly. "And I'm not sure if I like it or not."

Martha looked at her sternly. "You don't have to like a thing about me, suga dumpling. I ain't in to women's anyway." She paused. "Just stay away from that man up there. I might as well tell you now so you can alert the others. He belongs to me!"

After insulting Dora thoroughly, Martha continued to dance from the melodic choir's voice, oblivious to the fact that her children were there. Having had their shoes removed they were making a beeline in her direction with Zoom leading the way. Once upon her he asked. "Ma, what's going on? Why you move out all your stuff?"

Martha looked back at him and focused on the front again. Embarrassed she asked, "What are you doing here?"

By T. Styles   115

"We're here to find out what's wrong with you," Zoom said more firmly, gaining the attention of an unwanted audience. Dodson was driving him up the wall about his mother and to be honest Zoom hadn't expected him to care so much. In the past he always acted as if he didn't give a fuck so what changed? "Dodson wants you home."

"I do," Dodson admitted nodding his head.

"Son, this is a place of worship," the preacher said stepping up to the podium. "If you can't respect your own soul so be it...please don't disrespect your mother's."

Zoom turned his head and locked eyes with him. "I'm not talking to you or none of these other fake ass sanctified people up in here! I'm talking to my mother!" He pointed at her church crown.

"Ah hell nah!" yelled an elderly woman with a blue-white bush. She took the hymnbook she was holding and flung it at Zoom. It missed his head and almost hit Dora's instead. "You can't be in here disrespecting Pastor!"

"Zoom, get out of here right now," Martha said through clenched teeth. "You're upsetting people."

"And I told you not without you!" he paused. "Now get your purse, we 'bout to leave. You got to see about Dodson and Berry because I'm not they father."

Martha angrily got up and walked toward the exit causing Zoom, Berry and Dodson to follow. Relieved they were gone, the congregation erupted in applause.

When they were outside Zoom softly gripped his mother's hand. "Ma, a lot has been happening since you bounced. I don't know what's up but we need you back. Dodson got himself in a situation—"

Martha snatched away and her lips pinched together. "I told you." She looked at Dodson and Berry too. "I told all of you that I couldn't take much more of your shit. And you didn't listen. None of you listened! You took and took until I was left with nothing else to give!"

"And this is your answer? To leave us? I mean them?" Zoom asked compassionately, trying to leave himself out of the mix although he was hurting too. "We your children."

"You *were* my children." She smiled as if she had joined a different conversation...one with a big joke and heavy laughter involved. "I have nothing more to do with you and I love it that way."

Zoom wanted to hit her so badly his knuckles ached. "You know what...you never took up for us. Ever! Why do you think we hate you so much? A hate this deep don't pop up from nowhere! It's bred!" he stepped back. "You up in the church giving away all your paper meanwhile the bills are about to be due. Who gonna take care of that?"

She crossed her arms over her chest and said, "Ain't you slinging dope?"

Zoom was done. He walked down the steps and got in the car.

"So you saying you aren't coming home ever?" Berry asked as tears ran down her cheeks. "Not even for your special boy?"

Martha looked at Dodson who was beside himself with grief. For a moment there was a brief hint of guilt but it evaporated like steam from a teakettle. "I'm not your mother anymore...and never will be. Now get the fuck from in front my face! I'm trying to praise God!"

CHAPTER FIFTEEN
MOTHERLESS CHILDREN

Defeated, Zoom tromped into the house with Berry and Dodson on his heals. Having sat on the stoop since they left, waiting, Nay walked inside the apartment with them.

The day was harsh for the Gregory family and he wasn't sure things would get better. The bottom line was their mother made a decision not to be their parent anymore, so what would they do now?

"So ma really not coming back, Zoom?" Dodson asked. "She don't love us no more?"

"Yo, Dodson, for real, get the fuck up out my face!" he yelled. "I'm sick of you getting at me 'bout that bitch!" he paused. "Go wash up. I'm gonna put some hot dogs on for dinner." They gave him space and he moved toward the kitchen.

"Let me do that for you, Zoom," Nay said softly. She washed her hands and opened the freezer for the meat. While they cooked she grabbed Zoom a beer out of the fridge and sat it next to him at the table. "You drink that and try to relax."

"Something is off with my mother and I wish I knew what it was. I mean...I hear her when she says she doesn't want to be our mother no more but its like I'm looking into the eyes of someone I don't know. It's like she's sick."

"I'm not sure either...but maybe she just needs a little time, Zoom. Maybe she's tired. Mothers are expected to do a lot. They have to see to it that their kids are fed, loved and provided for, especially if they're single. And all of this must be done while they push their own feelings to the side. Not every woman can handle it."

"Well we ain't ask to be here." Zoom sighed. "I wish I saw this shit coming. I'da stacked more paper."

"Are you sure you didn't?" she turned the eye on the stove down when the water was boiling too hard. "Was your mother doing or saying anything in a cry for help?"

He sighed. "She don't know nothing 'bout crying for help." He looked into her eyes and she could tell the statement ran deep. "But we do." He rubbed his throbbing temples as he tried to come to terms with it all. "I have no idea what I'm doing."

"Things will work out. But you're going to have to step up because your sister and brother are depending on you."

"That's just it, I ain't up for this," he said sticking a stiff finger in the table. "I didn't sign up to be nobody's father." He pointed to the backrooms. "Them ain't my kids! I don't mind kicking a pair of shoes or two but the fulltime daddy daycare shit ain't for me."

Nay laughed. "You better get ready because you don't have a choice."

About an hour later everyone was sitting at the table eating hot dogs and fries. It was so silent in the apartment that they could hear the ice crackling in the freezer.

When Zoom took his last bite he looked over at his brother and sister. "I know ya'll know already that mom's not coming home. She made it clear and we gotta go on with our lives."

The Ungrateful Bastards   120

"I hate her," Berry said under her breath. "She ain't nothing but an old dumb bitch with stinky wigs!"

"That may be true but we still on our own," Zoom responded, finding it difficult to disagree.

"Who's going to take care of us now?" Dodson asked.

Zoom rubbed is bare chest, dropped his hand and scratched his braids. He was trying to think of anybody else but he was coming up short. Having stalled enough he said, "I am."

Berry's jaw dropped in disbelief.

"But I want mommy," Dodson said as tears started to cascade down his cheek.

"Didn't you hear what I just said, lil nigga?" Zoom asked angrily. "Ma ain't coming back." He hated dealing with emotional shit but he decided that he needed to put his feelings to the side and focus on his younger siblings. Until another adult came to the rescue. "I know you're upset but I promise I will never leave."

"You a fucking drug dealer," Berry yelled, digging into his ass. "What the fuck you gonna do 'cept get your stupid ass locked up?"

"Watch your mouth," Zoom said.

"You not my daddy! You will never, ever be my father so stop acting like it."

"Berry, you testing my—"

"I don't care!" She yelled. "You made me go to that church when I didn't want to. Then we got embarrassed in front of everybody when she didn't want to come back with—"

"That's your fucking problem and one of the reasons ma left!" Zoom yelled cutting her off. "You so busy blaming everybody else when you forgot your part in all this shit. Remember the fake rape charge you tried to put on dude? Had ma down the police department when you know we have to steer clear of cops! If she gone it's your fault too!"

She cried and the tears rolled down her cheeks. "That's not true!"

"You a liar, Berry. That was the thing that sent ma over the edge. It ripped her apart and she ain't been right since. The only thing you care about is that fuckin' car!"

Berry looked away guiltily.

"Zoom, don't say that," Nay said.

"Don't tell me what to say." He pointed at her. "This my family. You don't have one remember?!"

Nay got up from the table and looked down at him. "Nobody gonna talk to me like that. Not even you." She stormed out of the apartment and slammed the door.

Zoom wiped his hands down his face and exhaled. After taking several deep breaths he looked up at his brother and sister. "Whether you two know it or not things will be changing 'round here."

"You don't control me," Berry yelled jumping up. "Nobody does!"

Frustrated Zoom looked at Berry. "You know what, get out my face and go to your room." He looked at Dodson. "You too."

"But I'm not finished eating," he said, holding a half eaten hot dog.

"Swallow it or take it with you."

When they left Zoom cleaned the kitchen and when he was done he remembered something Perch said earlier in the month. On the same day he told him that his mother was doing drugs again. *I'm opening shop in Virginia. I need a loyal*

The Ungrateful Bastards   122

soldier. If you ready I can move you up there and give you more points on a package. All you have to say is the word."

As Zoom thought about his life he contemplated leaving. If Martha did it why couldn't he? It wasn't like his brother and sister weren't at the age to speak up for themselves. They would be placed in foster care for a few years and he was certain Berry would get a place on her own to reunite them both in no time.

The more he thought about it the more he realized leaving would be a good idea.

****

Upset at how he treated her, Nay busted through Zoom's building door, down the steps and into the street. She had no business dealing with him yet she couldn't separate herself. She found in him mystery and danger and his pain called to her soul.

She was in the middle of the block when she looked back and saw George walking quickly in her direction. "Can I talk to you for a minute, young lady?"

She wiped her tears, turned around and was startled. "No...leave me alone!" The last time she saw him Zoom was holding a gun to his face and robbing him in the hallway.

What could he possibly want accept his money back?

"Just five minutes of your time," he begged as she continued to walk briskly. "It's about Martha Gregory and the family. There are things you don't know. Things I have to tell you."

Nay stopped and stood in the middle of the street. "What...what about them?"

"My apartment is right around the corner and my car is on the curb." He pointed to a navy blue Cadillac. "Let me take you there and tell you everything you want to know. Judging by your tears I can tell you have questions."

Nay accepted and walked slowly to his car, all the while Berry watched from the window.

****

George pulled up in front of his house and walked around to the passenger side to let Nay out. They were walking toward his front door when Berry stepped out and leaned against his vehicle. Although they took the roads to get to his home, which was around the corner, the back roads had Berry there quicker by foot.

Sure they had problems in the family but there were some secrets that needed to remain just that...secrets. And Berry was going to see to it that it stayed that way.

"What you doing, George?" Berry asked calmly. "How come you got Zoom's friend in your 'llac?"

Nay looked at George and at Berry as if she'd been caught red-handed fucking. Clearing her throat she said, "He was just giving me a ride to my friends' house." Her eyes moved everywhere but on Berry's.

Berry frowned and gazed up the block. Squinting she said, "Didn't know you had friends 'round here. I don't think Zoom does either."

Nay felt afraid although she didn't understand why. "Thanks for the ride, George." She was about to take off.

The Ungrateful Bastards   124

"Ask them about 614," George blurted out. "When you get a chance ask Zoom about it. See if what he says sounds like truth."

Nay ran away and George walked toward his front door.

"Stay out of our lives," Berry said crossing her arms over her chest. "If we go down...everybody goes down."

George turned around and faced her. "I'm just worried about you all."

"What can we do with worry?" Berry rolled her eyes and walked away.

CHAPTER SIXTEEN
LEAVE ROOM FOR TROUBLE

After leaving the kitchen Dodson sat in his room on the floor, to finish his meal when Zoom walked inside. "Look, man, I'm leaving for a minute."

"Where you going?" Dodson asked, mouth full of food.

He stuffed his hands into his pocket. "To go find your sister. She left mad and I gotta bring her back."

Dodson's gaze flitted around the room before resting on Zoom. Filled with worry he asked. "You think she left for good? Like ma?" His eyes blinked rapidly before freezing.

"No she ain't leave like ma." He waved him off, tiring of his boyish way of seeing things. When Zoom was his age he was so much more mature and yet he knew the mental disability was to blame. "She just out there somewhere showing out. You stay in this room and don't get into trouble." He pointed at the floor. "You hear me?"

He nodded.

Zoom slammed the door and Dodson waited for a minute to be sure enough time passed. When he was certain he stood up and walked carefully toward the window. Gazing down toward the street he saw Zoom and Nay get into his car and drive off.

Closing the blinds he walked out the door and headed straight for his mother's dresser. Normally there would be change lying on top of it that Martha would put down after going to the grocery store, but when he remembered that he already spent what was there, and that she wasn't returning a pain he couldn't explain rolled through his lower belly.

Suddenly the days when Bear was at his house came to mind. There was still one game to play alone. He lifted the handset and dialed several numbers until someone he didn't know answered. In a sleepy voice the person on the other end said, "Myers Residence."

"Suck my dick, bitch," Dodson yelled before hanging up. Although the joke was far from funny it took several minutes before he regained his composure. Dropping to the floor he held onto his stomach.

His immature behavior when he was alone was the type of thing that drove Zoom crazy. But if Zoom was going to be the provider and the protector he couldn't be up under his siblings every five minutes, which left plenty room for trouble.

After the laugh subsided Dodson picked up the phone and dialed another number but no one answered. Looking for the same foolish high he continued to enter numbers, changing combinations until he reached someone else. "Hello," a soft-spoken woman said.

"Suck my dick, bitch!" Dodson yelled before hanging up.

As he did before he fell out in laughter but this time the high was short lived. When the phone rang immediately, expecting it to be Zoom, he cleared his throat and tried to appear serious. "Hello."

Silence.

"Zoom...that you?"

Click.

The person hung up and Dodson looked at the phone eerily. For some reason he didn't feel like playing anymore. But when it rung again he quickly answered, hoping it was his brother. "I know you were playing on my phone, nigger," the mild sounding woman he just hung up on said. "But when I catch you I'm gonna tie a rope around your neck and drag you up the block behind my truck!"

Dodson's eyes widened as he slammed the phone down. Instead of his nightmare ending there it rang multiple times until he answered. With the headset clutched in his hand and pressed against his ear he stuttered. "H-hello."

"I'm on my way to your house to cut your head off and spit on your neck stump!" the woman said again before hanging up.

Now the kid who was always so malicious sat on the sofa rocking side to side. Unwilling to hear a threat anymore he removed the phone from the hook and sat in silence. At that moment he decided to retire his phone playing days but what to do with his boredom?

After thirty minutes he placed the phone back on the hook, not because he felt any better but he was worried that Zoom might kick his ass if he tried to reach out but couldn't get through.

Trying to figure out what to do with his self, he remembered that a new boy moved into the building earlier in the week. The only problem was he didn't know the exact address.

Hoping to make a new friend, he opened the front door, left it cracked and knocked on a few doors. Nobody answered the first couple so he moved to the third and the moment he did, a man

The Ungrateful Bastards   128

he didn't want to see when he was alone walked outside and into the hallway.

The Creeper.

He'd seen him around the building but because he never went downstairs he didn't know where he lived.

Now he did.

Frozen in place, Dodson's arms dangled by his sides and his body stiffened. He wanted to run but didn't want the man to know that he was afraid either, instead he separated his lips and slowly asked, "Does...the...the new boy live here?"

The Creeper smiled and said, "You mean my nephew. Of course he does, come on in."

****

Dookie sat in a recliner chair as she had an uncomfortable procedure...chemotherapy. The port running into her chest was slightly raw and she was eager for one thing...to get it over with.

After selling heroin out of Wonderland for most of her young life Dookie didn't leave with just a few million dollars and real estate properties, she also contracted Mesothelioma, a form of cancer.

The building where she pumped drugs was heavy with asbestos fibers, which she breathed into her lungs on a regular basis. While most people won huge settlements from lawyers for getting the illness, she decided to ignore the money, for fear her enemies would find out and use it against her as a weakness. Besides, she was far from broke.

With the relaxation therapy being given she was just about to doze off when her boyfriend Meister walked into the office. Dressed in all black, with a dope rope swishing around his neck, a cell phone was pressed against his ear as he spoke loudly into it.

Her two-year-old son Prince walked in front of him touching everything in sight, including biohazard chemo cords, and she wanted to strangle Meister for not watching him better.

Looking at all the colorful equipment, Prince's brown eyes grew large when he saw his mother. Running up to her he crawled up into her lap; the sole of his black Nike boot almost pulled the tube out of her chest. "Mommy, why you still here?" he asked excitedly.

She smiled and rubbed his hair with her free hand, trying to hold him tightly and keep him still so he wouldn't rip out the cord stuck in her flesh. Looking up at Meister she said, "I was about to ask you the same thing." She kissed her son on the forehead and waited for the answer from her man.

Meister having caught whiff of her snappy attitude ended the call. "Look...I got a situation to handle at one of our shops. Had to drop the kid off early."

She placed a hand on both of Prince's ears so he couldn't hear her words. "Does your situation have a wet pussy and soft titties? And belong to my cousin Miranda?"

He rolled his eyes and stuffed his hands into his pockets. "Why you keep bringing up old shit?" he paused. "I said I was sorry and you said you forgave me."

"But you still cheating!" she yelled. "When you know my situation." She looked up at him with big eyes. "I'm sick, Meister. And I need to

The Ungrateful Bastards   130

know Prince will be taken care of on the days I have therapy."

He grew angry, shuffling around as if the floor was hot. Suddenly he walked closer to the chair and looked down at her. "Hold up...don't come at me like I don't look after shawty. You be too sick to do shit 'round the house. I'm the one who gets him up, gets him dressed and feeds him."

"You mean your mother," she corrected him.

"If my mother does it, it's the same as me." He pointed at the floor. "Little man knows how I feel about him."

"Prince," she paused. "I gave him the name for a reason. So use it!" She removed her hands off of his ears. "Just go... I'm tired of looking at you anyway."

Meister didn't leave. He stood guiltily in the middle of the floor. "I'll always look after him, Dookie. You never have to worry."

"And still I don't trust you."

He smiled. "Maybe that speaks to who you really are instead of me." He paused. "I know you never got over that bamma ass nigga Zoom. Everybody in DC knows. To this day that's why we never worked out."

"Just go, Meister." She looked at Prince. "Before I get angry and forget my son is in the room."

"You didn't deny it though did you?" he chuckled. "What happened between you and him that made you love him more than anything? Even your own son? Even me?"

CHAPTER SEVENTEEN
THE ITCH THAT NEVER STOPS

After getting his car fixed, Zoom had to look for Berry...

With no luck, a few hours later he entered a defile of Washington DC projects as he continued the hunt. The buildings on the right were cracked from top to bottom, as he and Nay continued to push further into the most violent portions of the city.

Earlier he found Nay walking down the street and he apologized causing her to reluctantly get into the car. Although in the back of his mind he felt she didn't want to come, as if she had something else to do.

From the passenger seat Nay looked over at him, wanting to ask about 614 but somehow she felt it wasn't the time. She was also trying to feel him out. Did Berry tell of her interrupted visit with George?

"Do you know her friends?" Nay asked as she rubbed her arms. "Anybody at all who could tell you something?"

He frowned upon hearing her voice, having forgotten she was in the car. "She be with that freak Liberty most times...and I can't stand that little bitch. Seems like every time she get with her she's getting into some more shit." Zoom glanced to the left at a group of young girls with tiny skirts and loud mouths. None of them resembled his flat butt sister.

"I know you mad but you going about getting her to listen to you the wrong way."

He looked over at her. "You got a sister?"

"No."

"A brother?"

"No," she giggled wondering what was his point.

"Then what the fuck would you know about how I go about something? That's why we had a problem earlier."

A tingling sensation crept up the back of her neck and rolled across her face. His quick attitude had her feeling out of place...again. "I don't have siblings but I'm a teenager. I know how it is to want your freedom and feel like it's been taken from you." She peered out the window. "If I don't know anything else in life I know 'bout that."

Zoom took a deep breath and tried to compare the situations but in his opinion they were just different. After their father died, his sister grew up in a world where she could say and have anything she wanted. Especially Berry because she was the only girl child.

"I don't know what happened to you, Nay. But I do know my sister. She a brat and that shit gotta stop if my mother comes home."

"You mean *when* your mother comes home. She won't stay gone for too long."

When his phone vibrated in his pocket he quickly answered. It was Perch and he wished he looked at the Caller ID first because he would've bounced the call. "Hey, man," Zoom said under his breath. "I'm busy right now."

"This won't take but a sec. So me and Gaze in the new Club Chains and then we see this fine ass shawty walk inside."

He wiped his hand down his face trying to determine what any of it had to do with him. "*Okay*?"

"Well after Gaze walked up on her to invite her to VIP, that's when I noticed who it was." He paused for effect. "Your sister's friend Liberty. And Berry out here playing herself hard too. You might want to get out here. We let a few dudes know she off limits but the disrespectful kind ain't got here yet. You may want to come collect her young ass."

"Say no more. I'll be there in a second." Zoom's face turned beet red as he turned his car around to hit it to the club.

"Where we going?" Nay asked rubbing her arms more briskly. In pain, she doubled over and rubbed her stomach before holding her arms again and leaning back in her seat."

Oblivious to her agony he said, "This dude just told me she's at a club." He was so angry he could barely see two feet in front of him.

"You got fifty dollars on you?"

Zoom finally focused on her and he could tell by her body mechanics that something was off. Besides, Nay never asked for money since they'd gotten serious. Examining her he asked, "What's wrong with you?" he frowned. "Why you looking all crazy?"

"I'm on my period," she yelled. "But that ain't answering the question. You gonna give me money or not?"

"Fuck you need money for?"

"I just need it," she barked. "If you so pressed I'll give it back in a few days."

Zoom was turned off and not in the mood. He had the paper but with moms gone each dollar was accounted for.

Fuck this bitch! He thought.

The Ungrateful Bastards   134

At the moment his mind was on his sister not some begging as chick on the rag.

Ignoring her question, Zoom pulled up at the club and tried to find a parking space but it was crowded. Where would he leave the car? The more he thought about the antics Berry was putting him through the angrier he grew.

When he saw an alley next to the club he decided to park illegally. And if he was in there too long Nay could move his ride. It wasn't like he was going to be in long. The plan was to bring her out kicking and screaming and take her home.

There wasn't a whole lot more to it.

After parking he gazed over at Nay who was still doubled over in pain. "I'm going in." He grabbed a fresh t-shirt and slipped it down his naked chest. "Can you move the car if the police come?"

Slowly her head rolled toward him. "Zoom, please give me some money. I'm begging you."

He felt bad but not enough to give her cash. "I'll see what I can do when I get back. Just move the car if the police come." he got out without another word and slammed the door.

As Zoom bopped toward the entrance he looked down at his gear...white t-shirt, blue jean shorts and red Nike Foamposites to match his red beads. As bland as he looked what if they wouldn't allow him inside?

Thinking on his feet he decided to text Perch.

Zoom: Walking to the door. You got me?
Perch: My man on the lookout for u. But u owe me again.

Zoom stuffed his phone back into his pocket and shook his head. Perch was always exercising his power at the wrong time and it fucked his mind up. Either he was going to help him or not, but he wasn't about to be obligated to him for the rest of his life either. Perch wasn't satisfied until he owned a nigga's soul.

Once in front of the club, he waited for a few minutes and before long Gaze stepped to the door, whispered to the bouncer who without word allowed Zoom behind the ropes. "Thanks, man," Zoom said giving Gaze some dap.

The moment he entered the loud music seemed to change his mood, pushing him on the angrier side. And active mind since birth, Zoom could already envision strange niggas pushing up on his kid sister and it drove him mad.

"Perch in VIP." Gaze pointed in the area. "And I'm going to the bar. Want something?"

"Naw, I'm good." Zoom replied, swatting him away like a fat fly.

On a mission Zoom walked around the club and it didn't take him long to spot his blood relative. She was pinned up against the wall with a dude who looked about 45 yapping in her face.

Liberty was at her side, also enjoying the conversation of someone older than her by at least ten years.

Irritated Zoom rushed over to Berry and gripped her by the forearm. "Let's go!"

At first she was confused on who was disrespecting but after realizing it was her brother she grew emboldened. "Get the fuck up off me," she yelled. "I told you, you not my father!"

Zoom zeroed in on the drink in her hand and snatched the cup. He took a big sniff. "And you out here drinking too?" He growled. "I'll fucking kill—"

His sentence was interrupted when the dude she was talking to approached. "My man, what the fuck you doing? I was talking to the shawty."

"Well the shawty is my fuckin' sister," he barked back. "And she only fifteen. You trying to go down over some pussy you'll never get? Or do you want to live to fuck another day?"

The moment the dude heard her age he jetted and the friend who was chilling with Liberty followed.

"Why did you do that shit?" Berry yelled snatching away from him as Liberty stood next to her. "I liked him!"

"I ain't trying to hear that shit! You don't need to be up in here! You ain't grown, Berry. You just pissed in the bed the day before yesterday so don't play yourself."

Embarrassed that he just told her business she slapped him on the cheek. "I was having a dream I was on the toilet!" she paused. "I hate you! Leave me alone!"

After being struck Zoom lost all reason. He gripped her by the hair and yoked her through the club like a cavemen claiming his bitch. Berry's body went limp due to his force. She never saw him that angry.

Without altercation from the security guard he was able to get her outside, tossing her in the backseat of the car like a bag of trash. Trying to avoid further humiliation, she didn't relent for fear it may have been detrimental to her health.

He removed his t-shirt and tossed it in the backseat in her face. And he was just about to

By T. Styles 137

ease into the driver's seat when he saw Nay was gone. "Where the fuck is this bitch at?" He said to himself. "I'm sick of these females!"

He stomped down the alley, hair beads clacking against one another as he hunted for her. "Nay," he yelled. "I found my sister! It's time to bounce! Where you at?"

When he walked further down the alley he was shocked. There on the ground, next to a dumpster was Nay on her knees serving a blowjob.

Caught, dick handed, she jumped up, wiped her mouth with the back of her hand and yelled, "I'm sorry, Zoom." Her hands extended outward. "Let me explain...please!"

CHAPTER EIGHTEEN
PRETTY LITTLE CRACKHEAD

The night seemed cold and dark as Nay walked down the street, flashes of Zoom seeing her tricking stayed on repeat in her mind. A new drug addict, free from the signs of long-term use, she did all she could to hide her habit but it caught up with her in the worst way.

When she saw a small diner she walked inside and up to the counter. "Can I use your phone?" she asked a cashier.

He pointed to a phone booth, something she hadn't seen in awhile. "It's fifty cents for a call," he advised.

"Alright...thank you." She walked toward it, dug in her pocket and pulled out some change. Her finger trembled as she hit the buttons. "Hello."

"Albert," she said softly. "It's me...LeNay."

Silence.

"What do you want?" he asked.

"I need some help, maybe some place to stay for just one night."

"You left the apartment door open," her sponsor said. "You knew you would be too old in a few months and you didn't finish out one month's work. I'm done."

"Please—"

"Don't call me again!"

He hung up the phone and she wept a little before picking herself up and walking out the door. She expected him to be unhelpful but it still hurt.

Once outside she dug into her pocket and removed the fifty-dollar bill she earned when

Zoom caught her giving head. Since Albert hadn't helped, the plan for the night was simple...cop some crack and grab a dollar room while she tried to figure out what was left of her life.

She was almost to the trap house when a Navy blue Suburban pulled up in front of her, blocking her path. Three women hopped out and grabbed Nay as she tried to wiggle out of their clasps.

Wondering what was going on she received an answer when the back door to the truck flung opened and Dookie eased out. Wearing tight blue jeans, a red top and red open toe sandals, Nay could finally see why Zoom use to be in love.

She was bad.

Dookie continued toward Nay, her steps were slow and deliberate. Standing directly in front of her she said, "Good evening, Dope Head. I knew I was right about you."

"I ain't on drugs!" she lied.

"First off I own these blocks. And I know a dopehead stroll when I see one," Dookie responded. "And the only reason Zoom being bothered with you is because you remind him of Martha. Men always gravitate to those like mama." She laughed lightly. "I'm gonna have to tell my boo charity ain't necessary. Besides, you look like you can take care of yourself."

Frowning she asked. "What you want with me?" The women maintained their hold.

Dookie rocked back on her heels. "For starters I want you to stay the fuck away from Zoom and my family. I need his mind together and not on you."

"Your family?" she laughed. "How they your family when you ain't nothing but a snake?"

Dookie lowered her brows and moved closer. "What you think you know about me, Dope Head?"

Nay felt a warm sensation inside her body she couldn't describe. She wanted her to know that she and Zoom talked about everything and it was time to bust her bubble. With a sly smile she said, "That you had your friend Ericko sent to prison on account of some shit you did."

Dookie laughed. "Is that what Zoom told you?" she paused. "That I had Ericko take a fall?" she shook her head. "It's true, our best friend did go down but he took that L on his own. In turn I took care of his family! I still take care of Ericko and his people now. But ask Zoom about 614...and see if the truth will come out."

Nay remained silent. That was the second time she heard those numbers and she wanted to know why they were so important. But with her and Zoom beefing she doubted she'd get an answer anytime soon.

"You're a liar!"

"You're wrong, Dope Head. That ain't why Zoom left me. That's just what he told people to hide the truth," She paused. "I know you think you're smart but there's a lot about that family that you don't know."

"You're lying!"

Dookie laughed harder. "Let me tell you how this is going to play out. You will walk away from this family, not only because I'm telling you but for your own good. They'll do anything to keep the '614' secret." She paused. "And so you know I'm not playing I'm gonna give you a little gift to remember me by." Dookie looked at her goons. "Beat her down...stop right before she stops breathing."

CHAPTER NINETEEN
MY BROTHER'S KEEPER

A large pillow was pressed over Zoom's head as he lay in bed, wearing jeans and no shirt. He thought he was dreaming when he heard knocking until the sound grew louder. Realizing it was the front door; he pushed the pillow to the floor, sat up straight, wiped his eyes and walked groggily toward the front door. When he looked out of the peephole he started not to open it upon realizing who it was.

He wasn't in the mood for this shit, besides yesterday was hard. After snatching Berry out of the club, he stayed up all night to make sure she didn't leave the house. He had all intentions on giving her the beat down of a lifetime if she disobeyed and luckily for him she was too tired to do anything, electing to cry herself to sleep instead.

As he sat in the living room and drank beer after beer, the only person he could think about was Nay. Her behavior in the alley was odd, unlike the nurturing, loving person he'd come to have a crush on.

Slowly he opened the door, rubbed his chest, walked toward the couch and plopped down. Earlier he removed the braids on the right side of his head, revealing a long curly bush on the other side.

He was so angry until he saw her face. She was beaten so badly her clothing was soaked in dried blood. He started to console her until he remembered how he last saw her. On her knees in an alley giving head.

As if he didn't care he asked, "What happened?" he started removing another braid.

Nay walked inside, closed the door behind her and stood in front of him in shame. "I was beaten up, Zoom." She said in a soft voice.

"By who?" He paused. "The nigga you served in the alley? Did you make him wash his dick first too?" Nay looked hurt but before she could answer in an irritated tone he continued, "What you want?" He leaned back in the couch.

"You."

He grunted. "I don't feel like playing games, Nay. I'm tired. Now either tell me what the fuck you want or bounce."

She took one step closer but gave him his space. "I have a drug problem. I've had it for a few months and I've never been more ashamed of it until I saw the look in your eyes. I know you don't believe me, Zoom. But I want to change."

He yawned and rubbed his chest before crossing his arms over his body. "And you telling me this for...?"

"Because I'm hoping you will help me." A tear rolled down her bloody face and stopped at the crease of her nose. "You've been my only friend for the past few weeks, Zoom. And I know that you don't feel like dealing with my shit now but..."

"I still haven't heard what this has to do with me."

She shuffled a little in place. "I'm on crack."

He moved uneasily upon hearing the words.

"And I...I want to stop but I need you," she continued. "Since I've been on drugs the only time I tried to stop was when I was with you. Nobody

By T. Styles   143

ever cared about me. Only about what they could get from me. Last night I was sick and I needed a fix so I did what I thought needed to be done...without thinking of how you would feel."

This was too heavy. The last thing he needed was to be dealing with a crack head. "Look, I feel bad for you but this can't be my life. I'm taking care of my brother and sister and you gotta bounce. I don't trust you around them."

He stood up and walked toward the door but she blocked him, placing her dirty hand on his arm. The same hands that hugged another nigga's dick the night before. Shaking her off, and with hate in his eyes he said, "Don't touch me! Get the fuck up out my crib!"

"Don't put me out like this, Zoom," she cried pressing her palms against her eyes. "Please."

"I'm not a doctor, Nay!" he yelled. "I can't do shit for you!"

She dug into her pocket and pulled out a small piece of paper. "I got accepted into rehab. All I need is your help until that day. I'm begging you. If you help me I'll never bother you again."

For some reason Zoom thought about his mother. Had his father not given her a chance when she was abusing drugs he probably wouldn't be alive. He felt compelled to help even though his intuition said to leave her alone.

"You can stay here until that day but you gotta sleep out here." She hugged him and he pushed her back so hard her lower back banged into the front doorknob. "Go take a shower." The smell of her body was atrocious. "I'll bring some of my sweatpants and a t-shirt." She rushed

The Ungrateful Bastards   144

toward the bathroom before he could change his mind.

"What am I doing with this bitch?" he said to himself. "Like I don't have enough problems…"

He grabbed some clothes from his room, opened the bathroom door and sat them on the toilet. She was in the shower already getting her body together when she heard him walk inside. "Thank you again, Zoom," she said behind the yellow shower curtain. "I won't let you down."

He grumbled a little and went to check on Dodson. He heard something bumping around in his room when Nay first arrived so when she was taken care of he went to see. Dodson was up, eyes wide open and as red as strawberries.

He looked frazzled. More frazzled than he did when Bear was killed.

"What's wrong with you, man?" Zoom asked stepping into the room.

"Nothing," he said shaking his head. He didn't want to say anything about his meeting with their neighbor The Creeper yesterday. "Just leave me alone!"

Zoom took a few steps backward and stuffed his hands into his jean pockets. "You know what, I don't even care what's wrong. Just get up and follow me. I gotta talk to you and your sister."

Dodson walked slowly behind him on the way to their sister's room. When they got there Zoom entered without an announcement. Also awake, Berry was sitting on the bed staring at the wall. "I want to talk to you," Zoom said firmly.

"About what?" She asked, forehead wrinkled and brows pulled closely together. It was clear she hated him at the moment.

"About the rules in this house." He leaned against the wall and crossed his arms over his chest. "Dodson sit on the floor because I'm talking to you too." When he was seated Zoom took a deep breath and wiped his hand down his chest. "I don't want tension in this house but I feel if I don't put shit down you'll think what I'm about to say is a joke."

"Go head, Zoom," Berry said as she leaned back into the wall and placed her feet on her bed to hug her knees.

"I do love you. But I'm not letting you fuck your life up just cause ma not in the picture. So here's how it's going down. When you come home from school the first thing you do is your homework. After that you can go out but you gotta be back by 9:00."

"Nine?" she yelled. "What the fuck!"

"The fuck is that things are going to change. Don't worry its only Monday through Friday. On Saturday you can stay out 'til 11:00 pm."

"I'm a teenager, Zoom!" Berry yelled as if he didn't know. "This shit ain't fair! You trying to treat me like a kid!"

"What's not fair is you playing yourself like a whore 'round the city." She pouted but then Zoom focused on Dodson. "I want you in the house by 7:00 o'clock during the week and at 9:00 on the weekends."

"I don't want to go outside no more anyway," he said softly.

Zoom shrugged. "Whatever...just remember what I said."

"What happens if we don't come in on time?" Berry asked seriously.

The Ungrateful Bastards 146

"You'll be locked out because I'm changing the locks."

Berry was so angry she could've murdered him.

"You not going to get away with this shit," she said. "I promise."

"Watch me."

With the law handed down Zoom walked into the living room.

Nay didn't follow right away, instead she went into Berry's room. "Sorry about your curfew. He's doing it because he loves you."

"Don't act fake," she said through clenched teeth. "I didn't tell Zoom about George." She looked at her bruised face. "Guess you met Dookie again huh?"

Nay smiled, closed the door and walked to the living room.

Zoom examined her clean but battered face, more curious than ever about what she'd gone through. "You gonna tell me who did this to you or not?"

Worried about the outcome she decided to be real. "Dookie...and Zoom, I don't trust her, she seems dangerous."

****

Reprimanding her soldiers, Dookie stood in the front of a project where she moved dope when suddenly Zoom pulled up, jumped out of the car and approached with vengeance.

He was bare chested, with a white t over his shoulder and pissed off.

Although she was in mid conversation, when he yanked her roughly by the elbow one of

By T. Styles   147

her soldier's, in hero mode, pushed him a few steps backwards.

Ready to kill, Zoom leaped up and stole him in the jaw, knocking him ass first to the ground. Blood splattered on Zoom's chest as he continued his mission. Zoom kicked and punched the man repeatedly as the others tried to pull him off.

It was of no consequence. Zoom didn't stop until he was tired, breathing heavily over his body.

When the soldier regained his footing, he drew his weapon and aimed it at Zoom who was unmoved. Fearing things were about to escalate to the final level; Dookie jumped in front of her goon and yelled, "Go, home!"

Scowling he said, "But this nigga just—"

"Get the fuck out of here, Francis!" she yelled louder. "I have it under control."

Francis and the other men stormed away, not without throwing Zoom looks that could murder.

When they were gone Dookie turned around and addressed Zoom. "You could've been killed just now. He's one of my best shooters."

"Don't know 'bout all that," he responded with an arrogant laugh. He wiped blood off of his chest with his white t-shirt before throwing it on the ground. "Don't take much skill to shoot a nigga standing right in front of you."

She placed her hands on her hips. "What do you want, Zoom?"

"I thought I made myself clear but its obvious I didn't. Stay the fuck away from me and anybody who knows me," he said flatly.

She smiled. "We grew up in DC together, Michael. It's gonna be hard not running into people we both know."

Through clenched teeth he said, "You know what the fuck I mean."

"This must be about your little girlfriend."

"She ain't my girl."

"So you mean you were about to get killed just now over nothing?"

He stepped closer. "I'm serious, Dookie. This ain't a game. I moved on with my life and I suggest you do the same." He pointed in her face.

Dookie stepped back and placed her hands on her hips. "She don't know about your family does she?" she paused. "She's still under the illusion that you're picture perfect."

Zoom looked her up slowly from her feet to her eyes. The last thing he thought his family was was perfect. Shaking his head, and having said his piece, he headed back toward his car.

Once inside he grabbed a fresh t-shirt out the back and slid it on. When he looked in the direction Dookie stood and didn't see her. Thinking she disappeared quickly he raised his head higher and saw her lying face down on the ground.

"What the fuck?" he yelled jumping out of the car to see what was wrong.

****

When Dookie opened up her eyes, the sounds of hospital machines were beeping in the background, she was surprised to see Zoom, leaning against the wall next to the door. "Your girl knows you here?"

"I told you already...she's a friend."

"That's why you won't tell her the truth?" she laughed softly. "Because she's just a friend?"

"Why didn't you tell me?" he skipped the subject.

Slowly she rolled her head away from him and toward the window. "Tell you what, Zoom?" she exhaled and looked at him again.

"That you have cancer."

She laughed. "Would it have made a difference?" she paused. "You made it known how much you hate me."

Before he could respond Meister walked into the room holding Prince in his arms. When he saw Zoom he shook his head and laughed sarcastically. Using bad taste Meister said, "It's a little too late to get back with her now don't you think?"

Zoom ignored him and focused on Dookie. "This the nigga you chose to be with?"

"You should talk," she said softly, remembering Nay's coked out ways. Focusing on Meister she said, "What you doing here?"

"Came to see you, babes," he said, bending down and kissing her on the lips. He sat Prince on the edge of the bed who was focused intensely on a red ball in his hand. "Plus he wanted to spend a few minutes with mommy."

She sighed deeply. "Meister, I'm in the hospital and he shouldn't be here. I don't want him to see me like this."

"I know... but I figured he'd brighten up your day," he continued. "Don't worry, I'll be back to pick him up later."

"I bet...do what you gotta do with my cousin," she said softly.

The Ungrateful Bastards   150

Meister touched her arm and walked toward the door stopping at Zoom. Looking into his eyes, he opened his mouth like he was about to speak. Instead he laughed at Zoom and walked away.

When he left Zoom said, "Cute kid."

She rubbed her son's head. "I know...he's two years old."

"I'm talking about your dude," he said jokingly, not feeling the nigga one bit.

She laughed. "He's not coming back you know?"

Zoom frowned. "Who?"

"My boyfriend."

"Why you telling me?" he shrugged.

"Can you take him with you?" she asked looking at her son. "I can't have him in here with me and I'm afraid CPS (Child Protective Services) will get involved if someone doesn't get him."

"Where your people?" he paused. "Like your cousin Miranda."

"She living foul."

Zoom peeled himself off the wall and said, "I see a lot of issues with what you want. Starting with the fact that I don't fuck with you and secondly I got problems of my own."

"I'll have somebody come pick him up. I promise. You'll only have him for a few hours."

"Dookie...this shit..."

"I'll never ask you for another thing again."

Zoom looked at her and the kid and exhaled. "This little nigga not my job."

"Why do you blame me for something that wasn't my fault? After all these years! The past is the past and I know you still care because you wouldn't be here. All I'm asking is for your help."

"I trusted you." He said through narrowed eyes.

"And I loved you. I still love you now." She paused. "What you think happened years ago didn't happen in that way. You believe everybody but me and that shit rips me apart."

Silence.

When she could tell he was going to believe what made him sleep at night she said, "If you don't want to help me why are you still here?" she continued. "I don't know why I expected you to step up anyway. Just leave...I'll be fine. I always am."

CHAPTER TWENTY
SWEET HUMILIATION

Irritated beyond belief, face quenched and mind twirling, Berry stomped down the street talking to Liberty on the cell phone. It pissed her off that she didn't have any wheels.

On the way to Liberty's house she was hoping she could quickly get community service over with. Since she didn't have a car anymore because her mother took hers, she had to kick rocks or risk getting locked up.

"My brother ain't been in charge but for a few weeks and already he tripping. He be laying up in that bitch like he's my father. I feel like I'm losing it, Liberty!"

"What happen?"

"The other day this dude I met on the way home from school called the house looking for me and Zoom slammed on him! Talking about I didn't do my homework first. Ma never carried shit like him."

When she saw a few dope boys looking her way she switched harder, in the hopes of catching a gold fish. Knowing all the while that if Zoom saw her he would crack her ribs.

"Just ignore his ass and do you anyway," Liberty suggested. "It ain't like he can do anything but threaten you."

"Come on, girl. You know I do me regardless...but I don't feel like him jumping up in my face either. You saw how he acted at the club. On everything I cherish, if he do some shit like that again we fighting."

She laughed. "You good because that couldn't be me," She said in pity. "I need my freedom and I don't take that kind of shit from my own mama. Because of him leaving me in the club I had to bounce with them dudes we met. The one who liked you kept trying to stick his finger in my pussy in the backseat. I had to fight my way out of the car!"

"I'm sorry, Liberty. I'm five seconds from unleashing on him so please don't pump me up. He thinks I'm scared but I'm not," she lied.

She was talking mad shit until a brand new silver Cadillac Escalade pulled up on her and slowed down. Berry's heart rate kicked up because if she liked one thing rich niggas who was driving was it. "Damn, Berry, you getting phatter by the day," Don Morton, a low-level drug dealer, complimented. She smelled the new car scent along with vanilla air freshener wafting from the window and her little puss jumped.

Hiding in the corners within the hood, he had been feeling Berry for a minute and watched her body develop from a little girl to a teenager. The chicken was ready to be plucked. He made his intentions known to Zoom one time in a respectful manner and almost got fucked up. Although Zoom was only 18, he was far older than his 15-year-old sister.

Before flirting, Berry looked down the street to make sure her brother wasn't coming. "You better stop playing, boy before Zoom see you." She kept the phone in her hand so that her best friend could hear every word. "Plus don't you got a girlfriend and stuff?"

He dismissed the notion of being taken away with a wave of his hand. "Naw. Even if I did I'm trying to get to know you. You gonna give me the number or what?"

The Ungrateful Bastards   154

Berry leaned into the car window, raised her flat ass in the air and quickly read off every digit. "Now that you have it, use it."

"Aight, mami. I'm gonna call you later. Maybe take you out to eat or somethin'." Which was code for give her some 'dick.'

"Do just that," she grinned.

When he pulled off she placed her ear back to the phone. With a grin on her face she listened as Liberty asked, "Bitch, who you just caught?"

"The nigga Don!" she said barely able to stay still.

Liberty was beyond excited and expressed it with the high pitch of her voice. "Girl, I can't believe his fine ass pulled up on you! You lottery status now!"

"I don't know about all that...let's see how he plays shit." She walked up the steps leading toward Berry's building. "But buzz me in...I'm out front."

Liberty hit the button allowing Berry into the secured building and took the hike to the fifth floor. The moment the door was opened Berry could smell food cooking in the oven and it made her stomach rumble. Up until that second she hadn't realized she was hungry.

"What your mama in here cooking?" Berry asked putting her purse on the sofa and walking into the kitchen.

"Pizza from scratch. Why? You want some?"

"Bitch, what you think?" Berry asked with her hands on her hips.

When the pie was ready they sat at the dining room table with Liberty's mother, Levine.

She was as beautiful as her daughter and Berry always liked her because she let them be teenagers and stayed out the business. With all that said today was different. Levine's presence reminded Berry of what she was trying to avoid, that she was abandoned.

After taking one bite of pizza Berry tossed the slice down and stood up suddenly, stomping toward the door. Her quick movements startled Liberty and Levine. Her heart was all over the place and she was feeling rage of the jealous kind. "We gotta go, Liberty. The bus gonna be here in a minute."

Levine wiped the corners of her mouth and walked over to Berry. Concerned she asked, "Are you okay, honey? You didn't finish eating."

Berry backed up a little and grabbed her purse from off the couch. "I'm fine. We just late that's all." She looked past her at Liberty. "You coming or what?"

Liberty stood up, grabbed her things and followed Berry outside. When they were walking to the bus stop silence hung in the air between them like a dick between two balls. Liberty couldn't take it anymore and decided to talk first because she hated beefing. "So when you think you gonna call Don?"

"Not sure." she shrugged.

When they arrived at the bus stop they sat down and Berry looked out ahead of her...a blank expression covering her face. She was trying to find a good reason to be angry otherwise she'd looked like a crazy bitch who was jealous that her friend had a mother and she didn't.

"What's wrong with you?" Liberty questioned. "Why you acting funky?"

"Nothing is wrong...damn! Why you keep asking me the same thing over and over? If something was wrong best believe I'd tell you and stuff."

The bus pulled up and Liberty decided not to press the issue. Besides, she hadn't had her morning blunt yet. "Whatever."

When the bus stopped they both got on but Berry walked to the back...Liberty sat in the front. When it pulled off Berry looked out of the window. The emptiness that accompanied her was hard to describe.

To make matters worse when she was halfway to her destination she saw her mother walking down the street with Dora. A huge smile covered Martha's face and it was as if she didn't have a care in the world.

How could she be so happy without her?

Berry placed her hands on the window and pressed her nose against the dirty glass. At that moment she wasn't a rebellious kid. She was a baby in need of a mother who had long ago disconnected.

When the bus continued and her mother went out of view she sat back in her seat and cried softly. Gazing up, she knew Liberty saw her too because she was staring her way.

Berry wiped the tear off of her face roughly with the back of her hand and put on a tough front. Emotions were out of place in DC. She had to toughen up and she knew it. In that moment she made a decision to stop crying for that old bitch. If she didn't want to be in her life she wouldn't press the issue.

Fifteen minutes later they made it to the community service site to fulfill their obligations. After being given their duties Berry was much angrier than Liberty upon learning that they would have to pick up trash off the side of the

By T. Styles 157

highway. This job was courtesy of Detective Millin because he wanted her humiliated. Her worst fear was one of her friends seeing them and her losing cool points.

After being given instructions she angrily picked up debris and stuffed it in the large yellow plastic bag. Since she wasn't speaking to Liberty she didn't have anybody to help her vent.

She was just about to focus on work when the Angry Woman and her husband drove by the site, with grins on their faces. When they saw her doing work he threw a plastic cup on the ground and both of them threw their fuck you fingers in the air.

Frustrated, lonely and annoyed, she tossed the poker down on the ground and yelled, "Fuck this shit!"

The supervisor, a mean man with bushy gray and black eyebrows, yelled, "Pick up that stick or I won't be signing off on your completion form! Keep in mind this is for your probation. Not the city of DC!"

"I don't care what you're signing off on! I'm done!"

CHAPTER TWENTY-ONE
THE WORD IS BOND

Zoom sat in bed in his room looking at TV while Nay was baking cookies in the kitchen. He invited Dodson to join him and Prince, but Dodson had been acting differently lately. He chalked it up to him missing Bear and decided not to press the issue. Besides, it wasn't like he didn't have enough problems.

Zoom felt stupid for allowing Dookie to guilt him into watching the kid on and off while she attended therapy. It was like she was trying to force a bond between them. On the days he said no, he'd come home and Prince would be sitting in the living room because Berry or Dodson would have him. Although he faked mad, there was something about the little dude that he liked.

Nay didn't like it but what could she say? They weren't together.

Just when he was starting to go with the flow he received a call from Liberty that Berry walked away from the community service site and she didn't know where she was.

A few minutes after that Nay said he needed to go with her to the rehabilitation center in Baltimore because they wouldn't accept anyone without a support system. That wasn't apart of their original plan and he felt lied to, now having to play the concerned boyfriend.

It was tough and he was five seconds from saying fuck it.

"They're ready," Nay said walking into the room with a tray full of chocolate chip cookies. "They're hot too."

"Did you knock on Dodson's door and ask if he wanted any?" he asked plainly, careful not to make her think that he had forgiven any of her dick sucking indiscretions.

She placed the tray on the table and picked one up to give to Prince who gulped it down.

"Damn, shawty," Zoom joked looking at the baby. "You can eat."

Prince laughed and chewed with his mouth open.

"I asked Dodson but he didn't want any," Nay said. "I thought you said they were his favorite."

"They are," he sighed. He took a cookie for himself but placed it on the bed.

She looked at it and sighed. "I hope I didn't bake them for nothing." Disappointment covered her cute face.

"You didn't." he focused on the TV.

"Zoom, as your friend and future girl, can I do anything for you? Anything at all to make you feel better? I don't care what it is."

"First off I never said we would be together." He paused. "And the only thing you can do for me is get clean and get on your feet."

"Outside of that, Zoom." She sat on the bed. "Can I help you with your siblings?"

"No," he sighed. "This family business and I'm gonna have to work through it. Plus I just got a notice that the rent will be due in two weeks and I'm sure other bills are coming too."

Her eyes widened. "So what you gonna do?" she looked at the baby. "With Prince?"

"Somebody is picking him up tomorrow," he said flatly. "Don't worry you won't have to take care of him."

"It's not that I mind," she said softly. "I just don't think that he's good for the family right now. Too much is happening and too quickly."

"Let me handle him," he said ruffling his hair.

She looked at Prince. "He looks like you..."

Zoom stared at him and said. "No he don't."

"He does..."

Irritated he said, "I'm busy, Nay. What you really want?"

"You gonna hustle again?

He remained silent.

"Zoom, you can't go back that route. What happens if you get locked up? Dodson and Berry might go into foster care and get lost in the system. Trust me, I know how bad that is for a kid. Before you hustle I would rather sell my body. I was doing it for drugs anyway...might as well use it for you."

He looked deeply into her eyes so that she would know he was serious. "I'm not that kind of dude, Nay." he paused. "Never have been and never will be. I'll get the money without you having to use your body."

She nodded, trying her best to find a way to help. "What you gonna do about Berry being out in the streets right now? It's getting late."

"I don't know. This shit is so fucking confusing. If I go out there and find her she's going to think she can break the rules and I can't have that shit either. I have to let her know things are different."

By T. Styles   161

"So you've answered your question. Let her come to you."

It was settled.

They spent the next two hours watching television with Prince but Zoom had no idea what was going on in the program. He was worried about his family but worry had no place in a man's world.

About thirty minutes passed until he finally dozed off on the sofa. When he heard soft knocking Zoom popped up.

"Somebody at the door," Dodson whispered entering the living room where they sat.

Zoom looked at the clock on the wall and frowned when he noticed it was 1:00 in the morning. He was sure it was Berry but now it was decision time. Did he let her in and give her the impression that she could pull this type of shit all the time? Or did he hold to his bottom lines?

Zoom walked toward the door and the knocking grew louder. When he glanced down he saw Dodson and he started to tell him to go to his room. But he wanted to use Berry's situation as a teaching moment. If Dodson did anything similar in the future the same rules would apply.

"Who is it?" Zoom asked.

"It's me, Berry.," she sounded drunk. "Open the door. My key won't work."

"That's cause I changed the locks," he advised. "What time was curfew?"

"Zoom, stop fucking playing around! I'm tired."

He immediately grew angrier. Certain she was drunk, it was evident that his sister played him as a bitch. It was time to call her on it. "So

The Ungrateful Bastards   162

you been out in the streets drinking? And carrying yourself like a whore?"

"I'm not—"

"Answer the fuckin question," he yelled. "You been drinking or not, Berry?"

She exhaled. "Yes. Now will you please open the door? I'm tired and I want to get in the bed and go to sleep and stuff."

He took several deep breaths. "You broke curfew so you stay out there. I'm not playing no more!"

Silence.

"Stay out here?" She repeated. "Zoom, open the fucking door!"

"Bitch, kick rocks," he yelled.

"But I don't have anywhere to go," she begged. "Me and Liberty got into it earlier today and I can't stay at her house. Come on, Zoom. Please."

"Not my problem."

Silence.

He didn't leave the door until he heard her soft cries, followed by footsteps walking down the steps in the hallway. Doubting himself, Zoom sat on the couch wondering if he made the right decision. Wondering if he came down on her too hard considering everything that was happening. But he felt like he was at the crossroads. He had to hold his guns now or lose her forever.

When it was 3:00 am the big brother in him went outside to see if she was sitting on the steps. He didn't know what he was going to do when he saw her but he wanted to at least know she was okay. But after he got dressed and went out he didn't see her anywhere.

Preparing to walk back inside, he was stopped when he heard loud rap music booming from the speakers of a car. "You Zoom?"

Zoom reluctantly walked down the steps and toward a black Honda Accord. "Who asking?"

"My name is Miranda...and I'm Dookie's cousin. I'm here for Prince."

He frowned and scratched his cornrows. He remembered her during the Wonderland years but she changed and was more attractive. "I thought Meister was scooping him later."

"He sent me instead," she replied. "Dookie died this morning. We getting all the family together...and that means the kid too."

CHAPTER TWENTY-TWO
UNDER ZOOM'S ADMINISTRATION

Berry was miserable...

After spending the night on the cold, pissy, dirty Laundromat floor in her building—her back, neck and buttocks throbbed. Making her own bed and lying in it for breaking the rules, she cried all night and as a result her temples throbbed. As much pain as she was in she knew one thing Zoom was not playing with curfew. His point was made and she heard him loud and clearly.

Pulling herself off of the floor, she slogged up the steps and faced her apartment door. Slightly humbled, she knocked and when Zoom opened it he allowed her to walk inside. She couldn't be certain, but as she looked up at him, there appeared to be peace on his face, as if relieved to see her. Not looking too much into things she said, "Hey."

Hand resting on his bare chest he asked, "Hungry?" He locked the door when she was fully inside.

She nodded yes as the smell of sausage, eggs and cinnamon toast caused her stomach to rumble.

"Go wash your hands," he said. "Nay said breakfast will be ready in a few."

As she made her way to the back she glanced around the apartment. A huddle of crystal navy blue beads sat in a pile on the living room table and she noticed Zoom's braids were fresh and figured Nay had just done them.

As he helped Nay with breakfast she stole a few looks at him. He was her brother and she loved him even if she wanted to play hard. Maybe it wasn't worth it to fight anymore...

In the bathroom she took a moment to gaze at her dirty face in the mirror. If she didn't get her life together, her night in the Laundromat would be foreplay of coming events and she realized she wasn't built for the hard knock existence. At least for now she decided to render to Caesar, hoping that her brother would do good by them.

After cleaning up and putting on a fresh shirt, she walked back into the kitchen. Nay pulled out a chair and she joined her, Zoom and Dodson for breakfast in silence. Much needed to be said but no one wanted the peaceful moment ruined. It was as if they made a silent pact to respect the calm and not say a word.

Stuffed, when Dodson finished eating he walked over to the living room sofa and grabbed a home movie from under the TV. Placing the DVD in the player his eyes lit up when he heard his father's voice booming from the speakers. Although he watched the same DVD a million times, it was as if it was the first. It was a sermon their father delivered and it always made him feel good, placing him at extreme ease when things got hard.

Also captivated, when Berry was done she eased up from the table and walked over to the sofa to sit next to her brother. Zoom followed shortly thereafter, taking a seat on the recliner.

Instead of interrupting, Nay cleaned the kitchen and gave them that private moment. Besides, the three of them were captivated by their late father's voice as they unconsciously took his message to heart.

The Ungrateful Bastards   166

Who was she to ruin it by intruding?

There Steven stood...strong behind the podium, delivering a message of love, family and devotion. He spoke of how life could get heavy and how family should always be able to count on one another in the toughest hours, when it counted most.

Suddenly Zoom snatched the remote, turned the television off and looked down at them. The news of Dookie dying fucked him up and had him acting sporadic. "Why we still playing this game?" he asked. "Why we still pretending that this man was anything but fucked up?"

Nay looked at Dodson not having an answer.

"No more pretending. I'm done with this shit." He opened several DVD cases and cracked every one with Steven's name. Standing over a pile of lies he said, "We not acting like our past matched theirs no more. We done with that shit."

****

The small community service cafeteria was crowded with hungry church folks as the annual fish fry, hosted by Martha, was underway. In addition to catfish and trout, there was cornbread, mac and cheese and greens. An assortment of desserts was also present.

Every now and again Martha would look across the way at the Pastor, hoping he approved of her contributions. And judging by how he continued to gaze her way he did. Besides, they were already up fifteen hundred dollars with more plate orders coming.

By T. Styles 167

Martha just finished her last batch of fish when Zoom, Dodson and Nay walked down the steps and toward her. The members, knowing they belonged to Martha, looked at her in anticipation.

The look on her children's faces was anything but pleasant.

Nervous, and hoping to get them out as quickly as possible, Martha wiped her hands on the towel on her shoulder and approached. "What are you doing here?" she asked in near panic. She looked back at the pastor who was also watching.

"Don't worry, we're not here to ask you to come home," Zoom said. "We wanted you to know that you did us a favor by bouncing. You were never down for us anyway."

"Come with me." Martha took them to a small private room. The last thing she needed was her business spilling out into the streets. When the door closed she said, "I don't know what's gotten into you but now is not the time to—"

"Why you let him do us like that?" Berry asked. "Why you let him treat us like shit while you stood by and did nothing?"

"I don't know what you're talking about." She paused. "This ain't about that girl dying is it?" she asked Zoom. "I heard what happened. God took her on account of cancer." She wiped her hands on her towel. "If it is about that you need to let her and everything she represented go. But leave me out of it!"

Zoom frowned. "This ain't got nothing to do with that shit." He corrected her. "This is about the past...and how we remember it all."

****

The Ungrateful Bastards 168

Steven Gregory held a bottle of beer in his hand as he stood in front of the dining room table that was stacked with their dinner. The smells causing their hungry tummies to grumble.

Martha, a small shell of herself, sat at the table too ashamed to look her children in their eyes, electing instead to stare at the floor.

In front of Steven, on their knees stood 9-year-old Dodson, 11-year-old Berry and 13-year-old Zoom, their stomachs growling after not eating in three days.

Standing in a soiled, sweaty t-shirt, Steven took a big gulp of beer and said, "I know you're hungry but you're also ungrateful, dirty, bastards!" He clutched a thick leather belt in his hand causing it to groan. "If you want to eat you have to earn your food around here. So let's see how much you remember." He paused and focused on Zoom. "Leviticus 20:26."

Zoom closed his eyes and recited the Bible verse. "You are to be holy to me because I, the Lord, am holy, and I have set you apart from the nations to be my own." Zoom opened his lids and hoped for the best.

Steven nodded in approval because he was correct.

Focusing on Berry he said, "Leviticus 15 versus 19 through 20."

Body trembling, she searched her mind for the correct answer because the wrong one meant not eating and possibly being beaten...again.

When she thought she was correct slowly she parted her lips and said, "When a woman has her regular flow of blood, the impurity of her monthly period will last seven days, and anyone who touches her will be unclean till evening." She

By T. Styles   169

paused and said, "Anything she lies on during her period will be unclean, and anything she sits on will be unclean."

Steven nodded in approval upon hearing the right verses quoted.

Focusing on Dodson, Steven said, "Ephesians 6:5."

Dodson closed his eyes and tried desperately to remember but as hard as he searched he couldn't recall the answer.

Zoom looked over at him wanting to help but feeling the pressure of his father, he remained silent.

"Dodson, answer the question," Steven demanded.

"I...I can't remember."

Zoom was beyond worried because Steven always beat Dodson the worst, resulting in his developmental issues early on in life.

Having tired of waiting, Steven drowned all of his beer and with a thwack, came down on the side of Dodson's head. Instead of stopping he unloaded on him until his bicep throbbed and pulsated.

Zoom wanted to help but feared Berry would be without food for the night too. Instead he looked at his mother, and pleaded with his eyes to make him stop. Too weak of a woman to assist, she mouthed the word 'sorry', got up and walked into her bedroom, closing the door behind her.

Zoom thought all was lost until the front door opened and Pastor Chris, one of Steven's friends entered holding a six pack of beer. Although he wasn't a real pastor, they called him one because he did a lot for the community.

The Ungrateful Bastards 170

He was at the Gregory house earlier, only stepping out a few moments to grab some beer. The last thing he expected to see was child abuse.

He tossed the beer onto the recliner, pulled Steven off Dodson and yelled, "All of you go get in my car!" The children hesitated and he yelled, "Now!"

Piling into his white Lincoln they waited with baited breath for him to come outside. When he finally did, and they saw Steven was not with him, they breathed a sigh of relief.

It may have taken Pastor Chris five minutes but eventually he returned with four beers in hand. He tried to give Berry and Dodson one to relax their nerves but they refused. But when Zoom was offered he accepted, also taking the ones his siblings didn't want.

It was his first taste of beer but it wouldn't be his last.

That night Pastor Chris made sure they ate and were safe but Zoom never got over how his mother turned her back on them when they needed her most.

****

Martha wiped her hands on the towel again and looked at her children. She could hear the crowd growing louder in the large community room at the fish fry. "I made some mistakes...but everything I did was for you," she said to them.

Zoom looked her up and down and shook his head. "We want you to know this...Never come back. You dead to us."

****

By T. Styles   171

Zoom shot up in bed, wet with sweat and mind running one hundred miles and hour. He had a dream that was dressed up more like a revelation and he couldn't shake it. "He's mine," he said into the darkness of his room.

Nay, who heard him from the living room, knocked on his door and walked inside without an invite. "You okay?"

"He's mine," he repeated wiping the sweat from his brow. "Prince..." he looked at her hoping she would get the point without further information.

Walking further into the room she said, "Is it because I said he looked like you? Because babies got a million faces when they growing up."

"No...I mean yes...I mean I don't think so." He looked at her and stood up, pacing in place. "I think that was why Dookie was pressing so hard to be in my life. She knew she would die and she wanted us reunited."

"Zoom, I think it's too early to be taking on a responsibility that big. Especially with your mother gone. Maybe you should give it a little time."

He blinked and said, "Are you ready?"

Confused she asked, "For what?"

"You're leaving for rehab this morning. You forgot?"

She had. "Oh...yes, I'll get dressed." Before walking out she turned around and said, "Are you sure you're okay. I don't like how you look and I'm worried."

"I'm fine...just go get ready...I got a lot to do."

"Okay..." She smiled and walked away.

Zoom showered, dressed and waited in the living room for Nay. He had a lot planned for the day and some of his actions included Prince. All he wanted was for Nay to hurry so that he could get things into motion.

About thirty minutes later Nay entered the living room with her bag in hand. Zoom grabbed his car keys and was about to leave until she said, "I'm not going."

He turned around and faced her. "What you talking about? That's been the plan since you've been here...to stay for a while and take your bed in the center. Why is that changing?"

"Zoom, I know what you're about to do...you're going to see if Prince is yours." She moved closer. "And if he is I want to be there for you. You already got Berry and Dodson, the last thing you need is Prince by yourself. Let me help."

"That wasn't the plan, Nay," he said angrily. "And when plans change it throws shit off. You were supposed to be in Baltimore and we should stick to that. Even if he is mine there's a process I gotta go through to get him."

She moved even closer, careful of his space because she knew he was still salty with her. "I'm going to get help...trust me. I know I can't get clean by myself. But right now my priority is you. Let me do what I can and I'll go later. I promise."

Zoom considered her words. She was right, if he was going to get his son he needed all hands on deck. That is if he was really his son. Besides, it was obvious Nay had no intentions on leaving anyway. "Okay, chill here," he opened the front door. "I'ma be right back."

****

By T. Styles

It took Zoom a minute but he finally remembered the place Dookie's cousin lived. What fucked him up was not his memory being on point, but that when he pulled up Prince was sitting in a sandbox out front of the building, playing with the same red ball he had when he first met the kid.

He was alone.

He parked, walked up to the sandbox and looked down at the kid. He felt like punching Meister in his face and if he saw him that was exactly what he intended. Gazing around he was angry when he realized that not one adult was in sight. "What you doing little man?"

"Ball," he said raising it in the air.

Zoom looked around once more, determined that the dangerous situation was not for the kid and picked him up. The moment he did Miranda came outside laughing on her cell phone. When she saw Zoom holding Prince she said, "I'm gonna call you back when I get more info on your case." She tucked the phone in her purse, and walked briskly toward Zoom. You can't take him! Meister on the way now to pick him up."

"Don't tell me what I can take," he said angrily, maintaining his hold on the child. "I let you get him thinking you were gonna do right by the little dude. Instead he out here by himself at two years old."

"I was in the hallway," she yelled.

"So running your mouth more important than watching the kid?"

"I was working!"

"And we still out!" Zoom announced.

"But Meister told me to let him—"

"I don't give a fuck what he said," he yelled. "If he wants him tell him to come see me. He knows where I live."

Zoom was halfway to the car when she said, "Wait a minute!"

He turned around to see what she wanted not feeling like the bullshit. Miranda deactivated her car alarm which was parked a few spaces up from his and removed a car seat. Realizing what she was trying to do Zoom opened his door for her and she hooked the car seat up before placing Prince inside.

When she was done she looked at Zoom and said, "Dookie told me about you."

He shrugged. "What she say?"

"Just that you would do right by Prince."

Silence.

"I don't know if he's really your son or not but I hope it's true...that you are his father," she continued. "Because Meister ain't shit. The only reason he wants him is because he's worth over ten million dollars."

Zoom frowned. "How you figure?"

"Dookie was a great investor...dope wasn't her only game. She owns five apartment buildings and a few Laundromats and they are all bequeathed to Prince. Meister wants him so that he can get the money... nothing less and nothing more." She moved closer. "As long as you have him Meister will never let it rest. And I might as well tell you that you should be in fear for your life too."

CHAPTER TWENTY-THREE
VOICES THAT DON'T REASON

Martha sat in the pew with wide eyes and open ears...accepting everything the minister delivered without filter. A self respecting Christian to some, to those who knew her most her mental illness was festering by the day, and more than all for the worse.

That very morning she woke up in the apartment she shared with Dora. She was on a newfound mission after receiving a vision. The vision occurred to her when she sat outside on Dora's balcony during the chilly weather.

Not wanting to wake her friend, Martha tiptoed to the sliding glass door and walked outside. Slowly she closed it behind her and breathed in the Washington DC thick air. When she was ready she dropped to her knees on the concrete, folded her hands before her lips, bowed her head and prayed for guidance.

The message she received struck her harder than a semi truck at one hundred miles per hour.

She finally had the answer on what to do about her children.

Martha was too far in her head to see the audience forming outside below. Had she been in her right frame of mind she would've understood why people were snapping pictures and making video for their personal collections. Because Martha was nude as the day she was born...void of one stitch of clothing.

In her room sound asleep, Dora received many phone calls before she decided to answer one. Had she picked up the others the message would've been the same...that her good friend Martha was outside showing everybody her natural business.

Grabbing two housecoats, one for herself and the other for Martha, she rushed to the balcony only to learn that the frantic calls were true. Dora helped Martha to her feet, wrapped the housecoat around her body any kind of way and pushed her into the apartment, sliding the door harshly behind them.

For a second Dora looked down at Martha's wrinkled skin, saggy breasts and graying vagina hair. Back in the day Martha would've never allowed anyone to see her in such disarray. But it was obvious that things changed.

Dora helped Martha put the housecoat on correctly and sat in a chair in front of her. Her mouth slackened before finally saying, "Martha, I love you. But you either gonna have to get yourself together or you have to get out my house. I can't deal with this no more."

She blinked a few times. "What do you mean? All I was doing was praying."

Dora scratched her jaw. "I understand all that, honey," she lied. "But what I don't get is why you out there naked."

Martha finally looked down at herself, realizing that Dora was correct. Instead of admitting her wrong she looked outwardly. "We weren't bought into this world with clothes you know?" she said defensively. "Those are all items that man made in an effort to make us feel bad about our bodies. Well I'm not ashamed of mine anymore."

But you should be though. Dora thought.

"I'm no longer going to allow myself to be subject to what man thinks," she continued. "My Glory belongs with the King." She raised her hand up high and slowly dropped it into her lap.

"Martha, you gotta tell me what you doing...you gotta tell me something that makes sense."

Martha flapped her eyelids and said, "Do you think it's possible that a mother can kill her children out of love?"

She looked at Dora who felt an awful tingling sensation in her chest. Worried she said, "Martha...are you okay? You not talking about hurting them babies are you? It's one thing to take a break but this is ridiculous."

Without another word Martha stood up and walked to her room believing she already received an answer from God. All she needed was another sign. When she was done she strolled into the kitchen, made coffee and toast for herself and Dora before sitting at the breakfast table to finish her meal.

Martha may have moved about like nothing happened but Dora was in fear for her life. After they both ate, with Dora's eyes glued on her the entire time, they went to service.

Martha's body expression changed the moment she entered the church. She went from being fully alive, to being stuck in a trance. Usually in agreement with her friend, these days Dora felt differently. Maybe Martha was taking things to literally, causing her to lose track of reality.

"Today, I want to talk about family," the Preacher said. "I want to talk about what happens in some families that can cause us to backslide and go into the wrong direction."

"Preach," Martha said before the man released a complete thought.

"I hear you, Sister Gregory," he grinned pointing at her. This did nothing but rile her up even more because he gave her a little attention. "And I'm going to do exactly that. Because it needs to be said here and now that some people are born into your family that you should stay away from."

The congregation clapped loudly.

"But ya'll not ready to hear me though!" he continued.

"Yes we are," yelled one woman.

"Preach!" screamed another.

"I said that some people are born into your family who you should stay away from. And if you're not careful these same people can be the cause of your one way ticket to hell!" He patted the corners of his mouth with a cloth napkin.

"Speak on it," Martha yelled again.

"Now I'm not going to be like some of them worthless ministers and tell you that you should live in a home where Godliness is the priority. See, I don't want my flock to be led astray. I want you to know what I stand for!"

The church erupted in violent applause.

"I stand for God! I stand for family! I stand for peace! And I stand tall as the leader of this church. Now let's talk about what I don't stand for."

The congregation's volume grew so loud it throbbed the eardrum.

"I don't stand for the devil! I don't stand for disobedience! And I tell you right now; if you know any one in your family who is ungodly you should smite them swiftly out of your life! Put them out of their misery for they know not what they do." He patted is mouth again. "But do it quickly! Do it now! And do not delay!"

CHAPTER TWENTY-FOUR
ANGRY TRUTHS

Zoom pushed the cart into the shopping line to pay for his groceries with Prince and Dodson in tow. As they waited their turn, their neighbor The Creeper walked into the grocery store, causing Dodson more fright.

Zoom didn't see what had his little brother shook but he did see Dodson's nervous stance. "What's wrong with you now?" he looked in the direction he was looking and finally saw the creepy neighbor. "Did he do something to you?" His nostrils flared, as he contemplated murder. "Did he hurt you?" he gripped him by the elbow.

He snatched away. "No!" he yelled. "Just leave me alone!" He stormed out of the grocery store.

Zoom looked down at Prince and sighed. His world was toppling down around him and the only thing he wanted was his break. When would things be looking up for him?

What am I doing? He thought to himself. *Why do I have a kid that's not even mine?*

When he made it to the register the cashier rung up all of the food and he handed her a debit card he used for small shit. When he got some cash he would put a few bucks on it but lately he hadn't been hustling. Daddy work was full time business.

"I'm sorry, sir, this isn't going through." The cashier said softly.

Zoom frowned. "I put five hundred dollars in there the other day," he said although he couldn't remember when. "Do it again." Zoom looked around to see who was watching and noticed the line grew longer and more impatient.

She tried to use it again and still, the same thing. "I'm sorry, sir. It's denied."

She handed it back and he snatched it away. Embarrassed, Zoom grabbed Prince from the cart and hustled to his vehicle, placing him in his car seat. He couldn't even storm off like he wanted because he had a baby.

Temples throbbing, he was about to pull off when there was a knock at the window. When he turned his head he saw it was Pastor Chris who he hadn't seen in years. Slowly he rolled the window down and said, "What you want?"

Pastor Chris leaned inside, smiled at Dodson and focused back on Zoom. "I saw what happened back there?"

"What the fuck do you want, slim?" Zoom yelled, startling little Prince and causing Dodson to sit up straight in the backseat.

"I know you're mad at me for not keeping you guys, but I didn't have the authority. I had to turn you over to your parents but you gotta believe I tried. That's why you stayed with me for a few weeks. I was trying to work things out."

"You knew what he was doing to us," Zoom yelled. "Everybody knew but nobody helped. And now you here for what?"

"You love judging don't you?" he frowned. "You think your fucked up background gives you the right to do all kinds of shit but nobody else gets a pass?" He laughed. "News flash, I had a fucked up life, your mother had a fucked up life and your father did too! Grow up and get over it!"

Zoom faced him. "That makes you feel better?" Pastor Chris was about to leave when

Zoom grabbed him by the collar and stuck his gun in his face. "Toss everything in your pocket on my lap."

When he tried to run Zoom cocked his gun and pulled him further inside. "I'm broke. I got a baby and my kid brother in this car. Which means I don't have nothing to lose. Now toss it...I'm not going to say it again."

Pastor Chris quickly did what he was told.

"Just so you know, Steven wasn't your real father," he said in anger. He would've told him at another time, perhaps over beers, but being robbed brought the worst out in him. "Why do you think he use to fuck ya'll up so much? You weren't his kids!"

"Fuck is you talking bout?" Zoom asked.

Dodson also sat up to hear what he was saying.

"Just what I said," he spat back. "The man you think was your father wasn't." he paused. "Your mother came with three babies in the marriage and he resented her for it. Had he known about ya'll he never would've married her." He looked at him and smiled. "The most ironic part is that you hate him so much yet you're just like him."

In shock Zoom released him.

"Tormented." Lighter in the pocket, Pastor Chris walked away.

Zoom took a few seconds, gun in his lap and thoughts on what he just heard. It explained why Steven hated them but why would his mother lie? He felt slight relief that he wasn't his father but who was he? He scratched in between one of his cornrows and tried to understand it all.

Needing to place his anger somewhere else for the moment he said, "What happened between you and the nigga downstairs? I peeped how you looked at him."

"He knows I was with Bear. He saw the murder and everything."

Zoom was shocked but relieved, having thought the worst...sexual abuse. "So he didn't touch you?"

"Touch me?" he paused. "No! He was blackmailing me for money I don't have."

"Is that why you been acting so strange?" he yelled. "Why wouldn't you say something to me?" he hit the steering wheel. "It's dumb!"

"Because you said you were tired of dealing with my shit. And I thought you would leave like ma. I don't want you to leave."

Zoom took a few deep breaths and tried to calm down. "What were you even doing around him? I told you to stay away!"

"I was looking for somebody to play with," he said scratching the part in his head. He received a fresh haircut earlier, which was another reason Zoom was light on cash. "And I thought the new kid in our building lived with him."

"Did he?"

"No," he said.

"It's time for you to grow up," Zoom said. "Nobody gonna protect you like you can protect yourself. Tonight you will be a man."

****

The Creeper walked into his dark apartment without turning the light on, as usual. Besides he knew where everything was placed.

The moment he reached his room and flipped on the switch, Dodson turned it back off before the creepy neighbor could see his face.

Since he lived on the first floor, it was easy to enter his apartment through the window and that's exactly what Zoom and Dodson did.

Not knowing what was happening, The Creeper was met with a slash across his face from Zoom's knife. He could've shot him but he was preserving bullets and losing the sound.

When he tried to fight, Zoom snatched him closer and stabbed him multiple times in the chest and back. Although not visible in the darkness Zoom's victim's clothing was thick crimson red.

Realizing his life was coming to an end The Creeper was about to scream until Zoom went across his throat, severing his vocal chord. Suddenly he had become responsible for all of Zoom's troubles, as he flashbacked to the boxing matches he had with Steven where he couldn't fight back.

The creepy neighbor was not moving but Zoom continued to stab him when he hit the floor until his thrashes when straight to the carpet beneath his body.

****

The next day Zoom eased out of his car as he tried to figure out what he was going to do about cash. Earlier in the day he went to have a paternity test done on Prince and if he was his son, money would get even tighter. That little paper he lifted off Pastor Chris wasn't enough to do shit for his financial woes...he needed more.

By T. Styles   185

Much more.

He was either gonna hustle and kiss Perch's ass or knock niggas over and stack his paper. He was sick of Perch so honestly he was considering the latter.

Shit was already bad but got worse when Meister pulled up in a black Porsche truck and stepped up to him. "Where my son at, yo?" he yelled, nostrils flaring.

Zoom smiled and focused on him. "You got five seconds to get the fuck up out my face."

"Nigga, you ain't hard!" Meister yelled. "You think you gonna come back after two years and take my fucking money, cuz?" he continued hitting his chest. "Over my dead body! That kid belongs to me." he tapped his waist so that Zoom could see he was holding. "Now where he—"

Suddenly the kid or the money was the least of Meister's concerns when Zoom pulled his gun, fired past his ear and then placed the hot burner on his forehead. "You want it like this? Right here in the street? 'Cause I'm eager to serve."

Forehead burning, Meister threw his hands up in the air. "Please don't do it, man. I just want to go home. I don't want no trouble."

Zoom laughed and bit his bottom lip. "Run that piece." Without waiting, Zoom snatched the gun from his waist and noticed it was a twenty-two. He laughed at the small handset he was carrying. "Fuck you gonna do with this? Tickle me? Open your pockets and toss it on my car." he laughed harder as he watched Meister release the day's payout. "Now get the fuck out of here!" Zoom lowered the weapon and Meister ran to his truck, with his life in tow.

The Ungrateful Bastards

CHAPTER TWENTY-FIVE
PEPPERED LIES

A few days later...

Berry was stretched out on her bed speaking to Don Morton on the phone. They had been phone boning for the past few days and he was eager to take things to the next level. But she was scared. After coming in late the other night and being forced to sleep on the laundry room floor, she didn't want to irritate Zoom too early.

"When you gonna get with me," he asked pressing her as hard as he could for sex. "Like a man should a woman? Cause I think you ducking and dodging."

She twisted the cord of her pink heart shaped phone. "It's not even like that. I said we can hook up this weekend."

"Why we gotta hook up so late when there are seven days in a week? I'm a grown man, ma. I need a woman who can get with me when the mood hits. You with that or not?"

She sat up straight. "Yeah...I just..."

"Afraid of what your brother gonna say?"

"No," she lied. "I just want to make sure you like me."

"I like you...I told you that...but I can't be dealing with no chick acting like a young bitch. I need a woman, feel me?"

She swallowed...feeling young and dumb. "Okay, so when you trying to see me?"

"Tonight."

"Cool," he said having gotten his way. "I'll hit you later with the plan. And don't let that nigga change your mind...you all woman now."

When she hung up someone knocked at the front door. Sliding out of bed she walked into the front room to investigate, with Dodson following.

Gaping through the peephole he said, "It's Dora..."

"Let her in," she frowned.

"But I don't want her in—"

"Let her in the fucking house!"

Dodson rolled his eyes and opened the door. She pushed her way inside without asking and sat on the edge of the sofa, not enough energy to sit further back. Looking up at them she asked, "Where Zoom?"

"What's wrong?" Berry questioned, put off by her behavior.

"Where is he?" she yelled causing both to tremble.

Dodson never liking her was now afraid. "I don't know." He shrugged. "Why you here?"

She looked at the floor and then at their eyes. "You seen your mama?"

They shook their heads no.

"Have either of you told anybody about 614?"

Now the hairs on the back of their necks rose. "No...I haven't." she looked at Dodson. "You?"

"No...I haven't said anything either."

"Then I don't understand what would spark this...if my theory is correct it doesn't make any sense." She swallowed and wiped her mouth, hand dropping down her side. "It's like your mother's gone mad."

Berry shrugged. "She's been that way for awhile now. That's why she not here no more.

And how come you acting like you don't know already?"

"No, honey," Dora said. "This is different...*very different.*"

Silence.

Dora slowly stood up and paced the floor. With her back in their direction she turned around. "Unless...she's faking it. To plan an insanity defense." She paused and looked around. "I knew I never should've gotten involved!"

"Why would she do that?" Berry questioned. "Ain't nobody came around asking right? About 614?"

"Not that I know of." She stepped to the children. "But she may be trying to put this little performance on us just in case." She paused. "That way everybody will look at her with pity."

Berry started crying. "I'm confused. We didn't tell anyone! We stuck to the plan like we all said that night!"

Feeling for them she grabbed one of their hands apiece and looked at them compassionately. "I know we had our problems. Before your mama married Steven I did the best I could to take care of all three of you. I might have been on drugs but you always had a home, a clean bed and a meal."

"And you still left us," Dodson said, finally revealing the source of his anger toward her. "You knew Steven was beating us and you didn't care or come get us."

"I know...I let them convince me that the three of you were nothing but some ungrateful bastards." She shook her head in shame. "I let them turn me against the kids I practically raised. I guess I was hiding my own guilt." she released their hands and flopped back on the sofa. "How could I do that to the children I named. The children that I loved?" She exhaled deeply. "All she wanted was to fit you kids into a mold that was good for the wife of a priest. An ex one at that! But she never told him about ya'll. She never told him she had children. Came into the marriage with three babies and that drove Steven mad."

"Wait...Steven wasn't our real father?" Berry asked.

"I knew that already," Dodson said lightly. "Tried to tell you earlier but you told me to get out of your room."

She rolled her eyes upon hearing the truth. "So the man who beat me, wasn't my daddy?" Berry asked stunned.

Dora shook her head no.

"Than who is?"

"We don't need to worry about all that right now." She grabbed their hands and pulled them toward her again. "I came over here to tell you this. Be careful of your mama. I think she's plotting to kill you."

****

Zoom sat in the car, quietly, with Nay in the passenger seat. Earlier he got the news he didn't want to receive, that Prince was not his son.

Looking at Prince in the rearview mirror, he couldn't believe how attached he got to him already. The main question that floated on his mind was if he wasn't his son, why did Dookie want them together so much?

Was it just because Meister was a bitch?

"You okay," Nay asked touching his hand softly.

"I'm fine..." he huffed. The sun hitting the black crystal beads on the ends of his braids.

"The police were all out here earlier. They found that creepy neighbor in his apartment stabbed to death. Guess somebody finally killed him."

He shrugged. "Such is the nature of DC."

She found his statement odd but knew where it came from. "I know you wanted him to be your kid, but maybe it's for the best." She shrugged. "If you had a son it would be impossible to get your life back on track. Especially with Berry and Dodson."

"I hear you," he said sighing deeply.

Nay looked away and then back. "Zoom, what's 614?"

He rotated his head in her direction. His mouth opened and closed as if the words had fallen out. Frowning he asked, "Where'd you hear that?"

"Does it matter?" she asked softly.

He focused ahead. When his phone rang he saw it was Berry but turned it off, opting not to deal with her. "614 is the day my father died." He paused. "Well, the man I thought was my father. Found out the other day he wasn't shit to me." he shrugged. "I don't care much now. Wouldn't have changed how I feel about him." He wiped his sweaty hands on his jeans. "He was the meanest nigga I ever knew. The only time he wasn't was when he was called to a church as a guest preacher. That's why Berry and Dodson like them DVD's so much. They were during the nicer times."

"But I thought he wasn't a priest no more."

"He wasn't." he scratched in between one of the rows of braids. "He called it motivational speaking although I never found out why." He paused. "All I know is he use to fight me like I was a grown man but only when I fought against him for beating Berry and Dodson. Other than that he left me alone. He would purposely not hit me as much because he wanted to turn my brother and sister against me."

"What kind of stuff he do?"

"He made Berry walk everywhere she went so boys wouldn't get to her. That's one of the reasons she likes cars so much," he laughed to himself. "She the only person I know who feel like their world comes to an end if they can't drive." He shook his head.

"He tried to make Dodson learn the whole bible even though he knew he couldn't cause of his developmental stuff. So he would hit him over the head repeatedly making his condition worse. And he would make me watch him beat them, telling me over and over that they were worthless and for a while I started to believe it. Until I saw him for the man he really was."

"When he died did you miss him?"

He looked into her eyes, taking a second to answer. "How could I? He never gave me nothing to love."

When Meister pulled up beside his car, he was surprised that Miranda was with him.

"I thought he was coming alone to pick up Prince?" Nay asked.

"I thought so too. Stay here." Zoom got out and grabbed the kid out of the seat. With the baby in his arms he approached Meister.

The Ungrateful Bastards   192

Miranda took the baby, looked at Zoom like she was scared and got back in the car. "You got the kid, now what?" he asked Meister.

"It's whatever you want it to be?"

A cop rolled past the building.

"What you want to do, bitch ass nigga?" Zoom yelled, eager to take some of his frustrations out on somebody.

Meister looked back at Miranda. It was obvious at that time that they were fucking. Realizing too much was about to go down and he might get embarrassed he said, "We gonna see each other real soon."

"Don't see me soon, see me now!" Zoom stepped closer.

Meister stared at him, too afraid to make any moves. "I heard there was something weird going on with the Gregory's. I can see now that it's true." He frowned. "I got the kid...I'll get you later."

"I wait patiently for the day," Zoom said as he watched him climb into the car and pull off.

****

Nay walked into the house and Zoom came in behind her, slamming the door hard. He was furious about what almost occurred with Meister and even angrier that he continued to threaten him.

Nay sat on the sofa and watched him pace in circles. "Niggas, won't be satisfied until you put that heat on 'em!" he yelled. "He a bitch though. If the kid wasn't with him I'da set his clock back."

Berry walked out of her bedroom and yelled, "Fuck is you yelling all loud for?"

"Get back in your room!" he pointed at her door.

"I gotta tell you what Mrs. Dora said about—"

"I'm not trying to hear no shit about that bitch," he yelled cutting her off. "Now go back in the room!"

"I hate you, you skinny, black bitch!" Berry finally obeyed, slamming the door loudly.

Nay felt bad because she knew his emotions were all over the place. First after learning the kid was not his and secondly his father was not his blood and now Meister. "Zoom, stay calm. Try not to—"

"Fuck calm! I should've pushed that mothafucka off earth! My gun stay loaded, that nigga faking!" he stopped in place and leaned up against the wall. Taking five deep breaths he closed his eyes and reopened them. "I need to get some money."

"For what?" she asked quietly.

His eyebrows rose and his stare was glassy. "I gotta leave DC, Nay. I gotta leave the city now or it's gonna change me for the worse."

"What you gonna do?"

"I'ma do whatever I must," he said firmly. "Including robbing some niggas."

"You just saying that," she hoped. As if she didn't already know he was fully capable. "What if you get killed or locked up?"

"Then B and Dodson gonna have to go into the system. What else can I do?" he stood up straight. "I'm gonna get some fresh air, I be back."

She grabbed her purse and followed. "I'm coming with you."

When they left Dodson ran to his window and looked out. From his view he saw Zoom walk outside and jump into his car. Even from the top floor he could hear his brother yelling.

Dodson turned around, fixed his pillow as if he were lying in bed and walked to Berry's room.

He had to talk to her.

He had to talk to somebody.

****

"I hate his fucking ass," Berry yelled to Liberty on the phone. "I been taking Zoom's shit for weeks but I'm done now!"

"What better time than tonight," Liberty said excitedly. "Wait...Don do have a friend right? I don't want to be no third wheel."

"He said yes, Liberty! Just make sure you look cute, because you representing me," Berry responded. When her bedroom door opened she rolled her eyes when she realized it was her little brother. "I'ma call you back. Some shit just rolled into my room." She hung up and focused on him. "What you doing in here?"

"I think Zoom gonna leave us like ma!"

She rolled her eyes and waved him off. "The last thing that nigga doing is leaving. He love getting on folks nerves too much."

"It's true! I heard him talking about it with Nay!"

"Dodson, just leave and get you some business and stuff! That boy ain't going nowhere and you need to stop acting like a baby because you ain't!" she paused. "Now get out of my face! I'm tired of looking at you."

By T. Styles   195

When he left she locked her door and fixed her pillows on the bed so that if Zoom entered he would think she was sleep. When she was done she picked up her phone and called Liberty. "I'ma have Don meet us at your house. I'm on my way!"

****

Hours later...

Zoom drove angrily down the highway in silence. Nay looked over at him ever so often but didn't bother interrupting his anger space. She figured he was entitled to feel the way that he felt...until thirty minutes passed and they were nowhere.

"Where we going?" she asked looking out the window trying to see familiarities.

Silence.

"Zoom, where we going?" she said louder.

He didn't respond but when she saw the Baltimore signs on the highway she received her answer. He didn't do a lot of things outside of DC and especially in Bmore. "I'm not ready to go to rehab...not when you need me the most!"

"You want me to put you out my car?" he looked at her and then the highway again. "Because I will."

"But Zoom!"

"It ain't nothing for you in DC until you get yourself clean! You can't stay up under me no more, Nay. You gotta make a way for yourself but you can't do it dirty."

Huge tears rolled down her face. "But I can't do this without you! You and your brother and sister are the only family I have! Please, don't do this Zoom! Not right now! Not after telling me that you gonna rob some niggas to take care of yourself."

"I rob niggas all the time. I'm gonna be alright." He paused. "Worry about yourself."

Silence.

No other words were said and when he pulled up to the facility and parked he exhaled. He cared about old girl and didn't want her feeling any other way but he didn't want bad karma on his heart. "All I want is you healthy, Nay."

"But you won't be here when I'm done, Zoom! I'm afraid!"

"I'll be here. I wouldn't do you like that."

"You promise?"

He wiped a rolling tear off her cheek. "You gotta trust me. My word is all I have. It's all anyone has."

CHAPTER TWENTY-SIX
THE PROBLEM WITH IT ALL

Zoom was on a block, in front of another project not too far from his building, slinging rocks. He was working for Perch just to make enough money to buy some groceries and stash some paper until he figured things out. Although he was doing what he felt necessary, he couldn't help but think there was another way.

He just finished servicing one customer, with another waiting, when through the corner of his eye he saw Dodson staring at him quietly, as if admiring. Although he was aware that Dodson knew what he did for a living, at the moment he was his only role model, and he made up in his mind to shield him. That was the sole reason for going to another building instead of pumping in front of his own like usual.

"What you doing out here?" Zoom yelled at Dodson, scaring the fiend in front of him. "Get the fuck in the house!"

"Are you coming home?"

"I'm not fucking around! Now leave!"

Dodson blinked a few times, looked at Zoom and ran away. After serving his customers, when he was alone, he plopped on the stoop. His head fell forward and he exhaled deeply.

"Fuck!"

****

It was three am when Zoom came into the house, wobbling after working all night. Instead of hitting it for the shower like he normally did, he pulled his gun out, placed it on the table and fell face first on the bed.

Dodson, who had been waiting on him to come back home, opened his door and walked in his brother's room. Relieved to see him he took a second to look at his sleeping body. He loved his brother and the idea of him leaving made his belly sick.

Seeing the gun on the table, he picked it up, stuffed it in his back jean pocket and walked out the front door.

****

Perch was in the dug out, an alley between two buildings in the Shane Projects. Playing craps as always, he was waiting on Gaze to roll so he could go next. Although winning in the rest of his life, owning five real estate properties and a gaggle of barbershops, he could never win the game of dice and for that he was obsessed, often putting himself in dangerous situations.

When Gaze played, Perch picked up the dice and was about to roll when Dodson walked up behind him with his mother's stocking covering his face. "Toss everything in your pocket on the ground," he yelled, remembering what Zoom did to Pastor Chris.

When Gaze tried to move Dodson shot at a spot in the brick near his head like he also saw Zoom due to Meister. He had limited experience with actual weapons, but he handled a lot of BB guns and had excellent aim.

"Don't move!" Dodson yelled at Gaze, fingers shaking.

Gaze threw his hands up in the air. "You got it, slim."

By T. Styles   199

Focusing back on Perch he said, "Empty your pockets."

Perch removed the comb from his head plucked his bush one time and said, "I know who you are." He focused on the shaved lines on Dodson's scalp that wasn't fully covered in his mother's stocking that he used as a mask. "Why you doing this, lil man? You think Zoom would approve?"

"You don't know me!" Dodson said with a dancing hand that could fire at any moment. "You don't know shit about me!"

"I know you a cool kid," Perch continued. "And I know Zoom don't want this for you. If you want a job I got you. But this ain't the way to fame, kid." He paused. "All I got in my pockets is a few bucks. Don't take something light when you could get the big payout."

"Fuck this kid," Gaze interrupted. "If I were you I wouldn't give him shit!"

Dodson pointed the gun at him and yelled, "No...fuck you! Fuck you!"

Worried he would shoot Perch said, "Dodson put the gun down."

Hearing his name Dodson fired twice, hitting Perch once in the head and chest. Shit went to another level quickly. Gaze tried to run and for his endeavors, received a bullet through the shoulder blade. Although his hurried movements didn't stop him from getting injured, he still got away.

"Oh no," Dodson yelled to himself as he saw his life unraveling.

All he wanted was to help Zoom out by snatching a few bills like he saw him do, so that he wouldn't leave. But now what? Things were so far out of hand that he didn't see a way out.

Mad about it all, and with Perch lying on the ground, Dodson moved closer and shot him again in the face. When he was done he dug into Perch's pockets, relieved him of his money as well as the cash on the ground from the dice game before running away.

****

Don Morton and his friend Miami sat in a dark restaurant with Berry and Liberty in a booth. The plan was simple, feed them liquor until they were too drunk and dazed to know their own names...and they were getting close.

"You want anything else, ma?" Don asked Berry, with his arm draped around the back of her chair. "Because you told me you could handle your liquor. I hope you ain't lie."

Berry giggled and said, "You got me out here fucked up!" she turned to him, face full of teeth due to grinning so hard. "Why you doing that?"

"We just want ya'll to feel good," Miami said, trying to push the dating game to its end point so they could go to the hotel to fuck.

"Let me get some food in me first," Berry said. "Then I'll be ready for another round."

"I'm already good on the liquor," Liberty said making the cutthroat sign with her hand. "Anything else and I'ma throw up and pass out."

"One more round please!" Miami joked upon hearing her statement.

The foursome laughed heavily before Don's phone rang. "Let me get this right quick, cutie," he said to Berry who blushed upon hearing the nickname. "What up?" he said answering the phone. He listened attentively for a few seconds and his eyes widened the longer he stayed on the line. Slowly his head rolled toward Berry before telling the caller he would get up with him later.

She was still smiling until she peeped the seriousness on his face. "You have to go home, ma."

Mouth hanging Berry asked, "Why?"

"The whole hood looking for your brother Dodson. He just murdered Perch."

CHAPTER TWENTY-SEVEN
THE NEXT DAY – SUNDAY MORNING
THAT WHICH IS LIKE ITSELF IS DRAWN

Mo murda, mo murda, mo murda...," Martha Gregory sang as she marched down the street on a mission.

A gang of wilted yellow dandelions hung out her brown church hat as she stomped. The service she attended earlier was a blessing and she left feeling inspired.

The edges of her worn imposter leather purse were busted open, revealing a grayish-white cotton fabric beneath. But she clutched it tightly against her, for fear that the many thugs who dressed the street curb of the Washington DC block would relieve her of her possessions, including the twenty-two dollars and sixteen cent she had to her name.

When she made it to a gathering of young men they parted like the Red Sea, unveiling Pierce Guns— a 22-year old hooligan with nothing to lose and limited respect for those he didn't know.

"You Guns," she asked with authority, clutching her purse closer when a vandal passed the blunt to his comrade that at first she thought was a gun.

"If he is, what you want with him?" Five-feet five Jordan Marx asked, blocking her path.

The moment he stepped her way, Martha raised her tattered purse and knocked him in the head repeatedly until he was as flat as a stick of gum. Although any of the men could've pulled her off they were all too intrigued to stop her.

When she was done, with most of her flowers now pressed against the grungy concrete, she stood up, wiped the sweat off her brow and took a few deep breaths.

Jordan was about to repay her with a blow to the jaw when a few of the men on the sidelines pulled him away. He would be forced to be the laughing stock of the neighborhood on this one because nobody was willing to see him hit an old woman, not under their watch.

"Are you Guns?" she repeated.

Guns removed a chewed toothpick from his mouth and threw it on the ground. Grimacing he said, "You doing a whole lot aren't you?" he asked.

"I come in peace."

He laughed. "You call that peace?" he looked at Jordan and shook his head. "Yeah...I'm Guns."

She nodded satisfactorily. "Then you just the man I'm looking for."

He ran his hand over his lips before dropping it at his side. "How so?"

"Because you're going to do a job for me." She cleared her throat. "A job I can't do myself, otherwise I wouldn't be here." She readjusted her church crown.

"And what's that?"

"You're gonna kill for me."

He laughed and looked at his homies. "And exactly who do you want dead?"

"My kids...and you have my sincere blessings."

Everybody on the blocked laughed thinking it was a joke. "Old lady, get the fuck up out my face."

The Ungrateful Bastards   204

Martha's eyes widened and she was confused. "But they told me to come here."

"Even if I wanted to kill your children, you went about shit wrong. Caused a scene that people will remember." He gazed around the projects taking in the windows. Although no one but them was outside, he knew they were all looking. "If you want something done you better do it yourself."

Martha looked at him again and slowly walked out of the crowd, with no killer to call her own. Before she was out of sight one of the thugs ran up behind her — a low level dude always looking to make a quick buck. "Miss Lady, can I talk to you for a minute?"

Martha turned around and gripped her purse closer. "Who you?"

"I'm just somebody who understands your plight," he responded. He opened his jacket and revealed a sawed off shotgun. "Guns is right...about doing it yourself you know? I can sell you this if you want to put the work in."

Martha thought about his offer. "How much?"

"How much you got on you?"

She looked in her purse and closed it again. "Twenty two dollars and sixteen cents."

He smiled, revealing his four yellow teeth. "Sounds to me like you got a deal!"

****

The hallway was quiet as Martha stood in front of her apartment door trying to gain entry. Looking both ways she finally removed her eyes from her purse and tried to open the top lock but it wouldn't turn, refusing her access. She attempted

By T. Styles   205

several times until she realized someone had changed it and her key wouldn't work.

"Hey Martha," Ms. Monroe said walking into the building. She was carrying two bags of groceries as she worked her way up the steps.

Dora, acting guilty, turned around and leaned up against the door. Looking at the woman she smiled and said, "Yes..."

"I'm so sorry to hear about what happened to your youngest boy. Hope ya'll work it out and he'll be safe."

Martha nodded and smiled; having no idea what she was talking about. The last thing on her mind was holding a conversation with a nosey bitch in the hallway. Besides, she figured she was referring to any number of things Dodson could've been responsible for.

"Thank you..."

When the woman walked up the steps Martha tried her key on the bottom lock and to her surprise it was already open. As always someone didn't lock the door and their oversight gained her access.

Once inside she placed her purse on the living room table, grabbed her gun and crept down the hallway. Standing in her youngest son's doorway, gun still aimed, she took in the furnishings in Dodson's room. She was trying to tap into an emotion that was familiar between her and her baby but nothing struck a nerve.

"May your soul rest in peace," she said before firing into the lump on Dodson's bed.

Quickly she moved to Berry's room, opened the door and fired once into her bed. She had to be quick, realizing that gunfire would give her away.

The Ungrateful Bastards 206

Finally she walked to Zoom's room, opened the door and pulled in a deep breath of disappointment upon realizing he wasn't there. She wanted to put his soul at ease too and now she wouldn't get the opportunity.

After doing her do, she grabbed her purse and hit it for the front door. Once outside she jumped in her car and pulled a couple of blocks up the street and parked. She took out her phone and called the pastor. "Praise be to God," he said as a greeting.

She immediately smiled. "Hey, Pastor. This sister Gregory."

"Sister Gregory," he paused. "How are you this morning?"

"I'm fine...just wanted to tell you that I have my children together. They never gonna bother us again."

"Sister Gregory, what you talking about?" he laughed softly. "I don't see how you could get them together in a few days. Unless you making miracles. Your bunch seemed like a handful...I'm confused."

"Why you confused...you tell me all the time how my kids are awful and you're right. I smite them in front of the Lord." She said with wild eyes. "I did it for them like you said. They did some things that ain't right and I want them to go to heaven. Best way to do that is for a Christian woman to send them. Right?"

Silence.

"Sister Gregory, I think you have the wrong impression about me and my ministry. I never wanted you to hurt anyone."

"Sure you did...for the Lord. Remember? You preached it."

By T. Styles 207

"Sister Gregory, the bible isn't to be taken literally. Nor is my ministry."

"But...I thought...I thought...if I did what the Lord wanted then you would look at me like a man would a woman."

"I'm a taken man. I have been seeing Sister Dora for three weeks now." He paused. "Didn't she tell you? I thought you two were so close. She told me herself."

"I'm...I'm confused."

"Sister, where are you now? I'm going to send someone to come get you."

Embarrassed, Martha hung up the phone, the realization that she wouldn't have another man of God heavy on her brain. And then there was the crime she committed against her own children. If she didn't understand his sermons right, or the bible, maybe she was going mad. Maybe she killed them in vain.

She was just about to get away from the scene when there was a soft knock at her window. When she turned around she was looking at the barrel of Jordan Marx's gun...the same man she hit over the head with her purse earlier in the day.

The moment she turned around, he fired multiple times in the car before fleeing the scene.

CHAPTER TWENTY-EIGHT
614

Zoom got up early that morning and hit the highway. Finished thinking about his life, and realizing his cell phone was turned off, he turned it on and noticed he had fifteen voicemails. The first one, from Berry, almost caused his stomach to buckle.

"Zoom, you gotta come home! Dodson done killed Perch and now niggas looking for him!"

Throwing the phone down in the passenger's seat Zoom pressed the pedal as hard as he could to make it back to DC to see about his family. All the while many questions circling his head.

What was Berry talking about? Why would Dodson kill Perch and was his little brother safe?

He started to call her back but figured it was best to get home than ask a bunch of questions over the phone. Besides he didn't want to crash worrying so much.

After twenty minutes he finally made it to his building and things were a disaster. There were the flashing lights of the cop cars, red ambulance vehicles on the curb and a large fire truck with blaring sirens also dressed the block.

Why all the display?

Not caring about a ticket, he pulled up in front of a fire hydrant jumped out and rushed toward his building. Right before breaking the huddle of police officers protecting the entrance he heard, "Zoom! Zoom!"

When he turned around he was relieved to see Berry. The past months she irritated him beyond belief but at the moment her face was the most beautiful thing ever. Running up to her he asked, "What the fuck is going on around here?" he looked around at the chaotic scene. "Why so much action out front our crib?"

Frantically she cried, "I don't know about this...I just got here. But Zoom, it's all my fault about Perch! Dodson tried to talk to me last night and I kicked him out of my room! Now he went and killed Perch and stuff."

He glanced around as if looking for answers. Every time the thought of Dodson killing Perch entered his mind he felt nauseous. Nothing made sense. "Where were you?" he gripped her shoulders. "Last night? You were supposed to be watching him!"

"I stayed at Liberty's house!" she placed her head on his bare chest as she hugged him tightly, his arms dangling at his sides. "Please don't be mad at me! I know you said to watch him but I wanted to go out." He hugged her back. "And I didn't come back home because they said niggas was looking for Dodson! I was afraid they'd get me too," she let him go, his chest wet with her tears. "What are we going to do now?"

Part of him wanted to smack her for leaving him alone but he knew he shared half of the responsibility. "But why would he do this shit...?" his voice trailed off.

"I think he was trying to get some money. He said something about you leaving and not coming back." She sniffled. "Maybe things got out of hand and he killed him..."

"How could he rob somebody without a gun?" Suddenly Zoom touched his hip and realized he didn't have his handset on. "Oh, snap! Where's my piece?"

She shrugged. "I don't know...I think he used it," Berry said with wide eyes.

He walked away from her, held the sides of his head and looked up at the sky. "FUCK!" he dropped his hands. "I need to get up there! To our apartment. He may be in there afraid! What are they even doing here? The cops and shit?" he looked up at the building.

"I don't know...I tried to get in too but they wouldn't let me!" she paused. "That's when I saw you pulling up."

When Zoom saw Pierce Guns and a group of dudes he use to be cool with looking at him with disdain, he went into protective mode. Dodson was wanted but he had to protect Berry too. "We gotta get in my car, Berry. I think the heat coming our way."

Berry saw Gun's huddle of goons and quickly followed Zoom to his car. While driving away Berry took the time to tell him everything Dora said the night before. As she spoke he recalled her trying to speak to him about Dora but he was too angry to listen. Meister pissed him off, sending his pressure to another level.

Upon hearing everything she said he sighed. "Why would ma want to kill us? She don't fuck with us but this is too crazy."

"Maybe to hide the murder." Berry whipped her long weave over her shoulder. "If we dead who gonna tell?"

"There were more people than us there that night." He reminded her. "Kill us and you have to kill everybody." He shook his head. "No...something else is up with ma."

****

614

That hot summer day, on June 14th, there was a feeling something was coming in the air. The sky was sparkling blue and the sun shined upon the flowers in the Gregory garden.

And suddenly, as if the sky were not as clear as water moments earlier, the clouds covered the sun and rain flooded onto the Gregory home.

Inside, in the center of the living room, a man who made a mistake while drunk pleaded to a child to keep his secret. "I messed up, Marine. But this past week I've been doing good. I'm off the sauce and I'm working on repairing my marriage." He grabbed Dookie by the arms and looked into her eyes. "Don't ruin it for me."

She walked away and stood in the middle of the floor. "But you raped me, Steven! I came here when Ericko got arrested to see Zoom, and when he wasn't here you invited me in. Made me think it was safe to be here and instead you raped me!"

He stepped closer. "But I wasn't myself!" he paused. "I wasn't the man I'm trying to be today. A man of God."

She sat on the sofa and looked up at him. "I can't do this...Zoom has a right to know."

Dripping wet, with an umbrella over her head, Martha entered the house. At first she didn't see Dookie because the umbrella concealed her view. Shaking the raindrops onto the floor she was surprised that she was there, without Zoom.

"Marina, is everything okay?" she asked Dookie suspiciously.

Dookie stepped to her, looked back at Steven and then Martha again. Rubbing her protruding belly she said, "I'm pregnant...and I *think Steven's the father." She exhaled. "And Zoom doesn't know."*

Martha stumbled backwards into the door. "What...I...I don't..."

"He raped me when he was drunk. I never said anything because I love Zoom so much. But I can't lie anymore."

Martha looked over at him, pain of the ultimate betrayal written all over her face. "But why Steven...I don't..."

Steven who hadn't had a drink in weeks walked over to his fully stocked bar. He popped off the top of a jug of whiskey. "Sobriety is for losers. I need relief now."

"Please leave, Marina," Martha yelled.

"But..."

"Just go!" she screamed.

Dookie grabbed her raincoat, looked at Steven and back at Martha. "I'm sorry...I just can't lie to Zoom anymore. He's going to ask me about the rape and I'm gonna be honest." She moved toward the door, opened it and walked into the rain.

Martha eased slowly toward the bar. "Pour me a drink?" she asked with a smile on her face which was out of place.

"I know this is another milestone for us to get over," he said grabbing a glass. "But if I can be deceived into marrying a woman with three kids, you can work with me on this." He poured her a half full glass of vodka.

"More," she smiled. "Liquor."

He did. "So what are you going to say?" he asked. "Are you with me in this like I've been with you?" he handed her the glass and she took a big gulp before putting it down. "Because marrying you wasn't a cakewalk either, Martha. You had the drug addiction, three ungrateful kids and a host of nosey ass friends. I deserve a pass for once."

"*And I stood by your side and supported you with your grief over being thrown out of the catholic church because you're a drunk!*" she yelled back. "*But why rape her?*"

There was a small black radio on the bar and Martha hit the play button. A CD was inside and Bone Thugz-N-Harmony's "Mo Murda" played through the small speakers. Normally the foul language would bother them both but there were other things in the air and she needed a mental break.

More important matters.

"*I didn't rape her I fucked her,*" he said correcting her. "*She wanted it...been walking around here teasing me...twisting her ass and giggling at my jokes.*" He laughed. "*I just helped her do what she wanted.*"

"*But she was Zoom's girlfriend.*"

"*Zoom is a young boy. He'll bounce back.*"

She shook her head and took a sip. "*You know, you were always manipulative. Even when we first met and you gave me money every month until I was too hooked to go anywhere else. You wanted to control me first and it worked. I gave you everything, even my children's lives.*"

"*Don't put that shit on me! You were willing and able to give up your kids,*" he paused. "*You didn't want them either. You don't get the mother of the year a—*"

Martha brought a bottle of vodka down over his head. The place where the blow was dealt left an opening in his temple vein. He fell to the floor and she beat him repeatedly, using different bottles from the bar.

Steven, wiggling on the floor, was losing consciousness just as Dora walked inside the house with Zoom, Berry and Dodson.

"What the fuck is going on?" Dora asked slamming the door, gazing at Steven's limp body.

The kids rushed over to Martha who was trembling with anger. "He was fucking Marina," she said to Zoom, omitting the rape altogether.

Zoom was devastated.

"And when I asked him about it he tried to hit me," she lied. "I'm not being hit no more." Covered in blood, she looked at Zoom. "Sorry, son. I know this is a lot but maybe it's for the best. That girl is too grown anyway."

Zoom felt gut punched, but too much was going on to talk. Earlier that day he was going to tell his mother that he was moving out with Dookie. Before doing anything Dookie said she had to clear some things up first, without telling him what.

"Martha, what is going on?" Dora asked. "We have to call 911!"

"This man is a monster and doesn't deserve to live!" she yelled circling Steven's squirming body. "He beat me! He beat my kids and he is an adulterer! No wonder he's not fit for the cloth! Either help me or walk out of here and get out my way!"

Berry, having animosity of her own toward Steven, walked up to him and kicked him in the gut. She kicked him for all the times he hit her, pulled her hair and cut her off from friends.

Dodson having equal hate kicked him in the head, for all of the times he hit him, called him stupid and starved him.

Finally Zoom kicked him in the chin, for all of the times he tried to turn him against his family. And for the affair with the love of his life.

By T. Styles   215

It was a family affair as they kicked and hit the man to death, stealing the life out of his body.

Dora, overwhelmed by the gory scene, but trapped in her loyalty flopped on the sofa...too stuck to move.

When they were done and out of breath, they stood in the middle of the floor and looked at each other.

"Now what?" Dora asked looking at the Gregory family, covered in blood.

"We have to get him out of here," Martha said anxiously.

"But how?"

"I have an idea." Martha walked to the back of the house and picked up the phone. The sound of the thunderstorm growing louder in the background. Dialing a number she waited for it to ring. "George, I need you to do me a favor."

"What is it, Martha?"

"Can't say it over the phone. Come over now. Please."

Twenty minutes later, he walked into the living room. Steven's body was not seen, he was just a hump in the middle of the floor covered in a rug. Led by Martha he walked toward the back.

Zoom eyed him the entire time, never liking him because he thought he was fucking his mother on the side. In his mind had he not been so concerned about Martha Steven would have treated them differently.

George stood in the middle of the bedroom. "What's going on out there?" he paused. "Why everybody looked crazy and the children dressed in robes?"

"Steven is dead."

The Ungrateful Bastards   216

His jaw dropped and he held one side of his head before stumbling backwards. "How...what...I'm confused."

"You know he was an abuser, George. Don't act like you didn't."

He shook his head and laughed, experiencing slight deliria. "I don't know what's going on but I'm not involved in this shit." He grabbed the doorknob preparing to leave.

He was about to walk out until Martha said, "Your kids are involved too. We all killed him and if you walk out on me you're walking out on them."

George trudged back inside and flopped on the bed. With hopeful eyes he asked, "They know I'm their father?"

"No...and they can never know. Plus you with Vicky now." She said. "And too much has happened to crack open secrets. Don't put them through that now."

"But I could help them if—"

"They my kids!" she yelled. "And all I want you to do is help me take Steven's body to the construction site you work at together. Put him in his car and let one of those metal pillars fall on the truck. I'll give you some of his death benefit and everything."

George's eyes widened upon realizing he really didn't know her. "Geez, Martha. Got it all figured out don't you?"

"Are you gonna help us or not?"

He shook his head. "Guess I don't have a choice."

Under the cover of night George drove Steven's truck to the construction site. When he was in the perfect position he pushed Steven's body in the driver's seat, operated the crane, which *held a large piece of iron and dropped it on the truck, crushing the corpse instantly.*

When they were done everyone came back to the Gregory home, tired and in a daze. Martha, having developed sudden confidence looked at Zoom, Berry, Dodson and Dora. George left having seen and heard enough for the night.

"What we have committed is murder," Martha said softly. *"And every one of us will be held accountable if this comes out. But there is away around that. Don't talk to police. Don't befriend new people and never speak of this night. If someone knows the truth you must deal with it quickly because there ain't no statute of limitation on murder." She paused. "One fall...we all fall!"*

****

"Dodson, where are you?" Zoom said to himself upon remembering his version of 614. He was still driving with Berry trying to figure things out. When he removed his phone from his pocket and saw Dora called him twice, he called back. His phone was on silent. "Do you have Dodson?"

"No, son...that's not why I'm calling." Her voice was so quiet he almost didn't hear her words.

"Then what's up?"

"Your mother has been murdered, Michael. A few blocks from the house. They think it's retaliatory because of what happened with Dodson of course no one is sure."

The phone dropped in his lap and he pulled over to the side of the road to catch his breath. "What's wrong?" Berry asked with wide eyes. When he didn't respond she nudged his shoulder. "Is Dodson okay?"

He stuffed his cell in his pocket, kicked open the car door and paced. Placing his hands on his face he leaned up against his ride and slid down on the ground, knees pulled halfway to his chest. Berry crept up slowly and sat on the hot concrete next to him. The running car made it even hotter but at the moment no one cared. "Zoom...what happened?" she asked touching his shoulder.

He removed his hands from his face. "Somebody killed ma."

Berry scooted away from him and sobbed uncontrollably. There on the side of the road, out in the open, they had to come to terms with a dark realization. It was one thing for Martha to abandon them but to know she was truly gone forever was mind bending.

Realizing she was worse off than he was he pulled her to him to console her but it was hard. "We gotta go forward, Berry. We all we got." When Zoom's phone rang again he answered. "Michael, it's George. I have to see you now..."

"I don't want to talk," Zoom said, pressing down the pain he felt from his mother dying.

"It's about Dodson." He paused. "Please come...now."

****

Zoom had his arm around Berry as they sat on George's couch after being devastated once again.

They just received the news that Dodson was murdered. After running from thugs who wanted blood for Perch's death, he was killed by his own mother while he lay in his bed hiding.

Berry would've been killed too had she been home but the fake pillows she propped up fooled Martha and although Dodson had done the same, he returned home after the murder in fear for his life.

The neighbor who saw Martha in the hallway earlier heard the gunshots and saw her leaving. Based on her witness testimony they connected Martha to the crime.

It took an hour before Zoom and Berry were consolable enough to talk and George understood, considering what they'd gone through.

Temples throbbing, eyes red from crying and anger, Zoom asked, "Why did the police call you? The man who was fucking my moms even though he got a wife?"

"I wasn't fucking your moms," he said softly. "Not anymore."

Zoom and Berry looked at one another.

"What you mean not anymore?" Zoom asked. "You finally admitting to it?"

"Back in the seventies we were all on drugs...me, your mother and Dora. We led a hard life and it caught up with us at the same time. I always loved Martha, even when she was with Steven. But after she got clean she had a vision she wanted for her children's father and I wasn't in the picture. So I stepped out of the way so that you all could have a good life."

Zoom rushed up to him. High off of learning his mother and brother died and liable to kill anything. "Wait...you trying to...you trying to sit here and tell me you my father?"

"I wanted to tell you...I wanted to tell you on June 14th but she didn't want me to." He

The Ungrateful Bastards   220

paused. "You all were the reason I got clean and still I wasn't good enough."

All Zoom felt was hate. "Why didn't you tell me yourself?"

"I wanted to tell you when I found out Martha was acting strange recently. I wanted to tell you to be careful because before she married Steven, your mother had mental illness. That's why I came to the house, before you robbed me. I predicted this would happen."

"Mental illness?" Berry said.

"Back in the seventies we fucked with it all...but one day our dealer had some other shit for us to hit. Some stuff he told us would make all our troubles go away. It was acid." He paused. "Me and Dora tried it with no problem, but your mother had a bad trip and haven't been right since. She started seeing things and all kinds of shit. Every now and again she would be out of touch with reality but when she was with Steven I couldn't check on her anymore so I didn't know what was happening. He was supposed to be good for you and I found out through Dora, after he was killed that he wasn't."

"So you trying to say my moms was crazy?" Zoom asked.

"The only time I knew her not to be was when she was working and trying to be a mother." He shook his head. "I always wanted to be in your lives but I didn't know how. Too much time passed and so many secrets committed. No one trusted anyone." He paused. "All because Steven raped your girlfriend."

Zooms eyes widened. "She wasn't raped," Zoom said strongly. "She fucked Steven."

George shook his head no. "Your mother wanted you to believe that, son. Because she wanted her away from you, so that she wouldn't have to live with the guilt. He raped that girl and the baby, the one I saw you with the other day, is Steven's child..." he exhaled, having laid a lot on him. "She was a strong girl...but don't let her strength convince you that she couldn't be abused."

Zoom walked away rubbing his throbbing temples. It was too much to take in even though all of the answers to his questions had been revealed. "Why are we here now?"

"You have to leave town. Gaze and his boys are looking for you because they think Dodson was sent by you." He paused. "I just got word that—"

Zoom's sentence was severed when bullets crashed into the window, shattering everything near...the TV, glass table and bookcase. They all fell on the floor for protection but the gunplay had yet to cease.

Who was trying to attack?

George crawled toward his sofa pulled out a .9 and a .45. He slid Zoom the nine and yelled, "Move toward the back door! I'll cover you!"

Zoom grabbed Berry by the arm and pulled her toward the back while George stood up and shot toward the windows. They dipped safely out the door and were able to get to Zoom's car parked a few blocks up from the house.

Zoom parked there because he was afraid of his car being spotted and now he realized he made a good decision. Once safely inside they pulled off. Berry was hysterical in the passenger seat and he tried to control her as best he could.

Dead mother. Dead brother and now gunplay.

The Ungrateful Bastards   222

"We gotta go on, Berry," he said holding her arm. "We gotta take care of each other because what's done is done!" there was no space for grief in his heart.

She continued to cry harder. "How...how...how do I know you won't leave me too?"

"I would've done it already."

She looked out of the window. "Well where we going?"

"Away from DC...but I have to make a stop first." He paused. "I have to do one more thing for a good friend."

****

Meister stood outside of Miranda's house leaning against his car, while talking on his cell phone. Prince was in his car seat sleep and Meister was waiting on her to come out so they could go to the lawyer's office. His mission was to see how he could get access to Dookie's money now instead of later. Afterwards throwing the kid in foster care.

Totally engrossed in his call, he didn't see Zoom walking in his direction with a black hood on his head. The drawstrings were drawn so tightly that the only thing you could see was his nose.

The moment Meister turned around Zoom was upon him.

"Put your hands in the air!" Zoom yelled, gun aiming in his direction.

Meister quickly obeyed although he talked shit. "You can't be serious!" he screamed. "Do you know who I am?"

"I'm very serious!"

By T. Styles   223

When his hands were up Zoom went through his pockets, removing all of the money he had on him. "Where's the kid?"

"What kid—"

"Where is the fucking kid?" he yelled in his face. "I'm not playing games! I'll kill your bitch ass!"

"In the car," Meister said trembling.

Zoom looked at the baby he was still sleep; pressing the barrel to Meister's head he pulled the trigger. Splattering the window with blood.

EPILOGUE
HOUSTON, TEXAS

A cold air blew across Elliot Martin's neck as he stood at the ATM removing money for the grocers. The moment he had cash in hand he saw a figure whose face was covered in a stocking standing behind him...a gun pointed in his lower back.

"You need to take out a little more than that, my man," Zoom said pressing the gun against his ribs.

"Okay, okay...whatever you do please don't hurt me." Elliot pressed the buttons on the machine and withdrew the max...five hundred dollars.

"Good boy," Zoom said snatching the cash. "Don't turn around!"

Slowly he backed away from him, gun still pointed until he ran down the street. Although Zoom was away from the ATM, where the car sat he could still see his victim. Suddenly the back door opened and a little girl, who saw the robbery, ran out and hugged her father.

She reminded him of Berry in the younger years.

Zoom feeling badly got away from the scene. "Fuck! Fuck! Fuck!" he yelled hitting the steering wheel. Had he known his kid was there he would've hit another victim as guilt sat on his heart. But he had a family that he needed to feed and it was every man for himself.

Pulling up in an abandoned garage he ditched the stolen car and got into his own, a beat up black Caprice. Once inside he changed into a blue Mechanic's uniform with the word

By T. Styles   225

Michael stitched on the front. Although he didn't work there, his common name allowed him to steal one he could use, to make it look like he had a job.

He told his family he was done with the hard life but with no skills he knew no other way.

Driving down the road he thought about his life. He didn't have any skills...he was a hustler from the day he was born. Who would hire him that would provide enough for his family?

Pulling up in front of a tattered house in Houston Texas, he parked his car and tucked the money he stole in his uniform. Next he removed his pistol, placing that in the back of his pants pocket. Finished he got out, wiped his hands on the dirty tires to give them that sooty look.

Appearing like he worked all day he walked into the house. Sitting at the table was Berry, Nay and Prince in his high chair.

Nay ran up to him and said, "Hey, baby! How was work?" she kissed him on the cheek.

He smiled only halfway, still guilty over his latest victim. "Good..." he slapped her butt and walked around her, heading for Prince. Smiling lightly he said, "What's up, little man? You gonna have to get a job and start helping around here soon," he joked.

Berry laughed a little too hard and he knew she wanted something.

"What's up, Berry?"

"You gotta enough money for my car and stuff?"

"You keep doing what you do in school and I'll get the paper," he promised. "The only thing I want you focused on is them books."

The Ungrateful Bastards   226

With Berry being in college, taking up Nursing Studies and Nay having six months sobriety, he wanted to do all he could to keep his family fed and safe, even though he was in hiding from Gaze and his clan in Washington DC.

Berry was even able to finish her community service in Houston, due to Martha and Dodson being murdered.

When there was a knock at the door Zoom rushed toward it and looked out of the peephole. A white man, who looked pretty official, was on the other side. Zoom's heart thumped in his chest but when he didn't see a police car he hoped for the best.

Opening it only halfway he said, "What you want?"

"I'm looking for Michael Gregory."

Although he wasn't deep undercover, running from thugs and not police, he still wondered who knew his address. "Who asking?"

"I'll take that as a yes," he handed him the envelope and walked off.

Zoom closed the door and opened the package. Inside was a court document saying that Zoom was the power of attorney for Prince Patterson, on behalf of the deceased, Marina Patterson, for a multi million-dollar estate.

Also enclosed was one letter.

Dear Zoom,

It took me some time to write because it took some time to find you. Unfortunately for me and those who loved him, Meister was murdered in front of my home.

I was and still am devastated.

At first I was concerned for Prince's safety and then I realized, there was only one person who cared about him more than anybody alive...you.

By T. Styles   227

No need to lie...I know you have him.

After some solid research I found out where you lived. The court case that you snuck in town for, to beat the drug charge, had this listed as your address.

To my surprise, after handling my cousin's estate, I discovered that Marina left Prince in the custody of his stepbrother Zoom.

Although I know brief information about the history of your family, I can only hope that you don't take the hate you had for Steven out on him. He's a cool kid.

Congratulations and keep Prince safe.

Love, Miranda.

Zoom looked up at Prince, Berry and Nay. Shaking his head he said, "Finally...hard times are over."

LIPSTICK DOM

Revised from the original novel Rainbow Heart and it's sequel Trying to Hide a Rainbow

T. STYLES

ESSENCE MAGAZINE BEST SELLING AUTHOR

By T. Styles

The Ungrateful Bastards 230

The Cartel Publications Order Form
www.thecartelpublications.com
Inmates **ONLY** receive novels for $10.00 per book.
(Mail Order **MUST** come from inmate directly to receive discount)

Shyt List 1	_____	$15.00
Shyt List 2	_____	$15.00
Shyt List 3	_____	$15.00
Shyt List 4	_____	$15.00
Shyt List 5	_____	$15.00
Pitbulls In A Skirt	_____	$15.00
Pitbulls In A Skirt 2	_____	$15.00
Pitbulls In A Skirt 3	_____	$15.00
Pitbulls In A Skirt 4	_____	$15.00
Victoria's Secret	_____	$15.00
Poison 1	_____	$15.00
Poison 2	_____	$15.00
Hell Razor Honeys	_____	$15.00
Hell Razor Honeys 2	_____	$15.00
A Hustler's Son 2	_____	$15.00
Black and Ugly As Ever	_____	$15.00
Year Of The Crackmom	_____	$15.00
Deadheads	_____	$15.00
The Face That Launched A	_____	$15.00
Thousand Bullets		
The Unusual Suspects	_____	$15.00
Miss Wayne & The Queens of DC	_____	$15.00
Paid In Blood (eBook Only)	_____	$15.00
Raunchy	_____	$15.00
Raunchy 2	_____	$15.00
Raunchy 3	_____	$15.00
Mad Maxxx	_____	$15.00
Quita's Dayscare Center	_____	$15.00
Quita's Dayscare Center 2	_____	$15.00
Pretty Kings	_____	$15.00
Pretty Kings 2	_____	$15.00
Pretty Kings 3	_____	$15.00
Silence Of The Nine	_____	$15.00
Silence Of The Nine 2	_____	$15.00
Prison Throne	_____	$15.00
Drunk & Hot Girls	_____	$15.00
Hersband Material	_____	$15.00
The End: How To Write A	_____	$15.00
Bestselling Novel In 30 Days (Non-Fiction Guide)		
Upscale Kittens	_____	$15.00

By T. Styles

Wake & Bake Boys   _____ $15.00
Young & Dumb   _____ $15.00
Young & Dumb 2:   _____ $15.00
Tranny 911   _____ $15.00
Tranny 911: Dixie's Rise   _____ $15.00
First Comes Love, Then Comes Murder   _____ $15.00
Luxury Tax   _____ $15.00
The Lying King   _____ $15.00
Crazy Kind Of Love   _____ $15.00
And They Call Me God_____ $15.00
The Ungrateful Bastards _____ $15.00

Please add $4.00 **PER BOOK** for shipping and handling.

The Cartel Publications * P.O. BOX 486 OWINGS MILLS MD 21117

Name:
_____

Address:
_____

City/State:
_____

Contact# & Email:
_____

Please allow 5-7 BUSINESS days before shipping. The Cartel is NOT responsible for prison orders rejected.

<u>*NO PERSONAL CHECKS ACCEPTED*</u>

The Ungrateful Bastards   232

Made in the USA
San Bernardino, CA
01 September 2017

5000 B.C.
and Other
Philosophical Fantasies

5000 B.C.

and Other
Philosophical Fantasies

Raymond Smullyan

St. Martin's Press
New York

Chapter 5, "Simplicus and the Tree," reprinted with
permission of THE UNIVERSITY of CHICAGO
MAGAZINE, copyright 1975. Chapter 6, "An Epistemological
Nightmare," appeared in *The Mind's I*, edited by Douglas
Hofstadter and Daniel Dennett (New York: Basic Books,
1981).

Design by Kingsley Parker

Library of Congress Cataloging in Publication Data

Smullyan, Raymond M.
    5000 B.C. and other philosophical fantasies.

    1. Philosophy—Miscellanea.   I. Title.   II. Title:
5000 B.C. and other philosophical fantasies.
B68.S65   1983   100   82-17071
ISBN 0-312-29516-2

First Edition

10 9 8 7 6 5 4 3 2 1

Contents

Foreword

When I was in high school, one elderly gentleman, hearing that I was interested in philosophy, said, "You say you are interested in philosophy. Tell me, how would you *define* philosophy?" Before I had time to answer, he continued, "Yesterday, someone from Columbia asked me how I would define philosophy and I told him . . ." The gentleman went on talking interminably without ever letting me get a word in edgewise. When he was finished, he said, "Well, it was nice talking to you," and left.

I am quite fascinated by the psychological phenomenon of a person asking a question without the slightest interest in receiving an answer. I am also reminded of Ambrose Bierce's definition of a *bore:* one who talks when you want him to listen. In this particular case, though, it was probably a good thing that the gentleman *didn't* let me answer because I would be sore pressed if I had to give an *informative* definition of philosophy. The literal definition, "love of knowledge," doesn't really give much feeling for what the subject is all about.

The pieces in this volume (at least most of them) are very much what the title suggests—philosophical *fantasies.* Many of them have the flavor of science fiction. There seems to be a new literary form in the air—a form that might aptly be called *philosophical fiction.* I am thinking not only of this book but of such books as *The Mind's I,* not to speak of Hofstadter's earlier work *Gödel, Escher, and Bach.* One advantage of this form, quite aside from the great entertainment value, is that important philosophical issues can be made perfectly comprehensible to the general reader. This book, for example, is completely self-contained. No prior acquaintance with philosophy is presupposed.

Not all the pieces of this volume are fantasies. Chapter 3, for example, is a free-wheeling, light-hearted, rambling collection of miscellaneous observations, anecdotes (some of them autobiographical), jokes, puzzles, and paradoxes. Chapter 4 will be found to contain a historical surprise for many a reader. The fantasies proper are mainly in Parts 3 and 5. Chapter 10 has a special and unusual status.

Although the spirit of this book is almost the opposite of that of a textbook, much of the material has been successfully used in introductory courses in philosophy. Many of the traditional philosophical questions are considered and many different viewpoints are presented—mainly through the various characters of the book. I do not take much of a position myself; I prefer to let my characters argue matters out among themselves. Of course, some of my own biases cannot help but show through on occasions, but I have tried to match opposing characters as evenly as possible.

I am interested in all this as much from a psychological and dramatic perspective as from a philosophical one. Many of the pieces are not so much analyses of philosophical problems as *dramatizations* of philosophical types. As such, I have thought of them largely as theater pieces and I have had great fun presenting them on stage, assisted by various actors and actresses. Audience responses have been most gratifying. I have long believed that the possibilities of successfully using philosophical themes for exciting live dramatic presentations have not yet been fully realized. If this book suggests new possibilities along these lines, then it will have fulfilled one of its principal objectives.

I wish to thank my wife, my friends and colleagues over the years, and Thomas McCormack and Kermit Hummel of St. Martin's Press for their many helpful suggestions.

1

Why Are You Truthful?

1

Why Are You Truthful?

MORALIST: I have gathered you good people together on this occasion because I know that you are among the most truthful people on earth, and so I propose that we hold a symposium on truthfulness. I wish to learn from each of you your reasons for being truthful. Adrian, what is your reason for being truthful?

ADRIAN: My reason is quite simple. It says in the Bible that one should be truthful, and I take the Bible seriously. Since my greatest duty on earth is obedience to the will of God and God commands me to be truthful, my reason for being truthful is obvious.

MORALIST: Very good! And you, Bernard, why are you truthful?

BERNARD: I also take the Bible very seriously. The one thing in the Bible that impresses me most is the Golden Rule: Do unto others as you would have others do unto you. Since I wish others to be truthful with me, I am accordingly truthful with them.

MORALIST: Excellent! And you, Carey, what are your reasons for being truthful?

CAREY: My reasons have nothing to do with religion. I am truthful on purely ethical grounds. I desire to be virtuous, and since truthfulness is one of the virtues and lying is one of the vices, then to be virtuous it is necessary for me to be truthful.

EPISTEMOLOGIST *(who is, strangely enough, in this group though he wasn't invited):*   I find this reason peculiar! Carey evidently doesn't value truthfulness in its own right but only because it belongs to the more general category of virtue, and it is this more general category that he values. Indeed, his very way of putting it: "To be virtuous it is necessary for me to be truthful," his very use of the word *necessary* suggests that he is reluctant to be truthful but is nevertheless truthful only as a *means* to another end, that end being virtue itself. This is what I find so strange! Furthermore, I think—

MORALIST: Sorry to interrupt you, old man, but it was not my intention that we criticize the speakers as they go along. I prefer on this occasion to let the speakers simply state their views; we can reserve critical analysis for another time. And so, Daniel, why are you truthful?

DANIEL: My reasons are also nonreligious—or at least nontheistic. I am a great admirer of the ethics of Immanuel Kant. I realize that his ethical attitudes were, at least psychologically, tied up with his religious ones, but many people who reject Kant's theistic views nevertheless accept his moral ones. I am one such person. I am truthful out of obedience to Kant's categorical imperative, which states that one should never perform any act unless one wills that act to be universal law. Since it is obvious that if everybody lied there would be utter chaos, I clearly cannot will it to be universal law that everybody lies. The categorical imperative hence implies that I, too, should not lie.

MORALIST: Very good! And you, Edward, what are your reasons for being truthful?

EDWARD: My reasons are purely humanistic and utilitarian. It is obvious that truthfulness is beneficial to society, and since my main interest in life is to benefit society, then accordingly I am truthful.

MORALIST: Splendid! And you, Frank, why are you truthful?

FRANK: In order to live up to my name. Since my name is Frank, then it behooves me to be frank with people.

MORALIST: Stop being facetious! This is a serious symposium! What about you, George, why are you truthful?

GEORGE: Because I am a selfish bastard!

MORALIST: What!

GEORGE: Exactly! The few times I have lied, I have ended up getting it in the neck! It's not other people I care about; I care about myself. I don't want any trouble! I have simply learned from hard and bitter experience that honesty is the best policy.

MORALIST: What about you, Harry?

HARRY: My ethical orientation is rather similar to that of George. But instead of using the rather harsh phrase *selfish bastard,* I would prefer to classify myself as a hedonist; I perform only those acts calculated to maximize my pleasure in life. I am not as fanatical as George; I place *some* value on other people's happiness but not as much as on my own. And I have much rational evidence that in the long run I will be happiest if I am always truthful.

MORALIST: So you are a hedonist! In other words, you are truthful because it gives you *pleasure* to be truthful, and you avoid lying because you find lying painful. Is that it?

HARRY: Not quite. I do not necessarily derive *immediate* pleasure from being truthful. Indeed, sometimes it is immediately painful. But I am a thoughtful and rational person; I am always willing to sacrifice my immediate pleasures for the sake of my ultimate good. I always plan ahead. Therefore, I am truthful since as I told you I have rational evidence that my being truthful is best for me in the long run.

MORALIST: What is this evidence?

HARRY: That is too long a story for us to go into now. I think we should instead hear the views of the other speakers.

MORALIST: Very good. What about you, Irving?

IRVING: I am also a hedonist.

MORALIST: That so far makes three of you! George, Harry, and you.

IRVING: Yes, but I am not like the others.

MORALIST: How so?

IRVING: You mean how not! By temperament, I feel very different from George, and unlike Harry I am not the rational type of hedonist. Rather, I am a mystical hedonist.

MORALIST: A mystical hedonist? That's a strange combination! I have never heard that one before. What on earth do you mean by a *mystical* hedonist?

IRVING *(sadly):*   I don't know!

MORALIST: You don't know? How come you don't know?

IRVING: Well, you see, since I am a mystical hedonist, I am also a hedonist. I feel that if I knew what I meant by a mystical hedonist, I would be less happy than I am not knowing what I mean. Therefore, on hedonistic grounds it is better that I do not know what I mean by a mystical hedonist.

MORALIST: But if you don't even know what you *mean* by a mystical hedonist, how can you possibly know that you are one?

IRVING: Good question! As you say, since I am unable to define a *mystical hedonist*, I couldn't possibly have rational grounds for knowing that I am one. Yet, in fact, I *do* know that I am one. This is precisely where my mysticism comes in.

MORALIST: Oh, my God! This is too complicated for *me!*

IRVING: Me, too.

MORALIST: At any rate, what is your reason for being truthful? The same as Harry's?

IRVING: The reason is the same, but my *justification* of the reason is totally different.

MORALIST: I don't understand. Can you explain this?

IRVING: Why, yes. Like Harry, I believe that my telling the truth is best for me in the long run. But unlike Harry, I have no rational evidence for this. Indeed, all the rational evidence I have is quite to the contrary. Therefore, the *rational* thing for me to do is to lie. But I have a strange intuition that I had best tell the truth. And being a mystic, I trust my intuition more than my reason. Hence, I tell the truth.

MORALIST: Most extraordinary! And what about you, Jacob?

JACOB: My truthfulness is a matter of contingency, not choice.

MORALIST: I don't understand you!

JACOB: I have simply never had the opportunity to lie.

MORALIST: I understand you even less!

JACOB: My attitude is as follows: Obviously, no one in his right mind would ever think of lying to his friends; it only makes sense to lie to one's enemies. If any enemy ever threatened to harm me, I would not for a moment hesitate to lie to divert his attack. But since I have no enemies and never have had any enemies, the opportunity for me to lie has never presented itself.

MORALIST: How singular! And what about you, Kurt; what are your reasons for being truthful?

KURT: I have only one reason. I am truthful simply because I *feel* like being truthful; I have no other reason than that.

MORALIST: But that is no reason!

KURT: Of course it is a reason! As I just told you, it's my *only* reason.

MORALIST: But your reason is no good!

KURT: Whoever said that I had a *good* reason? I said that it's my *reason;* I didn't say it was a *good* one.

MORALIST: Oh, but just because you feel like being truthful, it does not follow that you *should* be truthful. Of course, I believe that you should be truthful but not merely because you *feel* like it. There are many things I feel like doing, but I don't do them because I know that I shouldn't do them. Not everything that one feels like doing is necessarily right! So why is your feeling like being truthful an adequate justification of your being truthful?

EPISTEMOLOGIST: I thought we weren't supposed to argue with the speakers.

MORALIST: I shall ignore that remark. I repeat my question: Just because you feel like being truthful, why does it follow that you should be truthful?

KURT: *Should* be truthful? Who the hell ever said that I *should* be truthful?

MORALIST: Don't tell me now that you believe that you *shouldn't* be truthful!

KURT: Of course not! I don't give a damn what I should or shouldn't do!

MORALIST: Oh, come now; surely you want to do what you believe you ought to do!

KURT: What I *ought* to do! I couldn't care less! Look, man, I don't give one hoot for all your ethics, morality, religion, rights and wrongs, oughts and shoulds! As I told you, I feel like being truthful and that is my only reason.

MORALIST: But I am trying to explain to you that that reason is inadequate!

KURT: I don't give a damm whether it is adequate or not! It so happens I *feel* like being truthful! Do you mind?

MORALIST: No, I don't mind. I don't mind at all. Only you needn't be so belligerent about it! Now what about you, Larry? Why are you truthful?

LARRY: Why does a tree grow?

MORALIST: Look now, we are not here to play mystical games with each other. I asked you a serious question.

LARRY: And I gave you a serious answer.

MORALIST: Oh, come now, what does a tree growing have to do with your being truthful?

LARRY: More perhaps than you realize.

MORALIST: I wish that you would stop giving these cryptic responses! What are you, one of these Zen Buddhists or something?

LARRY: Yes.

MORALIST: Oh, no wonder you talk in this strange manner! But you can't tell me why you are truthful?

LARRY: Can you tell me why a tree grows?

MORALIST: I still don't see what the growth of a tree has to do with your being truthful.

LARRY: More perhaps than you realize.

MORALIST: So we are back to that again! You Zen men are the most frustrating creatures to talk to!

LARRY: In that case, why do you talk to us? But I'm glad you called me a *creature*. That at least shows that you have *some* insight into the true relationship between me and a tree.

MORALIST: Oh, really now, in what significant way are you like a tree?

LARRY: In what significant way am I different?

MORALIST: Oh, surely now, you regard yourself as a *little* more significant than a tree, don't you?

LARRY: Not at all.

MORALIST: But do you not realize that a tree is at a lower stage of life than a man?

LARRY: I find your use of the word *lower* ill advised. It is psychologically misleading and sets an emotional tone that is tantamount to begging the question. I would prefer to say that a tree is at an *earlier* stage of life.

MORALIST: Let's not be pedantic and quibble about words! In this context, *lower* and *earlier* mean exactly the same thing.

LARRY: Oh no they don't! *Objectively* they may have the same meaning in this context but *subjectively* they certainly do not. One would say that a child is at an earlier stage of life than an adult but surely not at a lower stage. This latter mode of speech gives the impression that an adult is superior to a child, which I don't believe many would wish to do.

MORALIST: All right, have it your way; so you're *not* superior to a tree. But why are you truthful? And please don't answer my question again with the question, "Why does a tree grow?"

LARRY: If you tell me why a tree grows, then perhaps I can tell you why I am truthful.

MORALIST: I still don't see the connection between the two! Why must I first tell you why a tree grows?

LARRY: Because I have great difficulty understanding your use of the word *why*. I was hoping that if you told me why a tree grows then I could gather enough data on your use of this word to help me answer your question more satisfactorily.

MORALIST: Oh, so our difficulty is semantical! In that case, I'll use a different word. What is your *reason* for being truthful?

LARRY: Does everything have to have a reason?

MORALIST: Well of course!

LARRY: Really now! Does a tree have a reason for growing?

MORALIST: Of course not. At least, I don't think so.

LARRY: Then why should I have a reason for being truthful?

MORALIST: Because you are not a tree!

LARRY: So because I am not a tree, it follows that I should have a reason for being truthful?

MORALIST: Oh heavens, you are only confusing matters! Look, a tree is not a conscious being; it has no free will and makes no choices. So one would hardly expect a tree to have a reason for growing, but one would expect you to have a reason for what you do!

LARRY: I grant you that if I were not conscious then I would not possibly have a reason for *anything* I do. But it does not therefore follow that because I *am* conscious I must have a reason for *everything* I do. In particular, I have absolutely no reason for being truthful.

MORALIST: No reason? None at all?

LARRY: None whatsoever!

MORALIST: Fantastic! In other words, you are in the same category as Kurt. You feel like being truthful and that is the only reason you are.

LARRY: No, no, not at all! You totally miss my point! As Kurt told you, his feeling like being truthful is, for him, his *reason* for being truthful. But I have *no* reason at all!

MORALIST: You mean that you don't even feel like being truthful?

LARRY: What a strange non sequitur! Of course I feel like being truthful; otherwise I wouldn't be truthful.

MORALIST: So I was right! That *is* your reason for being truthful.

LARRY: I am sorry, but you are still confused. I both feel like being truthful and am truthful but there is no evidence that either of these two phenomena is the reason of the other.

MORALIST: Look, I just can't believe that you have *no reason at all* for being truthful! You *must* have a reason; you just don't know what it is!

LARRY: At this point, I am not sure just which of several possible meanings of the word *reason* you have in mind. When you ask the reason for my being truthful, are you asking for my *motive* or *purpose* in being truthful, or are you seeking the *cause* of my truthfulness? Or are you perhaps asking whether I am truthful out of some *principle* like virtue or duty or obedience to God or the desire to serve humanity or to be personally well off? Which of these meanings do you have in mind?

MORALIST: Take your choice!

LARRY: I would rather you choose.

MORALIST: Very well then. Which of these principles you mentioned is relevant to your case?

LARRY: None of them.

MORALIST: Then what *is* the principle you follow?

LARRY: None whatsoever. I am not truthful on principle.

MORALIST: All right then, let's go over to another of your suggested meanings, cause. What is the cause of your being truthful?

LARRY: I have no idea.

MORALIST: Aren't you helpful!

LARRY: I am trying to be.

MORALIST: You certainly don't *seem* to be trying! At any rate, let's go on to the next possibility. What is your motive or purpose in being truthful?

LARRY: I am not aware of any motive, and I certainly have no purpose in being truthful. Does a tree have any motive or purpose in growing?

MORALIST: Why must you keep picking on that poor tree?

LARRY: Why do you keep picking on *me?*

MORALIST: I'm not picking on you! I'm trying to *help* you. I'm trying to help you to know yourself better.

LARRY: Why on earth should I want to know myself better?

MORALIST: Well, don't you want to?

LARRY: Of course not. Why should I want to do such a foolish thing?

MORALIST: What's so foolish about it? Recall Shakespeare's saying, "Know thyself."

LARRY: I guess it's all right for those who like that sort of thing.

MORALIST: And did not Socrates say that the unexamined life is not worth living?

LARRY: Isn't that a bit on the arrogant side? Who is Socrates to decide which lives are worth living and which not? Does a tree examine its life?

MORALIST: Socrates was talking about human beings, not trees!

LARRY: What is the difference?

MORALIST: Oh, so we're back to that again! Look, I don't have the time to spend with you playing these useless word games! Since you stubbornly deny that your truthfulness is to any purpose, then I think further conversation is futile.

LARRY: Good grief, how you have misunderstood me! I never said that my being truthful is to no purpose!

MORALIST: Of course you did! A short while back you distinctly said that you had no purpose in being truthful.

LARRY: That is true. Indeed, *I* have no purpose in being truthful. But that does not mean that there *is* no purpose in my being truthful. Of course there is a purpose—I feel a very important one —but this purpose is not mine.

MORALIST: Now I don't understand you at all!

LARRY: Isn't that amazing; you understand the matter perfectly with a tree but not with a human! That so beautifully reveals how differently you think of the two. You grant that a tree has no reason or purpose in growing since you say that a tree is not a conscious entity. Yet that does not mean that the growing of a tree *serves* no purpose. Now you will say that since I, unlike a tree, am a conscious entity, I not only *serve* purposes but have my *own* purposes, and indeed I often do. When I came here tonight, I had the definite purpose of speaking with you all. But that does not mean that everything I do I necessarily do for a purpose. In particular, my being truthful serves absolutely no purpose of *mine*. But I do not doubt that it serves a very important purpose. You see now why I compare my being truthful to the growing of a tree?

MORALIST: Yes, now for the first time I begin to get an inkling of what you are saying. I don't think I would agree with your point of view, but I do find it of interest, and I wish we had more time to go into details, but the evening is getting well on, and we should not neglect our final speaker, Simplicus. Actually, I planned this occasion primarily in Simplicus's honor as a tribute to a great and truthful man, one who is probably more truthful than all of us. All of us here tell nothing but the truth, but Simplicus also always tells the *whole* truth. Therefore, he should be most competent to analyze the real purpose of truthfulness. And so we ask you, Simplicus, what is *your* reason for being truthful?

SIMPLICUS: Me? Truthful? I had no idea that I was.

2

A Puzzle

Before leaving the subject of truth telling, I would like to tell you one of my favorite logic puzzles.

Suppose there are two identical twin brothers, one who always lies and the other who always tells the truth. Now, the truth teller is also totally accurate in all his beliefs; all true propositions he believes to be true and all false propositions he believes to be false. The lying brother is totally inaccurate in his beliefs; all true propositions he believes to be false, and all false propositions he believes to be true. The interesting thing is that each brother will give the same answer to the same question. For example, suppose you ask whether two plus two equals four. The accurate truth teller knows that it is and will truthfully answer *yes*. The inaccurate liar will believe that two plus two does not equal four (since he is inaccurate) and will then lie and say that it does; he will also answer *yes*.

The situation is reminiscent of an incident I read about in a textbook on abnormal psychology: The doctors in a mental institution were thinking of releasing a certain schizophrenic patient. They decided to give him a test under a lie detector. One of the questions they asked him was, "Are you Napoleon?" He replied, "No." The machine showed that he was lying!

Getting back to the twin brothers, two logicians were having an argument about the following question: Suppose one were to meet one of the two brothers alone. Would it be possible by asking him any number of yes-no questions to find out which one he is? One logician said, "No, it would not be possible because whatever answers you got to your questions, the other brother would have given the same answers." The second logician claimed that it was possible to find out. The second logician was right, and the puzzle has two parts: (1) How many questions are necessary?; and (2) more interesting yet, What was wrong with the first logician's argument? (Readers who enjoy doing logic puzzles might wish to try solving this one on their own before reading further.)

To determine which brother you are addressing, one question is enough; just ask him if he is the accurate truth teller. If he is, he will know that he is (since he is accurate) and truthfully will answer *yes*. If he is the inaccurate liar, he will believe that he is the accurate truth teller (since he is inaccurate in his beliefs), but then he will lie and say *no*. So the accurate truth teller will answer *yes* and the inaccurate liar *no* to this question.

Now what was wrong with the first logician's argument; don't the two brothers give the same answer to the same question? They do, but the whole point is that if I ask one person, "Are *you* the accurate truth teller?" and then ask another, "Are *you* the accurate truth teller?" I am really asking two different questions since the indentical word *you* has a different reference in each case.

2

On Things in General

3

Miscellaneous Fragments

1

Self-annihilating Sentences. Over a period of many years, the computer scientist Dr. Saul Gorn has compiled a delightful collection of sentences that somehow manage to defeat themselves. He has titled this collection "S. Gorn's Compendium of Rarely Used Cliches." With his kind permission, I reproduce a few choice items (with one or two minor modifications).

1. Before I begin speaking, there is something I would like to say.
2. I am a firm believer in optimism because without optimism, what else is there?
3. Half the lies they tell about me are true.
4. Every Tom, Dick, and Harry is called *John.*
5. Having lost sight of our goal, we must redouble our efforts!
6. I'll see to it that your project deserves to be funded.

7. I've given you an unlimited budget, and you have already exceeded it!
8. A preposition must never be used to end a sentence with.
9. This species has always been extinct.
10. Authorized parking forbidden!
11. If you're not prejudiced, you just don't understand!
12. Inflation is an economic device whereby each person earns more than the next.
13. Superstition brings bad luck.
14. That's a real step forward into the unknown.
15. You've outdone yourself as usual.
16. Every once in a while it never stops raining.
17. Monism is the theory that anything less than everything is nothing.
18. A formalist is one who cannot understand a theory unless it is meaningless.

2

Saul Gorn once told me his theory of asceticism: "It is well known that the longer one postpones a pleasure, the greater the pleasure is when one finally gets it. Therefore, if one postpones it forever, the pleasure should be infinite."

3

Many years ago, Saul Gorn and I were having supper at the Automat. Just as Saul finished, a waiter snatched away his plate. "Ah!" exclaimed Saul. "I finished just in time!"

4

On another occasion, Saul and I were with a group of friends. Saul asked us whether we wanted to go to a certain place. We finally decided not to go. Saul looked at us and said, "Then how do you expect to get there?"

5

Saul once told me that he was teaching a class in which two students were always talking to each other. Finally, Saul said, "It's pointless for you to keep talking because if you do, I'll have to talk louder, and then neither of you will be able to hear what the other one is saying."

6

This reminds me of an incident that occurred when I was giving an examination to an undergraduate class. At the beginning of the exam, I said to the class, "Will you give me your word of honor that you won't cheat if I give you mine that I won't report you in case you do?"

7

I am a firm believer that in studying mathematics one should never forget one's common sense. Many years ago, I was teaching an elementary algebra course. On one exam, I had a standard-type question that involved finding the ages of a mother, father, and child. After the students read the question, I said, "On this problem, I'll give you one hint." All eyes eagerly turned to me. I continued, "If the child should turn out to be older than either of the parents, then you've done something wrong."

8

On another occasion, I had to present the Pythagorean Theorem to a class in geometry. I drew a right triangle on the board with squares on the hypotenuse and legs and said, "Obviously, the square on the hypotenuse has a larger area than either of the other two squares. Now suppose these three squares were made of beaten gold, and you were offered either the one large square or the two small squares. Which would you choose?"

Interestingly enough, about half the class opted for the one large square and half for the two small ones. A lively argument began. Both groups were equally amazed when told that it would make no difference.

9

At one university where I taught, we were thinking of hiring a certain candidate. We invited him up for a talk. Sometime after the talk, the chairman asked him how he liked teaching. He replied, "I've never done any, but I don't think I'd like it."

At a departmental meeting a few days later, we were discussing why the candidate said that. "Oh," suggested one of the department members, "he probably dislikes lying even more than teaching!"

10

A Question of Semantics. At a seminar that he was giving, the late philosopher Alan Ross Anderson told the following fascinating incident: Anderson was working for the navy during World War II with a group deciphering Japanese code. They had great difficulty deciphering one word (represented by a number) that kept coming in repeatedly. It was soon apparent that the word was an adjective applying to people and nations ("This nation is———, but that nation is not———."). After much data were received, they finally decoded it as *pro-Japanese*. At the end of the war, the code book was captured, and the true meaning of the word was *sincere*.

11

The philosopher Nual Belnap, Jr., who collaborated with Alan Ross Anderson on a fundamental work in the field known as *relevance logic*, recently introduced me at a talk at Carnegie-Mellon University. He said, "In this introduction, I promised myself three things: First, to be brief. Second, not to be facetious. Third, not to refer to this introduction."

12

Someone once told me that he believed that logicians reason more accurately than other people; they make fewer mistakes.

"Logicians do *not* make fewer mistakes," I replied quite emphatically, "and if I'm wrong about that, then here am I, a logician, who has just made a mistake."

13

Recently, someone asked me if I believed in astrology. He seemed somewhat puzzled when I explained that the reason that I don't is that I'm a Gemini.

14

Because I have been a magician for many years, people have often asked me whether I ever have sawn a woman in half. I reply, "Oh, yes; I've sawn over seventy women in half in my lifetime, and I'm learning the second half of the trick now."

15

I performed magic most intensively when I was a student at the University of Chicago. I never did much stage magic; I was a close-up magician who entertained small groups at private parties and more often at the tables of various supper clubs. The following recollection is about my funniest.

At one table where I was performing, there was a man who was about the most blasé character I have ever met. He just sat there smoking his pipe, saying not a word, and *nothing* I could do got the slightest rise out of him. I made my tricks more and more startling, all to no avail. After about twenty-five minutes of increasing effort, I finally did my most spectacular effect, at which he took his pipe out of his mouth, slammed the table with his fist, and angrily shouted, "It's a *trick!*"

16

In those days, I particularly delighted in playing tricks on the philosopher Rudolf Carnap; he was the perfect audience! (Most scientists and mathematicians are; they are so honest themselves that they have great difficulty in seeing through the deceptions of others.) After one particular trick, Carnap said, "Nohhhh! I didn't think that could happen in *any* possible world, let alone *this* one!"

17

In item #249 of my book of logic puzzles titled *What Is the Name of This Book?*, I describe an infallible method of proving anything whatsoever.[1] Only a magician is capable of employing the method, however. I once used it on Rudolf Carnap to prove the existence of God.

"Here you see a red card," I said to Professor Carnap as I removed a card from the deck. "I place it face down in your palm. Now, you know that a false proposition implies *any* proposition. Therefore, if this card were black, then God would exist. Do you agree?"

"Oh, certainly," replied Carnap, "*if* the card were black, then God would exist."

"Very good," I said as I turned over the card. "As you see, the card *is* black. Therefore, God exists!"

"Ah, yes!" replied Carnap in a philosophical tone. "Proof by legerdemain! Same as the theologians use!"

18

Speaking of proofs of the existence of God, the funniest one I have ever seen was in a term paper handed in by a freshman. She wrote, "God must exist because he wouldn't be so mean as to make me believe he exists if he really doesn't!" Is this argument really so much worse than the ontological proofs of the existence of God provided by Anselm and Descartes, among others? (See Chapter 10.)

19

It has always puzzled me that so many religious people have taken it for granted that God favors those who believe in him. Isn't it possible that the actual God is a scientific God who has little patience with beliefs founded on faith rather than evidence?

20

This reflection on the nature of God may not be too unrelated to the problems raised by Pascal's wager. Pascal says that it is better to believe in God than not to believe because if God doesn't exist and one believes that he does, the loss is trivial compared with the infinite loss incurred if God does exist and one believes that he doesn't. (Failing to believe in a God who exists means eternal damnation, and such a loss is indeed infinite!) Therefore (reasons Pascal), from the objective viewpoint of pure probability, the rational thing to do is to believe in God.

Now, if it were really true that believing in God increases the probability of salvation one iota, then I would agree that one had best believe in God. But why should this assumption be true? I tend to feel that any God who could be so hideous as to damn a soul eternally couldn't be trusted on any issue whatsoever!

21

A delightful counterexample to the attitude described in §19 is that of a Protestant minister I once knew who said to me, "Why is it that the best people I know are atheists?"

"How do you ever expect to convert them *that* way?" I asked.

"Convert them?" he replied. "Who wants to convert them?"

22

When I was quite young I was present during a rather curious conversation. One person said, "I know there is a God!"

Another said, "And I know there isn't."

Isn't it remarkable that two contradictory propositions can both be known? In fact, how can either of these two propositions be known? If there really is a God, could that fact be not merely believed but actually known? Perhaps it could—by, say, some mystical insight. On the other hand, if there isn't a God, could that fact be known? Certainly not by any scientific means! Could it then be known by some mystical means? If so, it would be a rather fascinating type of mysticism that could perceive the nonexistence rather than the existence of something!

23

Curiously, people often confuse the following questions: (1) Is there a God?; and (2) is there an afterlife? Just because many religions believe in both is no reason to assume that the answers are necessarily the same! It could be that there is a God and no afterlife or that there is an afterlife and no God; or it could be that neither exist, or maybe both.

Recently, however, the two questions have become more separated. Indeed, people nowadays tend to be more skeptical about an afterlife than about the existence of God. I wonder why this is?

24

In *The Future of an Illusion,* Freud spends all his time discussing the desirability of civilization's maintaining or rejecting the "illusion" of religion.[2] He tries to project the probable psychological results of outgrowing the illusion, which he feels will be helpful, and he spends much time trying to dispel counterarguments.

To a realistic Platonist like myself, the real question is not whether religion is helpful or harmful but whether it is true. This question Freud hardly considers. He simply takes it for granted that religion is false, and he offers a purely naturalistic explanation of why people believe in God. Now, I have little doubt that even if there is no God people would still believe in one, quite possibly for the very reasons Freud gave. But this sheds absolutely no light on the more fundamental question of the truth or falsity of theism. As others have pointed out so well, a purely psychological explanation of the origins of a belief does not constitute the slightest rational evidence for or against the belief itself. (I wish more Marxists would realize this!)

I think that most parental decisions about giving children religious training, though often rationalized in terms of what is good for the children, are really governed by whether the parents themselves believe in God or not. However, this is not always the case. I knew a father who said, "I myself don't believe in God, but I still think that every child should have religious training." I have wondered why he had this attitude. Did he believe in deliberately lying to a child for its own good? Or did he perhaps believe deep down in God after all but was unaware of the fact?

On the other hand, I have never known anyone who believed in God but nevertheless felt that religious training is bad for a child. And so there is a curious asymmetry between theism and atheism. Though many atheists feel that the belief in God is bad, this badness is not a logical consequence of the doctrine of atheism, whereas in many if not most of the existing religions, the badness of disbelief (as well as the goodness of belief) is implied by the religion itself—indeed, is often explicitly part of the doctrine.

Freud seemed to have been deeply concerned about the general influence his book would have. The book is certainly an interesting one in its own right, but it is doubtful that it ever had or will have much influence at all, especially in either dispelling or cementing religious ties. Religious trends seem to come and go by laws of their own that we do not understand too well, and our choice in these matters is probably less significant than would appear.

25

A solipsist is one who says, "I am the only one who exists." (I am not sure that he actually has to say it; it is probably sufficient that he *believe* it!) At another seminar given by Alan Ross Anderson, about two hours were spent discussing solipsism. At the end of the period, I got up and said, "At this point, I think I've become an *antisolipsist;* I believe that everyone exists except me!"

26

The logician Melvin Fitting, with his typical sense of humor, once said to me, "Of course I believe that solipsism is the correct philosophy, but that's only one man's opinion."

27

This comment is reminiscent of the famous story about the lady who wrote to Bertrand Russell, "Why are you surprised to hear that I'm a solipsist? Isn't everybody?"

28

I have met some actual solipsists. One once said to me, "Smullyan, you don't exist!"

"Just *who* is it that you claim doesn't exist?" I replied.

29

Another solipsist once said to me, "I am the only one who exists."

"That's right," I replied. "I am the only one who exists."

"No, no!" he said. "I'm saying: *I* am the only one who exists."

"That's what I am saying; *I* am the only one who exists."

"No, no, no!" he excitedly shouted. "It is *I*, not *you*, who exists!"

"That's right." I repeated. "It is *I*, not *you*, who exists. We seem to agree perfectly!"

At this point, he became somewhat confused.

30

This exchange brings to mind the definition of *I* given by Ambrose Bierce in *The Devil's Dictionary.* [3] After defining the term, he continues, "Its plural is said to be *we*, but how there can be more than one myself is doubtless clearer to the grammarians than it is to the author of this incomparable dictionary." Despite the levity, the issue Bierce raises is a profound one that we will deal with more fully in Chapter 12, titled "Enlightened Solipsism."

31

I have sometimes wondered how a militant solipsist would react if everybody, instead of arguing with him, simply agreed with him! I once asked a professional psychiatrist what he thought. He replied, "I imagine that he would be terrified!"

32

Speaking of psychiatrists, I once heard the following anecdote about Freud. Someone asked him, "Would you hold a man responsible for what he dreams?" Freud replied, "Whom else would you hold responsible?"

33

The following exchange once occurred between a disciple of Freud and one of his patients.

PATIENT: Doctor, if you help me, I'll give you every penny I possess!

PSYCHIATRIST: I shall be satisfied with thirty kronen an hour.

PATIENT: But isn't that rather excessive?

34

Turning from psychiatrists to philosophers, a philosopher once had the following dream: First Aristotle appeared, and the philosopher said to him, "Could you give me a fifteen-minute capsule sketch of your entire philosophy?" To the philosopher's surprise, Aristotle gave him an excellent exposition in which he compressed an enormous amount of material into a mere fifteen minutes. But then the philosopher raised a certain objection that Aristotle couldn't answer. Confounded, Aristotle disappeared. Then Plato appeared. The same thing happened again, and the philosopher's objection to Plato was the very same as his objection to Aristotle. Plato also couldn't answer it and disappeared. Then all the famous philosophers of history appeared one by one, and our philosopher refuted every one with the same objection. After the last philosopher vanished, our philosopher said to himself, "I know I'm asleep and dreaming all this. Yet I've found a universal refutation for all philosophical systems! Tomorrow when I wake up, I will probably have forgotten it, and the world will really miss something!" With an iron effort, the philosopher forced himself to wake up, rush over to his desk, and write down his universal refutation. Then he jumped back into bed with a sigh of relief. The next morning when he awoke, he went over to the desk to see what he had written. It was, "That's what *you* say!"

35

There is a story about a philosopher who went into a closet for ten years to contemplate the question, What is life? When he came out, he went into the street and met an old colleague, who asked him where in heaven's name he had been all those years.

"In a closet," he replied. "I wanted to know what life really *is.*"

"And have you found an answer?"

"Yes," he replied. "I think it can best be expressed by saying that life is like a bridge."

"That's all well and good," replied the colleague, "but can you be a little more explicit? Can you tell me *how* life is like a bridge?"

"Oh," replied the philosopher after some thought, "maybe you're right; perhaps life is not like a bridge."

36

There is also a story about Epimenides, who once became interested in Eastern philosophy and made a long pilgrimage to meet

Buddha. When he finally met him, Epimenides said, "I have come to ask a question. What is the best question that can be asked and what is the best answer that can be given?"

Buddha replied, "The best question that can be asked is the question you have just asked, and the best answer that can be given is the answer I am giving."

37

Cartesian philosophy is the philosophy of René Descartes. Descartes first set out to prove his own existence. His proof is remarkably short; it consists of only three Latin words: "Cogito, ergo sum," that is, "I think, therefore I am." When I first heard this, I couldn't resist writing the following verse:

> I think, therefore I am?
> Could be!
> Or is it really someone else who only thinks he's me?

Descartes was a dualist; he believed that mind and matter are separate substances. Idealists like George Berkeley believe that nothing exists but mind. (The *absolute* idealist furthermore believes that there is only one mind in the universe.) At the opposite pole are the materialists (or realists, as they are sometimes called) who believe that nothing exists but matter and energy.

I have asked many children, "Do you believe that your mind is the same thing as your brain?" Interestingly enough, about half answered *yes* and half answered *no.* Among those who answered *no,* one said, "The mind cannot be the same thing as the brain because the brain is something tangible and the mind is not."

38

By now, I have defined just about all the technical terms that will be used in this book. I should add that epistemology is the theory of knowledge and should also say a word or two about logical positivism.

If I were to write a devil's philosophical dictionary in the style of Ambrose Bierce, I would define a logical positivist as one who rejects as meaningless any statement that he is incapable of understanding. Prejudicial as this definition certainly is, it is not completely without truth. Actually, the logical positivists set up (presumably) precise criteria of meaning, and any statement not passing these criteria is declared meaningless. But it can be argued that in setting up their criteria, they take into account only those meanings that they can understand.

Let me tell you a relevant true story: I once dined at a country inn. To my surprise, the walls of the dining room were lined with bookshelves that held a magnificent philosophical library.

"Oh, yes," the proprietress later explained, "my ex-husband is a philosopher and left me this library. He is a logical positivist, and it was logical positivism that broke up our marriage."

"Now, how could that be?" I exclaimed.

"Because everything I said—whatever it was—he kept telling me was meaningless!"

39

One of the basic principles of logical positivism is that no sentence should be regarded as meaningful unless there is, in principle, some method of verifying whether it is true or false. Of course, many people are logical positivists in this sense even though they have never heard the term *logical positivism*.

On the nicer side of logical positivism, I believe the pianist Artur Schnabel must have been one such person. I once attended three fascinating lectures given by Schnabel at the University of Chicago. During one of the question periods, someone asked him what he thought of his latest review.

"I don't read my reviews," replied Schnabel, "at least not in America. The trouble with American reviewers is that when they make a criticism, I don't know what to do about it! Now, in Europe it was different—for example, I once gave a concert in Berlin. The critic wrote, 'Schnabel played the first movement of the Brahms sonata too fast.' I thought about the matter and realized that the man was right! But I knew what to do about it; I now simply play the movement a little slower. But when these American critics say things like, 'The trouble with Schnabel is that he doesn't put enough *moonshine* in his playing,' then I simply don't know what to do about it!"

40

At another lecture, Schnabel said, "You may find this hard to believe, but Igor Stravinsky has actually published in the papers the statement, 'Music to be great must be completely cold and unemotional'! And last Sunday, I was having breakfast with Arnold Shönberg, and I said to him, 'Can you imagine that Stravinsky actually made the statement that music to be great must be cold and unemotional?' At this, Schönberg got furious and said, 'I said that first!' "

41

Sometime around 1940, the composer Leon Kirchner, then a student, was visiting me in New York. We listened to Schnabel's recording of Schubert's posthumous Sonata in A and were both deeply moved. (This is as good a piano recording as has ever been made!)

"Why don't we phone up Schnabel and congratulate him?" I jokingly suggested.

Leon immediately rushed to the phone. I went into another room and with great trepidation listened in on an extension. Schnabel was in and Leon told him how he and a friend had just listened to the recording and were so impressed by his remarkable understanding of the architecture of the piece that we *had* to phone him and let him know. Naturally, Leon and I were both extremely nervous at the idea of taking up the time of the great Schnabel. But what happened was this:

"Ah, yes," said Schnabel, "now you see, the first movement of the sonata is still a classic movement, whereas the second movement . . . " Schnabel went on and on, keeping *us* on the phone for about an hour as he traced the entire development of the sonata form!

42

On one occasion when I visited Schnabel, he was in a rather philosophic mood. "Oh, yes," he said, "I am a realist! It is because I am a realist that I can sit back and be an idealist!" Seeing my look of bewilderment, he added, "Because *ideals* are the reality!"

43

The composer Paul Hindemith was once conducting a rehearsal of one of his more dissonant orchestral compositions. At one point, he rapped his baton and said, "No, no, gentlemen; even though it sounds wrong, it's still not right!"

44

The pianist Leopold Godowsky once visited a composer-friend and found him composing merrily away with operatic scores all over the piano. Godowsky said, "Oh, I thought you composed from memory!"

45

I once heard a radio interview with the pianist Artur Rubinstein. On the whole, the interviewer struck me as incredibly trite and stupid. Out of the blue, he asked, "Mr. Rubinstein, do you believe in God?" There was a tense pause. "No," replied Rubinstein, quite definitely. "You see, what I believe in is something much greater!"

46

This anecdote reminds me of a riddle: What is it that's greater than God; the dead eat it, and if the living eat it, they die? (See §53, for answer.)

47

When Mark Twain was asked what he thought of the music of Richard Wagner, he replied, "Oh, it's probably not as bad as it sounds!"

48

Music and Mathematics. The mathematician Felix Klein was once at a party where the company was discussing the correlation between mathematics and music with respect to both tastes and aptitudes. Klein looked more and more puzzled and finally said, "But I don't understand; mathematics is beautiful!"

49

Pitch and Color. Our visual spectrum happens to be less than one octave, that is, the highest frequency of light that we humans can perceive is not quite twice the lowest frequency. (By contrast, our auditory spectrum encompasses several octaves.) If our visual spectrum were a little more than an octave, I wonder whether two colors an octave apart would have the same psychological similarity as two notes an octave apart.

I once put this question to a rather famous Italian physiologist. He replied, "Ah, that's a beautiful question!" I also put it to an equally famous musicologist. He answered in an irritated tone, "That's obviously unverifiable!" So you see, the musicologist was really a logical positivist at heart (in the bad sense), whereas the physiologist was not.

But is the question really unverifiable *in principle?* Is it inconceivable that science might one day find a means of extending our visual spectrum? Perhaps it is. But isn't it possible that we might one day meet intelligent beings from another planet whose visual spectrum *is* more than an octave and simply ask them?

50

Absolute Pitch. I was once riding in the front seat of a car driven by the computer scientist Dr. Marvin Minsky. In the backseat were two scientists from Bell Telephone Laboratories. The conversation turned to the subject of absolute pitch. Marvin said to them, "You know, Ray here has absolute pitch." One of the two asked me, "How accurate is your sense of absolute pitch?" For some odd reason or other, I didn't hear the question, so he said somewhat louder, "I say, how accurate is your sense of absolute pitch?" Upon which, Marvin turned around and said to them, "Oh, I forgot to tell you—he's also deaf!"

51

Once at a mathematics conference, one of the speakers gave me an account of a paper he was about to deliver. I found the account incomprehensible. As he was talking, Marvin Minsky walked by and said to him, "No, no; your trouble is that you're confusing a thing with itself!"

52

I love Marvin Minsky's quote on the jacket cover of the book *The Mind's I.* [4]

This great collection of reflections provides you with your own quite special ways to understand things such as why, if you don't read this book, you'll never be the same again.

53

The answer to the riddle of §46 is *nothing*.

54

I have told several philosophers that despite my great love for the Taoist philosophers Laotse, Chuangtse, and Liehtse, perhaps my favorite philosopher of all is Ferdinand the Bull. One of them took this seriously and earnestly tried to convince me that Ferdinand couldn't be a philosopher. "A philosopher is necessarily human," he said. I can't see why this must be true! Didn't Ferdinand have a pacifist philosophy?

55

I read in some philosophy book or other that perhaps the one true philosopher was the little girl of nine who was looking out a window and suddenly turned to her mother and said, "But what puzzles me is why there is anything at all!" The following comments, made by children I have known, have definite philosophical overtones.

Vincent (aged 3). When Vincent was about to go up in an airplane for the first time, he asked his father, "When we go up, will we also get small?"

Barry (aged 5 or 6). Barry once said, "I hope I never get to be ninety-nine!"

"Why?" I asked.

"Because when you get that old, you could die!"

Miriam (aged 8). Miriam is the daughter of a mathematical logician. She has either inherited or acquired many of her father's characteristics. At one point during dinner, her father said, "That's no way to eat, Miriam!"

She replied, "I'm not eating Miriam."

Jennifer (aged 6). Jennifer is the daughter of a philosopher. One morning, her brother Jon (aged 8) came down to breakfast and played one April Fools' joke after another on the parents. Then Jennifer came down, and Jonny tried an April Fools' joke on her.

"What's the matter with you, Jonny," she said. "Today's not April Fool!"

"It isn't?" he cried in astonishment.

"April Fool!"

On another occasion, Jennifer had just come home from a movie. She said to her mother, "Mommy, what is the best movie ever made? And I don't want you to tell me what you *think* is the best movie; I want you to tell me what *is* the best movie."

David (aged 10). My wife and I were once with David's family at a drive-in theater. The first feature was excellent, but the second feature looked as if it were going to be terrible. One of the adults suggested that we leave. David of course wanted to stay, and so an argument began.

"Why don't we take a vote?" I suggested.

"No!" said David. "That's not fair because the majority will win!"

Natalie (aged 8). Natalie is the daughter of a mathematical logician. The family was visiting us for a weekend, and one evening we all had a lively philosophical discussion about time. For some perverse reason or other, I took the position that time is unreal.

Next morning at breakfast, someone asked of two acquaintances which was the older?

"Bill is older by two years," I remarked.

"How could he be?" asked Natalie. "Didn't you say that time was unreal?"

56

Natalie's remark reminds me of G. E. Moore's famous proof of the existence of an external world. He held up a hand and said, "Here is a hand." Then he held up his other hand and said, "Here is another hand. Hands are objects, hence objects exist."

I am also reminded of a conversation I once had with the logical positivist O. Bowsma. I took an extreme view, holding that minds were essentially independent of bodies.

"I can easily imagine myself in another body," I said. "I am fully prepared for the possibility that next week I might find myself in a totally different body, say, one with three arms."

"You are *really* prepared?" asked Bowsma.

"Absolutely!" I replied.

"Tell me," said Bowsma, "have you bought yourself another glove?"

57

As the conversation continued, I became more and more wildly idealistic. Bowsma had an objection to just about every statement I made.

"Tell me," I finally asked, "do you believe I am being inconsistent?"

"No," he replied.

Another philosopher present said, "What you are saying is too *vague* to be inconsistent!"

58

There is a curious thing about inconsistency. In the formal mathematical systems mainly in use today, consistency is absolutely essential, for without it the whole system breaks down and *everything* can be proved. It has therefore been argued that if a person is inconsistent, he will end up believing everything. But is this really so?

I have known many inconsistent people, and they don't appear to believe *everything*. First, it is difficult to live long enough to believe everything. Second, even if we were immortal and inconsistent, we would not necessarily believe everything. I say this for the following reason: If we were *consistent* in our inconsistency, then we might end up believing everything, but it is more likely that an inconsistent person would be just as inconsistent in the way he carried out his inconsistency as he is about other things, and this would be the very thing that would save him from believing everything.

The inconsistent people I have known have not seemed to have a higher ratio of false beliefs to true ones than those who make a superhuman effort to maintain consistency at all costs. True, people who are compulsively consistent will probably save themselves certain false beliefs, but I'm afraid they will also miss many true ones!

59

Here is a little paradox:

> YOU HAVE NO REASON
> TO BELIEVE THIS SENTENCE.

Do you have any reason to believe the above sentence or don't you?

60

Have you heard the business executive's paradox? It was invented by the literary agent Lisa Collier of Collier Associates. The president of a firm offered a reward of $100 to any employee who could provide a suggestion that would save the company money. One employee suggested, "Eliminate the reward!"

61

My favorite paradox of all is known as *hypergame*. It is due to the mathematician William Zwicker.

A game is called *normal* if it has to terminate in a finite number of moves. An obvious example of a normal game is tic-tac-toe. Chess is also a normal game, assuming tournament regulations. Now, the first move of hypergame is to state which normal game is to be played. For example, if you and I were playing hypergame and I had the first move, I might say, "Let's play chess." Then you make the first move in chess, and we continue playing chess until the termination of the game. Another possibility is that on my first move in hypergame, I might say, "Let's play tic-tac-toe," or "Let's play casino," or any other normal game I like. But the game I choose *must* be normal; I am not allowed to choose a game that is not normal.

The problem is, Is hypergame itself normal or not? Suppose it is normal. Since on the first move of hypergame I can choose *any* normal game, I can say, "Let's play hypergame." We are then in the state of hypergame, and it is your move. You can respond, "Let's play hypergame." I can repeat, "Let's play hypergame," and the process can go on indefinitely, contrary to the assumption that hypergame is normal. Therefore, hypergame is not a normal game. But since hypergame is not normal, on my first move in hypergame I *cannot* choose hypergame; I must choose a normal game. But having chosen a normal game, the game must finally terminate, contrary to the proven fact that hypergame is not normal.

An amazing paradox indeed!

62

A Moral Paradox. The philosopher Jaako Hintikka makes the delightful argument that one is morally obligated not to do anything impossible. The argument, which ultimately rests on the fact that a false proposition implies any proposition, is this: Suppose Act A is such that it is impossible to perform without destroying the human race. Then surely one is morally obligated not to perform that act. Well, if Act A is an *impossible* act, then it is indeed impossible to perform it without destroying the human race (since it is impossible to perform it at all!), and therefore one is morally obligated not to perform the act.

63

But doesn't the following argument *(sic!)* show that one is morally obligated to do *everything* that is impossible?

Suppose that Act B is such that if one performs it, then the human race will be saved from destruction. Isn't one then morally obligated to perform the act? Now suppose that Act B is impossible to perform. Then it *is* the case that if one performs Act B, the human race will be saved, because it is false that one will perform this impossible act and a false proposition implies anything. One is therefore morally obligated to perform every impossible act.

64

For those who like logic puzzles, here are some nice ones.

Problem 1. There are three brothers named John, Jack, and William. John and Jack always lie (make only false statements) and William makes only true statements. The three are indistinguishable in appearance. One day you meet one of the three brothers on the street and wish to know if he is John (because John owes you money). You are allowed to ask him only one question, which has to be answered by *yes* or *no*, and the question may not contain more than three words. What question would you ask? (The solutions to this and the next four problems are given in §66.)

Problem 2. Suppose in the last problem we change the conditions and make John and Jack the truth tellers and William the liar. You still want to know whether the brother you meet is John. Now what three-word question will work?

Problem 3. This time we have only two brothers. One is named John, and the other is not. One of the two always lies, and the other always tells the truth, but we don't know whether John is the liar or the truth teller. You meet both brothers together, and you wish to find out which one is John. You are allowed to ask either one of them a three-word question. What question will do the trick?

Problem 4. Suppose in the last problem you are not interested in which brother is John but only in whether John is the truthful brother or the brother who lies. What three-word question will enable you to find out?

Problem 5. I once met these two brothers on the street. I had two distinct questions in mind. I knew that if I asked the first question,

I would then know the correct answer to the second question, whereas if I asked the second question, I would then know the correct answer to the first question. Can you supply two such questions?

65

A Gödelian Machine. Of the many mathematical machines I have used to illustrate Gödel's famous proof, the following is the simplest.

The machine prints out various expressions composed of four symbols: *P,N,R, ∗*. An expression is called *printable* if the machine can print it. A *sentence* is any expression of one of the four forms: (1) P∗X; (2) NP∗X; (3) PR∗X; and (4) NPR∗X, where X is any expression built from the four symbols. Each sentence is interpreted as follows: (1) P∗X is called *true* if and only if X is printable; (2) NP∗X is called *true* if and only if X is not printable (N is an abbreviation of *not*, just as P is an abbreviation of *printable*); (3) PR∗X is called *true* if and only if XX is printable (XX is called the *repeat* of X, hence the letter *R*); and (4) NPR∗X is called *true* if and only if XX is not printable.

We are given that the machine is completely accurate, that is, every sentence printed by the machine is a true sentence. The problem is to find a true sentence that the machine cannot print! (The solution to this problem and a discussion are given in §67.)

66

Solutions to the Puzzles of §64. For Problem 1: A question that works is, "Are you Jack?" and it is the only three-word question I can think of that does work!

Jack and William would both answer *no* to that question (Jack because he lies and William because he is truthful). John would answer *yes* (because John lies). Therefore, if you get *yes* for an answer, you will know that he is John, and if you get *no* for an answer, you will know that he is not John.

As for Problem 2: The very same question works! Only now a *yes* answer indicates that he is not John, and a *no* answer indicates that he is John.

Now, the solution to Problem 3: This is more subtle. The question, "Are you John?" is useless. Whatever answer you get could be the truth or could be a lie. A question whose correct answer you already know (such as, "Is water wet?") is no good. You will then know whether the one addressed is truthful or not, but you won't know whether or not he is John. The question, "Are you truthful?" is no good. You will get the answer *yes* from both brothers.

A question that does work is, "Is John truthful?" John would certainly claim that John is truthful (regardless of whether or not John is truthful). John's brother would claim that John is not truthful (correctly if John's brother is truthful and falsely if John's brother lies). So, a *yes* answer indicates that the one addressed is John. A *no* answer indicates that he is not John.

Another three-word question that works is, "Does John lie?" A *yes* answer to that question indicates that the one addressed is not John. A *no* answer indicates that he is John.

As for Problem 4: To find out whether John is truthful, the question, "Are you John?" now works! Suppose you get *yes* for an answer. If the speaker is truthful, then he really is John, in which case John is truthful. If the speaker is lying, then he is not John, hence John must be the truthful brother. So, whether the speaker is lying or telling the truth, a *yes* answer indicates that John is truthful. We leave it to you to verify that a *no* answer indicates that John is not truthful, regardless of whether the speaker is lying or telling the truth.

There is a pretty symmetry between the last two problems. To find out whether the one addressed is John, you ask him whether John is truthful, whereas if you want to find out whether John is truthful, you ask him whether he is John. This provides a solution to Problem 5: One question is, "Is John truthful?" The other question is, "Are you John?" Asking either question will enable you to know the correct answer, not of the question you ask, but of the other question.

67

Solution to the Gödelian Machine Puzzle. The sentence NPR*NPR* says that the repeat of NPR* is not printable (i.e., the sentence is true if and only if the repeat of NPR* is not printable). But the repeat of NPR* is the very sentence NPR*NPR*! So this sentence is true if and only if it is not printable. If the sentence is false, then it *is* printable (since the sentence says that it isn't), which would mean that the machine is capable of printing a false sentence. But we are given that the machine is accurate and never prints false sentences. So it must be that the sentence is true, hence what it says is really the case, which means that it is not printable. And so the sentence NPR*NPR* must be true, but the machine cannot print it.

The philosopher J. Michael Dunn once showed the above problem to his son, Jon. After the boy understood it, he said to his father, "One thing I would like to know. Why would anybody want to construct such a machine?" The father thought for a moment and replied, "Well, it would be nice if we could have an accurate machine that could print out all true facts about the world. But it seems that such a machine is not possible."

The whole point, of course, is that no accurate machine can possibly print a sentence that says that the machine cannot print it. In the very process of printing it the machine would falsify it! The situation is reminiscent of the scene in *Romeo and Juliet* in which the nurse comes running to Juliet and says, "I have no breath." Juliet replies, "How can you have no breath when you have breath left to say 'I have no breath'?"

68

I started this chapter with self-annihilating sentences, and it seems only fitting to end with what might aptly be called a self-annihilating conversation. The dialogue is not original. It was devised by Goodwin Sammel, a musician I first met in my University of Chicago days who has always taken an interest in mathematical matters. When he first heard about Gödel's theorem he came up with this exchange:

A: It's true!

B: It's not!

A: Yes, it is!

B: It couldn't be!

A: It *is* true!

B: Prove it!

A: Oh, it can't be proved, but nevertheless it's true.

B: Now, just a minute: How can you say it's true if it can't be proved?

A: Oh, there are certain things that are true even though they can't be proved.

B: That's not true!

A: Yes, it is; Gödel *proved* that there are certain things that are true but that cannot be proved.

B: That's not true!

A: It certainly is!

B: It couldn't be, and even if it *were* true, it could never be proved!

Notes

1. Raymond Smullyan, *What Is the Name of This Book?* (Englewood Cliffs, N.J.: Prentice-Hall, 1978), p. 208.

2. Sigmund Freud, *The Future of an Illusion* (Third edition, The International Psycho-Analytical Library #15, translated by W. D. Robson-Scott, The Hogarth Press, 37, Mecklenburgh Square, London, and the Institute of Psycho-Analysis, 1943).

3. Ambrose Bierce, *The Devil's Dictionary* (New York: Hill & Wang, 1957).

4. Douglas Hofstadter and Daniel Dennett, *The Mind's I* (New York: Basic Books, 1981).

4

A Query

I have one Catholic friend with whom I have had many a lively discussion. I once asked him which of the following two types, both of which act extremely well by Christian standards, he considered the better: The first type is sympathetic and kind by nature and acts lovingly toward his neighbor simply because he feels like it; he does not have to force himself to do so. He does not act the way he does because of any moral principle nor out of obedience to any commandments; he simply *feels* like acting as he does. By contrast, the second type, though he in fact behaves as well as the first, does not do so spontaneously but *forces* himself to do so because he believes it is the right thing to do. I asked my friend which type was the better. After thinking for a moment, he replied, "The first one sounds to me as if he is more in a state of grace, but the second one's actions have more salvation value."

An apparently similar viewpoint appears in Meister Eckhart's ninth talk of instructions, titled "How the Inclination to Sin Is Always Beneficial."[1]

Know that the impulse to wrong is never without use and benefit to the just person. Let us notice that there are two sorts of people involved. One is so constituted that he has little or no impulse to do wrong, whereas the other is often strongly tempted. His outward self is easily swayed by whatever is at hand—swayed to anger, pride, sensuality or whatever, but his better nature, his higher self, remains unmoved and will do no wrong, or be angry, or sin in any way. He therefore fights hard against whichever vice is most natural to him, as people must who are by nature choleric, proud, or otherwise weak and who will not commit the sin to which they are liable. These people are more to be praised than the first kind. Their reward is also greater and their virtue of much higher rank. For the perfection of virtue comes of struggle, or, as St. Paul says, "Virtue is made perfect in weakness."

The impulse to sin is not sin but to consent to sin, to give way to anger, is indeed sin. Surely, if a person could wish such a thing, he would not wish to be rid of the impulse to sin, for without it he would be uncertain of everything he did, doubtful about what to do, and he would miss the honor and reward of struggle and victory. Because of the impulse to evil and the excitement of it, both virtue and its rewards are in travail born. The impulse to wrong makes us the more diligent in the exercise of virtue, driving us to it with a strong hand, like a hard taskmaster, forcing us to take shelter in doing well. The weaker one is, the more he is warned to strength and self-conquest; for virtue, like vice, is a matter of the will.

Despite my general fondness for mystic writers, there are several things about the above passage that I find extremely disturbing. For one thing, certain parts are downright illogical! Is it really true that if a person had no impulse to sin he would be uncertain of everything he did and doubtful about what to do? Are saints and angels uncertain and doubtful about what to do? Aren't there other more useful and interesting things with which to occupy one's time than "exerting noble efforts to overcome one's sinful impulses"?

I think that Benjamin Franklin really hit the nail on the head in his astute essay titled "Self-Denial Not the Essence of Virtue."[2] He begins the essay as follows:

It is commonly asserted, that without self-denial there is no virtue, and that the greater the self-denial the greater the virtue.

If it were said, that he who cannot deny himself any thing he inclines to, though he knows it will be to his hurt, has not the virtue of resolution or fortitude, it would be intelligible enough; but, as it stands, it seems obscure or erroneous.

Let us consider some of the virtues singly.

If a man has no inclination to wrong people in his dealings, if he feels no temptation to it, and therefore never does it, can it be said that he is not a just man? If he is a just man, has he not the virtue of justice?

If to a certain man idle diversions have nothing in them that is tempting, and therefore he never relaxes his application to business for their sake, is he not an industrious man? Or has he not the virtue of industry?

I might in like manner instance in all the rest of the virtues; but, to make the thing short, as it is certain that the more we strive against the temptation to any vice, and practice the contrary virtue, the weaker will that temptation be, and the stronger will be that habit, till at length the temptation has no force, or entirely vanishes; does it follow from thence, that in our endeavors to overcome vice we grow continually less virtuous, till at length we have no virtue at all?

Franklin then further elaborates his point. He ends the essay with the following paragraph:

The truth is, that temperance, justice, charity &c. are virtues, whether practiced with, or against our inclinations, and the man, who practices them, merits our love and esteem; and self-denial is neither good nor bad, but as it is applied. He that denies a vicious inclination, is virtuous in proportion to his resolution; *but the most perfect virtue is above all temptation* [emphasis added]; such as the virtue of the saints in heaven; and he, who does a foolish, indecent, or wicked thing, merely because it is contrary to his inclination (like some mad enthusiasts I have read of, who ran about naked, under the notion of taking up the cross), is not practicing the reasonable science of virtue, but is a lunatic.

Notes

1.   Meister Eckhart, "How the Inclination to Sin Is Always Beneficial." In *Meister Eckhart, A Modern Translation*, Raymond Bernard Blakney (New York and London: Harper and Brothers, 1941), p. 12.

2.   Benjamin Franklin, "Self Denial Not the Essence of Virtue." In *Pennsylvania Gazette* (February 18, 1734).

3

Three Fantasies

5

Simplicus and the Tree— An Open Air Symposium

SIMPLICUS: I am enjoying this tree.

FIRST PHILOSOPHER: No, it is not the tree you are enjoying but the *light* from the tree. It is not the tree that is directly influencing your sense organs but only its reflected light. Therefore, you are enjoying the *light* of the tree.

SECOND PHILOSOPHER: No, no, it is not the *light* he is enjoying but rather the image the light forms on his retina.

THIRD PHILOSOPHER: This is superficial physiology! The retinal image could not affect him if his optic nerves were dead, and his optic nerves are but part of his brain and nervous system. Therefore, what he is really enjoying is the neural activities of his entire brain and nervous system.

FOURTH PHILOSOPHER: I think that it is misleading to say that he is enjoying this physiological activity; I would instead say that his enjoyment of the tree *is* this physiological activity.

CARTESIAN: All of you are wrong! His physiological process is only the material counterpart of an inner mental or spiritual process; it is this spiritual soul-activity that he is enjoying.

IDEALIST: Except that the evidence for what you call the material counterpart of this mental process is, as I have demonstrated, wholly inconclusive. I don't believe in the existence of this "tree." The proper way to phrase it, therefore, is that the mind or soul of Simplicus is enjoying his idea of the tree.

IDEALISTIC MYSTIC: I deny the existence of individual minds. There is no such thing as the mind of Simplicus! There is only one universal mind, called the *world soul, cosmic consciousness, God, the Absolute,* or whatever, and it is this universal or absolute mind that is enjoying the tree, which exists as one of its ideas.

REALISTIC MYSTIC:[1]   The viewpoint of my friend the idealistic mystic is about the opposite end of the spectrum from mine, and yet it comes closer to mine—in the sense of abstract identity or isomorphism—than any other yet expressed.

I start from the premise that reality is purely material. All that exists is the material universe, which for certain purposes *might* be broken down into material particles and their motions. Simplicus's enjoyment of the tree is therefore indeed an event or set of events in the nervous system of the body of Simplicus. This viewpoint, though correct, seems to me only partial. Simplicus is not a closed physical system. When Simplicus has a thought, the particles of the cerebrum of Simplicus move not only in relation to each other but also in relation to every particle of the entire universe. I therefore wish to look upon the thoughts of Simplicus as an activity of the universe as a whole. Thus, instead of saying that it is Simplicus enjoying the tree, I would say it is the whole physical universe that is enjoying the tree.

FIRST LOGICAL POSITIVIST: I wonder if the viewpoints of the idealistic and realistic mystics really differ in content or merely in terminology. How do I know that when the first says *material* and the second *mental,* or the first *physical universe* and the second *universal mind,* that they are not merely using different words to denote the same thing?

SECOND LOGICAL POSITIVIST: I doubt that this question itself has any cognitive content. How in principle could one verify whether they mean the same or different things?

PHYSICIST: This type of question is out of my domain. I would like to return to the viewpoint of the realistic mystic. Naturally, this viewpoint interests me in that it uses the terminology of science. It has, however, one serious weakness that borders on the downright ridiculous. All right, he may translate the statement, "Simplicus enjoys the tree," to, "The universe enjoys the tree." Now suppose someone else—say, Complicus—comes along and claims to enjoy the tree. Again the mystic translates the statement, "Complicus enjoys the tree," to, "The universe enjoys the tree." So when the realistic mystic says, "The universe is enjoying the tree," how can I possibly know whether it is Simplicus, Complicus, or someone else—or for that matter some dog—who is enjoying the tree?

REALISTIC MYSTIC: I should like first to remark that by profession I am also a physicist. Now certainly, when I do physics or am engaged in daily life activities I would use the more descriptive and specific terminology, "Simplicus is enjoying the tree," or "Complicus is enjoying the tree," rather than, "The universe is enjoying the tree." Just because I regard Simplicus's enjoyment of the tree and Complicus's enjoyment of the tree as special cases of the universe enjoying the tree does not mean that I regard them as identical events. So of course when it is necessary to be more specific (which is most of the time), then I *am* specific. But for other purposes—which might be termed *spiritual, mystical,* or *religious*—I believe it more fruitful to regard these particular events as an activity of the universe as a whole.

CHRISTIAN THEOLOGIAN: Since you brought up the word *religion,* may I ask whether you honestly believe it possible to incorporate into your purely materialistic framework the fundamental ideas of religion like God, soul, divine purpose, and reward and punishment? If all that exists is matter, what could it possibly mean for my soul to be immortal, and how could I anticipate punishment or fear reward?

PSYCHIATRIST: I think you meant *fear punishment* and *anticipate reward.*

REALISTIC MYSTIC *(amused):*   I certainly can incorporate all these ideas into a purely materialistic framework. By *God*, I of course mean the entire universe. The word *soul* or *mind* I happen to use most frequently. I am not a dualist in that I do not regard soul as a substance, as I do matter. Rather, *soul* for me is a combination of memories and dispositions. If I have a beautiful recording of a musical composition and the record should fall and break, it is no tragedy, providing I can get another copy. What is important about a particular record is not its particular atoms but rather the pattern that has been impressed upon it. It is this pattern that might well be called the soul of the record—its propensity to reembody the musical idea. Likewise, a man's soul consists of his memories and behavioral propensities. In this sense, it seems perfectly natural to also regard the universe as having a soul, which is its pattern. If you would prefer me to use the word *God* to mean this *soul* or *pattern* rather than its concrete embodiment, I would have no objection. After all, suppose if by magic each atom in the universe were replaced by an identical particle, or if this is empirically meaningless, suppose that all basic particles of the universe were thoroughly reshuffled but end in a pattern identical with the present one. I would hardly say that the universe had undergone any significant change; it would still have the same pattern or soul. I do, however, disagree with the idealist or dualist who thinks of soul as a substance, unless (is it possible?) he would allow a pattern to be called a substance. In this case, our difference is not metaphysical at all but purely terminological. This suggests the following thoughts on dualism versus monism.

I can see some sense in distinguishing a particular body from its pattern if there exists at least one other body with the same pattern. But since there is only one universe, it is hard to understand the difference between the universe and its pattern. This would mean that we can distinguish the mind of a man from the body of a man, or the mind of a dog from the body of a dog, but in the limiting case of God, the body of God might be the same as the mind of God. Stated in the language of the mathematician, matter and mind may be different locally but the same globally.

To return, however, to the theologian's second question, I first wish to remark that I have always found it exceedingly odd that many scientists—even those in the computer science field—are perfectly willing to use terms like *thinking, purpose, reward,* and *punishment* for both humans and computing machines but absolutely balk at the idea of applying these so-called anthropomorphic terms to the universe as a whole. Of course the universe is mainly inorganic, but so is a computer! I greatly fear that this is a sad reflection of the continuing egocentricity of mankind. Descartes thought that humans think but dogs do not. (His dog, however, thought otherwise!) People today who believe that humans think usually believe that dogs think as well. With plant life, people are doubtful, and when it comes to inorganic matter, there most people really draw the line! As if there is some social hierarchy— stones, plants, dogs, people! One calls stones *dead* and *inert.* Of course stones are dead in the purely biological sense. The word *inert* is, however, misleading, considering the fantastically rich life and activities of a stone's inner molecular structure. But to balk at applying anthropomorphic terms to the whole universe, whose structure is so vast and complex compared with any person or computer—indeed, it *includes* all people and computers—to refuse this terminology for the universe as a whole strikes me as totally unwarranted. No, I certainly have every whit as much right to apply such terms as *thinking, feeling,* and *planning* to the universe as a whole as I do to entities that are only parts of the universe. Let the tough-minded think of these terms as purely operational. My so-called mysticism consists not of any metaphysical meaning attached to this terminology but purely of my *emotional* responses that such terminology tends to engender. At any rate, in this terminology, it of course makes sense to refer to the universe as having a purpose or as punishing or rewarding us for our actions. For example, I would say that the universe punishes a baby—for its ultimate good—for sticking its hand into a fire.

As to survival after death, I have no definite opinion regarding it. In principle, there is no a priori reason why after my bodily death memories of my life may not remain in the universe and even eventuate in a reembodiment, and in principle it could be possible that I could then be rewarded or punished for my present behavior. But this is wholly speculative.

There is one aspect of religion—at least Western religion—that the theologian did not mention and that might be a bit more of a problem to incorporate into a purely materialistic framework. That is the notion that God created the universe. For this, I would need to retract my earlier statement that perhaps the mind of God is the same as the body of God. If I am allowed to distinguish the concrete universe from its abstract pattern or form, then I can certainly say that the pattern of the universe existed as a logical possibility before the universe, or better still, exists outside of time altogether. The creation of the universe by God can then simply mean the concrete embodiment of this pattern. This view may not be too far from the meaning of, "In the beginning was the Word."

CHRISTIAN THEOLOGIAN: Are you seriously advocating recasting all religion into a purely materialistic framework?

REALISTIC MYSTIC: Not at all! It is all the same to me whether religion is cast into a purely materialistic or a purely idealistic or a dualistic framework. I do not advocate any one more than any other. Personally, I happen to think in materialistic terms, though I am not a nominalist since my ontology does indeed include abstract entities like forms and patterns. My main point now is not that religion *should* be cast in materialist terms but only that it *can* be. My whole claim is that the kernel of religion—that part of religion that is of chief ethical and psychological significance—is totally neutral with respect to any metaphysical foundations.

FIRST EPISTEMOLOGIST: Enough theology! Let us come to a *practical* question. How does Simplicus *know* that he is enjoying the tree?

SECOND EPISTEMOLOGIST: Simplicus never said that he *knew* that he was enjoying the tree but only that he *was* enjoying the tree.

FIRST EPISTEMOLOGIST: But *does* Simplicus know that he is enjoying the tree?

SECOND EPISTEMOLOGIST: I don't know.

FIRST EPISTEMOLOGIST: How do you know you don't know?

SECOND EPISTEMOLOGIST: I don't.

FIRST EPISTEMOLOGIST: Then how do I know that Simplicus does know that he is enjoying the tree? For all I know, maybe he doesn't know that he is enjoying the tree.

RABBI: All right, so maybe he doesn't know he is enjoying the tree!

FIRST MEANY:[2]   I don't believe in fact that Simplicus *is* enjoying the tree!

SECOND MEANY: Exactly! The very fact that he says he is only proves that he isn't.

THIRD MEANY: Yeah, if he were really enjoying it, he would not have to say he was. When someone really enjoys something, he does not have to broadcast it to the world. When Simplicus says, "I am enjoying this tree," methinks the gentleman doth protest too much.

MORALIST: No, no, Simplicus obviously *is* enjoying the tree—just look at his face! What I question is whether he has the *right* to enjoy the tree!

SECOND MORALIST: Exactly! With all the starvation, misery, and social injustice in the world, what the hell is Simplicus doing there sitting under the tree when he should be out in the world helping matters?

ZEN MASTER: All this metaphysics, theology, epistemology, and ethics is certainly of interest, but do any of you here really think you have cast the faintest ray of light on the meaning of Simplicus's original statement? When Simplicus says, "I am enjoying the tree," it means nothing more or less than that Simplicus is enjoying the tree.[3] All of you have made the tacit but wholly unwarranted assumption that this statement expresses a relation between some subject and some object. Everyone has been discussing who has done what to whom, that is, what it was that was enjoyed and who it really was that was doing the enjoying. Can't you simply accept Simplicus's enjoyment of the tree as an event that is nonanalyzable? Every sentence when translated loses its essential meaning. The sentence, "Simplicus is enjoying the tree," simply means that Simplicus is enjoying the tree.

ZEN STUDENT: My master is right! The simple truth is that there is no Simplicus to enjoy and no tree to be enjoyed. In reality, there is just this one unanalyzable event of Simplicus enjoying the tree. This event is not a relation but just an occurrence in the great void!

ZEN MASTER *(slugging the novice):*   Oh, you great little snit! You the "enlightened one" know all about simple truth, reality, and the great void, don't you? And it is up to you to enlighten all these "poor ignorant" people with your great newfound wisdom, eh?

ZEN STUDENT: But master, how else can I get these people to understand the *essence* of Simplicus's statement?

ZEN MASTER *(giving him another blow):*   By holding your tongue! Damn it all, how many times must I tell you that there is no *essence* to be understood! If these people can't understand the perfectly plain statement, "I am enjoying this tree," then perhaps a few blows with my stick might enlighten them!

SECOND ZEN MASTER: I think everyone here should be given a blow with the stick regardless of whether he understands Simplicus's statement or not.

THIRD ZEN MASTER: Better still, I think everyone should be given a nonblow with a nonstick.

MORALIST *(in great alarm):*   This psychotic conversation has gone far enough! Unless this stops immediately, *and I mean immediately,* I will get very angry, and when I get angry, I can become *very* unpleasant!

SIMPLICUS: But the tree is so beautiful, why shouldn't I enjoy it?

Notes

1. I do not know if there is a school of thought called *realistic mysticism;* if not, let this be the beginning of one.

2. I obtained the term *meany* from the Beatles's movie *Yellow Submarine,* in which the villains were called *blue meanies.*

3. Shades of Alfred Tarski!

6

An Epistemological Nightmare

Scene 1. Frank is in the office of an eye doctor. The doctor holds up a book and asks, "What color is it?" Frank answers, "Red." The doctor says, "Aha, just as I thought! Your whole color mechanism has gone out of kilter. But fortunately your condition is curable, and I will have you in perfect shape in a couple of weeks."

Scene 2 (a few weeks later). Frank is in the laboratory of an experimental epistemologist. *(You will soon find out what that means!)* The epistemologist holds up a book and also asks, "What color is it?" Now, Frank has been earlier dismissed by the eye doctor as "cured," but he is now of a very analytical and cautious temperament and will not make any statement that can possibly be refuted. So Frank answers, "It seems red to me."

EPISTEMOLOGIST: Wrong!

FRANK: I don't think you heard what I said. I merely said that it *seems* red to me.

EPISTEMOLOGIST: I heard you, and you were wrong.

FRANK: Let me get this clear; do you mean that I was wrong that this book *is* red or that I was wrong that it *seems* red to me?

EPISTEMOLOGIST: I obviously couldn't have meant that you were wrong that it *is* red since you did not say that it is red. All you said was that it *seems* red to you, and it is *this* statement that is wrong.

FRANK: But you can't say that the statement, "It *seems* red to me," is wrong.

EPISTEMOLOGIST: If I *can't* say it, how come I did?

FRANK: I mean you can't *mean* it.

EPISTEMOLOGIST: Why not?

FRANK: But surely *I* know what color the book *seems* to me!

EPISTEMOLOGIST: Again you are wrong.

FRANK: But nobody knows better than I how things seem to *me*.

EPISTEMOLOGIST: I am sorry, but again you are wrong.

FRANK: But who knows better than I?

EPISTEMOLOGIST: I do.

FRANK: But how could you have access to my private mental states?

EPISTEMOLOGIST: Private mental states! Metaphysical hogwash! Look, I am a *practical* epistemologist. Metaphysical problems about mind versus matter arise only from epistemological confusions. Epistemology is the true foundation of philosophy, but the trouble with all past epistemologists is that they have been using wholly theoretical methods, and much of their discussion degenerates into mere word games. While other epistemologists have been solemnly arguing such questions as whether a man can be wrong when he asserts that he believes such and such, I have discovered how to settle such questions *experimentally*.

FRANK: How could you possibly decide such things empirically?

EPISTEMOLOGIST: By reading a person's thoughts directly.

FRANK: You mean you are telepathic?

EPISTEMOLOGIST: Of course not. I simply did the one obvious thing that should be done: I have constructed a brain-reading machine—

known technically as a *cerebrescope*—that is operative right now in this room and is scanning every nerve cell in your brain. I thus can read your every sensation and thought, and it is a simple objective truth that this book does *not* seem red to you.

FRANK *(thoroughly subdued):* Goodness gracious, I really could have sworn that the book seemed red to me; it sure *seems* that it seems red to me!

EPISTEMOLOGIST: I'm sorry, but you are wrong again.

FRANK: Really? It doesn't even *seem* that it seems red to me? It sure *seems* that it seems that it seems red to me!

EPISTEMOLOGIST: Wrong again! And no matter how many times you reiterate the phrase *it seems that* and follow it by *the book is red,* you will be wrong.

FRANK: This is fantastic! Suppose instead of the phrase *it seems that,* I said *I believe that.* So let us start again at ground level. I retract the statement, "It seems red to me," and instead I assert, "I *believe* that this book is red." Is this statement true or false?

EPISTEMOLOGIST: Just a moment while I scan the dials of the brain-reading machine—no, your statement is false.

FRANK: What about, "I believe that I believe that the book is red"?

EPISTEMOLOGIST *(consulting his dials):* Also false. And again, no matter how many times you reiterate *I believe,* all these belief sentences are false.

FRANK: Well, this has been a most enlightening experience. You must admit, however, that it is a *little* hard on me to realize that I am entertaining infinitely many erroneous beliefs!

EPISTEMOLOGIST: Why do you say that your beliefs are erroneous?

FRANK: But you have been telling me this all the while!

EPISTEMOLOGIST: I most certainly have not!

FRANK: Good God, I was prepared to admit all my errors and now you tell me that my beliefs are *not* errors; what are you trying to do drive me crazy?

EPISTEMOLOGIST: Hey, take it easy! Please try to recall: When did I say or imply that any of your beliefs are erroneous?

FRANK: Just simply recall the infinite sequence of sentences: (1) I believe that this book is red; (2) I believe that I believe that this book is red; and so forth. You told me that every one of those statements is false.

EPISTEMOLOGIST: True.

FRANK: Then how can you consistently maintain that my *beliefs* in all these false statements are not erroneous?

EPISTEMOLOGIST: Because, as I told you, you don't believe any of them.

FRANK: I think I see, yet I am not absolutely sure.

EPISTEMOLOGIST: Look, let me put it another way. Don't you see that the very falsity of each of the statements that you assert *saves* you from an erroneous belief in the preceding one? The first statement is, as I told you, false. Very well! Now the second statement simply says that you believe the first statement. If the second statement were *true*, then you would believe the first statement, and hence your belief about the first statement would indeed be in error. But fortunately the second statement is false, so you don't really believe the first statement; your belief in the first statement is therefore not in error. Thus, the falsity of the second statement implies that you do *not* have an erroneous belief about the first; the falsity of the third likewise saves you from an erroneous belief about the second; and so forth.

FRANK: Now I see perfectly! So none of my *beliefs* was erroneous, only the statements were erroneous.

EPISTEMOLOGIST: Exactly.

FRANK: Most remarkable! Incidentally, what color is the book really?

EPISTEMOLOGIST: It is red.

FRANK: What!

EPISTEMOLOGIST: Exactly! Of course the book is red. What's the matter with you, don't you have eyes?

FRANK: But didn't I in effect keep saying that the book is red all along?

EPISTEMOLOGIST: Of course not! You kept saying it *seems* red to you, it *seems* that it seems red to you, you *believe* it is red, you *believe* that you believe it is red, and so forth. Not once did you say that it *is* red. When I asked you originally, "What color is the book?" if you had simply answered, "Red," this whole painful discussion would have been avoided.

Scene 3. Frank comes back several months later to the laboratory of the epistemologist.

EPISTEMOLOGIST: How delightful to see you! Please sit down.

FRANK *(seated):* I have been thinking much of our last discussion, and there is much I wish to clear up. To begin with, I discovered an inconsistency in some of the things you said.

EPISTEMOLOGIST: Delightful! I love inconsistencies. Pray tell!

FRANK: Well, you claimed that although my belief sentences were false, I did not have any actual *beliefs* that are false. If you had not admitted that the book actually is red, you would have been consistent. But your very admission that the book *is* red leads to an inconsistency.

EPISTEMOLOGIST: How so?

FRANK: Look, as you correctly pointed out, in each of my belief sentences, "I believe that it is red," "I believe that I believe that it is red," and so forth, the falsity of each one other than the first saves me from an erroneous belief in the preceding one. You neglected, however, to take into consideration the first sentence itself! The falsity of the first sentence, "I believe that it is red," in conjunction with the fact that it *is* red, *does* imply that I have a false belief.

EPISTEMOLOGIST: I don't see why.

FRANK: It is obvious! Since the sentence, "I believe it is red," is false, then I in fact believe it is not red, and since it really is red, then I *do* have a false belief. So there!

EPISTEMOLOGIST *(disappointed):* I am sorry, but your proof obviously fails. Of course the falsity of the fact that you believe it is red implies that you *don't* believe it is red. But this does not mean that you believe it is *not* red!

FRANK: But obviously I know that either it is red or it isn't, so if I don't believe that it is, then I must believe that it isn't.

EPISTEMOLOGIST: Not at all. I believe that either Jupiter has life or it doesn't. But I neither believe that it does nor do I believe that it doesn't. I have no evidence one way or the other.

FRANK: I guess you are right. But let us come to more important matters. I honestly find it impossible that I can be in error concerning my own beliefs.

EPISTEMOLOGIST: Must we go through this again? I have already patiently explained to you that you (in the sense of your beliefs, not your statements) are *not* in error.

FRANK: Oh, all right then, I simply do not believe that even the *statements* are in error. Yes, according to the machine, they are in error, but why should I trust the machine?

EPISTEMOLOGIST: Whoever said that you should trust the machine?

FRANK: Well, *should* I trust the machine?

EPISTEMOLOGIST: That question involving the word *should* is out of my domain. However, if you like, I can refer you to a colleague who is an excellent moralist—he may be able to answer this for you.

FRANK: Oh, come on now, I obviously didn't mean *should* in a moralistic sense. I simply meant, "Do I have any evidence that this machine is reliable?"

EPISTEMOLOGIST: Well, do you?

FRANK: Don't ask *me!* What I mean is, Should *you* trust the machine?

EPISTEMOLOGIST: *Should* I trust it? I have no idea, and I couldn't care less what I *should* do.

FRANK: Oh, your moralistic hang-up again. I mean, Do *you* have evidence that the machine is reliable?

EPISTEMOLOGIST: Well of course!

FRANK: Then let us get down to brass tacks. What is your evidence?

EPISTEMOLOGIST: You hardly can expect that I can answer this question for you in an hour, a day, or even a week. If you wish to study this machine with me, we can do so, but I assure you that this is a matter of several years. At the end of that time, however, you would certainly not have the slightest doubts about the reliability of the machine.

FRANK: Well, possibly I could believe that it is reliable in the sense that its measurements are accurate, but then I would doubt that what it actually measures is very significant. It seems that all it measures is one's physiological states and activities.

EPISTEMOLOGIST: But of course, what else would you expect it to measure?

FRANK: I doubt that it measures my psychological states, my actual *beliefs*.

EPISTEMOLOGIST: Are we back to that again? The machine *does* measure those physiological states and processes, which you call psychological states, beliefs, sensations, and so forth.

FRANK: At this point, I am becoming convinced that our entire difference is purely semantical. All right, I will grant that your machine does correctly measure beliefs in *your* sense of the word *belief*, but I don't believe that it can possibly measure beliefs in *my* sense of the word. In other words, I claim that our entire deadlock is simply the result of our meaning different things by the word *belief*.

EPISTEMOLOGIST: Fortunately, the correctness of your claim can be experimentally decided. It so happens that I now have two brain-reading machines in my office, so I now direct one to *your* brain to find out what *you* mean by *belief* and the other to my own brain to find out what *I* mean by *belief,* and I shall compare the two readings. Nope, I'm sorry, but it turns out that we mean *exactly* the same thing by the word *belief.*

FRANK: Oh, hang your machine! Do *you* believe we mean the same thing by the word *belief?*

EPISTEMOLOGIST: Do *I* believe it? Just a moment while I check with the machine. Yes, it turns out that I do believe it.

FRANK: My goodness, do you mean to say that you can't even tell me what *you* believe without consulting the machine?

EPISTEMOLOGIST: Of course not.

FRANK: But most people when asked what they believe simply *tell* you. Why do you, to find out your beliefs, go through the fantastically roundabout process of directing a brain-reading machine to your own brain and then finding out what you believe on the basis of the machine's readings?

EPISTEMOLOGIST: What other scientific, objective way is there of finding out what I believe?

FRANK: Oh come now, why don't you just ask yourself?

EPISTEMOLOGIST *(sadly):* It doesn't work. Whenever I ask myself what I believe, I never get any answer!

FRANK: Well, why don't you just *state* what you believe?

EPISTEMOLOGIST: How can I state what I believe before I know what I believe?

FRANK: Oh, to hell with your *knowledge* of what you believe; surely you have some *idea* or *belief* as to what you believe, don't you?

EPISTEMOLOGIST: Of course I have such a belief. But how do I find out what this belief is?

FRANK: I am afraid we are getting into another infinite regression. Look, at this point I am honestly beginning to wonder whether you may be going crazy.

EPISTEMOLOGIST: Let me consult the machine. Yes, it turns out that I may be going crazy.

FRANK: Good God, man, doesn't this frighten you?

EPISTEMOLOGIST: Let me check! Yes, it turns out that it does frighten me.

FRANK: Oh please, can't you forget this damned machine and just tell me whether you are frightened or not?

EPISTEMOLOGIST: I just told you that I am. However, I only learned of this from the machine.

FRANK: I can see that it is utterly hopeless to wean you away from the machine. Very well, then, let us play along with the machine some more. Why don't you ask the machine whether your sanity can be saved?

EPISTEMOLOGIST: Good idea! Yes, it turns out that it can be saved.

FRANK: And how can it be saved?

EPISTEMOLOGIST: I don't know, I haven't asked the machine.

FRANK: Well, for God's sake, ask it!

EPISTEMOLOGIST: Good idea. It turns out that . . .

FRANK: It turns out what?

EPISTEMOLOGIST: It turns out that . . .

FRANK: Come on now, it turns out what?

EPISTEMOLOGIST: This is the most fantastic thing I have ever come across! According to the machine, the best thing I can do is to cease to trust the machine!

FRANK: Good! What will you do about it?

EPISTEMOLOGIST: How do I know what I *will* do about it; I can't read the future!

FRANK: I mean, What do you *presently* intend to do about it?

EPISTEMOLOGIST: Good question, let me consult the machine. According to the machine, my present intentions are in complete conflict. And I can see why! I am caught in a terrible paradox! If the machine is trustworthy, then I had better accept its suggestion to distrust it. But if I distrust it, then I must also distrust its suggestion to distrust it, so I am really in a total quandary.

FRANK: Look, I know someone who I think might really be of help in this problem. I shall leave you for a while to consult him. Until then, *au revoir!*

Scene 4 (later in the day at a psychiatrist's office).

FRANK: Doctor, I am terribly worried about a friend of mine. He calls himself an *experimental epistemologist.*

DOCTOR: Oh, the experimental epistemologist. There is only one in the world. I know him well!

FRANK: That is a relief. But do you realize that he has constructed a brain-reading device that he now directs to his own brain, and whenever one asks him what he thinks, believes, feels, fears, and so forth, he has to first consult the machine before answering? Don't you think this is pretty serious?

DOCTOR: Not as serious as it might seem. My prognosis for him is actually quite good.

FRANK: Well, if you are a friend of his, couldn't you sort of keep an eye on him?

DOCTOR: I do see him quite frequently, and I do observe him, but I don't think that he can be helped by so-called psychiatric treatment. His problem is an unusual one and is the sort that has to work itself out. And I believe it will.

FRANK: Well, I hope your optimism is justified. At any rate, I sure think that *I* need some help at this point!

DOCTOR: How so?

FRANK: My experiences with the epistemologist have been thoroughly unnerving! At this point, I wonder if *I* may be going crazy; I can't even have confidence in how things *appear* to me. I think maybe *you* could be helpful here.

DOCTOR: I would be happy to help but cannot for awhile. For the next three months, I am unbelievably overloaded with work. After that, I unfortunately must go on a three-month vacation. So in six months, come back and we can talk this over.

Scene 5 (same office, six months later).

DOCTOR: Before we go into your problems, you will be happy to hear that your friend the epistemologist is now completely recovered.

FRANK: Marvelous! How did it happen?

DOCTOR: Almost, as it were, by a stroke of fate—and yet his very mental activities were, so to speak, part of the "fate." What happened was this. For months after you last saw him, he went around worrying, Should he trust the machine, shouldn't he trust the machine, should he, shouldn't he, should he, shouldn't he? (He decided to use the word *should* in your empirical sense.) He got nowhere! So he then decided to formalize the whole argument. He reviewed his study of symbolic logic, took the axioms of first order logic, and added as nonlogical axioms certain relevant facts about the machine. Of course, the resulting system was inconsistent—he formally proved that he should trust the machine if and only if he shouldn't and hence that he both should and should not trust the machine. Now, as you may know, in a system based on classical logic (which is the logic he used), if one can prove so much as a single contradictory proposition, then one can prove any proposition, hence the whole system breaks down. So he decided to use a logic close to what is known as *minimal logic* that is weaker than classical logic. In this weaker logic the proof of one contradiction does not necessarily entail the proof of every proposition. However, this system turned out to be too weak to decide the question of whether or not he should trust the machine. Then he had the following bright idea. Why not use classical logic in his system even though the resulting system is inconsistent? Is an inconsistent system necessarily useless? Not at all! Even though, given any proposition, there exists a proof that it is true and another proof that it is false, it may be the case that for any such pair of proofs, one of them is simply more psychologically convincing than the other, so simply pick the proof that you actually believe! Theoretically, the idea turned out very well—the actual system he obtained really did have the property that, given any such pair of proofs, one of them was always psychologically *far* more convincing than the other. Better yet, given any pair of contradictory propositions, 'all proofs of one were more convincing than *any* proof of the other. Indeed, anyone *except the epistemologist* could have used the system to decide whether the machine could be trusted. But the epistemologist obtained one proof that he should trust the machine, and another proof that he should not. Which proof was more convincing to him, which proof did he really believe? The only way that *he* could find out was to consult the machine! But he realized that this would be begging the question, since his consulting the machine would be a tacit admission that he did in fact trust the machine. So he still remained in a quandary.

FRANK: So how did he get out of it?

DOCTOR: Here is where fate kindly interceded. Because of his absolute absorption in the theory of this problem, which consumed almost all his waking hours, he became for the first time in his life experimentally negligent. As a result, a few minor units of his machine blew out without his knowing! Then, for the first time, the machine started giving contradictory information—not merely subtle paradoxes but blatant contradictions. In particular, the machine claimed one day that the epistemologist believed a certain proposition, and a few days later claimed that he did *not* believe that proposition. To add insult to injury, the machine claimed that he had not changed his belief in the last few days. This was enough to make him totally distrust the machine. Now he is fit as a fiddle.

FRANK: This is certainly the most amazing thing I have ever heard! I guess the machine was really dangerous and unreliable all along.

DOCTOR: Oh, not at all; the machine used to be excellent before the epistemologist's experimental carelessness put it out of whack.

FRANK: Well, surely when *I* knew it, it couldn't have been very reliable.

DOCTOR: Not so, Frank, and this brings us to your problem. I know about your entire conversation with the epistemologist. It was all tape-recorded.

FRANK: Then surely you realize that the machine could not have been right when it denied that I *believed* the book was red.

DOCTOR: Why not?

FRANK: Good God, do I have to go through all this nightmare again? I can understand that a person can be wrong if he claims that a certain physical object has a certain property, but have you ever known a single case in which a person can be mistaken when he claims to have or not have a certain sensation?

DOCTOR: Why, certainly! I once knew a Christian Scientist who had a raging toothache; he was frantically groaning and moaning all over the place. When asked whether a dentist might not cure him, he replied that there was nothing to be cured. Then he was asked, "But do you not feel pain?" He replied, "No, I do not feel pain; nobody feels pain, there is no such thing as pain, pain is only an illusion." So here is a case of a man who claimed not to feel pain, yet everyone present knew perfectly well that he did feel pain. I certainly don't believe that he was lying; he was simply mistaken.

FRANK: Well, all right in a case like that. But how can one be mistaken if one asserts his belief about the color of a book?

DOCTOR: I can assure you that, without access to any machine, if I asked someone the color of a book and he answered, "I believe that it is red," I would be very doubtful that he really believed it. It seems to me that if he really believed it, he would answer, "It is red," and not, "I believe that it is red," or, "It seems red to me." The very timidity of his response would be indicative of his doubts.

FRANK: But why on earth should I have doubted that it was red?

DOCTOR: You should know that better than I. Let us see now, have you ever in the past had reason to doubt the accuracy of your sense perception?

FRANK: Why, yes. A few weeks before visiting the epistemologist, I suffered from an eye disease, which did make me see colors falsely. But I was cured before my visit.

DOCTOR: Oh, so no wonder you doubted that it was red! True enough, your eyes perceived the correct color of the book, but your earlier experience lingered in your mind and made it impossible for you to really believe that it was red. So the machine *was* right!

FRANK: Well, all right, but then why did I doubt that I *believed* it was red?

DOCTOR: Because you *didn't* believe that it was red, and you were unconsciously smart enough to realize that. Besides, when one starts doubting one's own sense perceptions, the doubt spreads like an infection to higher and higher levels of abstraction until finally the whole belief system becomes one doubting mass of insecurity. I bet that if you went *now* to the epistemologist's office, and if the machine were repaired, and you now claimed that you believe the book is red, the machine would concur.

No, Frank, the machine is—or rather was—a good one. The epistemologist learned much from it but misused it when he applied it to his own brain. He really should have known better than to create such an unstable situation. The combination of his brain and the machine each scrutinizing and influencing the behavior of the other led to serious problems in feedback. Finally, the whole system went into a cybernetic wobble. Something was bound to give sooner or later. Fortunately, it was the machine.

FRANK: I see. One last question, though. How could the machine be trustworthy when it claimed to be untrustworthy?

DOCTOR: The machine never claimed to be untrustworthy, it only claimed that the epistemologist would be better off not trusting it. And the machine was right.

7

A Mind-Body Fantasy

In Rudolf Carnap's article "Psychology in Physical Language," he argues that every sentence of psychology may be formulated in physical language.[1] As he expresses it, all sentences of psychology describe physical occurrences, namely, the physical behavior of humans and other animals.

I do not see that the second formulation is really implied by the first. It may indeed be perfectly possible that every statement in psychology may be *translatable* into a statement in physics. But this does not mean that statements in psychology are *about* physical occurrences. The following analogy will, I hope, add some insight into this point.

Imagine (if you can!) a world with the very curious property that any two objects have the same color if and only if they happen to have the same shape. So, for instance, all red objects are spherical and all spherical objects red; all green objects are cubical and all cubical objects green; and so forth. Imagine also that half the inhabitants of the world are completely color-blind, and the other half see colors perfectly. In this world, *color* is the analogue of *mental* and *shape* is the analogue of *physical*. Hence, the materialists are the color-blind, and the dualists are the color-sighted. (Unfortunately, I cannot fit pure idealists into this world, for who could they be other than people who could see colors but not shapes—and this is too outlandish even for me!)

Imagine the metaphysical controversies that might rage on such a planet! The color-sighted people would claim certainty that objects could differ not only in size and shape but also by something else equally important, which they called *color;* they would claim to know this by direct perception and not through any process of reasoning! The color-blind people would be completely skeptical; they would consider the views of the color-sighted occult or mystical, and with good reason! In this setup, the color-sighted people would have absolutely no way of demonstrating their color-vision to the color-blind! Whenever a color-sighted person could distinguish two objects by their color-difference, a color-blind person could just as well distinguish them by their difference in shape. So no empirical demonstration to the color-blind would be possible. Also, in this setup, all statements about colors would be translatable into statements about shapes (at least in the opinion of the color-blind!). Now suppose that the color-sighted developed a dual vocabulary employing both color-words and shape-words. (I will consider some objections to this dual vocabulary later.) Half the words of this vocabulary would be redundant to the color-blind. A color-sighted person would say, "This object is both spherical *and* red, which is saying two very different things about it." The color-blind person would reply, "I still cannot understand your distinction between the words *spherical* and *red.*" Imagine the theories that the color-sighted people might invent to account for the dual phenomena of shape and color! Some might regard shape and color as different aspects or modes of the same underlying substance. Others might marvel that God has preordained some miraculous harmony between shapes and colors. Then there would arise an identity theory that would maintain that despite the possible difference between the meanings of the words *color* and *shape,* colors and shapes themselves were nevertheless the same things. Of course, the color-blind people would have no idea what the metaphysicians were talking about.

Naturally, one can easily pick my analogy to pieces. For one thing, it could be asked, "What happens if a red sphere is cut into two hemispheres; do the two halves suddenly change color?" Of course they would have to in such a world! How? By some weird physical law or other. Also, in such a world, there could be no two sources of different monochromatic lights—let's say there was only a constant source of white light. Many other utter implausibilities would have to be explained, but the point is not whether such a world is remotely realistic *or even logically possible;* this is only an analogy whose purpose is (I hope) to provide some feeling for certain aspects of the mind-body problem.

There are, however, even more fundamentally serious difficulties with this analogy. In the first place, why should the color-sighted have ever developed a dual vocabulary? Next, how could the color-sighted have ever known that the others were color-blind? For that matter, how could a color-sighted person test someone else to find out whether or not he had color-vision? And for *that* matter, could anyone know whether *he* could see colors or not? In fact, could any distinction at all between colors and shapes ever have arisen; could these two different notions have developed?

I think that this question is highly important, but I do not claim to know the answer. I suspect that the answer is, "Yes, they would," but, curiously enough, by analogy with the mind-body problem. Let us for the moment assume there is a perfect parallelism between mental and physical events. Nevertheless, some people on this earth —perhaps the majority—do indeed make a radical distinction between the two and strongly claim that these are two very different notions, not one.

Of course, one way that color-shape distinctions could arise on this planet would be if some of the color-sighted inhabitants had come from a neighboring planet on which the optical and physical laws were like those on Earth. These few would have made a sharp distinction between color and shape *prior* to having landed on this strange planet. Imagine their utter surprise! Could they, do you think, be able to test the others for color-vision? Perhaps only by taking them back to their home planet!

I'd now like to consider a slightly frightening variant of our analogy. Again, our Planet *A* is such that any two objects have the same shape if and only if they have the same color. Again, half the people are color-sighted—by which I mean that they have that physiological equipment which those of us have who can see colors—and the other half are color-blind. Let us assume now that in fact *nobody* on the planet had ever suspected that there was any difference between colors and shapes and that the color-sighted people had no idea that they were any different from the color-blind. Furthermore, only one vocabulary had developed; let us say that *spherical* was used to mean both spherical and red (which are coextensive); cubical meant both cubical and green; and so forth.

Now suppose a band from that planet were to travel for the first time to another planet—a normal planet like Earth. Imagine the reactions of the color-sighted. They might well think that they were going crazy! They would see, let us say, a red, spherical Object *A*, a green, spherical Object *B*, and a green, cubical Object *C*. Objects *A* and *C* would be perfectly normal. But Object *B*! What kind of a hybrid monster is this! Imagine how they would try to describe it back home! "It is both spherical *and* cubical!" (By which, of course, they would mean, "It is both spherical and green.")

"What do you mean by this nonsense? How can something be both spherical and cubical?"

"Well, in one way it is spherical; in another way it is cubical."

"Oh, come on now, what kind of mystical, dialectical nonsense is this? We all know that the statement, 'A spherical object is not cubical,' is analytic—it is *necessarily* true."

"Well, in one sense it is analytic, but in another sense it is actually false."

And so forth.

If the travelers remained on the other planet for awhile, they would, of course, have to develop a dual vocabulary. When they returned home, they would then realize the distinction between color-vision and shape-perception. Would you say that they had had color-vision all along but didn't know it? (Perhaps this is similar to the belief of certain Eastern mystics that all of us are already in a state of enlightenment but don't yet know it!) Some readers will probably say, "Yes, they always had it," others, "No, they did not," and still others (who are positivistically oriented) that the question is meaningless unless it means that they had the potential to distinguish differently colored objects of the same size and shape on a normal planet. I believe, though, that after returning home most of the travelers would have said, "Yes, I had color-vision all along, but I did not realize it. I have not *gained* any new faculty, I merely have become aware of a certain faculty I always possessed." (Perhaps this is again not too far removed from what is meant by certain Zen-enlightened people who have claimed, "From enlightenment I have *gained* nothing.")

I hope my reader will at least *feel* some analogy to the mind-body problem. What baffles me most about this problem is how it is that we disagree among ourselves so radically about such a basic question! Dualists do not talk about sensations as opposed to physical events, as something occult or unknown but as something known directly and with absolute certainty. Monistic materialists claim this notion to be illusory, occult, or mystical, as are the notions of minds or souls. Why this fantastic difference? No amount of deductive or inductive reasoning ever seems to settle it! So, to what can the difference be attributed? I hardly can believe that the dualists have some extra *perceptive* faculty (like color-vision) that the materialists lack! Is it possible that settling the difference will take something as drastic as the discovery one day of a *lack* of parallelism between mental and physical phenomena?

Notes

1. Rudolf Carnap, "Psychology in Physical Language." In *Logical Positivism*, edited by A. J. Ayer (New York: The Free Press, 1966) p. 165.

4

To Be or Not to Be?

8

To Be or Not to Be?

I once posed the question, "What is the difference between an optimist and an incurable optimist?" Answer: "An optimist is one who says, "Everything is for the best; mankind will survive." An incurable optimist is one who says, "Everything is for the best; mankind will survive. And even if mankind doesn't survive, it is still for the best."

Then there is the pessimistic optimist who sadly shakes his head and says, "I'm very much afraid that everything is for the best." I think that the philosopher Arthur Schopenhauer can best be characterized as an optimistic pessimist. He happily and proudly nods his head and says, "See, everything is still for the worst," and he is optimistic that things will continue going as badly as he predicts.

Although Schopenhauer is usually called a pessimist, he can hardly be said to have a truly tragic sense of life, as have such writers as Leopardi or Unamuno. No, he has rather an *angry* sense of life. William James really hit the nail on the head when he said that Schopenhauer reminds one of a barking dog who would rather have the world ten times worse than it is than lose his chance of barking at it. It is indeed true that Schopenhauer is least convincing as a pessimist when he is most petulant.

I think a distinction should be made between what might be termed *essential pessimism* and *contingent pessimism*. I would define *essential pessimism* as the belief that life *has* to be predominantly painful, even under the best possible circumstances. By *contingent pessimism*, I mean the doctrine that as a matter of fact life is predominantly painful, but there is no a priori reason that it has to be. Thus, a contingent pessimist would say that this world is a pretty rotten one (and will likely remain so), but there is no logical necessity for this to be. Whereas essential pessimism leaves no hope for life at all, contingent pessimism leaves room for some hope, though perhaps only a slim one. It should be noted that the existence of only one predominantly happy life would constitute a disproof of essential pessimism but not of contingent pessimism.

Schopenhauer kept mixing up the two in a rather confusing way. I think that if he had left out his contingent pessimism, his essential pessimism would have come through more convincingly. As an essential pessimist, he tried to make the point that as soon as one desire is gratified, another one arises, and so the individual is as unhappy as before. As a contingent pessimist he kept ranting and raving about such things as how mendacious and hypocritical people are. But if Schopenhauer's essential pessimism is correct, why should these issues even matter? If people became less mendacious and hypocritical, how would that solve the real problem, which is life itself?

Von Hartmann. Now, the philosopher Eduard von Hartmann (a successor of Schopenhauer) strikes me as much more interesting. I am amazed that his book *Philosophy of the Unconscious* is not more widely known today than it is. His philosophical system is as wild as anything found in science fiction.

To begin with, he is far more convincing than Schopenhauer. He does not seem to take a perverse delight in how bad things are but instead seems genuinely concerned about what can be done to help matters. He has none of Schopenhauer's hysteria. His writings are completely sober, which adds to the convincing quality. He is far more an essential pessimist than a contingent one. He first sets out to dispel what he considers the three main illusions of mankind:

(1) That life is not really all that bad; (2) that there is an afterlife in which we will be happy; and (3) that through science and progress the world can be improved.

After many, many arguments to dispel these illusions, he considers the question, In virtue of all this, why shouldn't we commit suicide? He rightfully rejects Schopenhauer's silly reason that we would then never have the satisfaction of knowing we had done it. So why shouldn't we commit suicide for von Hartmann? It is because he believed that we are all but parts of one vast universal unconscious (gradually becoming conscious through evolutionary processes). We are but limbs of a single tree. Thus, if one individual commits suicide, the general problem would not be helped. What if we all committed suicide? No good. The collective unconscious that has come to life once would surely come to life again and suffer as much as before.

Then what *should* we do? Answer: We should develop science and cooperate with the spirit of progress as much as possible. Why? To make the world a happier place? No. This cannot be done, as the author has already argued. The real reason we should cooperate with science and progress is to aid evolution in accomplishing its true end. What is this end? Why, the entire purpose of evolution is that the collective unconscious develop enough knowledge to find a way of annihilating itself in such a manner that it can *never* come back!

This, in a nutshell, is von Hartmann's system. Wouldn't it be funny if it were correct?

I once asked the philosopher Bowsma why it was that when I read the pessimistic philosophers, instead of getting depressed, I feel enormously cheered up. He replied, "Of course, because you know isn't true!" I'm not sure that this is quite the reason; it may be so for Schopenhauer, whose arguments are so unconvincing (in a way almost fraudulent). But von Hartmann seems so utterly earnest and sincere that it is hardly possible not to take him seriously. Of course, he may well be wrong in any or all of his fundamental theses. It may be that present life is not as bad as he believes. It may be that there is an afterlife after all (who really knows?), and it may be that science and progress can make the world a happier place (though these days the prospects do not look so good).

The interesting thing, though, is that his system really ends on a happy note. He *does* have confidence that evolution will finally succeed in its end and all suffering will ultimately cease. So in the last analysis is he really a pessimist or an optimist?

9

The Zen of Life and Death

"You know," added Tweedledee very gravely, "it's one of the most serious things that can possibly happen to one in a battle—to get one's head cut off."

Alice laughed loud: But she managed to turn it into a cough, for fear of hurting his feelings.

Lewis Carroll, *Through the Looking Glass*,
Chapter 4

The subject of life and death appears to be of some general interest, and so a discussion of this topic may not be out of order. The only trouble is that just about anything one can say on this subject is probably wrong!

The Zen master Huang Po said about the mind, "Begin to reason about it, and you at once fall into error." I think that the same can be said even more aptly about life and death. All discussions of this subject somehow tend to miss the mark. Then why discuss it? I could give a Zen-like answer and say, "Why not?" The fact is that we *are* interested in these things and to repress these interests is kind of silly. Of course, many regard such discussions as essentially morbid. This is beautifully illustrated by Bertrand Russell's story of the man at a banquet who was asked what he thought would happen to him after his death. He seemed very uneasy and tried to avoid the question. But the questioner persisted and finally the man said, "I suppose I shall enter paradise and enjoy total bliss for all eternity, but must we talk about such unpleasant subjects?"

A somewhat related incident is the following. Once we had a dinner party. I jokingly said about one of the guests (a very close friend of mine), "Don't give him too much to drink; he gets hostile and belligerent." His wife then said, "He goes through several stages, one of which is that he becomes infuriated with the idea that one day he will have to die." My friend is only in his late twenties. Another guest, a gentleman in his early sixties, turned to him and said, "Are you not a bit young to be worrying about that? Do you really find life that wonderful?" My friend replied, "Oh, yes." He then went on to describe how he simply could not conceive of himself as not existing, the idea of which was infinitely frightening and repugnant. He then added, "I would be less disturbed by the thought of being eternally in hell than of not existing at all." I told my friend that I found it rather odd and puzzling that he should find nonexistence both inconceivable *and* frightening. Either one alone I could understand perfectly, but how could something be both nonunderstandable and frightening? The very fact that he could have such a positive emotional reaction as fear attached to a given notion would indicate that he had to have *some* idea of the notion. He admitted that this was indeed puzzling but found no reassurance in these considerations. I then suggested that what perhaps disturbed him was the thought that time should somehow continue without him, and I asked him, "Would it disturb you as much if tomorrow time itself would suddenly stop, so there never would come an actual time when you were dead?" He replied that the question was meaningless to him since he could form absolutely no notion at all of what it could mean for time itself to stop. I can't blame him too much for his reaction though I do not find the idea of time stopping so unconceivable. At any rate, I pressed this particular point no further although I did partake of the very lively discussion about life and death that persisted most of the evening.

The next day, my young friend and I reviewed some of the events of the previous evening. He told me with a mischievous smile that at parties, he would always bring up the subject of death and that the conversation would then remain on this subject all night, sometimes without his saying any more. What particularly impressed him was everybody's desperate attempts to convince him that there was really nothing for him to worry about! But he believed that the very urgency of their attempts indicated their own desperation at the thought that there really *was* something to worry about. I think that there is much truth in this observation. Since we all do have certain unresolved inner desperations about the matter, I think it helpful that we all *do* think about and discuss these matters as freely as possible. *Is* there really something to worry about? I believe not. But many will interpret this as a sort of wishful thinking, or "whistling in the dark." I will return to this question later.

One can approach the question of life and death in many ways. One is from the viewpoint of authority and revelation. Another is from the viewpoint of science and reason, that is, to consider all evidence for and against survival and then balance their probabilities and then decide which is the more "likely." Related to this approach is the analytic one: First determine whether the expression, "I can survive my bodily death," has any meaning at all before deciding whether it is true or false. Another somewhat related approach is to consider various meanings of the word *survive*. Then one can take the psychological approach by considering what are the psychological motivations behind one's attitudes toward the matter and to investigate how much of one's beliefs in survival or nonsurvival is simply the result of wishful thinking.

I believe that all these approaches are weak but shall consider some aspects of them, perhaps mainly to give the reader my feeling for their essential futility. Then I shall consider some mystical and

Eastern approaches to the question. These approaches strike me as not wholly satisfactory but nevertheless better than any others I know.

Authority and Revelation

Here I face a bit of a quandary. On the one hand, I never have had very much confidence in revelation and still less in authority. (As I once said to a friend, "Why should I believe in other people's revelations? I have enough trouble believing my own.") Yet my final attitude may come closer to revelation than anything else. That is about as much as I can say about this at the moment.

Analysis, Science, and Types of Survival

In the so-called analytic approach, one often examines a statement in terms of what it means before deciding whether or not it is true. Take, for example, the statement, "I will survive my bodily death." Some claim that the statement is true, others that it is false, others that it is certainly either true or false but we don't know which, others that it has no meaning whatsoever, and still others that if it has any meaning they don't know what the meaning could be. For example, the logical positivist Moritz Schlick regarded this proposition as perfectly meaningful and *possibly* true. As he said, "I can perfectly well imagine being present at and witnessing my own funeral." On the other hand, the logical positivist A. J. Ayer believed Schlick's statement to be not merely false but self-contradictory. (That's a rather drastic difference of opinion, isn't it?) Other logical positivists claim the proposition to be neither true nor false nor self-contradictory but simply meaningless. Since they claim not to understand what this self, soul, spirit, mind, or psyche is apart from the body, then they do not know just what it is that is said to survive or not to survive. Of course, a pure materialist might define the mind to be simply a person's memories and behavioral dispositions.[1] To such a materialist, one possible meaning of survival (and indeed the only one I can think of) is that at some future time after one's death another physical organism would be in the universe with the same memories and behavioral dispositions (a sort of resurrection). Such a materialist would most likely concede the logical possibility of this type of survival but would hold it as fantastically improbable. At any rate, surely this is *not* what Schlick meant! Otherwise, we would have the funny picture of another man at Schlick's funeral with the same memories, dispositions, and very personality of Schlick looking at the corpse of the old Schlick. (At least I find this situation funny, don't you?) No, this "physicalistic" type of survival, though of possible interest, is definitely beyond the scope of this enquiry. I am interested in discussing what might be called *psychic survival*, that is, the survival of the soul, psyche, or self.

What kind of survival do I have in mind? Actually, there is more than one notion of survival, and we should take a look at some of them. First, there is of course the Christian notion of the soul's surviving with all its memories and personal characteristics. Some Christians think of this survival in terms of bodily resurrection, others in the more Platonic terms of the soul leaving its body and entering a purely spiritual realm. The distinction between these two notions is not too significant for our present purposes; both are certainly concerned with individual or personal survival. Next we consider reincarnation. According to this notion, the spirit of the departed enters the body of a new living organism—human, animal, or possibly even plant—but *without* its memories. Many people who have a perfect understanding (though not necessarily belief) in the Christian notion of survival with one's memories find this Eastern notion of reincarnation—survival *without memories*—simply inconceivable! What on earth, they ask, could the self be without its memories and own individual characteristics? I myself don't have the *slightest* difficulty with this notion. I have a most definite concept of what I mean by *I*, and my memories and particular personal characteristics seem to me to be no more part of this essential *I* than the clothes I wear! If the reader asks me what then *do* I mean by *I*, I'm afraid that I can no more tell him than I can describe my sensation of red to a blind man. If the reader wishes to conclude from this that I only deceive myself in thinking that I have such a notion, that such a notion is really meaningless, of course he is free to. I think, however, that he should bear in mind that the inability to define a given notion in terms of a set of other "known" notions is not necessarily indicative of the meaninglessness of that notion; it may in principle simply not be so definable. I recall that someone once said to me, "After all, when you die, various babies will be born. How do you know one of them won't be you?" Several persons present simply could not understand what he was saying. I think that I understood perfectly! Of course, one of them *could* be me; the question is, *Will* one of them be me?

How attractive is this notion of reincarnation compared with, say, the Christian notion of survival with one's memories? This, of course, is a matter of individual taste. Personally, I find the idea of reincarnation extremely attractive. The idea of cyclic rebirth has a wonderful, sparkling freshness that appeals to me even more than the idea of continuing, as it were, on a straight line, which seems rather stale and tiresome. But this, of course, does not mean that I necessarily *believe* it. There is all the difference in the world between finding an idea attractive and believing it is necessarily true. This is beautifully brought out in the following passage of Suzuki on transmigration (reincarnation):

> I do not know whether transmigration can be proved or maintained on the scientific level, but I know that it is an inspiring theory and full of poetic suggestions, and I am satisfied with this interpretation and do not seem to have any desire to go beyond it. To me, the idea of transmigration has a personal appeal, and as to its scientific and philosophical implications, I leave it to the study of the reader.[2]

There is a curious variant of reincarnation that I wish to mention briefly. According to this variant, the soul is not a simple, indecomposable substance but a composite that after death simply gets recycled (just like the material of our bodies gets recycled). After death, instead of my entering the body of just one newborn baby (or other organism), I would split up into a multitude of them. If there is one thing I cannot imagine, it is the thought of my splitting up! (Even total annihilation is easier for me to comprehend than that!) Perhaps, though, I should modify this statement in light of the following past experience.

I am not sure whether it was during a dream or a hypnagogic reverie; I rather believe it was the latter. At any rate, I experienced myself as dead and turning into a cluster of bacteria—fresh, live bacteria! It was not as if I were detatchedly watching my *body* turn into bacteria; it was *I* who was turning into them and gaining my very life *through* them. Also—and this is most important—I did not at all feel as if I were a *victim,* as if the bacteria were preying upon me, sacrificing me for their own ends. *I* was the principal gainer of the transaction. Indeed, it was not quite clear to me where I left off and the bacteria began; the bacteria were *me!* Thus, I should have more understanding for the recycling hypothesis. The only difference is that I did not think of the bacteria as *individuals;* I did not have any sense that I was splitting up into these individuals. Rather, I thought of this bacterial cluster as a whole unit, and I was simply becoming this unit.

Next I wish to consider the so-called scientific arguments against the probability of survival. Frankly, these seem to me incredibly poor! What I now have to say is, of course, only pertinent to dualists, who think of mind and matter as distinct substances and who know perfectly well what it means for the soul to survive but who have grave doubts that in fact it will. I am thinking of one dualist who argued thus: In principle, it is conceivable that the soul survives, but in the light of scientific evidence, it is extremely improbable. Since the parallelism between psychical and physical events during our lifetime is so clearly in evidence, then scientific induction requires us to believe that the parallelism should continue after our death.

There are two aspects of this point of view that I wish to dispute. The first is this: Does scientific induction really require it? Suppose, for example, that a certain reaction between two chemicals is always observed provided that they are mixed in a platinum container. Scientific induction does indeed require us to predict that the same reaction will occur if they are again mixed in a platinum container but does not allow us to predict what will happen if they are mixed outside such a container. Similarly, the fact that a parallelism exists between psychic and physical events and that this parallelism exists during one's lifetime does not warrant the belief that it should probably continue to exist after one's lifetime.

I have a second objection, perhaps more serious yet. Suppose it be granted that the parallelism does continue to hold after death. Does this imply the annihilation of the psyche? It seems to me that it does not! After all, when the body dies, it does not just disappear. It gets eventually transformed (in all likelihood) to other living beings like bacteria, worms, and so forth, which in turn are transformed into the bodies of higher living mammals. Strangely, the dualist who disbelieves in the survival of the soul nevertheless believes that the body still exists after death. This certainly does not seem like a continuing parallelism but rather a drastic bifurcation: The body continues to exist, but the soul gets annihilated! In this regard, it is curious that one speaks of dead bodies but never of dead souls, except in the form of ghosts or sometimes departed souls. But a departed soul seems to mean something very different from a dead soul. The former is a soul that has gone elsewhere; the latter, one that no more goes elsewhere than a dead body goes elsewhere but rather somehow changes its state. I must confess that I hardly know what I mean by a dead soul, but if the parallelism between mind and matter should persist after death, then just as the body dies but does not go out of existence, the soul should also die but not go out of existence. If the body (or perhaps rather the material of the body) comes to life again in the form of other living organisms, then similarly the corresponding soul substance should come to life. So if anything, it would seem that if scientific induction requires us to project into the future an assumed parallelism between body and mind, then this should add support to something like reincarnation rather than annihilation. But as I said before, I do not believe that sound scientific methodology does require us to make this projection. Goodness gracious, if I have a remarkably consistent dream in which I observe a high correlation between certain experiences and others, what rational grounds exist for my expecting this correlation to continue after I wake up? To put the matter another way, it is not at all inconceivable to me that one day scientific technology will enable us to anesthetize the body of a subject and then connect a mass of electrodes directly to his brain and nerve centers, thus inducing a whole artificial life or sort of "dream world." (This idea is, of course, quite common in science fiction.) So if, for instance, the correct visual and tactile nerve centers are stimulated, the subject will have as vivid an experience of a material object as we have of objects in the (so-called) real world. Now, in this artificially induced life, the subject might also experience a "body" that he thinks is his own. He will observe a perfect correlation between his own perceptions and feelings with events that he observes taking place in his "body." Let us also assume that his "dream" is programmed to last, say, ten years. As part of his "dream," he observes other bodies, like the body that he calls his own, dying. Also let us assume that all memories prior to his "dream" have been obliterated; his "dream world" is the only world he knows. My point now is that under these conditions the subject would have the same grounds as we have for believing that upon the death of his "body" he would go out of existence, but of course he would be wrong. Furthermore, I have no reason to believe that this situation is not right now happening to me! I don't for a moment believe that it is, but I have no rational evidence that it is not. Some may say that it is highly improbable that I am now in the state of this subject. But I do not see any way of evaluating the probability of such an event, and what experiments could I possibly perform to throw any light on its probability? What experiments could a dreamer possibly perform in his dream to evaluate the probability of his dreaming? It seems to me none whatsoever! Thus I believe: (1) It is logically possible that I am in this state; (2) as a matter of fact, I am not in this state; (3) I have no evidence for this belief, but I believe it anyhow; and (4) probability has absolutely nothing to do with the matter. And so I believe about the question of survival after death: (1) that there is not the slightest rational or probabilist evidence that one survives; and (2) that there is not the slightest rational or probabilist evidence that one doesn't.

Wishful Thinking?

Now let us consider the psychological approach to the motivations of beliefs about survival from the point of view of how much of our beliefs concerning these matters are merely the result of wishful thinking. The unfortunate aspect of this approach—or rather about many of those who take it—is that they seem to regard the statement, "That's only wishful thinking," as a valid counterargument. I'm sure most of my readers are too sophisticated for that, but it is surprising how many people are not! At any rate, this approach is curiously one-sided when applied to the subject of life and death. The usual argument, of course, is, "First there is no evidence for the existence of the soul. Secondly, even if there is a soul, there is absolutely no evidence for its survival after death, and plenty of evidence against it. Yet many otherwise intelligent people in fact do believe in survival. Why is this? The only sensible explanation is that —whether they consciously know it or not—their desire for immortality is so intense, that it totally warps their objectivity about the matter."[3] Now, to those who dismiss belief in survival as mere wishful thinking, I would like to ask the following questions: What would you say about those who claim not to care whether or not they survive, or even express preference for nonsurvival, but who nevertheless strongly believe that they will survive? Would you say that really deep down they *do* want to survive and that they are only fooling themselves in thinking that they don't? What about those who believe in hell and that they are utterly evil and are frightened to death of their impending damnation, and who say, "I wish that we *didn't* survive, but the horrible thing is that we do!" I guess you would say that even the thought of hell terrifies them less than the thought of extinction, so it still is a matter of wishful thinking even though superficially it seems like fearful thinking. (As some Freudians say, fears are often disguised wishes.) What about those Eastern philosophers who believe in reincarnation but regard it as a curse rather than a blessing. All their endeavors are geared toward *avoiding* rebirth, and they believe and hope that with sufficient effort and insight rebirth can be avoided. Perhaps you would again say that deep down even the Easterner desires some form of survival but really knows that he cannot have it and so turns to the remarkable extreme of not merely saying that rebirth is undesirable (which is merely a sour grapes attitude) but makes it his most profound life purpose to try to prevent the very thing that he (unconsciously) most desires! Of course, one can also attack the Easterner for his wishful thinking along very different lines, but I imagine this line of attack would occur to relatively few Westerners. What I have in mind is this: Imagine someone brought up in the East who has absorbed the attitude that existence is suffering and has absolutely no doubts about rebirth, but who is a total skeptic concerning the possibility of avoiding it. He might well say, "We all know damn well that none of us wants to be reborn, and we all know—deep down—that we must be. So this Buddhistic and Hindoo talk that it is possible to avoid rebirth is sheer wishful thinking!"

A somewhat amusing incident comes to mind. I was once telling a friend (a gifted mathematician) that the hypothesis of survival seemed to me perfectly plausible. His immediate reaction (like that of Ayer) was that the idea was totally meaningless. But later in the conversation, he insisted that my belief in the possibility of survival resulted purely from the fact that I *wanted* to survive. Several years later, we met again, and I reminded him of the conversation. I said, "One thing puzzles me. I can understand what you mean when you say that my views on survival reflect wishful thinking. And I can understand—at least in part—when you say that my notion of survival is *meaningless*. But I cannot understand what you can mean when you put the two together. If, as you say, I wish to survive, then I must be wishing for *something*. Hence, I fail to see how that which I wish for—which I call *survival*—can be an empty notion. I can't see how I can wish for nothing." He replied, "I thought of that, and I was a little hard on you." I then pointed out that it was not that he was hard on *me* but that there was a purely logical difficulty to be straightened out: How can I wish for x when x is not merely nonexistent but *meaningless*? He replied, "What I really should have said is that what you are really wishing for is that your *body* live forever, and since you know that is impossible, then you have invented this notion of soul, and, as a substitute, hope that *it* will survive." I must confess that I am still puzzled! If I really have invented this notion of soul (or more realistically, if I have borrowed this notion from others who have invented it), then I have also invented the notion of the survival of the soul. I therefore have attached *some* meaning to the term, so how can it be meaningless?

If one must persist in using the ad hominem argument of wishful thinking, then I can think of another target that, it seems to me, has not yet been sufficiently or widely attacked. I am thinking of people like, for instance, Bertrand Russell, who reject survival as highly improbable but still maintain that there is nothing to worry about. They then proceed to give a whole host of reasons why survival is not even desirable and to explain the benefits that will accrue if individuals *don't* survive. These people pride themselves on their lack of wishful thinking. But it seems to me that their attitude can just as much be interpreted as a sour grapes attitude: "Who wants to survive, anyhow?" Of course, they are free from the (wishful) thought that they do survive, but the belief that they don't *want* to survive may be wishful thinking. I would like to put the matter another way. The groups to whom I refer evidently take the attitude, "It is only wishful thinking to believe that we survive. But we can be perfectly happy and content with the universe without this childish belief that we survive." My question now is, "Is it not possible that it is only wishful thinking to believe that we can be content without the belief in survival?" In a way, one might admire some of the existentialists who see this, and whose attitudes might be paraphrased, "Of course we don't survive, and of course we want to survive, so let's stop kidding ourselves that we don't want to survive. Instead, let us squarely face the infinitely painful fact that we do want to survive, but we can't. This is the true tragedy of life." To the great annoyance of many—and at the risk of being accused of rationalizing—I must nevertheless raise the question whether *this* attitude may not also be a form of wishful thinking, though perhaps of a somewhat different sort. Is there perhaps not such a thing as *masochistic* or *sadistic* wishful thinking? Is there not such a thing as *pessimistic* wishful thinking just as well as the (perhaps) more usual *optimistic* wishful thinking? For people who take a delight in how *bad* things are, is it so inappropriate to suspect them of wishful thinking when they exaggerate the bad aspects of life so ridiculously? While we are at it, is it not possible that *all* forms of thought are wishful thinking? Who knows, maybe one day some psychologist will prove that the real reason I believe in the laws of logic and mathematics is that I want to. At least, I cannot prove that some psychologist will not prove this.

At this point, things are getting a little ridiculous, aren't they? I think that the upshot of all this is that to be overly concerned about whether one's beliefs are or are not the result of wishful thinking is very bad, ultimately destroying, rather than aiding, the objectivity of one's judgment. Not only that, but this concern may well prevent one from knowing what he really thinks. How many fine thoughts have been repressed because it is feared that they may be only wishful thinking? This consideration is not unrelated to our next topic, for which I will coin the phrase *fearful thinking*.

I understand *wishful thinking* to be that thinking based on wish rather than evidence. Similarly, I would define *fearful thinking* as that thinking likewise not based on evidence but based purely on fear. Both wishful thinking and fearful thinking are equally lacking in objectivity.

Why would one engage in fearful thinking? I have already suggested masochism as one explanation. But another explanation may be more pertinent. I think tht one tends to believe that the worst will happen so as not to build up false hopes and thus be disappointed. So, for example, those who hysterically and fanatically insist that there is no afterlife are terrified lest they expect something good that in fact may not come to pass. Their fear, so to speak, is that they may live in a fool's paradise. Fearful thinking may be described as bending over backward to avoid wishful thinking. But I must again emphasize that it is just as open as wishful thinking to subjective error. To put the matter another way, I would say that just as those who insist that there is an afterlife may be engaged in purely wishful thinking, those who insist that there isn't are just as subjectively biased, only in the direction of fearful thinking.

Now let us forget about wishful and fearful thinking and ask ourselves honestly why we *are* in fact so disturbed by the thought of death. Many readers will reply, *"You* may be so disturbed, but *I* am not!" But I honestly find this rather doubtful. I believe that a few exceptional people are genuinely not disturbed but that many others only tend to repress their disturbance. After all, so many social factors encourage us to deny—even to ourselves—any fear of death. We are encouraged to "banish any such gloomy thoughts from our minds and to dwell on the beautiful things of life and on those lives to come." We are taught that fears of our own death are unmanly, cowardly, selfish, "egocentric," and so forth. One well-known writer said something to the effect that the charge of selfishness concerning our distress about death is unfair; it's not that we are worried about ourselves, we are worried about our loved ones, and we cannot bear the thought that they should perish. Although I *do* believe that we are also concerned about our loved ones, I find it a bit sad that people should be so worried about their selfishness. Of course we are very much worried about ourselves, and why shouldn't we be? All these moralistic charges of selfishness, cowardice, and so forth leave me quite unimpressed.

I now want to turn to an analysis of why we are in fact disturbed by the thought of *our* dying. My purpose is not to reassure the reader who is disturbed that there is nothing to worry about but rather to take a look at what in fact is really worrying him. The first thing that of course leaps to mind is the thought of those who *do* enjoy life: "What a pity it must end! Just think of all the good things I will miss." Then there is the rather deeper and more terrifying feeling that death is a state of loneliness, darkness, isolation, or separation from the rest of the world. It does little good to point out that it is really meaningless to talk of separation between something nonexistent and something existent, for we still have the psychological *association* of separateness. But the very feeling that after death we are separated from the rest of the world only indicates that we do think of ourselves as somehow existing after our death! Indeed, it is literally inconceivable to us that we can ever cease to exist. Here, I think, lies the true heart of the trouble! I believe it is not so much *fear* that is troubling us. The real trouble lies in our *trying to force ourselves to believe something that in fact is psychologically incapable of being believed!* One of Goethe's arguments for immortality is that a person cannot even conceive of his nonexistence; how then can he possibly believe it? This argument strikes me as quite remarkable. Not that I draw from it the conclusion that we *are* immortal, but I believe that Goethe came closest of all to the real reason why people do believe in immortality. This factor seems to be far stronger than the motive of wishful thinking. How can we conceivably believe in our nonexistence? Yet there are very powerful social pressures to make us feel that we should (e.g., considerations of trying to be rational, avoidance of wishful thinking, etc.). So I believe that *fear* of death is not the real issue; the real issue is the conflict between our deepest intuitions and the social pressures exerted on us to deny them. Stated otherwise, I grant that many of us are indeed disturbed by the thought of our dying, but I believe that our disturbance is not really fear—as it appears to be—but rather the result of our trying to force ourselves to believe that which we are not capable of believing.

Personal Views

In this section, I shall state some purely personal views on the subject of life and death. I have already considered this subject from several angles—analytic, scientific, and psychological. I believe that a certain degree of objectivity in these matters is of great value, but I don't believe that we should therefore neglect a purely subjective approach or that such an approach is worthless. After all, we do have our own intuitions in addition to our reasoning powers, and why should we allow either to be subservient to the other?

When I talk of taking a purely subjective approach, what I have in mind is to simply state what one really does believe without worrying about whether the belief is or is not rational or whether it is or is not the result of some form of wishful thinking. This is less easy than may be imagined. Even if we temporarily waive all requirements of justifying our beliefs, it is not all that easy to know just what our beliefs really are. At least I find it so—particularly about such topics as life and death.

Suppose I now honestly ask myself what I believe will really happen to me after my bodily death; will I continue to exist or will I go out of existence? To tell the absolute truth, both answers seem to me somehow wrong! The idea of going out of existence or of ceasing to exist is to me absolutely inconceivable, hence I (in the good company of Goethe) cannot possibly believe something that I cannot even understand—something that I can form no notion of. Therefore, I am forced to rule out the possibility of my ceasing to exist. From this, it might appear to follow that I believe I will continue to exist after my bodily death. But this is not so. I am open to the possibility that I will, but I have no particular reason to believe that I necessarily will. What about the proposition, "Either I will continue existing, or I will cease to exist." Do I believe that? My answer is emphatically, "NO!" Now, this might appear to be completely contrary to the normally accepted Aristotelian logic with its classical principle of the excluded middle.[4] If it does, I would not feel too bad, for although I fully accept classical logic in the exact sciences, I have some doubts that it is fruitful in the present area. But I don't believe that my drastic rejection of this (apparent) disjunction really does violate the law of the excluded middle. Its truth is really dependent on (at least) three tacit premises: (1) The word *I* really denotes something; (2) there really is such a thing as time; and (3) I am in time.

As to (1), we shall discuss this further in the next section. As to (2), the denial of the reality of time goes counter to common sense but is nevertheless a cardinal point believed—or rather felt—by many mystics. Suppose a mystic is asked, "Are you really serious about denying the reality of time? You really do not believe that some events occur before others?" Such a mystic—if he has a modicum of some philosophical orientation—might answer something like, "Of course, events occur in the phenomenal world—the world of appearance—and hence time may be said to exist in the world of appearance. But time does not exist in the world of reality." I do not wish to now go into this highly interesting question; for purposes of this essay let me grant that time really exists. But this still leaves open the question whether I am really in time.

If it surprises you that I have some doubts that I am really in time, let me say that it is of course obvious that I experience time, and I experience events in the normal time sequence. But does this necessarily mean that I—the experiencer—have to be in time for this to happen? Why can't I be outside time and experience moments of time nevertheless? Am I something that actually moves through time; or am I stationary, with time moving past me?

I realize that at this point I am becoming what the logical positivists would call ridiculously metaphysical, making one pseudostatement after another and asking one pseudoquestion after another. I hope that those of you who are positivistically oriented will at least give me credit for knowing what I am doing in the sense of realizing perfectly that the questions I am discussing *are not questions about the physical world* and are hence totally outside the scope of science. Therefore, scientific methods cannot be of help in this discussion, so if one wants to stick wholly to logic and the methods of the physical sciences, one will have to turn to a different topic.

To return to the topic of time, as I said, it is not at all certain to me that because I experience time I am necessarily in time. If I am not in time, then the entire question of whether I will survive my bodily death becomes meaningless—the question simply disappears!

But am I really outside time, or is my thought that I am only another example of wishful thinking? To tell you the truth, I don't know that either! To say that I am outside time does not strike me as quite right. To say that I am in time does not strike me as wholly right either. Is it necessarily true that I am either in time or outside time? I doubt that also!

Let me put it this way: I normally believe that I am inside time, but when I reflect on the matter, I am no longer so sure of this. Although it is wrong to conclude from the above that I am *outside* time, for my purposes it is enough that I do not believe that I am inside time; I therefore do not have to believe either that I will survive my bodily death or I won't!

I feel the same way, incidentally, about the question of my existence prior to my bodily birth. Did I really begin in the year 1919? I doubt that very much! Did I exist before 1919? I doubt that also. (This reminds me somewhat of the Kantian antinomy of whether the universe had a beginning or not.)[5]

This about sums up my real feelings about life and death. Do I really believe I am not in time? Not wholly and not constantly; sometimes I do and sometimes I don't. (Doesn't this sound silly: Some*times* I believe I am in time and some*times* I don't? But it becomes less silly when one distinguishes experiencing time from being in time.)

Some people might say that they can form absolutely no notion of what it could possibly mean not to be in time. I would like to ask them the following question: Can you conceive the possibility of there being more than one time series (as in some science fiction stories)? If so, can you imagine being in a different one than this one? Assuming there were more than one time series, what would immortality mean? Would it necessarily mean continuing forever in *this* one? If you believe that upon your bodily death, you would no longer be in this time series but would jump into another one, would that satisfy you? Perhaps you could conceive of there being many different time series and of your being in *any* one of them but not of being in *none* of them!

I am afraid that the whole problem of survival is intimately bound up with our very notions of time, which—except for purposes of science and practical, everyday living—are none too satisfactory. As I said at the beginning of this essay, I suspect that *all* thinking about these questions is somehow off the track, and I certainly don't except my own. My hunch is that those who believe in immortality are closer to the truth than those who do not but still miss the real point. It is possible that the entire question is still not adequately formulated. To this topic I now turn.

Some Eastern Approaches

When I say that the whole question of life and death may be inadequately formulated, I am thinking of the Buddhist notion that the *I* is simply a fiction, despite our usual intuitions to the contrary. If this is true, then the whole notion of survival takes on a totally different significance. Buddhist thought regards psychic reality as a stream of consciousness that has no *agent*. (This position is like that of David Hume, who did not believe in the existence of the so-called self.) If this is so, then fear of death—or the feeling that death is a tragedy—is really ludicrous. It would be like a group of people who are worried that a certain town is going to be bombed; The optimists say, "No, it won't be bombed, it will survive." The pessimists say, "That is only wishful thinking; the town will be destroyed." And then it turns out that the town they are all arguing about doesn't even exist!

Personally, I am somewhat dubious about Buddhist metaphysics. I find far more comprehensible the Brahmanic, or orthodox Hindu, notion that the *I* is not a fiction but is nevertheless quite different from what we think. It may be that the individual *I* does not exist, but the universal *I* does. Rather, it may be that what we think is the individual *I* is in reality the universal *I*. (My God, if the *universal I* disappeared upon the death of just one individual, then there *would* be something to worry about! It would mean that *nothing* would be left! I would not be surprised if deep down *that* is what we are really worried about!)

Again, it may be misleading to talk of the individual *I* and the universal *I*; perhaps we should talk of only one *I*. This seems to me the most important idea in Brahmanic philosophy. Let me elaborate a little.

Obviously, I make a distinction between your sensations, feelings, and thoughts and mine. But from this it does not follow that the agent who experiences your thoughts is different from the agent who experiences mine. The question is, Are the agents really the same? It may seem completely counterintuitive that they are. But this intuition really appears to be culturally induced. It seems that the intuition of most Westerners is, "Of course they are not the same. I am I, and you are you, and that's all there is to it." But the intuition of many Easterners really seems to be that you and I are literally the same person.

Is not this the central issue of Brahmanism? It strikes me as far more radical and thoroughgoing than the Hegelian and post-Hegelian ideas of the Absolute, which is something like an "oversoul" that, so to speak, *includes* your soul and mine but is somehow infinitely greater than both. By contrast, the Brahmanic idea is far more drastic. Indeed, it appears to come close to outraging logic itself. It is that you and I are not *parts* of some supreme being but that we are the *very same being.*

I hope that you realize the fantastic ramifications that this hypothesis has on the question of life and death! Assume for the moment that the hypothesis is true. It follows that I will *not* die upon my bodily death as long as one other live creature remains, for this creature is also me. I hence do not have to believe in my soul going to a spiritual realm or in reincarnation. I already *am* reincarnated; rather, I am already incarnated in all other conscious beings. So when my body dies, there will be countless copies of *me* left. Indeed, whether your body dies or my body dies, the effect will be no different on me (or on you, which is the same thing).

Is it not possible that all of us deep down feel that this idea has some truth in it and that's why we in fact don't fear death more than we do? Is it not possible that this is the real reason we treat each other as well as we do, and why we are as concerned as we are about protecting each other's lives? It is our *own* lives we are protecting!

In many ways, this viewpoint is quite remarkable! To use another analogy—an elaboration of one devised by Schopenhauer—imagine looking at a point of light through a crystal. We see a thousand images, but they are all of the very same point. Similarly, our individual selves are but multiple appearances of one fundamental self. An individual death, then, is like blocking off a single facet of the crystal, and an individual birth is like opening up another facet. So the images vary and change and come and go, dancing their "dance of life," but the real point of light remains totally unaltered during the whole procedure.

A similar analogy is drawn by the Vedanta. It likens the relation of the one true self and its individual selves to the one sun simultaneously illuminating a thousand rooms of a palace. The rooms are of course like the individuals. Each has its own individual light but not its individual source of light. Thus (this is *my* analogy), an individual death is like drawing a shade or curtain on the window of an individual room. The individual room, it is true, goes dark. But none of the sunlight is lost! Not even that portion of light that formerly illuminated the room is lost; it now illuminates the shade or curtain. If the pedantic reader asks, "But suppose the shade or curtain is dark brown or black?" my answer is, "Yes, then the *light* gets lost, but not the energy of the light, which is transformed into heat."

Some Chinese Thoughts on the Subject

Having touched a little on the Buddhist and Brahmanic approaches, I would like to conclude with some contributions made by Chinese philosophy to the subject.

When Confucius was asked to expostulate on the nature of death, he replied that we do not even know the nature of Life; how then can we talk of the nature of Death?"

Confucius's reply strikes me as quite sound albeit a trifle pedestrian. My favorite writers of all (on this as well as many other matters) are the Taoists such as Laotse, Liehtse, and Chuangtse. They give neither analogies nor any rational explanations whatsoever! In total defiance of all logic, they soar their merry way upward like birds in free flight.

For example, Laotse once said that he who dies but does not perish has life everlasting.

It is amazing how differently people react to this! Some (like myself) simply burst out laughing. Others become very solemn and serious and try to analyze what distinction Laotse could possibly have had in mind between dying and perishing. But I can assure you that any such analysis will totally miss the point! The line means absolutely neither more nor less than exactly what it says.

I love the incident from Liehtse about the group who came across a skull. Many of the group recoiled in horror. But one member said, "Both the skull and I know that there is no such absolute thing as life and death."

Finally, there is the following gorgeous passage from Chuangtse —one of the most remarkable passages ever written.[6]

Nan-po asked Nu-yu, "Sir, you are old, but have the look of a child. How is this?"

"I have learned Tao," replied Nu-yu.

"Can Tao be learned?" Nan-po said.

"Ah! How can it?" replied Nu-yu.

"You are not the type of man. Pu-liang—I had the ability of the sage but did not know the teachings. I knew all the teachings but did not have his ability. But still I had to teach him. It was three days before he was able to transcend this world. After he transcended this world, I waited for seven days more and then he was able to transcend all material things. After he transcended all material things, I waited for nine days more and then he was able to transcend all life. Having transcended all life, he became as clear and bright as the morning. Having become as clear and bright as the morning, he was able to see the One. Having seen the One, he was then able to abolish the distinction of past and present. Having abolished the past and present, he was then able to enter the realm of neither life nor death. . . .

Where else does one find a passage this wonderful? Apart from the marvelous phrase, "he became as clear and bright as the morning," there is the more immediately relevant phrase, "the realm of neither life nor death."

The concept of the realm of neither life nor death comes closer to what I have tried to say in this essay than anything I have been able to say. It is a perfect example of why I so love Chinese philosophy!

I can think of no better conclusion to this essay than to quote a passage of the Chinese Zen master Huang Po (T'ang dynasty). Of it, the translator John Blofield says, "This paragraph is, perhaps, one of the finest expositions of Zen teaching, for it encompasses in a few words almost the entire scope of that vast and penetrating wisdom."[7]

If an ordinary man, when he is about to die, could only see the five elements of consciousness as void; the four physical elements as not constituting an "I"; the real Mind as formless and neither coming nor going; his nature as something neither commencing at his birth nor perishing at his death, but as whole and motionless in its very depths; his Mind and environmental objects as one—if he could really accomplish this, he would receive Enlightenment in a flash. He would no longer be entangled by the Triple World; he would be a World-Transcendor. He would be without even the faintest tendency toward rebirth. If he should behold the glorious sight of all the Buddhas coming to welcome him, surrounded by every kind of gorgeous manifestation, he would feel no desire to approach them. If he should behold all sorts of horrific forms surrounding him, he would experience no terror. He would just be himself, oblivious of conceptual thought and one with the Absolute. He would have attained the state of unconditioned being. This, then, is the fundamental principle.[8]

Notes

1. See the viewpoint of the realistic mystic in Chapter 5, "Simplicus and the Tree."

2. Daisetz Suzuki, *Mysticism: Christian and Buddhist* in *World Perspectives,* Vol. 12, edited by Ruth Anshen (New York: Harper and Brothers, 1957), p. 126.

3. On the whole I admire Dean Inge's statement (William R. Inge, *Christian Mysticism* (London: Methuen & Co., 1912, p. 55n.): "The allegation that the Christian persuades himself of a future life because it is the most comfortable belief to hold, seems to be utterly contemptible. Certain views about heaven and hell are no doubt traceable to shallow optimism; but the belief in immortality is in itself rather awful than consoling. Besides, what sane man would wish to be deceived in such a matter?" Much as I admire this statement as a whole, there are three small points that disturb me somewhat. First, I wish Dean Inge had used a less harsh word

than *contemptible.* Second, I find it surprising that he should regard immortality as somewhat "awful." And third, I feel that his comment, "Certain views about heaven and hell are no doubt traceable to shallow optimism," warrants the same criticism that he is leveling at those who dismiss belief in survival as traceable to mere optimism.

4. This principle is that every proposition is either true or false.

5. If it did, then there must have been a time before the beginning. If it didn't, then an infinite past has come to an end, which (according to Kant) is also impossible.

6. *A Source Book in Chinese Philosophy,* translated and compiled by Wing-Tsit Chan (Princeton: Princeton University Press, 1963), p. 195.

7. John Blofield, trans., *The Zen Teachings of Huang Po* (New York: Grove Press, 1958), pp. 45–46.

8. Ibid.

10

What Is There?

This chapter is a bit technical. The reader who finds it too difficult can skip it without loss of continuity.

Ontology

One dictionary defines *ontology* as the science of being; the branch of metaphysics that investigates the nature of being and of the essence of things.

This sounds like a rather ambitious subject, don't you think? I am reminded of the following passage from *Sherlock Holmes in Tibet* by Richard Wincor.[1] Holmes is speaking.

On the 15th September 1891, the Vice-Chancellor advised me that I was to be one of several qualified Westerners to attend a special session conducted by Tibet's leading metaphysician, Lama Nordup. The session was scheduled in a fortnight's time; all of us were to clear out of Tibet a day later. Somewhat puzzled, I asked the Vice-Chancellor what the lama's subject would be. His reply (translated literally in these notes) was,

"The secret of life and death, and the mysteries of existence." This reply captured my interest somewhat, and I resolved to attend.

Quine starts his famous essay *On What There Is* with the words, "A curious thing about the ontological problems is its simplicity. It can be put in three Anglo-Saxon monosyllables: 'What is there?' It can be answered, moreover, in a word—'Everything.'"

A similar philosophy was expressed in Oscar Mandel's delightful book, *Chi Po and the Sorcerer: A Chinese Tale for Children and Philosophers.*[2] In one scene, the boy Chi Po is taking painting lessons from the sorcerer Bu Fu. At one point, Bu Fu says, "No, no! You have merely painted what is! Anyone can paint what is; the real secret is to paint what isn't!" Chi Po, quite puzzled, replies, "But what is there that isn't?"

Chi Po, though hardly a professional philosopher, was really expressing the same ontological viewpoint as Professor Quine—namely, that everything exists, and nothing else exists. Now, some of the medieval philosophers apparently had quite a different idea; they believed that existence is a *property* that some things have and some things don't have, and the nonexistent entities can have lots of properties despite their nonexistence. So whereas Quine and Chi Po would agree that there are no centaurs at all—existent or otherwise—these medieval philosophers would say that there *are* centaurs but no existent ones. In other words, they would say that no centaur has the property of existence; but that does not imply that there are no centaurs, for there still can be nonexistent ones.

The philosopher Immanuel Kant vehemently denied that existence is a property, and so Kant, Quine, and Chi Po are in perfect agreement on this point. Indeed, Kant (though a devout theist) believed that none of the ontological arguments (which purport to prove the existence of God by pure reason) were valid because in all cases they rested on the false assumption that existence is a property.

Quite frankly, I don't know whether existence is a property or not, but I am perfectly open to the possibility that it is. I take the position, however, that even if existence were a property, the ontological arguments of Anselm and Descartes are still no good. (I give my reasons for this in item #241 of *What Is the Name of This Book?*,[3] where I show that Descartes' argument proving the existence of God could just as well be used to prove the existence of anything—such as a unicorn.)

A far better version of the ontological argument was given by the unknown Dutch theologian Van Dollard in an unpublished manuscript discovered by Inspector Craig.[4] Van Dollard constructed an axiom system much in the style of the later axiom systems of Spinoza, but his system was far more rigorous! (Sometimes I wonder whether Spinoza ever had access to Van Dollard's writings. Probably not; Spinoza was far too honest not to have mentioned it!) To fully appreciate the subtlety of Van Dollard's thought, I must ask the reader to try to put himself in the frame of mind of the medieval philosophers who believed that existence is a property that some things have and other things do not and that nonexistent things can have various properties just as well as existent things. In Van Dollard's system, certain properties are called *perfections,* and a *god* is defined as any being that has all perfections. The system starts with the following two axioms:

Axiom 1. The property of existence is a perfection.

Axiom 2 (the ontological axiom). Given any perfection *P,* if all things having Property *P* also have the property of existence, then there is at least one entity having the Property *P.*

1

From just these two axioms, Van Dollard obtained a rather startling result!

Theorem 1 (the ontological theorem). Something exists, that is, there is at least one entity that has the property of existence. (Perhaps Theorem 1 answers Leibniz's question: Why is there something instead of nothing?)

Can the reader see how to prove Theorem 1? (All proofs are given in the appendix to this chapter.)

2

Van Dollard next gave the following two axioms:

Axiom 3. Given any Class C of perfections, the property of having all the perfections in C is again a perfection. (For example, for any two perfections P_1 and P_2, the property of having *both* perfection P_1 *and* perfection P_2 is itself a perfection. The same is true of any three perfections P_1, P_2, P_3, or indeed for *any* class of perfections [whether a finite class or an infinite one]. In modern mathematical terminology, this axiom would be more succinctly stated: The intersection of any class of perfections is a perfection.)[5]

Axiom 4. There is a class of perfections that contains all perfections. (We shall henceforth refer to this class as the *class of all perfections*, and denote it by P.)

From these four axioms, Van Dollard obtained a rather basic theorem in theology:

Theorem 2 (the weak bible theorem). There is at least one god —moreover, an existent one!

To help prove this theorem, Van Dollard first proved as lemmas the following two propositions (which are not without interest in their own right):

Proposition 1 (rediscovered by Descartes). All gods exist, that is, every god has the property of existence.

Proposition 2. The property of being a god is a perfection.

3

This is as far as Van Dollard could get without using the following axiom:

Axiom 5. For any god g, the property of being identical to g is a perfection.

Using this axiom, Van Dollard obtained his major result!

Theorem 3 (the strong bible theorem). There is exactly one God.

Can the reader see how to prove Theorems 2 and 3?

Discussion. Van Dollard's proofs (given in the appendix), unlike the proofs of Anselm and Descartes, are completely rigorous by the most stringent standards of modern logic. Of course, the proofs tell us nothing about whether Axioms 1 through 5 are actually *true*, but as pieces of formal reasoning, they are impeccable! That is to say, whatever meanings one gives to the term *the property of existence* and to the term *perfection*, *if* the axioms are true under those meanings, *then* Theorems 1 through 3 are also true under those meanings. In other words, Theorems 1 through 3 are really logical consequences of Axioms 1 through 5. Moreover, it is easy to give meanings to those terms under which the axioms *are* true, and so, if nothing more, the axioms are certainly *consistent*.

And What about the Devil?

Good question; what about the devil or devils in general? Are there any? If so, how many are there? Do they have the property of existence? Is it possible that some of them have the property of existence and others not?

Fortunately, all these questions were settled completely in a remarkable manuscript written by a learned church doctor, Alphonso G. (Unfortunately, I am not allowed to divulge his complete name or the name of the manuscript [which, incidentally, was also discovered by Inspector Craig].) The manuscript was branded heretical by the Church, and the author was condemned to be burned at the stake. Fortunately, Alphonso escaped from prison and hid away his precious manuscript—probably the only surviving copy!

It appears from Alphonso's philosophical investigations that there are also certain properties called *antiperfections*, and naturally a *devil* is defined as a being that has all antiperfections. Here are some of Alphonso's postulates concerning antiperfections.

Postulate 1. Nonexistence is an antiperfection. (Nonexistence is of course the property of not having the property of existence.)

Postulate 2. Given any antiperfection *A*, if there is no existent entity having Property *A*, then there is no entity at all having Property *A*. (An existent entity is of course an entity that has the property of existence.)

4

From these two postulates, Alphonso first proved this theorem:

Theorem A. There are no nonexistent entities. In other words: Everything exists! (This means that Quine and Chi Po were right after all!)

Alphonso then proved the following theorem, which may well be the most important theorem ever proved!

Theorem B. There is no devil, existent or otherwise.

Of course it was Theorem B that caused Alphonso's break with the Church.

5

Alphonso had one very talented Polish student, M. Askanas, who (like all of Alphonso's students) believed that there was no devil but would not accept his master's proof. It's not that he believed that there was anything formally wrong with it, but he couldn't bring himself to accept Postulate 2 since it leads to Theorem A, and Askanas was not open to the possibility that there cannot be any nonexistent entities. He therefore proposed an alternative postulate that (with Postulate 1) also yields Theorem B but not Theorem A. Preparatory to stating this postulate, Askanas introduced the following definition: For any Property P, an entity is said to have the Property $P+$ if it has both Property P and the property of existence. (For example, if P is the property of being a fruit, then every apple —existent or not—has Property P, but only *existent* apples have the property $P+$.)

Here is Askanas's alternative postulate.

Postulate 2'. For any Antiperfection A, the Property $A+$ is also an antiperfection.

This postulate strikes me as particularly plausible. Indeed, I would say that if A is an antiperfection, then the Property $A+$ is, if anything, even a *worse* antiperfection than A! For example, if A is the property of being a tyrant, isn't the Property $A+$ even worse? That is, isn't an existing tyrant worse than a nonexistent one

Surely, of the two, the existing tyrant can do the more damage!

Anyhow, as I have said, Theorem B can be derived from Postulate 1 and Postulate 2'. Can the reader see how?

Remarks. Someone once asked me if, instead of proving that there is a God and no devil, couldn't one prove that there is a devil and no God? The answer is: Of course; just change the axioms!

I have heard that in the twelfth century there was a rumor that Alphonso G. had another student who constructed a system that sounds most intriguing! According to the account, this system (like that of Askanas) proved there was no devil and left open the question whether or not there are any nonexistent entities. The system, like that of Van Dollard, proved there was a God—in fact, a unique God—but the most curious thing of all is that the system did *not* prove that there is any *existent* God! In other words, the system proved that there is a unique God, but whether or not God has the property of existence was evidently undecidable in the system. (I'm not sure whether this proposition was *proved* undecidable in the system, or whether it was just that no one was able to decide it.)

This system sounds quite fascinating, and I wish I knew more about it! But, as I have said, it may be only a rumor. Moreover, I'm not sure whether there really was such a rumor, or whether I merely *heard* there was such a rumor.

Medieval Ontology and Solipsism

It has just occurred to me that the medieval ontology that espouses the possibility of nonexistent entities casts a new light on the philosophy of solipsism.

Suppose a solipsist says to me, "I am the only one who exists." How am I to interpret this? From the viewpoint of Quine and Chi´o, the statement can have only one meaning: "There is nobody else but me." But from the viewpoint of medieval ontology, the statement could just as well mean, "I am the only one who has the property of existence."

These two possible meanings strike me as having a drastically different significance. Frankly, I find it almost impossible to believe the solipsist if he intends his statement in the first sense. (I say *almost* for reasons that are dealt with in Chapter 12.) But if the solipsist intends his statement in the second sense, how can I know that he is wrong? Since I don't quite know what this property of existence is, then how can I tell which people have it and which people don't?

Chaudhuri's Ontology

I shouldn't leave the subject of ontology without at least a brief mention of some Eastern thought on the subject.

Many of you have heard the classic Hindu philosophical pronouncement: Nothing exists. Should this be interpreted to mean that no entity has the property of existence or that there are no entities at all?

The only Eastern philosopher I know who has seriously addressed this question is a certain Dr. Chaudhuri (whom I read about in some private notes of Inspector Craig). He vehemently affirmed that the statement was meant only in the *first* sense and that a lot of misunderstanding on the part of Western philosophers was the result of their interpreting it in the second sense. "Of course there are entities," wrote Chaudhuri, "the only question is whether any of them have *reality!*"

I should mention that Chaudhuri translated all of his own works into English and that he used the word *reality* instead of *existence*. He referred to an entity as being either real or unreal, and we shall follow him in this respect. Obviously, he defines a real entity as one that has the property of reality and an unreal entity as one that does not. He stated his main theorem thus:

Theorem C (Chaudhuri's Theorem). Nothing is real.

Chaudhuri derived his theorem from two ontological axioms. He referred to certain properties as Brahmanic properties. (I'm not sure what he meant by a *Brahmanic property*, but I suspect that he meant the same thing as the medieval Western ontologists meant by a *perfection*.) Here are Chaudhuri's ontological axioms.

Axiom C_1. Reality is Brahmanic.[6]

Axiom C_2. Given any Brahmanic property, if there is any real entity having the property, then there is also an unreal one having the property.

From these two axioms, Chaudhuri's theorem easily follows. We leave the proof to the reader.

Appendix

1

Proof of Theorem 1. This is quite simple: Let E be the property of existence. By Axiom 1, E is a perfection. Obviously, anything having Property E has the property of existence (since E *is* the property of existence), and so by Axiom 2, there is something having Property E, that is, there is something having the property of existence.

2

We first prove Propositions 1 and 2.

Proof of Proposition 1. This proposition is a trivial one and follows from Axiom 1 alone: Let g be any god; g has all perfections. By Axiom 1, the property of existence is a perfection. Therefore, g has the property of existence.

Proof of Proposition 2. This proposition follows from Axioms 3 and 4: Let P be the class of all perfections. (There is such a class by Axiom 3.) Let G be the property of being a god. By the definition of a god, Property G is nothing more nor less than the property of having all the perfections in P. Then by Axiom 4, this Property G is a perfection.

Proof of Theorem 2. Again, let G be the property of being a god. By Proposition 1, every entity having Property G has the property of existence (this is the same thing as saying that all gods have the property of existence). Also, by Proposition 2, the Property G is a perfection. Then by Axiom 2, there must be at least one entity having Property G, which means that there is at least one god.

3

Proof of Theorem 3. We have already proved that there is at least one god, so all that remains to prove is that there is at most one god.[7]

Let g_1 be any god. We will prove that given any god g_2, it must be that g_2 is identical with g_1. Suppose that g_2 is a god. Since g_1 is a god, then by Axiom 5 the property of being identical to g_1 is a perfection. But g_2, being a god, has *all* perfections, so in particular, g_2 has the perfection of being identical to g_1. This proves that any gods g_1, g_2 must be identical, and hence there cannot be more than one god.

4

Proof of Theorem A. Let N be the property of nonexistence. It is obvious that nothing having Property N can also have the property of existence. Then by Postulate 2 there is no entity at all having Property N. In other words, there is no entity at all having the property of nonexistence. (This proof uses Postulate 2, but it does not require Postulate 1!)

Proof of Theorem B. From Postulate 1 alone it follows that there cannot be any *existing* devil (which is already a relief!) because by definition every devil has all antiperfections, and nonexistence is an antiperfection (by Postulate 1), and so every devil has the property of nonexistence. So if there were a devil, it would have the property of nonexistence. But by Theorem A, there is no entity at all that can have the property of nonexistence. Hence, there is no devil.

5

Askanas's Proof of Theorem B. Askanas's proof is a bit more subtle! We recall that we now have Postulate 1 and Postulate 2 available but not Postulate 2.

Again let N be the property of nonexistence. Since we don't have Postulate 2 available, we cannot conclude that no entity has Property N. However, by Postulate 1, the Property N *is* an antiperfection. Then by Postulate 2', the Property $N+$ is also an antiperfection. Now, nothing can possibly have Property $N+$ (because such an entity would have both the Property N of nonexistence and the property of existence, and this is a contradiction). But since $N+$ is an antiperfection, then if there *were* a devil, it would have to have Property $N+$. Therefore, there is no devil.

Notes

1. Richard Wincor, *Sherlock Holmes in Tibet* (New York: Weybright and Talley, 1968).

2. Oscar Mandel, *Chi Po and the Sorcerer: A Chinese Tale for Children and Philosophers* (Tokyo: Charles E. Tuttle Co., 1964).

3. Raymond Smullyan, *What Is the Name of This Book?* (Englewood Cliffs, N.J.: Prentice-Hall, 1977).

4. This is the same Inspector Craig of whom I wrote so much in *The Lady Or The Tiger?* (New York: Alfred A. Knopf, 1982).

5. Parenthetical remarks accompanying the axioms are mine.

6. If my aforementioned suspicion is correct, then except for terminology this axiom is the same as Van Dollard's first axiom.

7. This, according to a famous quip of Alfred North Whitehead, is the creed of the Unitarians.

5

Concluding Pieces

11

Dream or Reality?

To distinguish the real from the unreal, one must experience them both.

S. Gorn's *Compendium of Rarely Used Clichés* [1]

SKEPTIC: You claim that you see a chair. How do you know that you see a chair?

SUBJECT: I never said that I know that I see a chair; I merely said that I *see* a chair. I am not as sure that I know that I see a chair as I am that I see a chair. To me, seeing is more immediate than knowing.

SKEPTIC: Suppose I prove to you that you don't see a chair?

SUBJECT: No proof can convince me since I already know that I do see a chair.

SKEPTIC: Ah, I've caught you! You do claim you *know* you see a chair.

SUBJECT: I never denied knowing it; I merely said that I am less sure that I know it than that I am seeing the chair.

SKEPTIC: And you would still claim to see the chair even if I proved to you that you don't?

SUBJECT: Of course I would!

SKEPTIC: Then you are being irrational.

SUBJECT: Not really.

SKEPTIC: Can you prove that you are seeing a chair?

SUBJECT: Of course not! Or rather, I should ask, "Prove it from what premises?"

SKEPTIC: Can you at least prove that it is probable?

SUBJECT: Probable? I don't even know what it means to say that it is *probable* that I am seeing a chair. What I say is that I *am* seeing a chair.

SKEPTIC: But how do you know that you are seeing a chair?

SUBJECT: You asked me that before. Let me say this: First of all, I am not completely clear that I understand the meaning of *how I know* anymore than *how I see.* But to the extent that I do understand it, I can honestly say that I do not know *how* I know that I see a chair.

SKEPTIC: So you don't know *how* you know you see a chair, and you admit you can't prove you see a chair, yet you stubbornly maintain that you see a chair.

SUBJECT: Of course!

SKEPTIC: Then you are being dogmatic!

SUBJECT: Perhaps.

SKEPTIC: But do you really want to be dogmatic? Just think of what dogma leads to! Think of fascism, communism, and the Spanish Inquisition.

SUBJECT: Oh, come on now; these are examples of intolerance, not just dogmatism!

SKEPTIC: But what is the difference between dogmatism and intolerance?

SUBJECT: The present case is as good an illustration as any. One might label my dogged belief that I see a chair *dogmatic* (though I am not sure this would be correct), but surely no one in his right mind would label this belief of mine *an act of intolerance!*

SKEPTIC: The reason that I cannot accept your statement that you see a chair is that I doubt the existence of chairs. I think, however, that one can translate your statement into another form whose truth I would accept. I think that what you are *really* trying to say is that you are having a certain visual sensation—the so-called sensation of seeing a chair.

SUBJECT: If it makes you happy to translate it into those terms, by all means do so! *I* would not think of saying it this way. It *may* be also true—in fact, it probably is true—that I am having this so-called sensation. But again, as I see it, the notion of sensation is a far more sophisticated concept than just seeing and leads to a considerable number of philosophical problems and ambiguities. To a phenomenalist or idealist, a sensation is an immediate element of experience. To a materialistic realist, a sensation is a certain brain state or cerebral phenomenon, which seems to me to be something completely different. At any rate, the sort of statements that I most immediately understand are things like, "I see a chair," "I see a table," and so forth. I understand statements involving terms like *sensation* mainly to the extent to which I can translate them into such primitive statements.

SKEPTIC: But would it not be a more secure basis for philosophy to start out assuming only the things one really knows, like one's own sensations? No one but you can know whether you have a sensation or not. So if you say you have a given sensation, it cannot be reasonably denied. But you have absolutely no basis for claiming to know that the sensation is *of* something.

SUBJECT: This whole way of starting out philosopy is, to my mind, the worst one possible. To start out with one's *sensations* (or sense data) as the primary known realities! Children, who to my mind are the best philosophers, don't do anything like that. They talk about *objects*, not *sensations* of objects. Once you start out with sensations as the given, then you get involved in the whole nightmare of worrying about the very problem you raised: Are there objects corresponding to these sensations, or are there just free-floating sensations, so to speak? Then the problem arises as to what these objects are really like: How do they resemble our sensations of them, how do they cause the sensations of them, and for that matter what real evidence do we have for their very existence? Is our evidence probabilistic, or must we accept objects as an act of "animal faith"? Kant thought it a scandal of philosophy that the existence of external objects had never been satisfactorily proved. But to me, the search for a proof is utterly ridiculous. I directly perceive the objects; what more could I want? I don't *perceive* sensations at all. At least, the things I perceive I don't call *sensations* but *objects*, like this chair. I can assure you that if I did not perceive this chair directly, then absolutely *no* proof for its existence would carry the slightest conviction with me. I honestly regard it as pathological to require proofs of things one already knows.

An important consideration has just occurred to me. There is another way—a totally different way—of understanding the statement, "I see a chair," than the one I had in mind, that is, the way it would be understood by a physicist qua physicist, which is a statement about the physical world, made within the framework of physics. This *secondary* interpretation, which to my utter amazement is regarded as primary by some philosophers, states that my body is now facing the chair, I am awake with open eyes, light rays are reflected from the chair that form an image on my retina, causing physiological changes in my optic nerve, brain, and so forth. If this "physicalistic" interpretation of my statement is what you understood, then I can well understand your labeling my sureness of it an unfounded dogma—indeed, I would agree! I *believe* that this secondary interpretation also holds, but I cannot possibly *know* it in the absolute sense that I know the other. Indeed, I know this only secondhand, that is, on the testimony of scientists. I have never seen my brain or optic nerve and only know of them from authorities trust. Incidentally, my objections to analyzing the statement, "I see a chair," into objects and relationships does not apply to the "physicalistic" interpretation; indeed, this interpretation does put together things like human bodies, chairs, light rays, optic nerves, brains, and so forth. Although I also clearly understand this secondary interpretation, it is a far more involved business than the primary interpretation, and I am able to understand this secondary interpretation only by analyzing it ultimately in terms of experience statements in their primary sense.

SKEPTIC: Since you make this sharp dichotomy between what you call the primary and secondary interpretations of experience statements and claim such an important difference between them, how in discourse do you make clear which meaning you have in mind?

SUBJECT: With philosophers—particularly so-called materialists—this is usually the most difficult thing in the world! With most people —especially with children—there is no difficulty whatsoever since they usually understand experience sentences only in the primary sense. Of course, primitive people—as well as all people who lived before the rise of science and so knew nothing about optic nerves and brains—can understand such statements *only* in the primary sense.

The situation seems to me well-nigh tragic. People in their childhood understand only the primary interpretation of experience statements. But at some stage of their development, particularly those who study science, they become aware of the secondary interpretation. They learn that one sees a chair when and only when one's physical brain is in a certain state. This is an exciting realization. But unfortunately certain people—those who become materialists—tend to identify the two meanings and cannot subsequently separate them. It may be possible that they even forget after awhile the primary meaning altogether, but I think this in fact unlikely. If they did, it almost would be too frightening to imagine. It would be as if someone like Alberich traded love for gold, and after living in the world of gold for awhile totally forgot what love was even like except in the purely operational sense of understanding how people behave when they are in love. But as I said, I doubt that my fears have any real basis. To use an analogy, a blind physicist knows what the word *red* means only in the *secondary* sense; a sighted child, knowing no physics, knows the word in the *primary* sense. I doubt very much if a sighted adult who became blind could ever in his lifetime actually forget what *red* meant in the primary sense.

SKEPTIC: Isn't it unfortunate that the same words and phrases have these two very different senses and that our language doesn't have separate phrases for the two meanings?

SUBJECT: Extremely unfortunate! This is precisely one of the things that leads to so much confusion in philosophy!

SKEPTIC: Is there no way that you can explain your distinction of primary and secondary meanings of experience statements to, say, a hard-boiled materialist?

SUBJECT: They are obviously aware that I think that there are two meanings. The secondary meaning they already understand (at least I think they do). As for the primary meaning, those who are polite say, "I have no idea what you could possibly mean"; those who are more crass say, "You don't mean *anything at all*; you are just using meaningless words, you are simply talking nonsense!"

SKEPTIC: Could you give me an example?

SUBJECT: Yes. One way I can explain that my primary meaning of, "I see a chair," is totally different from the secondary meaning is this: Under the secondary meaning, it would be a total contradiction in terms to say that I might see a chair after my bodily death. But under the primary meaning, there is no contradiction at all. Whether I will see chairs after my death is (to my mind) simply an unknown fact, but it is inconceivable to me that the notion is *contradictory*. I am thinking of Schlick, who maintained that in principle there is no reason why he should not witness his own funeral. Ayer, on the other hand, held this notion to be self-contradictory. Clearly, Schlick was thinking of witnessing in what I term the primary sense, Ayer in the secondary sense. Obviously, Aye would not accept my argument at all; he would not agree that his difference with Schlick showed that there are *two* senses of the phrase *I see* or *I witness.* He would deny that what I call the primary sense has any meaning at all.

SKEPTIC: Tell me, would you commit yourself to saying that you *know* that you see a chair?

SUBJECT: Yes, I would.

SKEPTIC: You realize, of course, that this commits you to saying that you know that you are now not dreaming.

SUBJECT: Not at all!

SKEPTIC: What!

SUBJECT: I said, "Not at all." I regard it as perfectly possible that right now I *am* dreaming.

SKEPTIC: Good God! Surely if you are dreaming right now, then you don't still maintain that you *now* see a chair!

SUBJECT: I most certainly do! In a million years, I would not *dream* of making my assertion that I see a chair dependent on the fact that I'm not dreaming.

SKEPTIC: But if you are now dreaming, then the chair you claim to see *doesn't even exist!*

SUBJECT: It most certainly *does* exist; I *see* it! It is one of the objects I am now dreaming about (assuming that I am actually dreaming).

SKEPTIC: But surely you don't maintain that the objects you dreamed about, say, last night, really exist!

SUBJECT: They may not exist now, but they sure as hell existed last night; I *saw* them!

SKEPTIC: No, no; you are putting it the wrong way! It's not that last night you *really* saw *dream* objects; it's that last night you *dreamed* that you saw *real* objects, but in fact you were wrong!

SUBJECT: Not at all; last night I really saw objects.

SKEPTIC: Would you call these objects real or not?

SUBJECT: This brings us to the heart of the matter. Look, I don't use such words as *real, unreal, dream, nondream, real world, unreal world* in an absolute sense but only in a relative sense. Let me explain.

What do I mean when I say that right now I may be dreaming? This should be explained first. Well, last night I went to sleep and then saw all sorts of objects. This morning I woke up, and where are all these objects? They are nowhere to be found in the world I now experience. So I tend to declare them unreal and the state I was in last night a "dream state," or the world I experienced last night a dream world. When I say that I may be dreaming now, all I mean is that I am open to the possibility that at some future time I may be in a state in which I regard my present state as I did my state last night. In other words, the experience of having gone from one state into another, in which the former state seemed to be unreal, has happened to me many times, and I cannot see why it cannot happen to me again with regard to the very state I am in now. It could be that in the next day or hour I could again have the experience I call *waking up* and regard my present state as unreal. In fact, I don't expect this to happen the next hour, day, week, month, or several years. But when my body dies, I am less sure that I will not enter a state relative to which my present state is a dream. And this state in turn may prove to be unreal relative to some future state, and so forth ad infinitum.

At any rate, I no longer believe in any absolute notion of what is real. I only think of the reality of a state or of an object as relative to some other state. Thus, the very question of whether I am now dreaming in some absolute sense is (to me) meaningless. I can only consider such a purely empirical question as whether or not my present state will one day seem unreal. Every state is real relative to itself. To me, it is an open question whether or not every state may be unreal relative to some other state.[2]

SKEPTIC: I must say, your idea terrifies me! Look, before we started talking about dreams, I thought that the whole time you were defending the philosophy of common sense in an uninhibitedly dogmatic manner. You *see* chairs; therefore, there *are* chairs, and so forth. Then you pull this complete reversal and come up with this ultrafantastic *idealism!* I must say, I am completely bewildered, and it will take me awhile to get over the shock.

SUBJECT: I don't regard this idea as either fantastic or idealistic.

SKEPTIC: Of course it is idealistic to say that *nothing* has absolute reality, that reality is only *relative* to something else!

SUBJECT: This is not idealism.

SKEPTIC: Look, I'm not going to quibble with you over terminology. Maybe it shouldn't be called *idealism* but simply *crazy and fantastic.* All right, I admit that on purely logical grounds, your position is no more disprovable than, say, something like solipsism. At least, at the moment I am not clever enough to find an actual inconsistency in your doctrine. So on rational grounds, I cannot refute you. But on psychological grounds I find the doctrine extremely dangerous. Frankly, the idea that one day I might wake up or be in another state relative to which all the objects and people around me that I have come to know and love should turn out to be *unreal* fills me with utter horror and totally shatters my feelings of security.

SUBJECT: I am glad that you brought up psychological factors because I think that they are most relevant. My psychological reaction is the very opposite of yours; to me, the belief in some absolute reality would make *me* highly insecure!

SKEPTIC: Why on earth should it do that?

SUBJECT: Because once I believed in this thing called *reality,* then I would start worrying about whether the things that appeared real to me really were real!

SKEPTIC: Why can't you just *know* that they are real as I do?

SUBJECT: Hey, I thought *you* were the skeptic! It seems in some ways that I am more skeptical than you.

SKEPTIC: You sure are! Indeed, your whole method of philosophizing is the strangest mixture of dogmatism and skepticism I have ever seen! About certain things you are totally dogmatic and about all other things—all things that are not *your* dogmas—you are skeptical.

SUBJECT: But of course! How could I be anything other than dogmatic about things that I know and skeptical about things that I don't?

SKEPTIC: But tell me honestly, why are you skeptical that the things before you are real in any absolute sense?

SUBJECT: When you use the word *why*, I am not sure whether you are asking for a psychological explanation as to how I got this way, or whether you are asking for my epistemological reasons. Let me first consider the former, which brings us back to the very important point you raised about feeling secure. Don't you see that once I admitted an absolute reality, I would have all the nightmarish problems about whether I am *really* awake or not. But without this category, all these awful problems don't even arise!

SKEPTIC: But ignoring a problem does not solve it! I can't reject the notion of reality just to avoid facing problems. Besides, the very thought that there is no such thing as reality itself makes me insecure.

SUBJECT: Originally, you told me that my philosophy, though possibly consistent, was dangerous because it leads to psychological insecurity. In other words, your immediate reason for rejecting it was that it makes *you* feel insecure. But now when I tell you that it makes *me* feel secure, you say these are not legitimate grounds for accepting it. Are you being quite fair?

SKEPTIC: No, you are right.

SUBJECT: I would like to say more about feeling secure. It is difficult for me to believe that what really makes you (or me, for that matter) feel insecure is that the objects we both see lack this property of absolute reality. Isn't the real fear that at some future time we may come to believe or to *feel* the unreality of the objects we both now perceive?

SKEPTIC: That is certainly part of it, but not all.

SUBJECT: Well, let me put it this way. Suppose God himself (or any being you would take to be both omniscient and truthful) would now come down to earth and say to you, "There is indeed such a thing as absolute reality. But, for certain reasons, I am not going to tell you whether any of the things or people you now perceive are real. This much I promise you, however: Never will you have the experience of one day being in a state relative to which your present state will appear like a dream. In other words, if you are dreaming now, then—unlike the dreams you have had before—you will never know it, not even in the afterlife, if there is one." My question now is whether this answer would satisfy you.

SKEPTIC: I'm afraid not. This would mean that I never would know which things were real and which were not.

SUBJECT: Well, suppose God then said, "All right, I'll tell you after all. Everything you now see *is* real." Would that satisfy you?

SKEPTIC: It would still not satisfy me, because I might be afraid that I was only dreaming that God spoke to me.

SUBJECT: Hey, it seems that *you* are the one who is *really* insecure! Insecure, that is, in *your* philosophy, not mine!

SKEPTIC: I'm afraid you are right. Well, I guess what I need is to have *faith* that I am now not dreaming.

SUBJECT: Ah! That is precisely the difference between your approach and mine. I don't want my feeling of security to have to depend on any act of faith. I have always thought of faith as somehow "whistling in the dark."

SKEPTIC: But how without some act of faith can you know you are not now dreaming?

SUBJECT: I told you before that I use the word *dream* only in a relative sense. But a point that I think may be important has just occurred to me. When I suggest the possibility that reality is only relative, that every world (or state) may be unreal relative to some other world, does this idea make you feel that the present world (the one we are now in and see) is less real than you would normally feel, or that other worlds are more real? In other words, do you feel that

I am trying to make the present world more fantasylike, dreamlike, or chimerical or that I am trying to make fantasy worlds appear more real?

SKEPTIC: Why, the former, of course. If I believed that every world was unreal relative to some other world, then I would feel that *all* worlds, including this one, were unreal.

SUBJECT: Oh, if that is your reaction, then I certainly don't blame you for totally rejecting the idea. I was thinking of it the opposite way! I was not trying to "derealify" this world but rather to "realify" so-called nonreal worlds. Why can't you see it in this light?

SKEPTIC: I don't know; the idea is quite new to me. I would have to think about it.

SUBJECT: You see, there is one important difference in our attitudes. Suppose for the moment that there really is an afterlife and that in the first state we enter the present world is unreal relative to that state. Your reaction will be very different from mine. You will say, "How surprising; I thought my previous state was real, but I was wrong; I was *deceived.*" I will say, "Just as I thought, the last state was real and interesting while it lasted, but was *impermanent.* Too bad, I guess nothing lasts forever."

I really think that the notion of permanence is the key to the whole business. Let me ask you another question. Suppose you were on another planet—call it Planet A—on which all the inhabitants, including yourself, slept half the time (instead of roughly a third of the time, as we do here). Now suppose at the end of each day on Planet A you undressed, went to bed, fell asleep, and found yourself in a totally different body—call it Body B—on a totally different planet called Planet B. You would spend a day on Planet B, at the end of which your B-body would undress, get into bed, go to sleep, and then you would return to State A. Let us assume that your existence in State B were just as consistent and coherent as in State A. When in State A you put some object on the desk and went to sleep, the next morning it was still there, and the same held for State B. Assume also that this state of affairs has been going on all your life; indeed, you were unable to recall whether your life started in

State *A* or State *B*. I repeat, each state had the same coherent internal structure. Let us say that science and psychology were about equally advanced in both worlds. The scientists of World *A* would assure you that your thought processes were nothing more nor less than certain physiological events in your brain—call it Brain *A*. They would tell you that when you went to sleep and "dreamed" you were on Planet *B*, this "dream" was nothing more than certain physical events taking place in Brain *A*. But the scientists of Planet *B* would tell you exactly the same thing in reverse; all your thoughts were nothing but events in Brain *B*. Moreover, they would tell you that Brain *A* doesn't really exist at all; those on Planet *A* would tell you that Brain *B* doesn't really exist except as a figment of the imagination of Brain *A*. I can even imagine the psychiatrists of both planets each diagnosing you as schizophrenic for believing in the reality of the other state; perhaps each would offer you some medication that would permanently cure you of your "illusion" concerning the other state.

Now, you must admit that under these circumstances your whole notion of reality would probably be very different. What would you believe? That either State *A* or State *B* was real and the other illusory, but you couldn't decide which? Or maybe that both states were real—that there could be, so to speak, two disjoint realities? Or perhaps you would suspect that both states were unreal and that your *real* state—State *C*—was something very different yet? Or maybe that *no* states are real? Don't you think that you would reject the very notion of reality as meaningless and would simply settle for the realization that each of the two states was internally real but that neither one was real relative to the other and that the only common bond would be that you experience them both?

SKEPTIC: Of course, *had* I lived such a life, my views on reality would probably have been very different. But the fact is that I have *not* lived such a weird life. So why should I let my views be influenced by the hypothetical situation you have just been spinning out, which itself is just a sheer fantasy? I'd like to know what you are really driving at. Tell me honestly, why are you so intent on trying to relativize the notion of reality? You said before something about having some epistemological reasons for rejecting any absolute notion of reality. What now are these reasons?

SUBJECT: My reason for rejecting it is very simply that I have absolutely no reasons for accepting it. Indeed, I don't even know what the notion really means! I have no idea how I can use the notion. Suppose I enter a new place and see a wooden chair. At least it *looks* wooden to me, but then it occurs to me that it may not be really wooden; perhaps it is cleverly painted papier mâché. In this sense, the word *really* means something quite definite to me; I know how to go about testing it. So I go over to the chair, inspect it more closely, feel it, and so forth, and conclude, "Yes, it really is made of wood." But now, what in the world would it mean for me to ask, "But is this chair real, or is it only illusory?" What test can I possibly perform to find out if the chair has this mysterious property of being real?

SKEPTIC: Why is it that you, who are usually so hostile to positivism, take such a positivist attitude toward this question?

SUBJECT: Because in this regard, I feel that the positivists have something of value to contribute. Incidentally, concerning my "hostile" attitude toward positivism, I think that I should state clearly that I divide positivists into two types, which I call *dogmatic positivists* and *skeptical positivists*. The dogmatic positivist will say about any word, phrase, or sentence whose meaning he cannot understand that it is meaningless or nonsensical. The skeptical positivist will instead be skeptical that it has any meaning or will wonder what the meaning could be. I am perfectly sympathetic to the skeptical positivist; it is only the dogmatic positivist of whom I am totally intolerant. After all, since I am dogmatic myself, it is only natural that I cannot tolerate any dogmas that conflict with mine.

But coming back to the notion of absolute reality, I, like the skeptical positivist, do not really understand what the notion is and indeed have some doubts that the notion has any real meaning. But I am not prepared to say that it is meaningless. The notion of absolute reality somehow reminds me of the notion of absolute position in space or absolute motion in space. When people first hear from the physical relativist that there is no such thing as bodies moving through something called *space*, but that bodies move only relative to each other, the reaction is often something of a shock; the new idea somehow seems counterintuitive. The dogmatic type of relativist will say, "There is no such thing as absolute motion; this is just an antiquated notion." The more modest and reasonable type of relativist, when asked, "How do you know that there is no such thing as absolute motion through space?" will reply, "I cannot say for sure that there is no such thing but merely that I do not know what it is and can see no possible way to use it in science. The subject matter of physical science is simply the description of how objects move relative to each other. And nowhere can I see how the hypothesis of absolute motion can be used in this study."

I have similar feelings about a chair's being real. Saying that it is relatively real is quite different. Again, this notion is related to the notion of permanence. I will put it this way: I certainly do have a notion of something appearing real or seeming real to me. For example, the chair I see before me certainly seems real to me. The chair I saw yesterday while I was awake seemed real to me then and still seems real to me in retrospect. But the objects I saw last night in my sleep seemed real to me then (at least as far as I now remember) but do not seem real to me now. So it is perfectly meaningful to ask whether I may *in the future* be in a state in which the chair I presently perceive will then seem unreal to me.

SKEPTIC: But this again is something you cannot now test.

SUBJECT: Of course I can't possibly test the chair to find out whether *in the future* it will seem real to me any more than I can now test it to determine whether in the future some rock will be hurled through the window and demolish it.[3] But both notions seem to me perfectly meaningful.

SKEPTIC: Perhaps your idea of relative reality is not so bad after all. It also may not be a bad idea to define something to be absolutely real to a given observer if it is in your sense permanently real, that is, if at no future time will it seem unreal.

Still, I am vaguely disquieted. I must say that I have a lingering intuition that there is something more to reality than a mere reduction to a permanent set of appearances. Do you honestly maintain that you have *no* such intuition?

SUBJECT: To be absolutely honest, I do have such a lingering intuition. But for that matter, I must also confess that I still have left *some* remnants of my childhood intuition concerning absolute motion.

SKEPTIC: So how do you reconcile these intuitions with your relativist position?

SUBJECT: I, as it were, hold such intuitions in abeyance. Incidentally, my intuition concerning absolute motion is much weaker than my intuition concerning absolute reality. Indeed, by now it has practically disappeared. But with the notion of absolute reality I am less sure that there is nothing to it. What should one do with such intuitions, intuitions that conflict with reason or with stronger intuitions? I do not believe in being overly brutal and harsh—even with oneself—and tearing out those intuitions that one regretfully realizes are not in complete harmony with one's general world view. I have far too much respect for *any* intuition to wish to "murder" it. So I let such intuitions, so to speak, lie asleep. I say to myself, "It is difficult to know what absolute reality can be, other than what I have suggested. But then again it appears possibly to have some other meaning. But I don't know how to work with such a meaning. So I will suspend final judgment until I have more knowledge."

SKEPTIC: I think your attitude is very reasonable. Still, I would love to know just a little more about your intuition of absolute reality. Strange, isn't it, that *I* have been defending this notion, and you have been attacking it. Yet you have so convinced me that this notion is unsatisfactory that I have to appeal to *you* for help in finding out what *I* mean by *absolutely real!* What is it you are looking for, and how will you recognize it if you ever find out? Or do you feel that in principle you never can?

SUBJECT: No, I would not say that in principle I never can find it, though I have as yet no idea of how I can or even just what it is that I seek. I am not one to go along with the idea that it is hopeless to find something unless one knows precisely what it is that one is looking for. So it is with the notion of absolute reality. I told you all my skeptical reasons for doubting that there is really anything to this notion, and so I am unable to use it in my actual life. Yet, as I have confessed, I still sometimes have the haunting feeling that I am overlooking something crucial, that I may be missing something of extreme importance. How can I find it? God only knows! There is nothing more at present that I can possibly do. But who knows? Maybe one day the idea, if there really is any idea, might dawn on me. Perhaps through further advance of science, through a more refined logical analysis of the question, or through something like a sudden mystical insight, it might happily happen that I will say, "Ah, of course! How simple! So that's what reality *really* is!"

Notes

1. S. Gorn, *Compendium of Rarely Used Clichés* (unpublished and used with permission of the author).

2. To the mathematical reader, the situation as described has a resemblance to conclusions some mathematical logicians have drawn from the Skolem-Löwenheim theorem. This theorem is to the effect that no axiom system (of first order logic) can compel the domain of interpretation to be nondenumerable. This led Skolem and others to believe that the very notion of nondenumerability has no absolute meaning.

3. This reminds me of the beautiful Haiku poem:

> There is nothing in the voice of the cicada
> To indicate how long it will live.

12

Enlightened Solipsism

ANDRICUS: I can well imagine why some Eastern mystics and philosophers find so strange our Western idea that one *should* love and treat one's neighbor as oneself. I am thinking of the type who believes that one's neighbor *is* oneself! Naturally, someone who believes this needs nothing like ethics or morality to treat others well but would do so for the very same reasons that one treats oneself well. Under this belief, the very notion of sacrifice would be meaningless. This is an interesting example of how a purely metaphysical hypothesis can have fundamental ethical ramifications without appealing at all to anything like principles of morality.

MORALIST: It would be a fine kettle of fish if people had to have *such* an idea to behave ethically!

FIRST PHILOSOPHER: This idea only substantiates what I have always said, namely, that if you start out with nonsense, you usually end up with nonsense! The hypothesis that my neighbor *is* myself is so patently absurd that it seems an utter waste of time to even consider its further ramifications.

ANDRICUS: But I ask, is it all that absurd? Does it have no meaning whatsoever? Even if strictly speaking it is false (or even meaningless), may it not at least suggest something of value that perhaps a more conventionally meaningful sentence would not suggest?[1]

SECOND PHILOSOPHER: If you claim that there is any meaning in the sentence, "My neighbor is myself," then it is incumbent on you to demonstrate this fact!

FIRST PHILOSOPHER: Three cheers!

ANDRICUS: Softly, my friends! I make no claim whatsoever. I feel, however, that there is something extremely important in this sentence. All I wish to do is to discuss with you certain ideas that have occurred to me in the process of trying to understand it. Before this, however, I wish to mention a closely related point. Many people feel that this is an unjust world since some lives are fraught with so much suffering and others with so much joy.

FIRST PHILOSOPHER: Obviously! Everybody in his right mind knows that.

ANDRICUS: Well now, consider a hundred booths in a building, each one containing an occupant watching a private movie. Suppose some of the movies are very good and others very bad. At first sight, this situation seems very unjust; why should some be more privileged than others to see good movies? But suppose upon learning more about the setup we found out that the overall plan was that the occupants were to rotate, and hence everyone would see all one hundred movies, but each in a different order. Then we would revise our opinion about the situation's being unjust.

FIRST PHILOSOPHER: This is obviously an analogy; what are you driving at?

ANDRICUS: It seems to me that it is logically possible that the physical universe simply repeats its history over and over again and that we sentient beings (minds, souls, egos, spirits, psyches, call us what you will) simply interchange roles, that is, each of us inhabits the body of some living organism during one universal cycle; in the next cycle, we switch organisms. Thus, we all "see the same show" but in different orders. If this were true, then clearly the world would *not* be unjust.

FIRST PHILOSOPHER: *If* this were true; that's a pretty big if.

ANDRICUS: I am not claiming the hypothesis to be true; I am only claiming it to be *possible*. If I am not wrong in this claim, then an important conclusion can be drawn: Some pessimists claim that the existing world is *necessarily* unjust; there is no possible way of justifying it. Now, if my hypothesis is true, then the world is not unjust. Hence, if my hypothesis is possible (which no one has yet disproved), then it is possible that the world is not unjust, and hence the pessimists' claim that the world is necessarily unjust is false.

SECOND PHILOSOPHER: The world obviously *is* unjust, and it is clearly up to *us* to make the world *more* just! Your theory constitutes the perfect apology for the quietist who wishes to sit back and let things remain as bad as they are. Just think! If your theory were true, then the world would already be perfectly just and would remain perfectly just in the future regardless of what we did. In other words, there is nothing we could do to make the world any more just, so we might as well sit back and continue in our rotten ways!

ANDRICUS: Ah, but that is precisely my second point! Just think, if my hypothesis were true—or more important, if it were generally believed—how much better would we treat each other! My neighbor's fortunes and misfortunes are nothing more than my own past or future fortunes and misfortunes.

MORALIST: At this point, I vigorously protest! Apart from the utter metaphysical absurdity of the hypothesis, I vehemently deny that its *belief* would lead to more moral behavior! I wish to categorically state once and for all that if I refrained from hurting my neighbor simply because I believed that I would one day be hurting myself, then my act would have no moral worth whatsoever.

ANDRICUS: Well now, that depends upon one's basic orientation toward morality. Tell me, are you a Christian?

MORALIST: Yes.

ANDRICUS: Well, does not Christianity motivate people toward good deeds by talk of rewards and punishments in a future life? Would you regard it of no moral worth for a man to try to live a good life to obtain salvation or escape damnation?

MORALIST: Of course God metes out punishments and rewards in the afterlife. But the truly moral man does not pursue the good for the *purpose* of obtaining rewards or avoiding punishments; he pursues the good only for the sake of the good.

ANDRICUS: You grant that Bishop Berkeley was a good Christian apologist?

MORALIST: Of course!

ANDRICUS: Well, perhaps you are aware that in his essay, "Future Rewards and Punishments," he actually stated that a man who did not believe in future rewards and punishments would act a *foolish* part in being honest. He continued,

> For what reason is there why such a one should postpone his own private interest or pleasure in doing his duty? . . . But he that, having no such view, should yet conscientiously deny himself a present good in any incident where he may save appearances is altogether as *stupid* as he that would trust him at such a juncture.[2]

MORALIST: I am aware that Berkeley unfortunately wrote these words. Look, I certainly regard Berkeley as a model Christian in almost all respects. But this particular sentiment I regard as most un-Christian! Christianity in the true sense of the word teaches that though moral acts do carry future rewards, one should perform them not for the sake of the rewards but simply because they are right. This was clearly recognized by Immanuel Kant. Indeed, Kant had the insight to realize that even when one performed a helpful act for a neighbor merely out of sympathy or compassion, the act had no moral worth since it was then performed only out of *identification* with one's neighbor's feelings, and hence, in the last analysis, only done out of consideration for one's own feelings. In other words, such an act is only a disguised form of selfishness.

ANDRICUS: Oh come now, if you carry that type of analysis far enough, then any action can be regarded as another form of selfishness. It could be equally argued that your very attachment to what you call *morality* is only a form of selfishness; in other words, you perform moral actions only because of the satisfaction you get from doing what you know to be right.

MORALIST: I protest! This is an old and vicious hedonist trick. The hedonists try to rationalize their selfishness at any costs; obviously, they cannot successfully do so. Hence, to assuage their guilt feelings for their selfishness (which shines through their philosophy however they may try to hide it), they point an accusing finger at the decent moralist and claim that he is just as selfish as they!

ANDRICUS: I think that you misunderstood the point I was trying to make. I was not claiming that your pursuit of the good is not moral but only that if your argument were correct, then it could also be turned against you. In other words, I was merely attempting a sort of reductio ad absurdum argument against your position. I know that some hedonists also do this, and though I am definitely not a hedonist, I think that they are right in this respect. In other words, if you are going to bring moral charges against hedonists—even those who act altruistically not out of moral principle but simply out of human kindness—if you charge them with selfishness for doing this, I do not see how the same charge cannot be leveled against you for the pursuit of morality itself.

MORALIST: But there is all the world of difference between the two.

ANDRICUS: Is there really? I guess your point is that virtue is its own reward and that one should pursue virtue only for the very reward implicit in virtue itself.

MORALIST: No, that is still not right. One should not pursue virtue for *any* reward whatsoever—not even the reward implicit in virtue itself. Of course, I believe that virtue is its own reward but that does not mean that one should pursue it for the sake of that reward. One should pursue virtue only for its own sake.

ANDRICUS: I think you are demanding something that in principle is impossible. You are essentially demanding that a person do something without having *any* motivation whatsoever. It is as if you were saying, "I want you to do this; but I don't want you to *want* to do it!" You are really giving contradictory commands—you are placing your listener in a double bind. The effect on a sensitive person can be psychologically shattering in the extreme. I think it is this aspect of so-called morality that more than any other has given rise to such strong antimoral feelings in the world.

FIRST PHILOSOPHER: How did we ever get sidetracked on the subject of morality? On moral grounds I am afraid I agree with Andricus rather than the moralist. I am basically a utilitarian and a pragmatist. I fully agree that if either the mystical hypothesis, "Your neighbor is yourself," or Andricus's hypothesis, "Your neighbor is your past or future self," were generally believed, then certainly people would treat each other far better than they do now, and this would indeed make for a better world. Whether moral worth should then be imputed to their motives, I leave for the moral metaphysician. The *fact* is that the world would be a hell of a lot better. But my pragmatism does not go so far as to make me believe something is true just because the belief in it makes the world better. The mystic belief is simply nonsensical, and Andricus's hypothesis, though not *logically contradictory*, is empirically ridiculously implausible. Surely there must be *some* saner way of getting people to treat each other better!

ANDRICUS: I also did not want to get sidetracked on moral issues, but I'm afraid that it was mainly my fault for remarking on the ethical ramifications of the concept of my neighbor is myself. But now that we are on the subject of morality, there is something else I wish to say before I come back to the metaphysical and epistemological aspects of the question.

What strikes me as the fundamental difference between the Eastern and Western concepts of morality is this: The Western mind tends to regard one's duty and one's natural inclination as opposing forces. These then are forces in eternal conflict. This conflict is clearly reflected in the Christian theology of God *versus* the devil. Virtue then consists of fighting, resisting, or overcoming temptations. One speaks of the triumph of good over evil. My response is,

"What a way to live!" The very idea of good triumphing over evil structures the situation in such a warlike manner! This is an excellent example of the type of duality that is regarded as so unfortunate by the Easterner. By contrast, the Eastern mind sees no real conflict between egotism and altruism; the apparent conflict arises only from what they call *ignorance*. The entire approach is not to have altruism *triumph* over egotism but to integrate or fuse the two, or rather to realize that they are really one.

I think that the whole situation is beautifully expressed in the Eastern story of the student who asked the master about the true nature of sacrifice. The master replied, "Do not speak to me, my boy, of sacrifice; it is all in the mind! There is much opportunity to do good in the world, and he who does not avail himself of it is robbing himself. Does the sun make a sacrifice by shining forth rays of warmth and light?"

SECOND PHILOSOPHER: Please, Andricus, *can't* we leave the subject of morality and return to the original topic? Your hypothesis was that our minds rotate bodies over various lifetimes, and hence that my neighbor's experiences are either my past or future experiences. Do you seriously regard this as an explanation of what the Eastern mystic means when he says, "Thy neighbor is thyself"?

ANDRICUS: Of course not! No Eastern mystic would accept such a crass, literal-minded interpretation. Only a Westerner like myself would even think of such a thing.

FIRST PHILOSOPHER: Why do you speak so disparagingly of we Westerners? Do you think we are congenitally inferior to the Easterners or something?

ANDRICUS: Of course not. The difference is neither congenital nor a matter of inferiority or superiority. But there *is* a very important difference, as I can assure you from having spent many years in the East. It is that our whole training since early childhood, our whole basic orientation toward life, is so different that we appear almost to have different basic categories of thought. Indeed, some feel that much of the profound wisdom of the East is not even translatable into Western terms. I myself do not go along with th view; I think it is translatable though there are enormous difficulties involved.

At any rate, the hypothesis I suggested was intended only as a first approximation of the notion, "My neighbor is myself." What I now wish to consider is the following variant of this hypothesis: Instead of there being many individual minds in the universe that rotate bodies during successive lifetimes, there is only *one* mind, which inhabits one body at a time—a different one during each physical cycle.

FIRST PHILOSOPHER: This hypothesis strikes me as even crazier than your first!

ANDRICUS: Me, too! It is a rather weird variant of solipsism. Suppose my body should now say, "My mind is the only one in existence." These two physical events would occur over and over again in the various universal cycles. Once and only once when *my* body says it, it will be true; once and only once when *your* body says it, it will be true; and so forth for each body that says it.

SECOND PHILOSOPHER: Since you admit your second hypothesis is even crazier than your first, why did you even bother to formulate it?

ANDRICUS: Mainly in preparation for my third hypothesis, which is as follows: There is only one mind in the universe. This mind very rapidly oscillates through all the living organisms of the universe. it spends, say, a trillionth of a trillionth of a second in your body, then in mine, then in the next fellow's, then in the body of a dog, and so forth. It oscillates so fast that the effect seems continuous, like a single beam of light oscillating all over a television screen.[3]

FIRST PHILOSOPHER: And this, you take it, is an explication of what the Eastern mystic means by the statement, "Your neighbor is yourself"?

ANDRICUS: No, certainly not. Again, this is far too literal, Western, and "science fictitious" to satisfy the Eastern mystic. Indeed, he has—or claims to have—*direct* understanding of the notion, "My neighbor is myself"; no explanation is needed.

FIRST PHILOSOPHER: And do you claim to understand this directly?

ANDRICUS: Yes and no. I might first of all go one step further in the hypothesis: Imagine the one mind oscillating faster and faster. Is it so impossible to pass to the mathematical limit of the situation, which is that the same mind is *simultaneously* in all the different bodies? Indeed, even without passing to this limit, if the oscillation is rapid enough, then for all practical purposes the mind *is* simultaneously in many bodies.

FIRST PHILOSOPHER: Can you honestly say that this idea of your mind being in several bodies *at the same time* does not go counter to your intuition about time?

ANDRICUS: To be perfectly honest, yes! But then I suspect that there is something wrong with our very intuition about time. But we have heard nothing this entire conversation from our friend the epistemologist. Why so silent?

EPISTEMOLOGIST: I have remained silent because my objection to the original statement, "My neighbor is myself," is on such trivially obvious grounds that it seemed almost pointless to voice it.

ANDRICUS: Why not voice it anyhow?

EPISTEMOLOGIST: All right, if you really wish me to I will. How can the statement, "My neighbor is myself," possibly be true? The simple fact is that if a pin is stuck into your body, *you* feel it and *I* don't. It would seem to me that if you and I were identical, then we would either both feel the pain or neither of us feel the pain. How can you say that two things are identical when you affirm something about the one and deny it about the other?

ANDRICUS: Obviously, this is indeed the main objection to the idea and is precisely why the idea is difficult for me to accept.

EPISTEMOLOGIST: Now I don't understand you. Do you accept this Eastern idea or don't you?

ANDRICUS: I told you before, yes and no, by which I mean that in a way I do and in a way I don't. Obviously, the kind of identity the epistemologist used is the Leibnizian notion, which is the notion used by most modern logicians. According to this notion, two things are identical if everything that is true of one of them is also true of the other. In this sense of identity, of course my neighbor is not identical with myself, for the very reason mentioned by the epistemologist.

EPISTEMOLOGIST: Of course I was using the notion of identity in the standard sense. What other sense is there? Any false statement can be made true if one simply changes the meaning of all—or even some—of the words involved. Perhaps you mean by *identical* just what most of us mean by *different*. In *that* nonstandard sense of the word *identical* I will grant you that my neighbor is identical with myself, which now simply means that my neighbor is different from myself.

ANDRICUS: Please now, you hardly think that I am so simpleminded as not to be aware of this completely trivial way of making any statement true. Do you honestly believe that when I affirm the statement, "My neighbor is identical with myself," that by *identical* I mean *different?*

EPISTEMOLOGIST: No, of course I don't believe you are doing anything quite that preposterous! But what *are* you doing? Since you admit that you are not using the notion of identity in the standard sense, you must be using it in some other sense. So instead of tampering with language, why don't you instead use the standard word, or group of words, to describe the notion you have in mind?

ANDRICUS: I assure you that I am not being perverse or trying to be mysterious. The honest fact is that I don't *know* of any other word to convey my meaning.

EPISTEMOLOGIST: And I can assure you that I am not trying to be skeptical for the sake of being skeptical, nor am I trying to be un-understanding. I genuinely believe it possible that you are trying to explicate an extremely important notion, but so far I cannot understand it. Is there *nothing* you can say to make the task any easier for us?

ANDRICUS: There may be something, though I don't know how much it will help. In the first place, though I admitted that my use of the notion of identity is not the Leibnizian notion that logicians use, it does not quite follow that my use is nonstandard; I very much doubt that the Leibnizian notion is the only standard one.

EPISTEMOLOGIST: What other standard notion is there?

ANDRICUS: There is the following: Ask an average adult whether he is the same person he was when he was a child, or whether he is a different person. Some will answer, "Of course I am different; I am taller, fatter, older, wiser, and so forth." Others will answer, "Of course I am the same person. Obviously, I have changed in the meantime, but still I am *really* the same person." My point is that enough people will give the latter answer for it to qualify as standard. Now, this notion of being the *same* person I was when I was a child is obviously not the Leibnizian notion of identity. The adult I and the childhood I do not have all properties in common. In particular, if someone sticks a pin into my present body, the childhood I did not feel it, and if someone sticks a pin in the childhood I, the present I does not feel it. Yet there is, I think, a very real and very important sense in which the childhood I and the adult I are the same. It is *this* notion of identity that comes far closer to the notion of sameness inherent in the statement, "My neighbor is myself."

EPISTEMOLOGIST: I think I understand this other notion of identity (though there are those who would question it). But the two contexts are so very different! In the case of a child becoming an adult, there is an obvious continuity that can easily and naturally give rise to this notion. But comparing you with your neighbor, this continuity is obviously absent, hence how can this other notion of identity apply?

ANDRICUS: Good question! I would answer it by saying that although this other notion of identity would naturally occur to one as a result of continuous transformation, it does not therefore follow that the notion is applicable only in this situation; it may also apply to myself and my neighbor.

FIRST PHILOSOPHER: I think that using pure reason we cannot make much more headway with this problem. At this point, I am afraid that I must ask you an irritatingly practical question. What evidence do you have that your neighbor is yourself?

ANDRICUS: None whatsoever!

FIRST PHILOSOPHER: Then why in heaven's name do you believe it?

ANDRICUS: Why? I don't believe I know why. It just seems right to me.

FIRST PHILOSOPHER: And from the fact that it *seems* right to you, you have the audacity to conclude that it *is* right?

ANDRICUS: Of course not! Of course I know that because something seems right to me it does not follow that it is true. You act as if I started from the premise, "I believe it," and drew as a conclusion, "It is true." But I have done nothing of the sort. The statement, "I believe it," is neither a premise nor a conclusion; it is simply a fact, since I *do* believe it—at least I do much of the time.

FIRST PHILOSOPHER: You mean to say that you believe it some of the time, and some of the time you don't?

ANDRICUS: I'm afraid so!

FIRST PHILOSOPHER: What do you believe at this very moment; do you believe it or not?

ANDRICUS: I'm afraid that at this very moment I feel so silly and on the defensive that I really cannot say whether I believe it now or not.

FIRST PHILOSOPHER: I find it rather ironical that all of us here have been wasting our precious time in what we honestly thought was a genuine objective philosophical discussion, and then it turns out that all you have been saying has led up to a mere *personal* idea, and moreover, one that by your own admission you do not even consistently maintain.

ANDRICUS: In all fairness to myself, I must correct you. I told you at the very beginning of the conversation that I made no *claim* whatsoever; I am merely trying to *understand* the Eastern mystic viewpoint.

SECOND PHILOSOPHER *(to First Philosopher):* I'm afraid Andricus is right about that, and I must say your attitude can hardly be described as *sympathetic*. But I can also understand your disappointment in expecting a purely objective analysis of the question.

FIRST PHILOSOPHER: Well, I'm sorry if I was overly abrupt, yet I cannot but feel that you, Andricus, instead of consulting us philosophers about this problem should have consulted a psychologist or psychiatrist since your problem is obviously not philosophical but purely psychological.

SECOND PHILOSOPHER: I perfectly agree that the problem is psychological rather than philosophical. Fortunately, I have had some psychiatric training, so I think I can be of some help here.

Look, Andricus, you obviously have some enormously strong *motivation* for wanting to understand and even believe the statement, "Thy neighbor is thyself." You have gone to fantastic lengths in first discussing its ethical ramifications and then bringing in all these weird science fiction fantasies to, as you say, *suggest* its meaning. Then you admit having no *evidence* for its truth and not even a clear knowledge of what it means to be true, and you admit that whatever understanding you *sometimes* have of it is elusive and inconstant. Despite all these difficulties—which you yourself evidently realize—you nevertheless cling to the idea as you would to something very precious. So I must ask you to ask yourself very honestly, What is your *real* motive for embracing this principle?

ANDRICUS: Without having to be as introspective as you suggest, I can certainly think of a very good motive, but I would call this motive philosophical rather than psychological.

SECOND PHILOSOPHER: What motive is that?

ANDRICUS: I was just about to tell you. The statement, "My neighbor is myself," seems to me the only alternative to—of all things—solipsism!

FIRST PHILOSOPHER: Good God, you can't be serious!

MORALIST: Now really, you are going a bit too far!

EPISTEMOLOGIST: How can this statement possibly relate to solipsism?

ANDRICUS: I was just about to tell you. All my life I have never been able to understand how any mind could possibly conceive of anything outside its own experience. How can one mind even *think* of another; what sort of image of it could it possibly have? How could I in all honesty believe in the existence of other minds when I cannot even *conceive* of them?

EPISTEMOLOGIST: What's wrong with the standard argument by analogy? You see other bodies acting sufficiently like your own for you to make a probabilist inference that they have other minds, too.

ANDRICUS: Please, you don't understand! No probabilist argument could help me in the least! In the first place, probabilist arguments have never carried with me the slightest conviction when applied to conclusions that themselves are not empirical.

EPISTEMOLOGIST: I am not sure I understand you.

ANDRICUS: I mean to say that when it comes to predicting directly observable events like the cast of a die, the outcome of spinning a roulette wheel, or the rising of the sun tomorrow, probabilist arguments really carry with me intuitive conviction; they really are causative factors in producing within me psychological *expectation*. But when applied to conclusions that might be called *metaphysical* in nature, as for example, whether external objects really exist, whether minds really exist, whether minds or souls survive bodily death, or whether other minds exist, probabilist arguments just don't carry with me the same type of intuitive conviction. I understand perfectly what is meant by saying that if I throw a die, the probability is 1 in 6 that the number 5 will come up, or that the probability of 17 coming up on a roulette wheel is 1 in 37. But what on earth does it mean to say that the probability that external objects exist is such and such, or that the probability is so and so that other minds exist?

FIRST PHILOSOPHER: But how could we know such things except on a probabilist basis? Everyone who has seriously thought about the matter knows, for example, that solipsism is not logically refutable. From the statement, "My mind is the only one in existence," one certainly cannot derive a logical contradiction. Therefore, I cannot know with logical certainty but only with very high probability that other minds exist. This probability is high enough for my comfort.

ANDRICUS: The probability that other minds exist is high enough for you? Just how high is it, anyhow? Would you care to give a *numerical* estimate of it? Of course not! I still say that probability, as well as logic, is utterly irrelevant to the problem. Most people believe as a matter of course that other minds exist; it would not even occur to them to doubt it, nor to consider, of all things, its probability. Indeed, if an average person should be asked by a philosopher, "How do you *know* that others minds exist?" he will usually look at the philosopher as if he is crazy (and, in a way, he may be right). It is only when one feels the need to justify one's metaphysical beliefs—say, the belief in other minds—that one brings in logic and probability, but these are only afterthoughts or rationalizations and, I maintain, very bad ones at that. The fact is that such beliefs almost always occur *prior* to the arguments found for their justification.

MORALIST: I also believe that the probabilist arguments used to justify the existence of other minds are very poor—indeed, down-right immoral. It is simply not very nice to doubt the existence of other minds!

FIRST PHILOSOPHER *(to Moralist):* I'm sorry that I cannot go along with this. Whether other minds exist or not is a fact, and I cannot use a moral argument to establish a question of fact. Besides, to say that it is not nice or that it is immoral to doubt the existence of other minds makes sense only if other minds do in fact exist. If there really were no other minds, why would it be morally wrong to know or to believe this fact? It seems to me that you are putting the cart before the horse. To know whether it is morally right to believe in other minds, it must be first settled whether there *are* other minds, and this, I maintain, can be settled only on the basis of high probability.

ANDRICUS: And I maintain that it cannot. But it is silly for us to argue this point now. If *you* find a probabilist argument necessary for maintaining your belief in other minds, it should hardly be my function to try to deprive you of it. But as I have said before, such an argument carries absolutely no conviction with *me*.

FIRST PHILOSOPHER: In that case, what reasons *do* you have to justify your belief in other minds? Or are you still a solipsist?

ANDRICUS: I still have not made my situation clear to you. I don't require any reasons or justification whatever for the belief in other minds!

FIRST PHILOSOPHER: Then you are not being rational!

ANDRICUS: Call it what you like; we can argue about this another time, since the question of my rationality is so irrelevant to what I am trying to say. As a child, I never had the slightest doubt about the existence of other minds; I took it completely as a matter of course, as most people do. Would you call them irrational for having this belief just because they have never figured out reasons to justify it?

FIRST PHILOSOPHER: Then I am more puzzled than ever. If, as you say, you don't need rational arguments to justify this belief, then what on earth stops you from having it? Why do you have a problem with solipsism at all? Since you don't need any probabilist argument, what stops you from simply accepting the existence of other minds without any inductive evidence?

ANDRICUS: Because of what I told you before. To me, the problem never was, "*Are* there other minds?" but "*Could* there be other minds?" Once I believe that other minds *could* exist, then I would not have the slightest doubt that other minds *do* exist.

FIRST PHILOSOPHER: This is the weirdest argument I have ever heard! You mean to say that you believe that everything that is possible is actual, that everything that *could* exist *does* exist?

ANDRICUS: Of course not! Why do you jump to such a silly generality? I am not saying that everything that can exist does exist. I am just saying that other minds happen to be one of those things whose possible existence would *to me* be enough to ensure their actual existence. In other words, my mind happens to be so constituted, whether rightly or wrongly, rationally or irrationally, that if I can accept the possibility of other minds, then I automatically accept their actuality. I am *not* here drawing any inference or proposing any argument; I am just telling you how I do as a matter of fact think. Normally, I don't do this, but you must recall that I was asked the *psychological* question of what are my *motivations* for my interest in the statement, "Thy neighbor is thyself."

SECOND PHILOSOPHER: So far, so good. I personally could not make the step from the *possibility* of other minds to their actual existence, but if you say that *you* can, who can quarrel with the fact that you do? But I still cannot understand your difficulties in the first place in believing that other minds are even possible. Why should they be impossible?

ANDRICUS: Because, as I told you before, how can I even conceive anything outside of my own experience; hence how can I possibly believe it?

MORALIST: Isn't your attitude just a bit on the egocentric side?

ANDRICUS: Of course it is, and of course I know it! But do you think that knowing it makes matters any easier or less painful? As was said before, how can any *moral* argument clear up an epistemological difficulty? A moral argument might indeed succeed in making one feel guilty for holding certain views, but it cannot possibly succeed in locating the actual source of one's error. Also—since morality has again come up—I think that as an ex-solipsist I should tell you that there is much moral and psychological misunderstanding of the actual state of mind of the solipsist. You act as if the solipsist is an aggressive individual who is trying to aggrandize himself by rejecting others. Has it never occurred to you that a solipsist may be an extremely lonely creature who is desperately trying but does not know how to succeed in *accepting* others?

MORALIST: Oh come on now with your sentimental hogwash! The typical solipsist goes swaggering around with a superior smile saying, "I alone exist, you do not!" Can you seriously expect me to believe that he is anything like the psychological type you describe?

ANDRICUS: The *typical* solipsist? How do *you* know what the typical solipsist is? I doubt very much whether the type you describe is the typical solipsist. I'm afraid that the typical solipsist does not go around publicly announcing his solipsism but bears it shamefully in silence. I wonder whether even the type you do mention is really so vain and proud, underneath it all, or whether he is not covering up a desperate fear and insecurity?

MORALIST: It seems these days that one can excuse any vanity by simply saying that it is only a cover-up for an underlying humility.

SECOND PHILOSOPHER: Leaving aside these moral questions, I would like to return to the basic matter. How does the statement, "Thy neighbor is thyself," help you to believe that the existence of other minds is possible?

ANDRICUS: Because if this statement is true, it means that other minds *do* exist! There can be millions, trillions of them, only they are all identical with my own!

FIRST PHILOSOPHER: Good grief! This is the most utterly insane solution of the solipsism problem that I ever have heard!

MORALIST *(gleefully):* The man's egotism knows no bounds! *Now* he is saying that *his* mind is the only one in existence, and no other minds exist in the universe; if they do, the only way that they can exist is if they are identical with his! So *his* mind is still the only mind in the universe! If this is not egotism pushed to its utter and fantastic logical extreme, I don't know what is! Perhaps it should no longer be called *egotism* but *superegotism!* I have never before in my entire life heard such a self-aggrandizing doctrine! Furthermore, his brand of solipsism (and after all, it *is* a brand of solipsism) should perhaps be called *supersolipsism.* Compared with standard solipsism, I would say that it is even worse and more vicious!

ANDRICUS *(to Moralist):* Strange as it may seem, I tend to agree with everything you have just said except for your final remark. My viewpoint might indeed be described as pushing egotism to its extreme logical limit. But what is necessarily so bad about that? I have long suspected—as have many others—that altruism is, in the last analysis, nothing more nor less than egotism expanded to its ultimate limit. I also like the terms that you have just coined: *superegotism* and *supersolipsism*. But when you compare supersolipsism with what you call standard solipsism and declare it to be even more vicious, I believe you overlook an important point. When two standard solipsists get together in an argument, each claims the other to be wrong. But I as a supersolipsist can attend a congress of a thousand solipsists, each one shouting, "I am the only mind in existence," and I can happily agree with *all* of them! Each may *think* that all the rest of them are wrong, but I can know that *all* of them are right since they don't actually contradict each other but only think that they do. Each one thinks that he is using the word *I* in a different sense, but in reality they are all using it in the same sense; they mean the same thing by it but don't know it. If I should have the really good fortune of attending a congress of a thousand supersolipsists, it would be even better. Now, when each one said, "I am the only mind in existence," each one would not only *be* right but would know that all the others were also right! I think that rather than call them *supersolipsists*, I would prefer to call them *enlightened solipsists*. Yes, from now on I shall refer to such people as enlightened solipsists. Just think of it! A whole world—a whole universe—peopled with enlightened solipsists! What could be more beautiful!

EPISTEMOLOGIST: I am sorry to interfere with your idyllic fantasies, but I am afraid that there are a few sober questions I must ask you. Your solution of the solipsist problem is certainly nonstandard, to say the least (though I do not think it is wholly original).[4]

The solution is both crazy and ingenious, and I am not wholly insensitive to a certain poetic value. But—with my hard-boiled empiricist training—I cannot let its poetic value seduce me into believing that it really makes any sense. I think that both the craziness and the ingenuity of your viewpoint are more apparent than real. In the last analysis, I think that all you are doing is using words in a nonstandard sense. You say that other minds exist, but they are all identical with yours. To a logician, this is, of course, a straight contradiction since the very word *other* means *not-*identical. But then you get out of it by saying that you are *not* using *identity* in the logician's sense. And when asked in what sense you are using it, you have great difficulty in being precise. Some will say that your inability to define *identity* in your sense indicates that you don't mean anything by it. I am willing to be more charitable and admit that *maybe* you do mean something by it but simply cannot explain what it is.

At any rate, it is clear that you are using language in a highly nonstandard manner. I think the crux of it is this: When you say, "Other minds exist, but they are identical with mine," how do you know that you mean anything more or less than I mean when I say more simply, "Other minds exist"? I think this is really the key question.

ANDRICUS: I would not be the least bit surprised if we meant exactly the same thing.

EPISTEMOLOGIST: In that case, why don't you simply delete the part, "But they are identical with mine," since this is superfluous and only confusing to others?

ANDRICUS: Confusing to others? Unfortunately, it is confusing unless I try to explain. But superfluous? It is not superfluous to me. For without adding this, I simply find it psychologically impossible to believe in other minds! I realize perfectly well how irrational I sound, but which is really more important, that I *talk* rationally or that I actually believe in other minds?

MORALIST: Why this dichotomy? Can't you both be rational *and* believe in other minds? I am perfectly rational, and I believe in other minds. Why can't you be like me?

ANDRICUS: Why *can't* I be like you? I don't know *why* I can't be like you, but the fact is that I simply can't. Who knows, maybe one day I *will* be like you, but for the present I can't. I sincerely envy you—or anybody who is able to integrate rationality with belief in other minds. But so far I have simply not yet found the means to do so.

FIRST PHILOSOPHER: You mean to say that you think that the belief in other minds is irrational?

ANDRICUS: Of course not! What I said was that *I* find it impossible for *me* to both be (or sound) rational and to believe in other minds, which is very different!

SECOND PHILOSOPHER: But what about when you were a child? You told us that in those days you had no difficulty believing in other minds. Did you then have to say, "Other minds exist, but they are all identical with mine"? Did you then have to get enraptured by the notion of enlightened solipsism?

ANDRICUS: Of course not. Those were my days of innocence and true knowledge. As I told you, those were the times when I accepted other minds as a matter of course without any doubts whatsoever—though of course I never verbalized this.

EPISTEMOLOGIST: So what happened to you in the interim?

ANDRICUS: What happened to me? My troubles all started in adolescence when I read the philosophers. Then for the first time bugs were put into my brain: How do you *know* other minds exist? Is it *certain* or only *probable*? What could it *mean* for other minds to exist? How can you possibly think of or believe anything outside your own experience? Having swallowed all this poison, the only way I know how to return to sanity is, unfortunately, by violating language, and talking about such things as enlightened solipsists.

Yet I don't know. Am I really so much worse off than I was before? Just think of it! A world full of enlightened solipsists! What could be more perfect?

Notes

1.   One of my objections to the positivist invitation to reject metaphysical statements since they are cognitively meaningless is that these statements may nevertheless suggest other statements that are meaningful, even in the positivist sense—that may never have occurred to one who had not first seen the others. Similarly, in

mathematics a false proof of a theorem might well suggest a correct one that would never have occurred to one who had not first seen the false one.

2.   George Berkeley, *Complete Works*, Vol. 4, ed. Alexander Campbell Fraser (Oxford: Clarendon Press, 1901), p. 161. Italics are mine.

3.   This is perhaps somewhat reminiscent of the idea of only one physical particle in the entire universe that oscillates all over the universe.

4.   It is not too far from the views of certain mystics, and in a strange sort of way, not too far from Wittgenstein.

13

5000 B.C.

Part I

ANCIENT METAPHYSICIAN: For years I have been trying to find out what keeps the earth up; why does it not fall down? The number of so-called wise men who have claimed to give a satisfactory answer to this problem is appalling! One told me that the earth is resting on another body. When asked upon what this body rests, he described another body. When asked upon what this second body rests, he said, "I have given satisfactory answers to two questions, and that is enough. One can't keep questioning forever!"

This reminds me of an equally exasperating theologian who claimed that there must be a God; otherwise, there could be no explanation for the creation of the universe. But when asked, "How was God created?" he likewise answered, "One can't keep asking questions forever." I replied, "I promise not to keep asking questions *forever;* I think it is unfair of you to stop the enquiry just at the point where you are ahead. So I merely wish to ask but *one* more question; how was God created? If you answer that satisfactorily, I am perfectly willing to end the enquiry there." He replied, "Some things are simply a mystery." I was somewhat softened by the candor of that reply, but as I explained to him, why not simply say that the existence of the universe is a mystery, and let it go at that; why must God be brought in? To put the matter another way, I certainly believe that some things *may* in principle be mysteries, but of what use is a hypothesis for explaining a mystery when the very hypothesis raises another mystery just as baffling as the one it explains?

However, I diverge. Coming back to the question why the earth doesn't fall, I could conceive of the possibility, although I find it rather counterintuitive, that there may be *infinitely* many bodies, each resting on the other, going infinitely far downward with the earth resting on top. Alternatively, perhaps the earth could be resting on a *single* infinite body that extends infinitely downward. Now, this possibility, though rather difficult to believe, does not appear a priori to be completely out of the question. But even if true, I still cannot understand why the earth together with this body wouldn't fall down together as a unit. No, the whole situation is extremely mysterious, and I am honestly very depressed these days at the fact that I simply cannot make any progress in this direction.

FIRST PHILOSOPHER: Perhaps this question is another mystery. That is, it may be totally beyond the powers of any human being ever to find out why the earth stays up.

METAPHYSICIAN: Of course, it *may* be beyond our power, but why should we give up so easily?

SECOND PHILOSOPHER: It may be that in essence your question is unanswerable! The very question itself presupposes a premise, which in fact may be false.

METAPHYSICIAN: What premise is that?

SECOND PHILOSOPHER: The assumption that everything that happens must have a cause or a reason! The earth *does* stay up: That is indeed a fact. But it does not follow that there must be a *reason* for this fact. It may simply be that the earth stays up, and that's all there is to it!

METAPHYSICIAN: Before I answer, let me ask you, Is there any significant difference between your viewpoint and that of the first philosopher, who claimed that the reason why the earth stays up is a mystery?

SECOND PHILOSOPHER: Of course they are different. The first philosopher never doubted, as far as I could tell, that there is a reason why the earth stays up but merely expressed skepticism as to whether the reason can ever be found. I am proposing the more radical hypothesis that there is no reason. There certainly is a difference in these two viewpoints. Indeed, there is a great difference between believing that something exists but not knowing how to find it and believing that the thing doesn't even exist and hence that it is hopeless to even look for it. I believe the latter.

METAPHYSICIAN: I have certainly considered it *possible* that the earth stays up without any reason whatsoever. But I regard such a hypothesis as extremely sterile. If I were to accept it, then I certainly would never find the answer even if there was one and it were in principle discoverable.

FIRST PHILOSOPHER: But you said yourself that you have made absolutely no progress in this direction, so why do you keep paining yourself against such hopeless odds?

METAPHYSICIAN: It is true that I haven't made any overt progress in the sense of having yet come up with any solution. It may be that I have made some latent progress—time will tell. But the point is that if I should adopt either the viewpoint that the answer is an unsolvable mystery or that there is no answer, then I certainly won't find the answer if there is one, whereas if I have faith that there is an answer and that it can be found, then at least I might find it.

ANCIENT POSITIVIST: Has it ever occurred to you that in *principle* you can never find an answer because you are not even asking a question?

METAPHYSICIAN: What on earth are you talking about?

POSITIVIST: I am suggesting that your so-called question is not really a question at all.

METAPHYSICIAN: I still can't understand you!

POSITIVIST: I am saying that the sequence of words, "Why does the earth stay up," though it sounds superficially like a question, is really no question at all; it is merely a meaningless sequence of words.

METAPHYSICIAN: Which words of the sequence are meaningless?

POSITIVIST: I did not say that it is a sequence of meaningless words but that it is a meaningless sequence of words. Of course each word of the sequence is meaningful, but the sequence as a whole is meaningless; it is simply not grammatically formulated.

METAPHYSICIAN: What in the world does *grammar* have to do with why the earth stays up?

POSITIVIST: It is your use of the word *why* that is causing the trouble. This word is of course meaningful in certain contexts but has no meaning in your context.

METAPHYSICIAN: Why not? Or am I again asking a meaningless question?

POSITIVIST: Ignoring this flippancy, I will answer you. When one asks *why* a certain phenomenon occurs, he is simply asking what known general laws account for it. But to ask why the very laws of the cosmos are as they are has no meaning whatsoever. This is really what you are doing in asking why the earth stays up. It is a perfect example of what should be termed a *pseudoquestion*, that is, a sequence of words that sounds like a question but in reality is meaningless.

METAPHYSICIAN: May I ask how you know that the question is meaningless?

POSITIVIST: The answer to this, though elementary in principle, is technically rather involved. After much time and thought, I have finally succeeded in giving an absolutely precise definition of *meaningful;* I have a perfectly exact set of rules called *formation rules for language* with the marvelous property that, given any sequence of words, the rules can decide in a completely mechanical manner whether the sequence is meaningful or not. And it is a simple, demonstrable fact that your pseudoquestion is not meaningful in this perfectly precise sense of *meaningful.*

METAPHYSICIAN: I don't for a moment doubt that you are right! I certainly take your word that according to the rules you have in mind my question is meaningless. But what does this prove? Merely that the question is meaningless according to *your* definition of *meaning*. It does not show that it is meaningless according to *my* notion of *meaning*.

POSITIVIST: What notion is that? Can you precisely define this notion and rigorously prove that your question is meaningful according to a *precise* definition of *meaning?*

METAPHYSICIAN: It seems that you are asking me two somewhat different questions. Do you want me to define *my* notion of *meaning,* or merely to define *some* notion of *meaning* according to which my question is meaningful? The latter is trivial. Of course, given *any* sequence of words, one could easily frame *some* definition of *meaning* according to which the question is meaningful and another according to which it is meaningless. But this strikes me as a completely empty game. The former is of more interest. No, I don't believe that I can define *my* notion of *meaning*. Every definition I have yet heard or yet considered somehow fails to hit the mark; it almost always leaves out something that I would call *meaningful*.

POSITIVIST: Ah, then you admit that you don't have a precise notion of meaning!

METAPHYSICIAN: It is not clear to me that the inability to define a notion necessarily indicates the lack of precision of that notion. A dog cannot define a bone, but he knows what to do with it, and I would say his notion of a bone is as clear and precise as yours or mine.

No; I certainly think that one should carefully distinguish between the following three things: (1) meaning something by a word, or group of words; (2) knowing what one means; and (3) being able to explain what one means.

POSITIVIST: Well, if you cannot explain to me your notion of meaning, perhaps I can form some idea by considering some examples. Suppose someone asked you, "Why is red?" Would you label this as meaningless or meaningful?

METAPHYSICIAN: I certainly can perceive absolutely no meaning to that question whatsoever. No one has ever asked me such a question (except perhaps in jest). If someone seriously asked it, I would surely be quite puzzled. As I said, *I* can see no meaning in it; it is meaningless to *me*. But I would hate to label it as downright meaningless. I don't consider it very nice to stigmatize another's words as meaningless.

POSITIVIST: Oh come now, you are just being excessively polite! Why should the truth be hidden just to spare another's feelings? You know damn well that, "Why is red?" is completely meaningless!

METAPHYSICIAN: I know that it is meaningless to me, and I am quite sure it is meaningless to almost everyone. But from this, I cannot conclude that it is meaningless to *him*.

POSITIVIST: I am not talking about the *subjective* notion of being meaningful to a given person; I am speaking about *meaning* in a purely objective sense.

METAPHYSICIAN: The only sense I can significantly attach to *objectively meaningful* is *subjectively meaningful to a large number of persons*. If this is all you mean by *objectively meaningful*, then of course the question, "Why is red?" is objectively meaningless in this sense. But I doubt that is what you do mean since this definition would fail to exclude my question, "Why does the earth stay up?" No one to whom I ever have previously asked this question has failed to understand what it *means;* they have merely not known the answer. Indeed, you are the first person I have ever met who rejects the very question itself as meaningless. That you do this strikes me, I must confess, as utterly astonishing!

POSITIVIST: The question has the same fault as so many other "questions" asked by metaphysicians. For example, consider what is perhaps the most ancient, and about the most senseless, metaphysical question of all: "Why is it that there is something instead of nothing?" Would you regard that as a meaningful question?

METAPHYSICIAN: Of course I would! How could one possibly fail to understand this question?

POSITIVIST: I should have guessed you would call this question meaningful; it is so analogous to your so-called question. Let me put it this way: Do you agree that for a question to be meaningful there must in principle exist at least a possibility of an answer?

METAPHYSICIAN: Of course.

POSITIVIST: And do you further agree that there must in principle exist some possible experience that the questioner could have that would constitute an answer?

METAPHYSICIAN: Yes.

POSITIVIST: Then let us stop kidding around. I ask you point-blank: What conceivable experience could you envision that would constitute an answer?

METAPHYSICIAN: I have no idea what such an experience could be! If I knew that, I might be well on the road to finding the answer.

POSITIVIST: So you mean to say that you can regard a question as meaningful even though you have no conception of what kind of an experience would constitute an answer?

METAPHYSICIAN: Of course I would say that! I have many times been puzzled by questions and had no idea what the answer could even be like until I found it. Indeed, I have sometimes even had a wrong idea about what the answer could be like, and when I found the real answer, I realized that I could never have anticipated what it would be like in a million years.

POSITIVIST: If you find an answer, will you know it?

METAPHYSICIAN: Obviously. What a silly question!

POSITIVIST: But how will you recognize the answer when you have found it?

METAPHYSICIAN: I don't know *how* I will recognize it; I will just recognize it, and that's all there is to it!

POSITIVIST: Will you be capable of communicating your answer to others?

METAPHYSICIAN: I am no mystic. If I could not communicate my answer to others, I would not regard the answer as altogether satisfactory.

POSITIVIST: I still would like to know *how* you will recognize an answer when you find one.

METAPHYSICIAN: You sound like an inquisitor! Let me ask you honestly, Why are you so intent on convincing me that my question is meaningless?

POSITIVIST: Please don't get so upset! My motives are not as harsh as you might suspect. I am not trying to show that you are stupid or to belittle you in any way. I am indeed trying to influence you to give up this question, but for your own good!

METAPHYSICIAN: Now what kind of nonsense is this!

POSITIVIST: It's not such nonsense. I cannot help but be concerned at the great number of talented minds like yours who have fallen into purely linguistic traps and are wasting time torturing themselves on speculations that in principle can never lead anywhere. I think that if you would have the patience to listen to my admittedly formalistic and rather dull theory of meaning, then you would fully realize that your question is meaningless and would soon give up asking it.

METAPHYSICIAN: The former perhaps, but certainly not the latter. Perhaps your motives are as good as you say, but if you are going to take this approach, then even from a purely psychological viewpoint, I don't think it is sound. All right, suppose that by superior logic you could drive me into a corner and compel me to admit—totally against my own intuition—that my question is meaningless. Do you think for one moment that this would in any way dispel my *feeling* for the meaning of the question? Do you really think that I would be any the less puzzled by why the earth stays up or would in any way cease to try to find out?

ANCIENT PSYCHOLOGIST: I definitely agree with the positivist that your question is pathological, but I disagree with his method of treatment. It is obvious to me that you are suffering from a purely concrete problem that you do not wish to face, so you have transferred all your compulsive anxieties to a purely abstract level on which you feel more safe. But you will never be able to get rid of the question by remaining on the level of philosophical abstractions. You can succeed only by solving the concrete problem that gave rise to it, in which case the philosophical question will disappear by itself. If only you had been brought up right, you would never ask such questions to begin with.

EASTERN MYSTIC: It is as I have been saying for years! If only the metaphysician would follow my exercises in breathing and meditation, then after a few months the question would disappear as if by magic.

PSYCHOLOGIST: I am afraid this approach is not very realistic! The metaphysician is obviously suffering from a concrete problem that was incurred in his early childhood. No amount of breathing or meditating is going to unearth this problem.

MYSTIC: I would say that his problem was incurred long, *long* before his childhood, but let that pass for the present. Even if his problem does have the genesis that the psychologist claims, it does not follow that the only or even best way to cure it is by remembering it. I have simply observed, in a purely hard-boiled empirical sense, that my exercises do relieve this type of problem without giving the kind of insight so valued by the psychologist. From my point of view, his true problem far transcends any events of his childhood. His real problem consists of his existential anxiety in not knowing who he really is and not knowing his true relationship to the cosmos. For this, no mere analysis of the events of his present life cycle will avail.

POSITIVIST: I think both your approaches are unnecessarily and highly indirect. It may indeed be true that the *genesis* of his problem is what the psychologist or what the mystic claims. But this is only the genesis. The problem itself is on a purely linguistic level and is perfectly capable of being treated on this level. After all, the metaphysician is an extremely intelligent human being and is capable of reason. He, like so many of us, has been enslaved by linguistic habits that lead to the asking of pseudoquestions. But this can be explained to him on a completely conscious and rational level.

PSYCHOLOGIST: I say you are wrong! No rational, linguistic analysis will help cure his malady. His problem is psychosexual, not linguistic.

MYSTIC: I say you are both wrong; his real problem is existential.
POSITIVIST: No, no; his real problem is linguistic!

Part II

At this point, the metaphysician quietly left the company, who were far too engrossed in diagnosing his condition even to notice his absence. After wandering about for awhile, the bitter irony of the whole situation really came upon him. The whole company unanimously considered that the solution to his problem was to cease asking the question rather than to successfully find an answer; they disagreed only on what technique could be used to help him cease his enquiry.

A few weeks after this episode, the metaphysician discovered the secret of time travel! He came to the twentieth century, where I met him a few months after his arrival. He had already mastered English perfectly. We struck up a close friendship almost immediately, and he spent his remaining few months of the twentieth century as a guest at our house in Tannersville. He adored my dogs, who barked joyously on his arrival. He loved romping with them in the mornings; the afternoons and evenings he spent mostly in our library. He mastered most of the extant philosophy in a phenomenally short period.

One day, as we were sitting in the library, I asked him how long it took him to find out the answer to his main question, "Why does the earth stay up?" He replied, "Almost immediately on arrival. Every schoolboy knows today that the word *up* has no absolute meaning." I then asked him, "Do you today regard the positivist as right or wrong when he declared your question meaningless?" He smiled and replied, "In a way he was right, but for the wrong reasons! He totally misled me by saying that the word *why* was the cause of the trouble. It was obviously the word *up* that was the true cause (though nobody in my time could have suspected it). Since the word *up* has no absolute meaning, then of course the question, 'Why does the earth stay up?' has no absolute meaning. But yet I now know the answer! The most remarkable thing that I have learned from this whole experience is something that I never would have dreamed or suspected, namely, that it is not always necessary for a question to be meaningful to obtain an answer. I now obviously know *why* the earth doesn't fall down; there simply *is* no such thing as down. But I could never have known the meaninglessness of this question without first having found the answer! So if I had listened to the positivist, I might have assented to the fact that the question is meaningless, but I never could have really believed it and never could have known *why* it is meaningless. Besides, had I listened to him, I never would have traveled to the future with the hopes of finding an answer."

The one topic my friend was secretive about was his method of time travel. When I expressed utter amazement that this could have been discovered in 5000 B.C., he smiled and said, "Your twentieth-century science fiction is totally off the path concerning the correct method. It does not require technology, elaborate machinery, or sources of great energy. The true method of propelling oneself into the future is so ridiculously simple, so obvious, so under our very noses, that virtually no one can perceive it." He then went on to say that he did not withhold the secret to be mysterious but felt certain that if the method were generally known, man would make a vast exodus to the future and too few people would remain to support the future, hence all would perish.

In his last few days with me, his philosophic interests centered mainly around the twentieth-century positivist and analytic schools. His bitterness knew no bounds. For example, upon seeing the title, "The Elimination of Metaphysics," he exclaimed in horror, "Eliminate metaphysics! Who in his right mind would want to eliminate such a beautiful subject!" To a large extent, I share his feelings. But I still felt duty-bound (partly out of loyalty to friendships I have had with empiricist philosophers) to offer some defense. I pointed out to him that a vast amount of metaphysical trash has been generated in the past, some of it downright fraudulent, and that we shouldn't be too hard on those of intellectual integrity who—though perhaps somewhat misguided—have made a sincere effort to combat this nonsensical activity. He replied, "I am fully aware of this, but they are throwing out the baby with the bathwater. Of course their program, if successful, would eliminate much phony metaphysics, but it would also eliminate some of the most beautiful, sincere, and sublime metaphysics produced by the human race." He also felt that many of the positivists were in a way just downright stupid. He asked, "Can they for one moment have any doubt that any of the earlier competent metaphysicians would have totally agreed with them that their metaphysical questions *were* metaphysical and had no *cognitive* meaning whatsoever? But obviously, to a metaphysician cognitive meaning is but a tiny part of meaning in general, so why should the lack of cognitive meaning of their enquiries encourage them to give them up?"

He also made another point that struck me quite forcibly. He sensed, particularly of the early positivists, a certain *heartlessness* to their approach. As he eloquently expressed it, "They remind me of hardhearted parents whose child is crying and complaining of some sort of pain or disturbance but whose knowledge of language is yet too limited to express exactly what or where the trouble lies, and the parents then respond, 'Unless you can formulate your trouble more precisely, don't bother me with your complaints!'"

I tried to point out to the metaphysician that, particularly in more recent years, the analytic tradition had something to contribute that was of real value even to the metaphysicians themselves, namely, that some light might be thrown on certain philosophical disputations as to whether they are real or only verbal. To use an analogy, imagine two societies living side by side in which one of them, for some strange reason, had got the words *circle* and *ellipse* interchanged. Imagine now two children, one from each society, standing before a geometrical figure and bitterly arguing, "It is a circle"; "No, it is an ellipse"; "No, it is a circle"; "No, it is an ellipse"; and so forth. Clearly, their difference is not real but semantical. To go one step further, imagine two children of whom we do not know whether they belong to the same or to different societies looking at a figure that is *very* slightly elliptical; almost a perfect circle, but so faintly elliptical that about half the people would be sensitive enough to perceive it as an ellipse, and the other half would see it as a perfect circle. Now suppose the two children were having the same argument. We could not possibly tell (without further questions) whether they *saw* it differently or only disagreed verbally. (Similarly, if they agreed verbally, we could not know whether their agreement was *real* or merely verbal.) It is here that something in the spirit of analytic philosophy could be helpful. We could, for example, ask the one who claimed it circular, "Is it *very* circular or only slightly circular?" The metaphysician saw the point.

It was sad when the day of parting came. He could not go back to his own time: Backward time travel, he assured me, was totally impossible. But he longed to investigate further into the future. Much as I knew I would miss him, I did not press him to stay. We said our parting words, and warmly shook hands. He then sat in a chair opposite me, smiled, waved goodbye, and quite suddenly vanished.

Afterthoughts

Some General Comments

Several people have asked me where I stand in all these matters. For example, in my piece "Simplicus and the Tree," do I identify myself with the realistic mystic? Well, I certainly find several aspects of this position of interest, but it is hardly my own. It seems to me that he is essentially an Aristotelian who identifies soul and pattern, which I assuredly do *not* do! To me, pattern is something purely abstract, whereas soul (or mind or psyche) is as concrete as anything can be. I believe that one of the most tragic philosophical errors of our time is the identification of the abstract with the concrete. For example, a well-known computer scientist recently said, "What's the difference between the universe and the set of differential equations that describes it?" How anyone can identify something as concrete as a universe with anything as abstract as a set of equations is totally beyond my comprehension. No, I am surely *not* the realistic mystic. If anything, I would tend to identify with the first Zen master. I heartily agree that statements such as, "I am enjoying this tree," are perfectly comprehensible without any analysis. In a strange sort of way, I also identify with Simplicus.

When I once read "An Epistemological Nightmare," to one well-known logician, I was utterly amazed that he could not see why it was funny. He regarded the experimental epistemologist as perfectly sensible! Really now, to have more confidence in a machine's report of the nature of one's experience than in the experience itself. How crazy can one get? Besides, even from a purely logical point of view, one's knowledge of the machine's report is obtained only through other experiences (seeing where the needles of the dial point, etc.), and so why should *those* experiences be held more trustworthy than the experiences being tested? I was thinking of adding another scene to this chapter in which there was a second epistemologist present using a brain-reading machine on the first epistemologist at the same time the first one was using a machine on Frank. Then when the first one says to Frank, "Wrong, the book does *not* seem red to you," the second one asks the first, "How do you know he is wrong?"

When the first answers, "The dials of my machine are reading 17–06–42–87," the second asks, "How do you know the dials are reading those numbers?"

The first replies, "It seems that way to me."

The second epistemologist then says, "It *doesn't* seem that way to you!"

Do I make my point?

What Can One Expect from Philosophy?

Aside from my obvious dislike of moralists, the one bias I have clearly shown in this book is my negative attitude toward logical positivism, but even here I have some reservations. I recently read Brand Blanshard's book *Reason and Analysis* in which he attacked positivism and much of positivist-oriented analytic philosophy.[1] Needless to say, I was delighted with his views and with his skillful use of positivistic techniques against positivism itself. But for some amazing reason, the overall effect of reading it has been to make me more sympathetic to positivism than I was before. Let me explain.

I believe that much of the antagonism toward positivism has resulted, so to speak, from the tone of voice or style of its writings rather than their objective content. For example, the very title, "The Elimination of Metaphysics," would immediately put anyone with metaphysical interests into an antagonistic frame of mind. It is a pity that Carnap did not choose some alternative title, such as "On the Necessary Limitations of Metaphysics." Such a title would surely antagonize no one; indeed, it would attract even the metaphysicians themselves. I think the fact is that positivists, particularly the early ones, have been quite hostile to metaphysics (which is quite understandable in view of some of the loose and sloppy work done by metaphysicians) and that their hostility clearly showed through their writings and aroused counterhostility on the part of many readers. This counterhostility may well have prevented, or at least delayed, recognition of what I feel are the useful and positive aspects of positivism. This now brings me to my central point.

Suppose I have a world view that is internally perfectly consistent, that is, logically consistent, consistent with all the experiences I have ever had, and consistent with all my feelings and intuitions. For the moment, let us make the further assumption (totally unrealistic as it almost certainly is) that the view is consistent with any experience I ever will have in the future. Let us call such a view a *perfect world view*. Now suppose that you also have a perfect world view but that yours is logically incompatible with mine. It seems to me that the valuable contribution of the positivists (and, for that matter, the pragmatists) is the realization of the question, "How *in principle* could you or I ever show each other to be wrong?" In other words, can we really hope to get anything more from philosophy than consistency? But suppose that you and I are both Platonists and that we are not at all satisfied that our views are merely consistent; we both believe in a real world, and we each affirm our views to be true of this real world. These Platonic principles, let us assume, are themselves perfectly consistent with the rest of our perfect world views, and so we both adopt them. The positivists might tell us that we are both wrong in asserting that each other's views are false since there exists no way of verifying them (from the outside). But you and I both add as further axioms to our systems, "The positivists are wrong," and let us say our systems are still consistent. Now what can the poor positivist do? In principle, he cannot convince us that our rejection of positivism is wrong. I might also add that although it may be true that in principle we cannot convince each other, it may be *consistent* for us to claim that we can. So we add as further axioms to our systems, "There is some principle that (if only we could find it!) can show that the other one is wrong," and we still have consistent systems. I think this is equivalent to our each denying that the other's world view *is* perfect. It could well be that our world views are in fact perfect, yet it might be consistent for each of us to deny that the other's world view is perfect. (Indeed, it might even be consistent to deny that one's *own* world view is perfect!) Actually, if I believed your world view to be perfect (though false), I think I am now sufficiently influenced by the positivists to realize that my arguing with you could be of no avail. Thus, I think that our very process of arguing with each other indicates our lack of belief in the perfection of each other's world views; we hope either to show the other view to be inconsistent or to produce some new experience in the other person that will change his mind or call forth to full consciousness some latent intuition. This, I think, is what metaphysicians of the past have been up to. As Carnap has rightly pointed out, metaphysicians are not content just to present their systems (unlike artists and poets, who only present their works of art), but they try to *refute* the metaphysical systems of others. I have just proposed what I believe this refutation to really be.

Suppose now that you and I believe that each other's world views are perfect (but false). Although it is senseless for us to argue with each other (even on the friendliest possible basis!), does it make no sense for us to philosophize together at all? No, I believe there is something very valuable left to be done. Let me, for the moment, describe the situation from my viewpoint. Since your world view is consistent, then (making an analogy to mathematical logic) there is *some* interpretation of all your terms under which everything you say is true. Let us assume that our terminology is the same, that is, we use the same words but not necessarily with the same meanings. Indeed, our meanings must be different since some of your statements are refutable in my system. But at any rate, since your system is consistent, then everything you say is true under *some* interpretation of our language. So instead of my saying, "You are wrong," it would make more sense for me to say, "You are wrong according to *my* meanings of our words." The important point to realize (and I don't know if I can convey to the reader the startling impact of this realization) is that according to a mere reinterpretation of the language, *everything you say is true about the real world!* Even if you should deny the existence of a real world and the notions of truth and meaning, *there is some interpretation of all this* that is true about the real world and that may be of extreme interest and value for me to know. The point, then, is, in mathematical language, to construct a model of your language within mine. Put less precisely, though more expressively, the point is for me to be able to see the world through your eyes. After having gone through such an experience, it is more than likely that my own world view might become considerably enlarged. After all, even in a perfect world view, one has not necessarily decided the truth of every statement; there may be many alternative ways of extending it to produce a more comprehensive perfect world view. The very process of modeling another's consistent world view within one's own might be just the thing to decide hitherto undecidable propositions.

To the reader with some knowledge of mathematical logic, I acknowledge that I of course realize that my fanciful analogies have their weak points. For example, I have treated a world view as if it were a formalized first order language, which of course it isn't (at least I hope it isn't! I would feel rather sorry for one whose world view is!). Also, the notion of a *perfect* world view is of course highly idealized; I doubt that anyone even has a world view consistent with all the experiences he has already had! But I believe that all I have said about perfect world views should apply a fortiori to those that are not perfect.

The technique of philosophizing that I am suggesting might be put in the form of a maxim: "Instead of trying to prove your opponent wrong, try to find out in what sense he may be right." This is a sort of tolerance principle, not too unrelated to that of Carnap.[2] To repeat my main point, much may be gained from constructing possible models of other world views within one's own. I believe that this is in the spirit of much of modern analysis. But I would like to see this applied more to some of the great metaphysical systems of the past.

Notes

1. Brand Blanshard, *Reason and Analysis*, The Paul Carus Foundation Lecture XII (La Salle: Open Court Publishing Co., 1964).

2. Indeed, it can be thought of as a semantic counterpart of Carnap's principle of tolerance. His principle says that a language should be regarded as acceptable if it is consistent—or, equivalently, if it has a model. My principle is to try to find such a model—or rather an interesting model of the language.